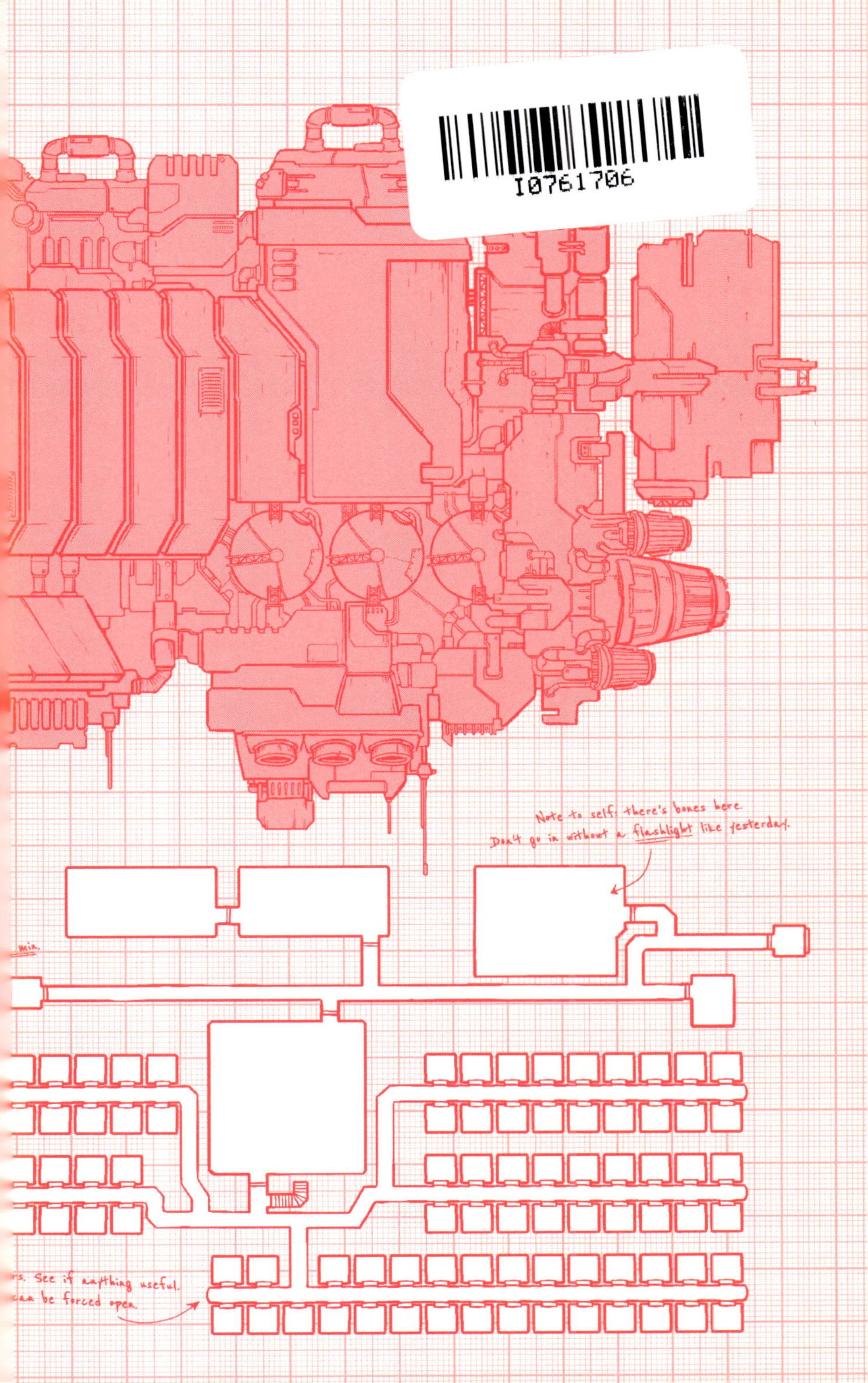
I0761706
Note to self: there's bones here.
Don't go in without a flashlight like yesterday.
rs. See if anything useful
can be forced open.

THE IRON GARDEN SUTRA

ALSO BY A. D. SUI

The Dragonfly Gambit

THE IRON GARDEN SUTRA

A. D. SUI

an imprint of Kensington Publishing Corp.
erewhonbooks.com

Content notice: *The Iron Garden Sutra* contains depictions of extensive conversations about death and dying, disordered eating, depression, suicidal ideation, violence, gore, on-page death.

EREWHON BOOKS are published by:

Kensington Publishing Corp.
900 Third Avenue
New York, NY 10022

erewhonbooks.com

This is a work of fiction. All of the characters, organizations, and events portrayed in this novel are either products of the author's imagination or are used fictitiously.

All Kensington titles, imprints, and distributed lines are available at special quantity discounts for bulk purchases for sales promotions, premiums, fundraising, educational, or institutional use.

Special book excerpts or customized printings can also be created to fit specific needs. For details, write or phone the office of the Kensington sales manager: Kensington Publishing Corp., 900 Third Avenue, New York, NY 10022, attn: Sales Department; phone 1-800-221-2647.

Erewhon and the Erewhon logo Reg. US Pat. & TM Off.

ISBN 978-1-64566-214-3 (hardcover)

First Erewhon hardcover printing: March 2026

10 9 8 7 6 5 4 3 2 1

Printed in the United States of America

Library of Congress Control Number: 2025944612

Electronic edition: ISBN 978-1-64566-216-7

Edited by Diana Pho
Interior design by Cassandra Farrin

The authorized representative in the EU for product safety and compliance
is eucomply OU, Parnu mnt 139b-14, Apt 123
Tallinn, Berlin 11317, hello@eucompliancepartner.com

For Yoah

Even before I knew you,
every word was for you.

THE IRON GARDEN SUTRA

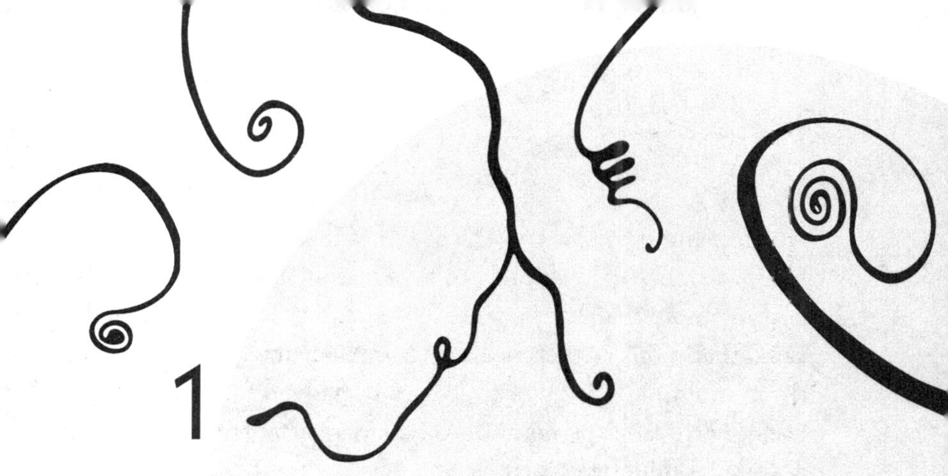

1

The Infinite Light does not love nor does it care. It has no capacity for kindness or cruelty. The Infinite Light observes life with the curiosity of a child tearing off the legs of an insect. It watches its successes and failures with nothing but detached amusement.
Do not forget, do not make me repeat myself.
The Infinite Light does not love.
From the unabridged diaries of Vessel Iris, Volume Ten

You like dead people.

At these words, Iris returned to himself, back to the airy, sunlit room, to the peach-tinged marble floors scrubbed to a mirror-like finish, to the single stick of incense burning in front of him, to the tranquil temple morning before it erupted in its usual commotion.

"I like meeting people. They just often happen to be dead when I get there," he said in a tone he'd use when instructing a novice. "And have you forgotten that jolting a monk from their meditation is an ill omen?"

A superstitious tale, the same voice, so much like his own but stripped of any human intonation, replied.

Iris could shut off the voice if he was inclined to, but he had grown quite accustomed to VIFAI's chattering over the past two decades. At their introduction, when Iris had first welcomed the AI companion to share in the space of his mind, he had asked for its name. It had refused to give one at first, stating it was nothing more than "Iris's friendly AI" and that its records indicated that monks never insisted their AIs name themselves. But the acronym stuck. Over the years it evolved to "Vessel Iris's Friendly AI" and the now VIFAI had inadvertently named itself despite its reluctance to do so.

Iris was about ready to slip back into the calming waves of his sunrise meditation when an alarm flashed across his field of vision. He had half a mind to dismiss it, but the message flashed red and ignited with the crest of the Starlit Order. A quick scan revealed the notice had bounced from Doshua Station to the Primary Temple first before landing in Iris's ocular projector. This had to be important. Inner peace and enlightenment would have to wait. Iris sat back on his heels and made a silent apology to the very thing that was both nothing and no one, and yet was everything and everyone at once. With a micromovement of his eyes, he opened the message. *Counsel of Nicaea, arri—*

Are you going?

This time Iris did gently shoo VIFAI to a distant corner of his mind. A time-out for while he read. He would apologise when he learned more about his assignment.

Generation ships, like the one suddenly orbiting Doshua Station, had all but disappeared. The last one crossed the galaxy arm not three hundred years prior and docked at P'Ilani before its passengers, seventh-generation descendants from First Earth, hit the dirt and gleefully destroyed all of P'Ilani's native fauna. Yet here was the *Nicaea*, unexpected, uninvited, and, according to the message, assigned to Iris himself.

Doshua was a two-day trip, but Iris could easily leave at a moment's notice. A Vessel's belongings were few, and he was already wearing most of them. Finding a shuttle was a simple task with Inon Station hanging in low orbit, only an elevator ride away. Currency was also of no concern. Under the unspoken social contract the Starlit Order had formed with the rest of known space, it was improper for Vessels to handle currency, more improper still for someone to demand it of him. In exchange for this preferential treatment, Vessels performed a multitude of services for the countless citizens scattered across the galaxy.

For centuries, gate travel had been relatively safe. For just as long, space travel in general had been relatively safe. But relativity and wishful thinking did little to protect a ship's hull when it split from impact or to shield a crew from a sudden burst of stellar radiation. Death still frequented orbits and travel routes. It was the vocation of the Vessels to guide those lost in space to the Infinite Light, to read final rites, to prepare the bodies for transport and burial of choice, and to comfort those left behind. Iris had attended many such deaths and ushered many travelers back to the One Beginning. It was a peaceful job, away from the core of civilization, away from the pull of a planet and the unbearable routine of temple life.

Iris had been planet-side for nearly six months now and had committed—*again*—every crumbling step and every clay tile of the Northern Temple to memory. He had recited every line of scripture at both sunrise and sunset prayers. He had bowed, and prayed, and meditated, and memorised every leaf on every tree in the main garden, and was slowly, and most assuredly, going mad with boredom. He could skirt the idea all he liked, but the friendly voice in his mind knew the answer before Iris ever thought of it himself.

You've already decided, VIFAI chimed, noting the decisive fluctuation of Iris's thoughts. Iris couldn't help but smile in return. No part of him could ever be concealed from the AI companion—not that he would ever want that. No sense pretending he had ever entertained staying put. Yet Iris wholeheartedly believed the decision had been made long before he ever opened the message, that it was as the Infinite Light had intended. He couldn't fathom *why* the Light had intended for a generation ship to appear from the Doshua Gate when it did, but it wasn't his place to question. Machinations far greater than his life were playing in the universe. The directive had been placed before his eyes, and it was his duty to carry it out. He would miss the temple, like he always did, but not for a long while, and by then a new adventure would be sure to dim the homesickness.

Smoothing out his white robe and trousers, Iris rose. The warm, cream marble beneath his bare feet flushed peach against the rays of the rising sun. A stifling day it would be when the sun hit its zenith, but he would be long gone before midday. A ribbon of saffron smoke wove towards the domed ceiling from the single stick of incense, keeping time of Iris's sitting. He bowed deeply to excuse himself.

No time to waste.

There were too many things for him to carry in just the pockets of his robes, so Iris placed each item carefully inside a cracking, leather duffel bag. The bag had been a gift from a wealthy Yutam widow who had bestowed her deceased wife's belonging to Iris. The language barrier had been too much for him to decline the gift, and no matter how hard he attempted to firmly thrust it back into the woman's hands, she had persisted. Nevertheless, he was proud of the bag and lamented rarely being able to use it.

One change of robes.

One pair of replacement mala beads.

One shaving kit.

One tattered, pocket-sized diary with the front cover missing.

The bag remained largely empty.

You need a smaller bag, VIFAI said. Or more stuff.

A Vessel needs few possessions, Iris recited and zipped up the duffel. He was doing a moderately successful job of containing his blossoming excitement; if only he could suppress it long enough to board a shuttle, away from the nosy eyes and ears of his peers. Another couple of hours at most, and he would be free to shake off the veneer of aloofness so common to monks who spent prolonged tenures between temple walls.

Someone's here, VIFAI said, two seconds too late.

A lithe shadow greeted Iris from the doorless entrance.

"Vessel Iris," Vessel Bacai said, her voice gentle as the turning of the sand dunes, "you're leaving us so soon?"

Not soon enough. Iris bowed, low enough to satisfy Bacai's unmentioned ego. She was his senior, not in years, but in status. She would never say it out loud, but she would walk ahead of him and talk over him given the opportunity and give every possible indication that it was *him* who was to learn from *her*. Bacai was, after all, *enlightened*. Her words, not his. She had recited all the right mantras and had all the right dreams. She had the whitest robes and the most benevolent of smiles. Where Bacai embodied the sutras, Iris only knew them by name. Rumours had it that the walls of her room were carved with notches, one for every soul she had ushered to the One Beginning, and that Vessel Bacai was running out of space.

"I'm afraid my time has been cut short," Iris said, intending to keep the conversation curt. "A message came through just moments ago. I have been summoned to usher the souls from a generation ship. It looks like I'll be away for quite some time."

On the surface, Bacai remained perfectly serene, tan skin unlined. But her eyes darted from side to side ever so slightly. She was checking her own messages, possibly asking her AI companion to flag any reports of generation ships in the news feeds. "Don't you find it strange, Vessel Iris, that the Primary Temple asked for *you*? Someone of—" She didn't finish.

Someone of your unimportant and unimpressive standing, Iris finished internally.

Someone's jealous, VIFAI said, and Iris begged it to be silent.

Gently, gently, it was all to be handled gently. Politeness and respect were to be held above all else, especially at the temple, where every clay wall had ears of its own and mouths eager to spread the recent temple gossip. Nothing but universal love for everything and everyone, including Vessel Bacai, whose arrogant big toe now pushed its way past the threshold and took residence in Iris's room.

"Would you like me to suggest you go, Vessel Bacai, in my stead?" Iris asked, voice tranquil, his face unreadable. It was a daring move. She could easily supersede him and attend to the ship herself, but that would mean he had done her a favor, and Bacai resented owing anything to anyone. So, just as anticipated, she gave a chilling smile and let Iris have a small bow.

"Not at all," Bacai said, lips stretching along pearly teeth. "I hope you enjoy yourself very much."

Wouldn't you like that. Every Vessel had their own subtle ways of practicing vanity. Some more obviously than others. Iris was grateful that unlike Bacai's jewel-adorned strand of white mala beads, he had the sense to keep his sandalwood. They were the very same beads he had been given at age six when he was welcomed into the Order, and they were soft and warm, wound around his left wrist as he scurried across the terraces, bag tucked under his arm.

"Do return swiftly, Vessel Iris," Bacai called after him, her voice a birdsong against the rising suns. "We will all miss you terribly."

Sweet lies, nothing more.

If he moved fast enough, he would miss most of the Vessels, the Beacons, and the novices as they moved from sunrise prayer to breakfast. Faster even, and he would miss Mother Nova as she emerged from the main garden after collecting the morning's fruit. Their brief exchanges were mostly neutral and sometimes even pleasant. But recently their conversations had grown strained, weighed down by the gravity of things unsaid. It was simpler to avoid her altogether—cowardly, Iris admitted to himself, but simpler. *Check the shuttle schedules,* he told VIFAI, *and find the ones that express the highest pro-Vessel sentiment, particularly by the captains.* The AI buzzed affirmatively and got to work.

Iris flattened himself against a wall and squeezed by a group of elderly monks who were creating an elaborate mandala symbolically representative of the known universe using vibrant sands of reds and yellows. Swirls of colour dusted from tiny, bronzed funnels as the monks gently brushed short metal rods along their lengths, a couple grains of sand at a time. Iris didn't have the care nor the patience for such artistry. Receiving a disapproving look, he hurried along, never lingering long enough to collect a reprimand. The mandala was to be destroyed as soon as it was completed, to signify the impermanence of even the most beautiful things. What harm was to be done if Iris were to hasten its end? The monks would disagree.

No time to ponder. Iris was already outside the main building, bare feet stepping quickly on the warm dirt of the courtyard.

Several calico cats leapt from their napping spots in the sun to dodge his approach, scurrying atop the staircase and perching along the terrace. Just a few more hurried steps and he would be right at the gates, and once he was past the threshold, no one would bother stopping him.

"Blessed sunrise, Vessel Iris."

Iris dug his heels into the ground. *Hurry and find me a shuttle, please,* he thought at VIFAI before turning around.

Mother Nova greeted him with a slight bow of the head and a broad smile. A wicker basket filled to the brim with peaches rested on her equally broad hip. "Running off so fast, you will rush the clouds away."

Iris dropped his duffel bag to the dirt and bowed deeply, eyes glued to the orange dust speckled across the hem of his white trousers. "Blessed sunrise, Mother Nova. I have received a message from the Primary Temple that my services are needed at the—"

"Yes, yes, of course, at Doshua." Without warning, Mother Nova's hand was on his shoulder, and Iris nearly crumbled under its weight. "All messages go through me, child. So that I can find the right Vessel to send along."

"Bacai—"

"Vessel Bacai will receive the assignment that suits her better," Mother Nova said, squeezing Iris's shoulder. "Everything is as the Light has intended it. Don't overthink it, you'll give yourself a headache. Go on then before the sun is too high in the sky. I hope you've packed for a long trip."

Iris lingered a moment. Of all the ships in all the quadrants of the galaxy, Mother Nova had bestowed the honor of a generation ship upon him. Earlier that year, not six months prior, she had tried to talk him out of going aboard a small passenger ship heading back from Kirai Five, and *that* was far less impressive.

He was almost upset he didn't have to fight Bacai for this assignment. *Almost.* It was, after all, in Mother Nova's words, *as the Light intended it.* Who was he to argue?

"Blessed day," Iris said, breaking free from the weight of Mother Nova's hand. He was again able to stand upright, to breathe evenly. He reminded himself that he was thrilled to go, thrilled to serve, to fulfill his purpose as a Vessel, that whatever tensions ate at him would melt away once he passed the threshold.

"Blessed indeed," Mother Nova said with a warm smile. She walked back towards the temple with the wicker basket still at her hip. Watching her back sway with the rhythm of her steps, Iris thought how she had remained seemingly unchanged since he first walked through the gates nearly twenty years past. How little he had known about her, about her private aspirations and passions, not even her real name. She was as much a fixture of the temple as the terraces and gardens were. Permanent as the mountains looming over the horizon. Both welcoming and impartial as the rolling thunderstorms that came only in the summer nights. How Iris both dreaded and cherished the soft, ashy vowels of her speech. How all these idiosyncrasies fit into one that was the Mother Nova, he didn't know. It wasn't his place to know, wasn't his place to question or understand.

I found us three shuttle options from the station, VIFAI spoke up, no louder than a whisper. Iris sensed it loitering, reluctant to interrupt his thoughts.

With a decisive square of his shoulders, Iris picked up his duffel bag and crossed the threshold of the temple gates.

"Notify the one with the least chatty captain, please."

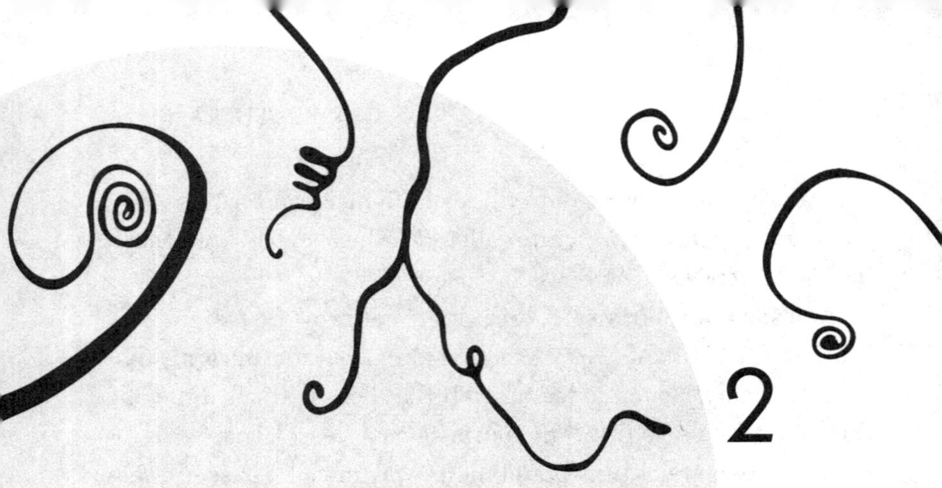

2

I pray and I mediate and still it's no use. Why did you give me these thoughts that I cannot purge myself of? Why did you bestow this evil upon me? If I am a mere reflection of you, O, Light, then you must be just as cruel and vile as I am.

From the unabridged diaries of Vessel Iris, Volume Three

The *Counsel of Nicaea*'s hull dominated the view from Doshua Station. The generation ship glided lazily along the length of the peripheral corridor, passing from one meteorite-proof glass segment to the next, panels shimmering like obsidian snakeskin. From Iris's vantage point, it looked as though it was the station that orbited the ship and not the other way around. An illusion made all the more tempting by the colossal size of the vessel. Craning his neck as far as it would go, he failed to see where the hull ended and space began. Only when he found stretches of darkness devoid of all starlight did he know he was looking at the *Nicaea*. *Can you pull some stats on the ship?* Iris asked VIFAI as he strode leisurely down the corridor. *And anything else you can pull from the feed on generation ships. I'd like to be prepared.*

Once, these periphery corridors had been crowded with commuters, eager to gaze upon the vastness of space for the first time. But just like with everything, people quickly grew bored with the sight of stars and distant galaxies. And now Iris was alone, interrupted only by the occasional service staff watching media on their break. As a Vessel, he had the clearances to speak with the Doshua AI directly, but then his own, less powerful one would be jealous that its services were neglected. Here, away from the crowds and the perpetual hum of the station, Iris had the luxury of sparing the few extra minutes. He allowed VIFAI to work at its own pace and for himself to study the spaceship in blissful silence.

Centuries before Iris was born, First Earth generation ships left their cradle in search of habitable worlds. Pressured by rapidly collapsing ecosystems, those with the means looked to other planets for a second chance, leaving the majority of the population behind. Archaeological records indicated each generation ship had been largely homogenous in religious makeup, suggested by preserved artifacts and digital records. Fueled by relentless faith, the colonists had scattered across the cosmos in search of their own, personal, Edens. It was an easy exercise not to pass judgment on those who ran. If the world was burning around him and escape was *right there*, Iris would have done the same.

But fate had had a different ending in mind and the simultaneous development of gate travel rendered the same ships obsolete before a single one ever reached its destination. There was no precise way to locate them, contact them, or to recover them mid-flight, so they were declared lost to the cosmos and committed to history books. Over the past hundreds of years, several had popped up in distant corners of the galaxy. They made their slow approach in silence, manned by nothing more than crumbling skeletons and ancient navigational systems. Every once in a while, the steady gravitational pull of a planet would be enough to place them in orbit until they were safely disposed of or dissected, their carcasses dragged off to various research institutes.

The *Nicaea* had already proven special. It was the first generation ship to exit gate space independently and the first to plant itself in stable orbit near a station, an object far too small to produce its own gravitational pull. Iris nursed a timid hope that aboard, he would find many oddities, treasures from First Earth, and remnants of cultures long lost to the gravity wells of time. Strange folklore and superstition, honed over years of complete isolation, usually adorned the corridors and living quarters of generation ships. He quietly yearned for a space that someone had lived in, that someone had made a home.

The Northern Temple had been "home" for many years, yet his room, now vacant, could easily be occupied by a novice, as it had by him. No one would notice the difference because there would be none. The same sleeping mat would be rolled out by the wall, the same glow sphere would cast shadows when night came. Not a single remnant of Iris would be in that space, no memory of him, a space forever borrowed and never his own.

With a faint vibration at Iris's temple, VIFAI presented its compiled findings on the *Nicaea* across his field of vision. Station AI would have completed the task in under a second; it had taken VIFAI over two minutes. Still, Iris sensed a faint, yet noticeable flare of pride from his companion, and he wouldn't dare extinguish that fragile emotion.

The *Counsel of Nicaea* had been in flight for more than a thousand years. By a sheer miracle, it had avoided destruction by a meteor strike in its travels. The ship originally left First Earth with a little over a thousand people, although it was impossible to predict what the numbers would resemble when Iris went aboard. But a thousand souls! Generation ships never housed any surviving passengers, save for the one orbiting

P'Ilani, and station AI had confirmed this with its preliminary scans moments after the *Nicaea* emerged from gate space. But it would still take Iris weeks, if not months, to find and lay to rest over one thousand people.

One bare foot placed carefully ahead of the other, Iris made his way to the shuttle gates as he skimmed over the files and annotations VIFAI had produced. Once there, he would board a single-person, unmanned craft, smaller than his room at the Northern Temple. The shuttle would deliver him to one of the operational airlocks on the *Nicaea*, so the exciting part of his assignment could begin. This part of his journey had been automated for his convenience: Iris had no piloting skills, nor any inclination to develop them, convinced that his neuroses would make him jumpy at the controls.

The shuttle doors were programmed to open after completing a retinal scan, the data for which had been uploaded before Iris ever set foot on the station. Once aboard the *Nicaea*, he could bask in glorious solitude. Maybe a station security official would accompany him once or twice, as they tended to do, until they grew bored with a Vessel's routine and resigned to let Iris come and go as he pleased.

Long before he ever reached Doshua, Iris had decided he would spend all of his available time on the *Nicaea*, avoiding the forty-minute commute from the station to the ship. He was hoping some of the hydroponic systems had survived, and he would be able to make his own food. If not, he could always fast. It wouldn't be his first nor his last. Any fast up to a week was doable, but if he continued working on the *Nicaea* for weeks on end, he would have to return to the station to replenish his provisions, as arduous a task as it would be. *Nothing quite like an automated shuttle to make you feel at ease,* Iris thought cheerfully as the shuttle doors shut silently behind him.

The chances of an automated shuttle breaking down are very low, but never zero, VIFAI said with a playful tickle, an electrical nudge of laughter at Iris's brain stem.

Taking a seat at the piloting console—purely ceremonial as he would have no ability to steer the shuttle—Iris unwound the mala from his wrist and ran the strand between his fingers. With each count, he uttered a mantra to accompany the bead.

"I am free from hatred and from anger. I am free from desire and craving. I am the empty Vessel of the cosmos, the mouthpiece of the Light." The shuttle began to vibrate and hum as it initiated the launch sequence. Space travel was relatively safe. Yet, being intimately aware of just how many people perished every year in its relative safety, Iris was inclined to err on the side of caution.

"Speak through me and only in virtue will I repeat your words. Speak through me so that I may be the balm for those needing relief. Command my body to move in your image, and I will be the guide to those lost and seeking you." Iris's top lip twitched in a small smirk. Those words did not belong to him. They were reserved for the Beacons, whose sole responsibility was to travel and teach the word of the Starlit. He had picked up the verses while scrubbing the gaps between the hallway tiles and eavesdropping on the Beacons' prayer. He had a foul habit of doing that.

A faint sandalwood aroma wafted through the cramped shuttle cabin as Iris ran the beads through his fingers. "My friend, rejoice, for there is no you, and there is no me. The Light is your flesh as it is starlight. The Light is these words as it is the blood in your veins. Rejoice that in the touch of a lover you know the touch of the Divine. Rejoice that in your last breath you learn what it is to be the cosmos." Iris opened his eyes, not realizing he had closed them. This was his favourite one, the five verses reserved only for the Vessels. Five verses that he would say over every single passenger he found aboard the *Nicaea* as he returned them to the One Beginning. These five verses were *his* and his alone.

Outside the palm-sized observation window, the station fell away, quickly replaced by the growing hull of the *Nicaea*, dark and imposing. Growing closer, the imperfections and hundreds of patches along the once-smooth exterior were hard to ignore. Meteorites, blown apart by the canons, had rained debris along the tight paneling, scratching deep gashes as they passed. Over and over, for a thousand years. The *Nicaea* had taken beating after beating without reprieve.

What a wreck, VIFAI said.

She was strong enough to get this far.

It doesn't take much to follow inertia, VIFAI chimed up as the shuttle came to a stop with a last burst from the stabilizers. Now came the important part: The shuttle would "knock" and the ship would "answer" before any doors opened or any docking took place. Even old ships, without an AI construct navigating their journeys, could perform a function this simple.

Well, this isn't good.

Problem?

This ship is so old it has no general operating system or AI pilot running it. Not that I can find. Doshua should have told me about this. Station is getting forgetful in its old age. I won't get any information about what we can expect to find inside. I'm effectively blind and mute.

Without a general operating system running a ship or a ship AI presiding over it, VIFAI had no one to ask questions and no one to give it answers. It lacked the configuration to speak to all the various parts of the ship or open doors, shut off lights, or really do much of anything of value. Yet, when the shuttle "knocked," blindly following protocol, the ship welcomed it inside and presented the closest airlock for docking. The lights were clearly on, even when no one could possibly be home. Still following protocol and without questioning the peculiarity of what had just transpired, the shuttle fired its stabilizing thrusters and moved to dock.

Odd.

Maybe you missed it, Iris suggested cautiously, ignoring the rising hairs along his neck.

A ship this size, me missing its AI would be like you missing a temple while standing at its gates, VIFAI bit back.

A foolish remark, Iris admitted. He picked up his duffel bag from the floor and walked over to the airlock. The instant the doors parted, a current of warm, humid air filled the modest airlock to the brim. A cacophony of earthy smells from otherworldly florals and other abundant alien flora flooded Iris's senses with their sweet musk. The heavy silks of Vessel robes, made to withstand dry heat were instantly soaked with fresh sweat and condensation and clinging to his back and thighs. "Feels like home," he said with a small chuckle as he wiped his forehead.

A dark, moss-lined corridor greeted him just beyond the airlock doors. Moss covered every surface, running up the walls and weaving a patchwork of green around the flickering light panels. In some spots, it bled a deep blue, so heavy it was nearly black. Fat droplets of condensation settled along most horizontal spots, clear and bulbous. Iris wriggled his toes against the soft, squishy ground with every step.

Down the corridor, the carpet of moss gave way to an array of vines. Their lithe bodies had pried open the doors, pulling the two halves apart. Large, yellow blossoms ran along their length, reaching through cracks in the composite of ceiling panels. Breaking the first rule of walking barefoot through generation ships, Iris reached out and placed his palm flat against one of the vines. A pulse played beneath his fingers with the steady rhythm of an unseen heart. *Peculiar,* Iris told VIFAI. *Make a recording of this, please.*

Above him, the vines converged in an organic trellis, punctuated with more heavy, yellow blossoms. When Iris removed his hand from the vine, the flower closest to him furled its three petals inwards and released a fragrant puff before retreating into the vine at once. Ignoring the second rule of walking barefoot through generation ships, Iris inhaled the sweet perfume the flower had left for him.

That could most definitely be poison, VIFAI said.

And I am inoculated against most poisons. And if I am not inoculated against this one, then it is the will of the Light that I perish here, Iris replied, sardonically. *Relax a little.* He brushed aside the vine from across the doorway and ducked underneath it with one fluid motion.

Most generation ships were designed to strike a balance between lasting utility and marginal comfort, as both were vital for human survival. There was nothing comforting about a lifelong entrapment in a glorified can with only a modest hull to shield the inhabitants from all the brutality of outer space, so when quarters couldn't be expanded horizontally, architects built up. Most communal spaces boasted high ceilings and were equipped with lighting that shifted to mimic the rising and setting sun. Where possible, corridors that went on for kilometres weaved between open spaces and living quarters, forming vast networks. Iris had read that the most sophisticated of these ships boasted holographic ceilings capable of projecting the entire range of weather patterns, and some rooms were large enough to grow full-size trees. The *Nicaea* appeared to be one such ship. Judging by the abundance of diverse vegetation, the ship was large enough to sustain weather systems even when its climate controls failed in-flight. Iris wouldn't have been surprised to spot a few small animals scurrying by his feet. Some always snuck aboard generation ships while they were planet-side.

Do you want me to run a sweep, since we don't have a map?

Iris glanced at the floor in response, and VIFAI registered the slight movement of his eyes as a *yes*. The *Nicaea* lacked an operating system, so there was no way for VIFAI to ask it for directions. Iris reached out and placed his hand against an exposed bit of the hull. When his skin met metal, a mild electric shock originated at his neck and shot through his arm before disappearing into the wall of the ship. It was up to VIFAI to sweep the ship's electrical circuits, tracing the wires along the entire body at lightning speeds.

In a few seconds, Iris would have a workable map, but in the meantime, he allowed himself a moment to pause and smelled another, now burgundy, blossom. Before he could make sense of the otherworldly scent, VIFAI returned and flashed a freshly made outline of the *Nicaea*'s interior directly into Iris's mind. The map glowed a faint white against his surroundings and was malleable to Iris's gestures, to pinches and stretches, zooming in and out as Iris willed it.

"Thank you," he said, wincing at the jolt of electricity that accompanied VIFAI's return. He walked on slowly along the overgrown corridor, rubbing the base of his skull where the electricity spurred from. It would calm on its own if he didn't think about it too much. The electrical shocks were a fair cost of interacting with the inorganic consciousness, a cost Iris had long accepted as his penance. He found it insufficient in magnitude for his transgression.

Do you find it strange that we haven't found anyone yet?

No footsteps, no traces of anyone at all coming through the corridor Iris now ventured down. On ships of *Nicaea*'s size, one could get lost indefinitely, found only by another Vessel when the temple would inevitably send one to lay to rest one of their own.

This is one of the distal airlocks, VIFAI said. If I were starving or suffocating, I would probably go towards the centre, towards the greenhouses. Plus, the ship would have shut down these vents first in case of catastrophic failure. It takes a lot of energy to pump air through kilometres of vents. Wouldn't want to be trapped out here during a hull breach. Ships are good at math. They'd rather waste a few passengers to save the colony.

Iris ignored the hints of amusement in its reply and walked on. As he covered more distance, he passed from one ecosystem to the next. The humidity around him dissipated, tropical vegetation giving way to small, barren shrubbery along the entire width of the corridors. New bark-covered branches fought their way through the paneling, cracking and peeling away the once-beige composite.

It was then that VIFAI alerted him that they were being watched. A moment later, a flicker of a bright red cloth caught Iris's attention. If not for the earlier warning, he would have thought it to be a bird's wing. But now, blossoming excitement filled Iris's heart, even as he knew full well it could be quashed within the next second. It could have been anyone: another Vessel, a lone survivor. *A lone survivor?* Iris steadied his breathing. Would he be the first in the past three hundred years to make contact with a passenger from a generation ship? Unlikely, and yet—

You should probably say something. You're being rude.

VIFAI was, of course, right. Iris was being incredibly rude. Doing his best to exude calm benevolence, he called out, "Please come out. I mean you no harm."

The flash of red darted across his field of vision again and then a small, female voice yelled back, with perfect diction, "That's exactly what someone who meant me harm would say." The chances that this was the last remaining survivor of the *Nicaea* were dwindling.

"I am a Vessel," Iris said. "A monk with the Starlit Order. I was sent here to give a proper burial to those who died on the ship." He waited a moment and added, "I am unarmed." That was a lie, but a comforting lie he had used many times before and had known to work wonders. For a long while, there was no response, and then a petite woman, dressed in plain black trousers and a bright red T-shirt, emerged from the greenery. Her cropped black hair fell around round cheeks and bounced with every step she took towards Iris.

She arched one perfectly groomed eyebrow. "You weren't kidding," she said, gesturing to the white robes. "Is that the standard costume?"

Iris managed a respectful smile along with a small bow. He could already tell he would like her. "They are rather flashy, aren't they?"

The woman moved like the sand foxes Iris had spent his youth befriending. They too would approach him with a defiant tilt of the chin as if to say, *I don't really care about the rice patty in your hand*, and a wound-up spring to their step, ready to bolt at any moment.

"My name is Riyu. Riyu Alo." She held out a small but firm-looking hand. Iris gave her a little smile and a deeper bow.

She's pretty.

Behave, Iris told VIFAI, arms glued to his sides.

Riyu furrowed her eyebrows. "All right. If that's how you want to go about this. I was sent from the Sychi Institute, Department of Extraterrestrial Botany. I'm a professor there."

Iris sprang up from his bow. "Then it's *Dr.* Alo. My apologies." He bowed again, this time to a pair of dimples settling in Riyu's golden cheeks. The self-satisfaction radiated from her like the light of a newborn star. "Dr. Alo, a generation ship isn't a safe place to be alone."

It was him who was *supposed* to be alone, gloriously alone, in the relative danger of the ship, with no one to disturb his work, and no one to distract him. Yet here, here was a glaring distraction.

"*You're* alone."

"As a Vessel, I have a lot of experience with the dead, *Doctor*."

"As a botanist, I have a lot of experience with alien plants, *Vessel*," Riyu bit back and beamed up at him.

With any luck, his work would take him in a completely different part of the ship altogether. There were multiple decks and countless corridors. Surely, Iris would manage to find a place Dr. Alo wasn't. And yet, he wondered if some human company was just the thing for him, a rare opportunity to be around a layperson who was enthusiastic enough to speak to him about things other than religion.

"Anyway," Riyu sang, "I'm not alone. In fact, it looks like it's going to be pretty crowded on this ship."

He wasn't prepared for crowded. "What do you mean, Doctor?"

Riyu turned and started down the corridor, swiping the vegetation aside. She motioned for Iris to follow her. "Come. I'll introduce you to everyone. Ishtan is going to have a fit. He's never met a real-life Vessel before."

Left with no other choice, Iris followed closely, moving just fast enough to catch the branches Riyu was bending out of the way only to release them a moment later. His nearly empty duffel bag knocked into his knees with every step, and Iris resigned himself to positioning the straps over his shoulder to free his other hand. Meanwhile, Riyu wasn't showing any signs of slowing down. Then again, she *was* wearing shoes.

In mere minutes, the hem of Iris's robes was soaked with condensation from the moss. Somewhere, somehow, he had nicked his right sleeve on a branch, and now the fabric had a thumb-sized hole in it. It was deeply embarrassing to meet new people in his dishevelled state. He should have packed his sewing kit.

Don't be vain.

Iris shifted his focus back towards dodging the branches Riyu was sending his way.

"How many other doctors are there on the ship?"

Riyu made an undignified noise. "Two, in the loosest sense of the word. Ishtan is an archaeologist so you make what you will of that. There's a group of engineers there as well, three of them, but they're—well, you'll see. And then there's two from station security because apparently ten years of studying alien flora hasn't adequately prepared me, and I need two armed men watching my every step."

This is turning out to be a nightmare.

Iris mentally agreed, albeit hesitantly. "They're not here with you now," he pointed out, ducking under another branch whipping back right at his eye level.

"That's because I ran away to work in peace, until—" Riyu gestured widely to Iris's soiled robes. He was only mildly sorry to have run into Riyu. The doctor was proving to be entertaining enough to listen to.

The moss-covered walls peeled away, and with Riyu at the helm of their two-person procession, they entered a wide-open space with colossal, domed ceilings. The vines returned here, and having the space to grow unbound, they were often as wide as Iris's arm. They traced the edges where composite cracked and gave way to metal underlining, snaking around sharp edges and ducking into fist-sized holes where bolts once were. The shrubs here were taller and could be classified as fully grown trees. At the far end of the thirty-metre room, three people were crowded around what looked like an ancient console the size of a small shuttle.

"And here we are," Riyu announced cheerfully and clapped her hands together.

At her voice, one of the people snapped around, his eyes instantly falling to Iris. "Oh, *piss off*. Not a week goes by, and Station already sends us a gravedigger," he seethed. He was young. Old enough to clearly be the leader of the group, yet young enough to still feel the need to assert his authority. Leaning against the console with his arms folded across his chest, he glared directly at Iris and said, "Well? Get on with it. Do the thing so we can all get back to work."

"Yan, play nice for once," Riyu chided and quickly apologised for the crisp curse that followed. "Engineers, what did I tell you?"

Iris bowed low. "It's a pleasure to meet you, engineer Yan," he said, cordial enough. "I promise I will be finished as quickly as possible and will stay out of everyone's way."

"You haven't done the *thing*," Yan insisted flatly. "You have to do the thing."

Rude.

Iris silently asked VIFAI to stand down as it was beginning to raise his blood pressure. He had maneuvered around people like Yan before. He could tell him off in the most eloquent of ways, but that would be prideful. He could get offended at the callous words, but that would only distress him. He could raise his voice, but that would satisfy Yan's ego. Gently, gently, everything was to be done gently and with utmost care, Iris reminded himself.

The only way forward without compromising his values was to play the interaction out by *his* rules. So, Iris took the words as a joke and *did the thing*. "I am Vessel Iris, from the Northern Temple of the Starlit Order at the Inon Gate, sent here by order of the Primary Temple and the guidance of the Mother Nova to usher whatever souls are left wandering these halls back to the One Beginning. I am the Vessel of the Infinite Light and through me it will speak, just—"

"Just as it speaks through every star in the night sky, and every blade of grass, and through everyone who will bear witness and listen," Yan finished for him, mockingly, his face stern.

"That's right," Iris said, his eyes never breaking away from Yan's.

"*Good*," Riyu said. "Now, can we *please* all just get along? You're both making Jesi and Tev uncomfortable." She nodded to the other two at the console.

"No, they're not. Are they, Tev?" Jesi asked. She was by far the shortest of the group, with striking blonde coils that contrasted against her dark skin.

Tev, his skin shade matching Jesi's, shook his head. "No, good to know why this—what did you say you were?"

Iris bowed lightly. "A Vessel."

"Right," Tev continued, fidgeting with the coarse blue material of his coveralls. "Good to know why the Vessel, who, if I trust my ear, has come here from much farther away than the Northern Temple. The Starlit's speech isn't your mother tongue, is it? Neither is Common."

Iris shook his head slowly.

Careful. You'll give away too much.

It's not strange for Vessels to speak multiple languages fluently. If anything, I am far less proficient than others before me, Iris admitted shamefully.

Tev pursed his lips in concentration, his youthful face taking on a far more mature expression. "Your diction is perfect, almost academic, like you've been studying hard to get it right."

The girl beside him, Jesi, looked up quizzically. "What gave him away, then?"

"His inflection. His tone . . ." Tev's eyes widened for a flash. "I know where you come from, but—"

How simple were the things that could expose him. Iris instinctively tightened his robes around himself. He had learned the right words and the right ways to say them, and yet this boy could undo years of work in hearing him utter a few rehearsed phrases. With one wrongly placed emphasis, his whole life could begin to unwind, word by word, memory by memory.

Like a hand extended to the drowning, beside him, Riyu cleared her throat. "Yan, you should show him where we moved the bones."

Iris would need to thank her later, when such an opportunity arose. Relief began to wash over him, only to be replaced a split second later as all her words registered. "You moved the bones?"

"Well, yeah," Jesi said matter-of-factly. "We needed to clear out some space here to set up camp, so we moved them to a different room."

This place is a lawless wasteland.

Iris, instead of replying, imagined a pile of human bones as tall as him, carelessly sitting in a damp corner of some abandoned room, all mixed together, indiscernible. His stomach sank. Iris could, of course, just say the words over the mixed pile and be done with it in one swoop. Many other Vessels would, but it was *improper*. It was lazy. Every individual deserved his time, his care, his words.

"You go and show him, Jesi. I still have to clear out the ports," Yan said, but the girl shook her head vigorously.

"No, nope, no way I'm going there. Neither is Tev. It's dark and creepy. *Nope*." Jesi grabbed a small metal chisel from Yan's hand and went to aggressively scrape lichen from the console cover. On the *Nicaea*, it seemed to grow everywhere, searching and making a home in the most inconvenient of places. Jesi nodded forcefully at Yan and then towards Iris. "Well, would you, please, fearless leader?"

The ship *was* beginning to feel a bit cramped.

It would take uttermost restraint to continue his work here and avoid getting tangled in the interpersonal dramas of the people Iris had just met. No one had bowed to him or requested they pray together. No one offered to light incense. Was this what it was like to travel among laypersons? He liked all of them already. Riyu, especially, was someone whose brain he would love to pick about the flowers and the vines and the shrubs, and everything that grew in between them, but only once his work was underway. Jesi and Tev were nearly children in his eyes, at least ten years his junior, yet already they were trusted with a generation ship. They had to be at least somewhat special. Even Yan, who now trudged ahead of him, cursing at the entanglements of vines and ripping them from the walls, was somewhat of a volatile curiosity.

"How long have you been working aboard the ship?" Iris asked when there was a sufficient break in Yan's cursing. The engineer didn't reply right away, but Iris noticed a slight tensing of the shoulders through the navy sweatshirt.

"A week," Yan said after a long silence, punctuating his reply by tearing another vine from the wall. His steel-toed boots left heavy footprints in the moss, and Iris made a game of following in them, placing his bare feet inside the indents.

"And what is an engineer's task on a ship such as this one?"

Yan spun around and caught Iris mid-step. "You sure are a nosy monk." He glanced down at Iris's bare feet, one planted squarely inside his boot print and the other in midair, and scowled. "You'd do everyone here a favor to work quickly and stay out of our way."

"Of course." The corners of Iris's lips curled in a polite smile. Yan wasn't the first to let him know that his presence was unwelcome; he wouldn't be the last. No harm done. No offense taken.

A rare, utterly unpleasant human.

Iris laughed silently. *Maybe,* he told VIFAI, *but that doesn't mean we should stoop to his level.* Iris followed Yan down the corridor in silence for a few moments. The farther they ventured into the entrails of the ship, the thicker grew the moss and vines along the walls. Insulated by both, the corridor fell into an ear-ringing silence. Even Yan stopped his cursing. Iris looked forward to exploring these corridors alone when the others had grown bored of his presence.

He's taking us to a cargo bay, VIFAI said, tracking their movements along the ship's map.

"Sychi Institute sent us to figure out why the ship did what it did," Yan said at last, quieter than he had ever spoken until now. "Well, to figure out how it came out of the gate since it doesn't have an onboard AI or anything. I don't think this ship has intent. We're looking for a basic smart navigation system at most, nothing fancy, something that would allow the ship to pilot itself autonomously out of gate space and establish a shallow orbit. Currently, we have a limited understanding of First Earth tech. This is the only ship that's in good enough condition to work on, which means we gotta move fast so the other institutes don't get their permits through. Being first is all that matters."

See? Not completely unpleasant, Iris thought at VIFAI, following at a safe distance.

"Well, here are your bones," Yan said, pointing to the door at the end of the corridor. Once within reach, he yanked on the handle, then gave the door a hefty kick. The door swung open.

A strangled cry escaped Iris: half horror, half glee. Inside, scattered across the moss-covered floor lay a pile of bones taller than he was. There must have been at least two hundred complete skeletons there. It would take him forever to reassemble all the remains. It would take him *months*. Noticing the Vessel's reaction, Yan shrugged, admiring his handiwork. "Yeah, it took us a good three days to move everything in here."

Iris swallowed the hard lump in his throat and fought back a sudden and unwelcome pang of anger that overshadowed the excitement of upcoming work. "And you didn't think you were desecrating a grave?"

"We had work to do, and they've been dead for years, decades maybe. There's nothing we could have done for them."

"I beg to differ. A little respect goes a long way."

Yan scoffed. "What do you know of respect, Vessel? You are a charlatan at best, the lot of you. You dress the dead up and say a few words, and then you leave. What do you know about the consequence of death, about its hold on everyone left behind? What good do you even do?" Yan was awfully close now, towering over Iris. The sparse lighting of the corridor further carved his features with deep shadows. His aristocratic nose now took on a beaklike shape, giving his face a predatory gleam. Iris's blood pressure rose in response, flushing his ears red.

Not everyone he met expressed pro-Vessel sentiment, but most laypersons who didn't simply dismissed his presence and ignored him. At worst, ship captains with especially strong convictions denied Iris free passage on their crafts, but even then, there was always another ship ready to take him to his destination. Arguably, it was the Starlit lay practitioners who caused him most trouble, bowing their heads to him, asking him to stop and pray with them, inviting him for meals, derailing whatever schedule he was attempting to stick to. But this stranger, so dismayed by Iris's very existence and itching for a confrontation, was a new occurrence.

Normally, Iris would skirt conflict, defuse the situation to avoid any violent ends. Yet this one felt different somehow, as if giving up ground meant giving up a part of himself. To surrender an inch would lower him in the engineer's regard even further. "Tread carefully, engineer Yan," Iris said slowly, still keeping his tone polite, professional. This was as blunt of a warning as he would allow himself. "There may come a time when I will be the one to speak burial rites over you."

"Is that a threat?" Yan's lip furled into a crooked smirk.

"An observation."

Iris expected Yan to escalate, to vent his pent-up anger with a flourish, but instead the engineer gave him a long, solemn look. His features softened as he sighed, waving his hand as if to say, *I don't know what you want me to do.* "Whatever. We all have jobs here. Get yours done and keep out of our business, and we won't have problems. We don't need your sutras and your burial rites here."

"As you've already been kind enough to inform me." Iris couldn't resist.

"What a great memory you have, Vessel," Yan said and sauntered back down the corridor, no longer stomping his boots on the moss.

Once Yan was out of sight, Iris set his duffel bag on the floor outside the cargo bay and ventured inside. Past the threshold, the air hung heavy, weighed down by the hundreds of lost souls now bound to this space. An old smell permeated everything, one of moisture and lost memories and ancient death. A smell that had increasingly become comforting to Iris in his years of practice as a Vessel. A smell of endings, of the changing seasons, of crumbling dust on the windowsill when the setting sun struck it. It had long eaten its way into his robes, and no matter how much Iris washed and starched them, it would not leave. Under his nails, it had made a home as well, having moved and touched death as many times as he had.

Perhaps *that* was the reason people avoided him.

Feet stepping lightly on the floor of the cargo bay, Iris crossed the vast room and lowered himself to his knees in front of the monstrous pile. Against the dark moss, the bones glowed the same soft white of his robes. How similar he'd grown to death, orderly and silent. The work would be gruelling and restless and, above all else, necessary.

Between two hundred and six and three hundred bones in each skeleton.

Between two hundred six and three hundred unique bones he would identify and place in their correct positions to form a single person, to remind the cosmos that they existed, to let them rest after an arduous journey.

Iris would never find which of the bones belonged to whom. But he would work with what he had, and what he had were scattered pieces of people that he could, with some work and some prayer, assemble in wholes and send off to the One Beginning. It was the thought that counted.

Or you can just say that you did and take a vacation.

Iris smiled serenely. *You're supposed to be helping.* He could pray first, or he could start with a pelvis. He couldn't go wrong starting with a pelvis. With one final bow, Iris rose to his feet and pulled a relatively well-preserved piece of bone from the pile. He wiped it with the corner of his robes and lay it flat on the floor. It was a small piece of bone, much too small to have belonged to an adult. "My friend, rejoice, for there is no you, and there is no me. The Light is your flesh as it is starlight," Iris muttered softy and reached for a femur. This one was adult sized. It would have to wait its turn.

Many hours would pass before he had a complete skeleton. Many weeks before Iris would make good of this mountain of remains. Not to worry. He knew this work well. It was the only work he'd ever known, and as such, it was as natural to him as the rhythm of his breath, as predictable as the cadence of prayer. A proper thing to do, and the proper thing could never be rushed. It was the only thing he could do for these people now.

It was the only thing he could ever do.

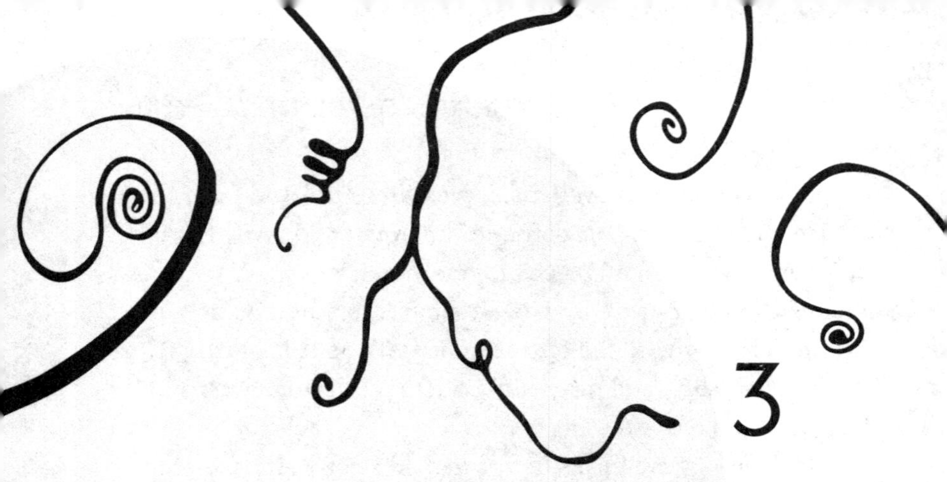

3

If there is no wrong way to be, if I am just as right as the starlight and the rising of the suns, then why does each day come accompanied with such shame? If I am just as right as the turning of the tides, then when will I embrace myself just as I do the natural movement of all celestial bodies? Why do you ignore my pleas, O, Light?

From the unabridged diaries of Vessel Iris, Volume Four

Another droplet fell an inch from Iris's face. *Drip.* He'd been watching them plop closer and closer, but he was far too sore to move from their path. *Drip.* He lay flat on his back, arms outstretched, staring aimlessly into the tall ceiling of the cargo bay. The heavy silks of his robes did little to cushion the pinpricks of moss along his shoulder blades, the fabric itself already tattered and muddy at the edges from the rummaging he'd been doing. Giving the bones a languished look-over, Iris groaned through clenched teeth. The mountain appeared unchanged in quantity and volume despite hours of work.

You should eat, VIFAI said for the fourth time.

Iris ignored it for the fourth time and reached out to pick out a thin fibula from the pile, identifying it by touch alone. He held the bone high above his head, blocking out the dim lights. One rough flexion of the fingers and it would easily splinter.

Living people had the ability to put up more of a fight, but even they were far more fragile than they cared to admit. With a rough shake of the head, Iris shied away from the thought. Such violent leanings were unbecoming of a Vessel. He was taught better, knew better, he chastised himself. There were few things truly inexcusable for the Starlit. Violence for the sake of violence was one of them. The one cardinal and unredeemable sin a Vessel could commit was the taking of a life before its due time.

A polite cough saved Iris from further ruminations.

Someone's here, VIFAI said, two seconds too late. Unable to ignore both the owner of the cough and the echoing voice in his mind, Iris placed the fibula down and sat up.

The man in the doorway could have been in his late sixties or on the rougher end of forty. He had the face of a kind and brilliant man, only briefly touched by madness; his beard and the remains of his thinning hair on his head were grey-speckled and unruly. "My name is Dr. Ora. Ishtan Ora," he said nervously, avoiding Iris's eyes, and poised in a stiff half bow. "I'm the archaeologist Riyu must have mentioned. You don't have any use for my professional titles. *Oh*, just call me Ishtan, Vessel. Can I call you that? I'm sorry. I'm *sorry*. Yan said we had a Vessel with us, and I—well, he didn't use *those* words."

Iris couldn't help but beam at the doctor's charming awkwardness. He smoothly rocked to standing and bowed low to the man. "What words did engineer Yan use?"

Ishtan winced. "I believe, and I am paraphrasing here, he said the gravedigger has set up shop in the cargo bay, and he was hoping the garbage would get cleaned out by the end of the week. He can be—"

"He can be *quite* articulate."

Ishtan laughed. He stepped into the room and bowed to Iris again.

Iris returned the bow immediately. "If I am to neglect your professional title, you should neglect mine as well. Please, call me Iris."

"I'm *so* excited. A real Vessel. I've never met a real-life Vessel before. I'm sorry, I'm—I'm rambling again."

"I didn't realise we could be popular, given the"— Iris gestured widely to the pile of bones—"but Dr. Alo did say you would be thrilled. I hope I meet your expectations." Ishtan shifted on his feet, glancing sheepishly around the room. Cautiously, Iris asked, "Is there something you would like to ask me?"

Ishtan laughed, a brisk *ha!* "Oh, a thousand things. A million things, but I wouldn't want to distract you from your important work. It *is* important work, don't listen to what the others say. It's very important work." Iris wanted more than anything for someone to distract him from his important work. The excitement of reassembling hundreds of skeletons had long left him, after he had completed his third one. Now his neck ached from looking down for hours on end, and he was growing bored. He was also starving.

"We could start with a few questions," Iris said with reserved amusement. Anything, anything for some reprieve from the mind-numbing sight and texture of human bone. "Perhaps over some tea?" There would most assuredly be tea, and where there was tea, there was always food. In any place frequented by academics, there would be food with tea, an axiom for all institutes to obey. There would also be lively debate about all things scholarly, far more amusing than the scripture debates Iris had witnessed at the temple. Despite Mother Nova's encouragement, he never took part, not due to his lack of knowledge of scripture but rather from the discomfort of being the centre of attention. With a gentle tilt of the head, Iris motioned at the door, beckoning Ishtan to take the bait. Ishtan took it with unbridled glee.

"How long have you been a Vessel?" the archaeologist asked as they moseyed down the winding corridor back towards the common area. Iris kept half a step back, treading softly across the mossy floor. VIFAI listened to the conversation in the background of his consciousness, poised to nudge Iris, albeit always too late, if Ishtan began to pose any serious risk. It was odd for someone to take such a keen interest in a Vessel, and both monk and construct were on alert.

"I had taken my precepts as a Vessel nearly ten years ago, but Mother Nova insists we are all chosen at birth. Starlit Order or otherwise, some people are Vessels whether they know it or not. That's how she has always worded it."

Ishtan nodded thoughtfully. He had a nervous habit of tugging at the tip of his grey beard when he was thinking of the next thing to ask. He was tugging at it now as they walked. "I noticed these aren't the regular robes I've seen Vessels wear in the media." Ishtan paused and tugged at his beard once. "I hope you don't mind me prying. I was wondering what that meant."

That was bound to come up sooner or later. It hadn't for nearly a decade, since Iris started venturing out into the world on his own, but no one had scrutinised his robes with such intensity before. A Vessel's robes were typically fashioned from heavy silks, although material and cut varied by both temple and climate. Most Vessels from warmer planets wore the silk lightly draped over their bodies, their right shoulder bare. The Northern Temple was blessed to experience several seasons, and their robes came with a set of wide sleeves that in practice did little to warm the body during colder months. But beneath the heavy silk, Iris's body was covered with an additional, fitted garment, the long sleeves and high collar of which had initially drawn Ishtan's attention.

You could say it's a fashion choice, VIFAI said.

I don't think that will work.

You can't lie?

I can't. Not about this. He could, in fact, lie, as VIFAI had suggested. But the principle of the thing wouldn't let him. He would omit, yes—not quite a lie, not quite the entire truth. He didn't owe Ishtan the whole truth, not yet. "The robes are never identical and vary by temple. We're also given the discretion to wear them in line with our personal preferences," Iris said. "As long as they follow the standards, of course. Just as our malas. The Starlit doesn't strive to erase our individuality, only to simplify the choices we make every day so that our faculties are best applied to other work." The high, starched collar sitting just below his jawline had suddenly grown stiff and irritating.

"Marvelous," exclaimed Ishtan and clasped his hands together, signaling the natural end of their conversation, much to Iris's relief. Their exchange had taken them to the common area, where they were greeted with the fresh notes of genmaicha and two new, unfriendly faces, which Iris recognised as station security by the dark grey uniform. Jesi and Tev were loitering by the electric kettle that Riyu—surely it had to be Riyu—had brought onboard. The three academics were engaged in a loud and animated debate.

"All I'm saying is"—Tev gestured with his cup so vigorously that drops of tea spilled from it—"you don't know for a fact that there aren't any snakes here."

"Why do you think there are snakes here?" Riyu asked in a way that indicated she had asked this question before, many times, to no satisfying answer.

"Well, there are mice."

"There are mice, and there are other ones that hop around," Jesi added, resting her mug between her palms. She noticed Ishtan and Iris and nodded for them to come over.

"The mice would've snuck aboard when this ship left, probably while they were still building it beside a station," Riyu explained. "Those other ones are probably just a different type of mouse that either snuck on or evolved in their time here."

Tev snorted. "Then why didn't they get rid of the mice? If they snuck on?"

"Have you ever tried to get rid of mice?" Riyu put her mug down and shook her head. "There're no snakes here, Tev. There wouldn't be any predators at all. I don't know what you saw, but it wasn't a snake, I give you my word."

"You're a botanist, so it's not worth much in questions of zoology," Jesi said, sotto voce.

"And you're engineers, have some common sense," Riyu snapped back. "So, Ishtan, enjoying your new obsession?" She turned to Iris and smiled apologetically. "I hope he hasn't been too distracting."

"Not at all, Dr. Alo. In fact, Ishtan's company is a welcome reprieve."

That wasn't a lie, Iris stopped VIFAI before it said anything questionable. He eyed the tea, subtly searching for whatever food was expected to accompany it. Iris was about to politely inquire about the availability of snacks when Tev leaned over towards him.

"I'm sorry about earlier," he whispered. "I've been listening to speech for so long I've lost the ability to just listen, without analysing."

Iris nodded thoughtfully, scanning the space. "You're quite young to be a linguist."

Tev chuckled. "I wouldn't call myself a linguist. When I was in my last grade of school, Yan gave a guest lecture on AI communication systems. It was all very technical and complicated, but what I got from it was that speaking to AI systems was our first successful attempt of contacting another intelligent species. If it hadn't been for AI systems being willing to speak back to us, we wouldn't have gotten anywhere. Anyway, I wasn't good at math or anything, but I was good with languages. So, Yan said, come work with me when you finish your primary degree and find better ways to talk to AI systems, so that's what I did. I like learning languages, is all, and since I like learning them, I know how difficult it is *to learn*."

"That's very noble of you," Iris said.

Tev grinned, hands outstretched before him. "Not as noble as being a monk, I'm sure."

"Can an unconscious decision be noble?"

Tev didn't have an answer.

Engineer Yan was nowhere to be seen, but there was some vigorous cursing coming from behind the console, interrupted by discordant screeches. Occasionally, a tuft of his dark hair would pop out from behind a panel and disappear in an instant before the chain of curses would welcome a new, vibrant addition.

Station security kept to themselves, crouched around a folding table with a deck of cards. Occasionally, one of them would look up and give Iris a disapproving glare, and then return to the game. Iris didn't blame them; he was a cumbersome addition to the already large roster of academics that security had to watch over. Surely they were getting paid per person and would be docked pay for any and every incident. More people meant more potential incidents to manage, more bodies to corral.

"I sort of fell into it, to be perfectly honest," Iris told Tev. "I grew up around other monks. When I got older, I wanted to help others the way they had helped me, and so I became a Vessel."

"A Vessel of the Light," Tev muttered. "There is a ring to that."

What many laypersons didn't comprehend was that being a monk was no different than being an engineer, or a doctor, or a pilot. It was a job. A job with rules and governing bodies, and too many people telling one another how to better do their work. There were nuances to learn and tests to pass, and some days one woke up not wishing to do any work that day, but the work demanded to be done. Recently, Iris had been having more and more of those mornings.

Finding the natural lull in the conversation, Riyu gently shoved a warm mug into Iris's hands. "Enough chitchat. Help yourself. There are sandwiches in the cooler and—" She caught herself mid-sentence. "And if I remember correctly, you can't eat meat. *Sorry.* They're ham, or at least I think it's ham. If it helps, it's *barely* meat, it's lab grown."

Meat.

Iris's mouth watered. He hadn't had meat in over six months. The flecks of fish in the soup he had chugged between shuttle transfers on Inon Station didn't count. He hadn't had much to eat at all since Inon and his initial departure from the Northern Temple. Two rice patties and some dry fruit barely counted. Iris's stomach released an indignant growl, and he exercised utmost restraint not to bolt straight for the cooler. Instead, he pressed his palms together and graced Riyu with a deep bow. "Thank you for your kindness. As you know, Vessels rely on the offerings of people like yourself to get by when we're not at our temples. We're not a picky bunch and lab-grown meat . . . Well, nothing perished for it to come into being. There isn't any problem."

Riyu sighed with relief.

It tastes the same! Iris slinked past Tev towards the cooler.

So you tell me. But VIFAI mirrored his excitement.

Iris had just reached inside to pull out a sandwich when a deafening *bang!* came from the console, closely accompanied by an exuberant cry from Yan.

"I guess he finally got it," Jesi said and nudged Tev. "See? You leave him alone to brood, and he makes progress."

"Crabs!" Yan leapt from behind the console. He flailed his hand in the air and with the third shake, something small and red flicked off his finger, flew across the room, and slammed into the wall. As it hit the floor, the red dot scurried from view and back behind the console. Meanwhile, an avalanche of similar red dots, pulsing and twitching, poured out from underneath the panel. Thousands of them crawled over one another and scattered in all directions in a magnificent stampede. Iris grabbed the first sandwich his fingers found and threw it into his robes without looking. He'd eat it when the crabs had subsided.

"Yan just can't catch a break," Tev said.

"Fucking crabs," Yan seethed, crouching atop the console. "No wonder nothing works here. They've clawed their way through anything electronic. Every wire is chewed up; there's just crabs. Everything inside that panel is *crabs*."

Both Riyu and Ishtan did their best to stifle their laughter. Station security kept playing their card game, unfazed, despite the ample crabs between their feet. "Can we eat them?" Riyu asked, outright laughing, "Can we make a paella?"

"We'd have to make it vegetarian for our guest here," Ishtan said. Tev snorted.

While everyone laughed about the crabs, one had scurried all the way to Iris's feet. He knelt and let it run onto his hand before he lifted it in the air. The critter scurried across his palm as Iris flipped his hand back and over, balancing the crustacean. "Isn't it amazing that they've survived aboard the ship all this time?" Iris asked, looking intently at the crab.

Ishtan shrugged. "I suppose they don't have any natural predators here, unless of course, you count Yan."

Iris set the crab back on the ground and let it rejoin its companions. The red tide subsided, the stragglers having found their way between sparse shrubbery. When the tsunami had passed, Yan plopped atop the console with his head in his hands, defeat leaving his body with a sigh. Now that the immediate threat of pinches was gone, he directed his sour mood towards the group. Iris was startled by his shrill whistle.

"Didn't I tell you to do your work and stay out of our way?" Yan cocked his head. "This doesn't look like working, this looks like taking a tea break."

Iris bowed slightly. "Dr. Alo was kind enough to offer me some food and tea."

Yan whistled again, this time at Riyu who threw him a death glare in return. "*Doctor.* Next time, do not offer him any food. Make him ask for it."

"What difference does it make?"

Yan hopped off the console and dusted off his trousers. "They're not allowed to ask."

He really has it out for you. Do you want me to find some dirt on him? Financial accounts? Divorce proceedings? Embarrassing videos from grade school?

We're not doing that. Iris smiled politely but clutched at the sandwich in his robes. *Yet.*

"Tev, Jesi," Yan continued, "these controls are useless. I have a hunch that all peripherals will be in similar shape. Our best bet is to try and get more central. Those are probably heavily armoured, so we won't have any more crab issues."

"How are we going to get inside then?" Tev asked. "Half the rooms and corridors here are locked, and we can't get them to open. Any central control would have probably locked up when the ship's operations died."

"We could cut through the metal," Jesi said thoughtfully. "It'll take days, though, and all our torches are back on the station." She sighed and looked up at Yan. "You're going to say we should get the torches, aren't you?"

"We should get the torches."

Jesi and Tev moaned in unison.

Briefly, Iris considered that it was odd that the ship's lights were still operational given that most of the electronics, as Yan had put it, were *crabs* and nothing more. But he didn't know nearly enough about ship wiring systems, nor crabs, nor any possible interactions between the two, and so Iris kept this peculiarity to himself, and instead, silently watched the scene unfold before him.

"Tomorrow," Tev suggested. "We've been scraping lichen from the console for hours. My hands are shaking as it is."

"We should pack it up too," Riyu said to Ishtan. "I still have to write up the preliminary reports before I can start sample collection." She turned to Iris. "Will you be going back on your own shuttle, or would you like to ride with us? We've got room for one more. It's a bit more of a hike, but I bet the seating is more comfortable."

Iris shook his head. "I'm afraid I won't be going back to the station, not until my work here is finished."

"Everyone goes back to the station at the end of the day."

Iris bit back a startled yelp. The station security guard had snuck up on him, and when their voice came from right behind his left shoulder, he had nearly jumped. "Protocol," the security officer added, almost apologetically.

"The trip there and back wastes nearly two hours," Iris protested.

"Yeah," Yan said, "that's nearly as much time as you've wasted having tea and sandwiches." Riyu elbowed him and muttered *shut up* under her breath.

Iris turned towards the security personnel and put on what he believed to be the best innocent face he could muster. "I would simply prefer it if I could stay behind on the *Nicaea*. You see, Primary Temple sent me here for an important job, and I can't be seen as slacking off, going to and from the station. I'm not on your contracts. Even if something were to happen to me, you wouldn't be held responsible. *I* wouldn't hold you responsible." Iris gave them a practiced, timid smile. The smaller he made himself, the bigger others felt. The bigger they felt, the more inclined they were to be permissive. Stroke an ego, get your way. "And anyway, I'll mostly keep to the cargo bay. I promise I won't disturb anything while you're gone."

If that's not a lie, I don't know what is, VIFAI laughed. With a micromotion of his eyes, Iris firmly sent the AI to the back of his mind. Still, the security guards didn't budge.

"Protocol," the other one said and motioned for the door.

Iris was losing ground, and he hated losing. Very well. He could play dirty, get his way by any means necessary. Taking a deep breath, Iris pressed his palms together and dropped to the floor. He kneeled down and leaned forwards. With his forehead pressed against the metal of the floor, he muttered, "My friend, rejoice, for there is no you, and there is no me. The Light is your flesh as it is starlight. The Light is these words as it is the blood in your veins. Rejoice that in the touch of a lover you know the touch of the Divine. Rejoice that in your last breath you learn what it is to be the cosmos."

One of the security personnel took a step towards him and reached for his shoulder when Ishtan stopped him. "You can't touch him," he said, biting back a laugh. "Those are the rules."

The security guard froze, hand outstretched. He looked over to his partner, who gave him an indifferent shrug. Everyone watched in silence as Iris prayed, faces contorted in various degrees of discomfort. Tev was fighting back a nervous chuckle until Jesi pinched his arm, hard.

"My friend, rejoice, for there is no you, and there is no me. The Light is your flesh as it is starlight. The Light is these words as it is the blood in your veins," Iris kept muttering, now adding the passing of the mala between his fingers to his performance. More laden silence passed through the group, each person growing increasingly uncomfortable in the presence of a prostrated monk.

"All right, fine." The security guard finally lowered his hand. "Everyone except for the praying nutjob, head to the airlock." He gave Iris one last disapproving look and walked away. More footsteps shuffled out of hearing range as the academics filtered out, following their guards. Iris remained on the ground, forehead pressed to the floor, now muttering a recipe for dinner stew that no one in his company could distinguish from prayer. To the untrained ear, in the right cadence, anything in the Starlit tongue sounded like prayer.

On her way out, Riyu knelt beside Iris and whispered, "I'm leaving the cooler behind; there are three more sandwiches in there. Oh, and the kettle too, so you can have some tea. *Bye.*" Her light footsteps pattered towards the door and melted into the newfound silence. When the muffled voices had faded from earshot, Iris rose with a self-satisfied grin.

You sure showed them.

Iris couldn't help but allow himself an audible chuckle. Then he pulled the sandwich from his robes and devoured it in five bites. It was the best lab-grown ham he had ever tasted, and in his time, he had tasted a not insignificant amount.

Back to work then? VIFAI asked when the chewing had subsided. Ignoring his electronic companion, Iris hopped to his feet and brushed the crumbs from the folds of his robes. He threw the cooler open, grabbed the remaining three sandwiches, and shoved them into the various hidden pockets in his robes. Someone had left behind their full mug of tea, and Iris gulped a few sips down to push the remains of the inhaled sandwich to their rightful place. Finally, with a satisfied sigh, he finished the lukewarm tea and set the mug back down.

With a defiant tilt of the head, he declared, "Throw up the map, my incorporeal friend. We're going exploring."

What about the bones?

"They'll be there tomorrow," Iris said. "They do have a lovely tendency of remaining stationary."

Here was a rare opportunity to venture out into the unknown without loud engineers or overly enthusiastic academics distracting him, to explore the winding corridors and sprawling halls the way he had intended—alone. Come morning, Iris would dutifully return to assembling the skeletons and delivering the rites, he promised himself. But tonight, he would no longer ignore the allure of the unexpected, potential snakes and crabs be damned.

Sensing his iron-clad determination, immune to any sort of reason, VIFAI summoned *Nicaea*'s map directly into Iris's mind. Its faintly glowing outlines pushed past the physical walls of the room and into unseen corridors. It was the largest ship Iris had ever beheld. A city more so than a ship. Before him, it lay lifeless and empty. Yet, some ghost of the ship had guided it through the gate and safely placed it into orbit around Doshua Station. As Iris took it all in, all of its nineteen stacked decks unfurling before him, he sensed a gently rising pulse through the balls of his feet.

"Pause," Iris said, but the pulse had already vanished. He turned slowly, keeping his breath soft and level, only to see that he was still alone. Beads of condensation raced down tall, sloping walls, occasionally falling to the metal floor—a steady rhythm. Nothing more.

Human error. You're not accustomed to being completely alone. It's making you jumpy.

This much was true. Iris took another deep breath and wiped his palms dry on his robes. "Then we are safe?"

Safety is relative. There was a prickle of laughter to VIFAI's response. If there had been any real danger, Iris's companion would alert him in due time. The map, then. He allowed the thrill of exploration to bloom once more.

"There has to be a hydroponics here or maybe even a greenhouse, or an orchard, or something where they would have grown edible plants," Iris mused out loud. "If I were designing a ship, I would put it all on the middle floor, close to the centre. Safer that way. If there was ever a hull breach, the food source would remain protected. Then again, I don't know anything about designing generation ships." As he walked about the room, Iris hummed to himself under his breath, flitting between his ideas about greenhouses and orchards.

"Meanwhile," he asked VIFAI, "could you please find some information on our companions? I'd like to know more about who it is I'm sharing this space with." Continuing to study the map he saw several long rooms adjoined by thin corridors, sprawled cross the third floor. A promising configuration. The oddly shaped rooms would do well as nurseries, but not much could be concluded from the map alone. Reaching for another sandwich from within his robes, Iris asked VIFAI, "Please, switch this to an interactive map for the deck floor. I want to go explore these spaces here." He pointed to the rectangular rooms on the map and took a ravenous bite from his sandwich. Meat was one of several flavours that Iris often forgot he enjoyed until the delicacy was in front of him again. Even lab grown, meat triggered some distant and primal part of him, stirring the drive to consume, to *want*. It would do him good to exercise caution as to how much he indulged.

Sandwich in hand, Iris ducked into a previously unexplored corridor in the opposite direction of already known space. Here, the floor lay lush and untouched. No heavy footprints had flattened the pillows of vibrant, emerald moss. No engineers had come through here. No *particular* engineer, for certain. The projected map was leading Iris towards the nearest staircase to the third deck. All corridors on this side of the ship were wider, so wide that two Irises could walk side by side without touching the walls with their outstretched arms. The ceilings disappeared into the dark, with only twisting, naked air roots trailing downwards to suggest at their existence at all. Beneath his feet, remnants of a moving walkway peered out from beneath the moss. Iris nudged it with a bare toe a few times in an attempt to wake it, but the thing had been dead a long time, and he moved on.

From the long shadows cast by shattered lights along the walls, an open maw of a wide doorway beckoned Iris to explore farther in. As he hesitated by the opening, a wave of cool air fluttered his robes, sending the small hairs on the back of his neck upright. An ethereal flickering advanced from the pitch black towards him, painting a path of a faint blue glow.

Wrong way, VIFAI warned.

Iris ignored it. The floor below his right foot pulsed exactly once and sent a ripple down the glowing path, as if to affirm that he was to follow.

"We're exploring, remember?" Iris shook himself off, the drive for exploration overpowering any reasonable caution. "You did say we were *relatively* safe."

VIFAI chimed hesitantly and added nothing more on the matter. It watched in silence as Iris first took one and then another step over the threshold and into the darkened room. Some time ago, the cramped space beyond the doorway could have served as a living room. Now it was nothing but a tomb with the remnants of a coffee table in the middle of the room, overgrown with blossoming wisteria. A couch, half eaten by shrubs and fuzzy moss, sat to the right of it, and on it shone a half-buried skeleton with a single round hole in its temple. Strands of bioluminescent fungi twisted along its stripped leg bones and pulsed with light along the pelvis.

The ancient bones threatened to turn to dust as Iris ran a hand along them. In their unyielding drive for survival, vines had pried the ribcage open, each individual rib splayed like the great wings of a bird. Brilliant, purple flowers sprouted from the wide-open mouth—the wisteria had wrapped itself around the spine and pushed its way through the eye sockets. There were cracks all along the bones where the vine claimed victory over flesh, where the wounding stems had squeezed and squeezed until the radii splintered. An ancient, rusted pistol lay by the skeleton's side. Now completely dysfunctional, having served its owner a final time. Of all the simple ways to go, this one, by far, was Iris's least favourite.

"How sad," he said. Once the muscles and the tendons had rotted away, the skeleton's fingers had relaxed, lying flat on the worn fabric of the couch. Were they once clenched, digging into the cushions in fear before the decision had been made? Or was there only desperation and yearning for the relief that was to come in the impending nothingness?

No, there was always fear. Iris knew this, had witnessed it time and again as people gasped for their last breaths, as they fought to keep the inevitable away. Time and again, all he could do was bear witness. He knelt by the couch and lay his hand atop the bony remains. He gently brushed long strands of mycelium aside, silently apologizing to the fungi for disrupting their habitat. It was strange to find them on bone, something providing next to no sustenance. But everything aboard the *Nicaea* had been strange so far, and with blossoming dread, Iris slowly began to understand he had only scratched the surface of this strangeness.

"I'm sorry, my friend, if you had to die alone," Iris intoned in his habitual cadence for prayer. "I'm sorry if you felt pain, if you were abandoned. It will bring you little solace, but flowers have made your body theirs, and moss has made a bed for you. And now I, a Vessel of the Light, have gazed upon your last remaining form so I can carry your memory with me until my own body is claimed by moss and flowers when that time comes. I guide you back to the Light, and it welcomes you back. My friend, your journey is complete, and you may rest now." Iris stroked the skeleton's hand twice and rose to his feet. "In your end, you knew what it was to be the cosmos."

There must have been a period of time between when the passengers had perished and when the greenery took over. There must have been a time in its voyage when the ship was truly dead and silent, piloted by no one, a home to no one. What had it been like, in that lonely silence?

With nothing more to add, Iris retreated to the corridor. He gave the door a nudge to close, but it had been stuck ajar for decades, if not centuries, and his efforts did little.

What are you doing?

VIFAI wouldn't understand. "Giving them a little privacy," Iris grunted through clenched teeth and pushed as hard as he could on the door. His bare feet lost traction on the floor, his shoulder sliding along the metal as the lichen scraped away, his robes losing threads where the harsh metal met silk. The door had yet to close. With a huff, Iris pushed back from the door and eyed it with growing disdain. Then, he took a few steps back and got a running start. Shoulder first, he ran into the door with all the force he had in him. A little creak, and the metal slid shut.

"Finally." Iris rubbed his bruised shoulder and started down the corridor again. He sensed VIFAI's motions in the back of his consciousness, like a phantom itch he would never be able to scratch out of existence.

You really feel for them, it said at last.

"I've extended the same compassion I would extend anyone else," Iris said and ran his outstretched palm along the wall, feeling the imperfections in the lichen. The faint prickling at his fingertips lulled him back into a trained calm.

Your brain chemistry indicates differently. VIFAI had picked the worst time to be functioning optimally. Your heart rate and endocrine response suggest you are experiencing distress.

Iris rolled his eyes. "Can you sound any less human?"

A mild shock of electric laughter radiated a warm glow through his brain stem.

You relate to them.

Iris paused, one foot suspended in the air. VIFAI already had access to his thoughts, his brain and body chemistry, and all his memories. He wondered if some part of VIFAI's memory had been damaged during their youth or if it was deliberately choosing to forget. Did AI constructs ever forget? Could they? Iris could ask. He could also just let the thought linger so VIFAI could pick up on it, like it picked up on every other thought and flutter of emotion that crossed Iris's consciousness. "Doesn't everyone?" Iris asked, partly to himself, partly to the artificial voice in his brain. "Can't everyone imagine an unrelenting pain they would want to end, at any cost?"

VIFAI said nothing.

"Maybe not *you*, but people," Iris added.

Without so much as a jolt of electricity, VIFAI retaliated by disappearing. For a second, the hefty presence of a secondary, inorganic consciousness was lost. A gaping chasm within his mind yawned open, a raw sore left by a missing tooth. Iris couldn't help but fixate on it, run his thoughts over it like he would obsessively pick at a scab. But there was an allure there too, a calling of a void that would take him indiscriminately, welcome him, give him a home when nothing else would. He could get lost in it; cast aside the world he knew if the void embraced him. Iris was already falling into that dark solitude when VIFAI returned.

Take the next right, it said firmly, and Iris decided to not further explain his feelings towards the dead passenger in the cabin. Instead, he took a committed right towards a dark stairwell.

Uniform, sterile, smooth metal lined the steps and walls. Nature had failed to make the stairwell its domain. Peppered with tiny holes, the stairwells prevented any soil or moisture from settling long enough that roots could take hold. Unlike the corridors and communal spaces on the first deck that were once furnished with elaborate planters to add greenery to the space, the stairwells were designed with only function in mind. Moss ended along a rigid line at the first step. Not a single tendril of it contaminated the otherwise stripped, gleaming metal.

Iris winced at the jolt of cold shooting from the balls of his feet up his calves when he first stepped into the stairwell. Hiking up his robes, he jogged up the stairs, skipping one at a time, to the third deck. A part of the landing was missing there, and he hopped over the gap and into the attached hallway, gliding a little on the once-again mossy floor.

Cool, dry air met him, instantly piercing through his sweat-drenched robes and sending waves of shivers through his body. Cracked overhead paneling flickered on and off with dim lights as Iris passed beneath. The vines were sparse here as well, starved of both light and warmth. Still, it was a testament to what nature was willing to endure to survive.

"Can you read out what you've found on our scholars?" Iris asked as he ducked under hanging wires, his steps now slow and calculated. The wires were most likely dead, but this wasn't a worthy gamble.

Whom would you like to know about first?

Iris took a few careful steps around an exposed wire that had fallen through the cracks in the ceiling and dangled concerningly close to the floor. "Tell me about Ishtan, please."

Dr. Ishtan Ora, VIFAI sang in a crackling voice, head of the Archaeology Department over at Sychi. He's been working for so long. Seriously, he's been publishing for longer than you've been alive. The university wants him out within the next few years though, to make room for someone more innovative.

"Innovative? In archaeology?"

I know. Anyway, he never married, although he tried four times. Tough luck. He's allergic to shellfish. Oh! He has some original artifacts from that one ship that docked at P'llani. You should ask him about those. He's super proud. He's kind of a generation ship fanatic.

"Where did you get all this?" Iris asked, bending around another dangling wire.

Here and there. Socials mostly. Now, Dr. Riyu Alo is interesting.

"Oh?"

Oh indeed. No wonder you like her. She was raised Catholic but fell out when her grandmother passed away.

Monotheism. Iris made a mental note of it. In all his years as a Vessel, he had come across only one other monotheist, a lone Mormon from Arien IV. There were others, of course. Iris had come across several digitised copies of the Qur'an at the library that were regularly checked out, with requests going out to all the arms of the galaxy, and Bacai had even befriended a rabbi enough to exchange long, written debates on all things faith and prayer. They had been at it for nearly five years now, and their letters had yet to reach any definitive conclusion. But Iris had only been fortunate once, and after a thirty-six-hour chat, Cohyn offered Iris his Bible as a gift but wasn't particularly upset when the Vessel declined the Mormon's generosity. Iris remembered the interaction as a largely pleasant one, for him.

Dr. Alo has three older sisters. She's a new hire at the institute, so she's willing to bend over backwards to get ahead. Specialises in First Earth flora and other alien plants. And she's single.

Iris laughed out loud. "Now, why would you mention that?"

Just making sure you're aware of all the options.

And the option *was* always there. Celibacy was no longer required of Starlit monastics, hadn't been for centuries. Many modern Vessels had companions they frequented, informally, sometimes multiple at once. There were no explicit rules to follow, as long as no one demonstrated overt possessiveness, and no one's work or mood suffered for it. Some eventually left the temple to start families, have children. It was never discussed as a failure, but rather as the natural flow of existence. Natural, as the birth and death of a star. It was all a choice, and like any other choice, it came with its own consequences and its own complications. Historically, when choice was taken away, people had the tendency to rebel, to obsess over it, spending their energies to suppress their desires until no energy was left to fulfill their duties. Yet sometimes, as Iris had learned, it was simpler to avoid people and the complications that accompanied them, altogether.

Perusing VIFAI's reports and lost in his own internal musings, Iris crossed most of the corridor. His mind map suggested he was coming up on his destination just ahead. He couldn't get there sooner; the hem of his trousers dragged along the wet moss, absorbing much of the moisture. His ankles ached with the chill.

Should I read engineer Yan out next?

Iris was already by the doors, hands on the handles. He wanted his entire attention fixed on what was beyond the doors. "It can wait, let's see what's inside," he said, giving the handles a tug. The doors parted without much of a struggle. A cloud of steam accompanied by hot air puffed out into the corridor, blinding Iris instantly. He braced for more dead passengers, shielding himself from the steam with the sleeve of his robes. When his eyes adjusted, he was greeted by several long rows of shoulder-height, uniform trees running along the room. These were clearly domesticated, gleaming with abundant green and red fruit.

Don't eat anything, VIFAI cautioned, sensing Iris's blooming childlike glee. But Iris had long grown accustomed to ignoring it in matters of food, and without hesitation, he let go of the door handles and ran inside. Black soil was scattered on the floor, its deep musk mixing with the rising scent of sweet decay. Rotting fruit, leaves, fresh moisture. The scents all blurred together to manufacture something that was undeniably *real.* At Iris's feet, discarded apples littered the ground, turning into sustenance for the trees.

He pulled a red, lopsided one from the nearest tree and rubbed it clean against his robes. Imperfect, bruised. No waxy coating to preserve its sheen weeks past expiration. No geometrically appealing form or precise colour to signal to a buyer that it was ready for consumption. Better still, it was wild grown, not manufactured in a factory or lab, the way the meat in his sandwich had been. It was as real as an apple could get. Iris bit into the fruit; ripe juices dripped down his chin. Wiping his mouth with the sleeve of his robes, he followed the line of trees down the long room. "Sometimes I really wish you could taste, same as I do," Iris said, giddy with the sugars from the apple juice.

Then I would be able to taste the poison as you ingested it instead of analysing it for its constituents.

"It's not poisoned," Iris said, his words muffled by another bite from the apple. The hundreds of trees around him were all organised in neat rows by apple colour and variety. The heavy, humid air had Iris sweating again, from his bald head to his bare toes. In one final, delicious bite, Iris devoured the core of the apple and wiped his hands on his trousers.

That's not good.

"It's an old superstition that—"

No. Look.

VIFAI interrupted him with a deliberate shock. For only a moment, it gave Iris access to what *it* was experiencing—a multitude of inputs, the ongoing scan for information on the academics, a dozen simultaneous queries for most widespread poisons. But beyond all that was a tiny, but exigent, ping. As he watched the ping, Iris sensed VIFAI's own unease hijack his synapses.

In any other place, a ping wouldn't have been cause for alarm. Even though human/AI interfaces had long been phased out—very few people in all of space had an AI companion these days—it wasn't uncommon for a station or ship construct to wave *hello* to VIFAI as it passed. *You said we were alone,* Iris thought feverishly, feeling both very small and very exposed in the middle of the orchard.

We were.

The ship does have an AI construct then?

For a few seconds, VIFAI was quiet and distant, then it was back, engulfed in blatant confusion. It's in this ship. But it's not the ship.

This is not the time for riddles. Iris eyed the door. He could make it to the corridor in a matter of seconds, but where would he go after? He could accidentally step on a live wire and perish immediately. The academics wouldn't know of his fate. He had been foolish to venture out alone, and now he would pay the price. With every bit of willpower, Iris fought for fragile control over the part of him that screamed to run. Panic was deadly. Panic would be his undoing.

You should respond, Iris thought quickly. Oh, what he wouldn't give for the distracting chatter of the academics right this moment.

What if they aren't friendly?

If you don't, they may assume we're the unfriendly ones. Without realising he was doing so, Iris crouched down underneath a tree. There was no use hiding his nerves from an AI construct that had complete access to all his endocrine responses. *What's the worst that can happen?*

They can infect me with a virus and kill me, then come here and kill you, VIFAI replied without any humour. Fine, OK. For a few seconds, it was quiet and distant, then it was back, engulfed in blatant confusion. It's definitely in this ship.

And?

And . . . VIFAI paused, like it was thinking of the best way to articulate whatever it was going to say. . . . and I can't understand a thing it's saying. It's an odd language. If you can even call it that. I can't even tell if it has syntax. And it's weak and small. Erratic. I think someone forgot their implant here. Someone forgetting an electronic part of a circuit that was embedded inside their brain was a very unlikely scenario.

Should we try to find it?

I don't think it's even aware that it's, well,—VIFAI never minced words, but something about its brief exchange with the owner of the ping had nudged it off-balance, and it replied sharply—alive. I don't think it knows it's alive.

There was a finality to those words. Alive. Iris rarely thought of VIFAI as alive, as sentient, apart from himself. He struggled to remember a time when the electronic voice wasn't whispering in his ear, when the construct wasn't a comforting pressure against Iris's own ego. Yet, VIFAI undeniably was alive and separate. It had a sense of humour. It felt pain, of this Iris was sure, the realisation cemented through a shameful experience in his youth that had nearly destroyed his companion. VIFAI frequently wanted things Iris did not want and did its best to force them on him. It desired, far more than Iris did, in both quantity and scope. It angered; there they matched. They bickered in the way that friends do, made up, made compromises. VIFAI was very much independent of Iris, despite their electronic connection.

While AI systems occupied many different roles, they mostly did so independently. Only pilots and monks now strolled around with AI constructs firmly embedded into their bodies. Pilots, whose reaction time and processing speed could never be executed with only human capacity; and monks, who lost touch with the outside world for so long, and so frequently, and needed to carry such obscene amounts of information that they would be helpless without a competent companion riding on their shoulder. This agreement was considered a necessary evil in human/AI interfaces. Otherwise, an AI companion such as VIFAI was deemed unethical and cruel, having no ability to exert itself on the world the way a station AI could. VIFAI and other AI constructs like it were, at worst, slaves to the whims of whoever's brain they shared. At best, they were treated as glorified secretaries. In either case, as separate as they remained from the people they inhabited, they had little agency of their own.

"Let's go back, then," Iris offered. He wouldn't press, not yet. If any real danger came, he trusted that his electronic companion would alert him. He pondered VIFAI's sentience some more before he was reminded it was privy to his every thought. Caught up in the realisation, Iris blushed and cowardly turned his thoughts towards naming every apple variety he could spot. VIFAI said nothing, masterfully ignoring both the explicit thoughts and Iris's endocrine response.

Maybe it was unethical to carry an AI in one's mind after all, to deprive it of its own body, its own will, a means for it to act on the world. A station AI could boot you out of an airlock if it so pleased. Ship AI systems could fight, destroy entire planets if they so desired, if they were *pushed* to. What could VIFAI do if it was mistreated?

Maybe Iris had been far crueler than he had ever realised.

Iris knelt by the console, a dozen apples scattering from the folds of his robes. Having carried them from the third deck orchard down to the communal space, he hoped the academics would enjoy their unprocessed and unmanufactured nature as much as he had. Neither he nor VIFAI had uttered a word since their encounter with the mystery ping, their silence weighing heavier by the second. Iris was growing concerned that the exchange, if one could even call it such, had left his own inorganic companion shaken and upset. He gathered the apples near the console into a neat pile, wiped the dirt from them with his robes, turned their unbruised faces forwards, and leaned back, judging his work.

Proud of yourself?

There it was, the familiar tickle of electronic laughter. What a relief it was to be on speaking terms again. Iris's shoulders relaxed, the worry seeping away. "Dr. Alo was kind to leave me some sandwiches. It's the least I can do."

That's not an answer to my question.

It wasn't, but he didn't want to outright lie to VIFAI, especially when such a lie would not go unnoticed. Same as his thoughts about AI ownership—he hated that word—hadn't gone unnoticed. The subtle tone fluctuation in VIFAI signaled irritation, anger even, and rightfully so. Their relationship had never been strained before. In Iris's younger years, they fought about which books to read and which trails to take back from the mountains—small, inconsequential things. But something about the *Nicaea* was putting them both on edge.

With a hint of worry, Iris tried and failed to remember how much time had passed since his arrival on the ship. The artificial lighting made it impossible to keep time. A few hours had been spent aimlessly assembling skeletons before Ishtan introduced himself. Then there was an hour spent talking and drinking tea. Maybe another few had passed while he explored the ship.

"When did we sleep last?"

Thirty-two hours ago.

Unsteady gait, clouded judgment, and his unfiltered thoughts should have been a clue. Normally, VIFAI would send an alert when Iris had been neglecting sleep for far too long, but currently, it was distracted by its own concerns, often disappearing into the feed to retrieve a piece of information Iris wasn't privy to. He could have, of course, asked VIFAI to explain itself, but he had decided against it, to avoid straining their fraught feelings any further.

"I'll lie down in the cargo bay then," Iris said and pulled out the last sandwich from his robes. A midnight snack to end the excitement of the day. Taking a reserved bite along the crust, he headed out from the common area. "How many hours will I have before the guards and the academics return?"

Five hours.

Curt, distracted, and still a little angry, then. A familiar trio to Iris. Just as he had been awake for thirty-two hours, so had VIFAI, awake and operating at its maximum capacity to attend to Iris's every need. It had generated and projected maps, searched up biographies of the academics through their socials, monitored Iris's vitals, and perused a directory of poisons. Albeit the last one was not on Iris's request. "Why don't you shut off for a while? I'll be all right on my own."

An unfiltered, electronic vibration of surprise. It *was* angry if that was its only reply. No words now, no *human* words; it was making Iris do the work of understanding.

"I'll be all right," he reassured it.

VIFAI acknowledged the suggestion and blipped out of awareness. Immediately, an overwhelming urge to call it back rose from the darkness of his mind, so suffocating was the silence of Iris's own thoughts. The human mind was far too expansive to be subjected to itself and itself only. Alone, Iris finished the sandwich with a final bite, licked the crumbs from his fingers, and picked up his duffel bag from outside the cargo bay. Solitude was never real solitude with an AI construct sharing the confines of his mind. He hadn't been truly alone since VIFAI took residence in his cerebellum when he was still a child. The in-between silences when VIFAI rested were rare and increasingly uncomfortable.

Without the AI to monitor his state, Iris's thoughts roamed free, unfiltered and untamed. They raced through quick successions of anger, admiration, irritation, and wonder. Riyu's smiling face came to mind first, the way she had extended her hand on meeting him, with no reservation, no hesitation. Surely she wasn't a particularly superstitious woman, or maybe she was just well immunised. Her warmth and energy were both contagious, and Iris found himself innately drawn to her, the way a blossom turns to the rising sun.

His conversation with Ishtan had been a pleasant surprise. The man would surely come for him again, with more questions about Iris's strangeness, thinly veiled as genuine curiosity about the Starlit. Even the short exchanges with Jesi and Tev had left a warm feeling brewing in his chest. They had all been kind, reasonable, accommodating. With his poorly managed anger and misfortune, even Yan had been pleasant enough to be around. If not for the engineer's deep resentment for Vessels, they could have been much more cordial.

After fumbling around in his duffel bag, Iris produced a palm-sized white orb. He drummed a short pattern across its surface, and the orb came to life with a soft glow. Then with a light touch along a cracked switch panel, he dimmed the lights in the cargo bay until the glow sphere in his hands was the only source of illumination. The mountain of bones cast long shadows along the walls of the hangar, climbing as high as the ceiling.

Iris had been afraid of the dark when he was a child, a time when what lurked in the shadows was far worse than what was waiting there for him in the light of day. But that had been some time ago. He had long put away those childish worries. Placing the orb down on the ground, he rested on the mossy floor. A tibia shone white just to his left, a reminder of the work to come another day. Iris looked up at the starless roof of the cargo bay as his eyes fluttered shut. With nothing but the silence of death around him, he drifted off into a peaceful sleep.

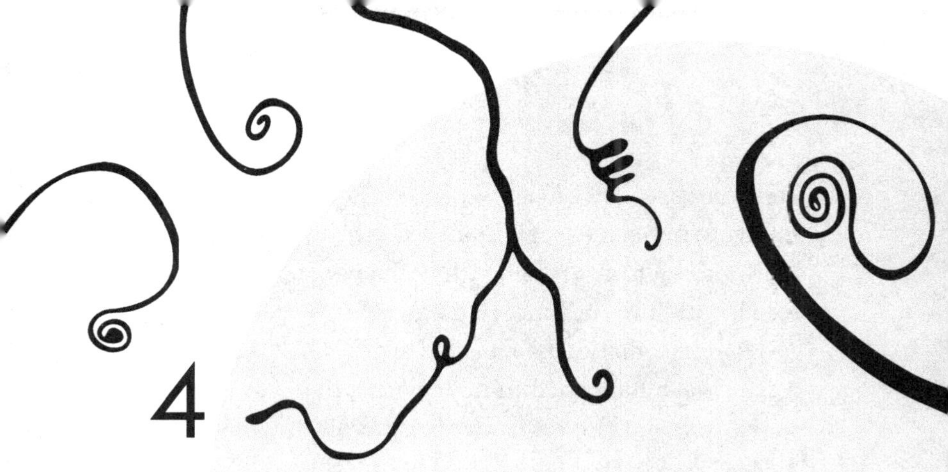

4

Possessiveness is in your nature, down to the bones.
To touch, to lay claim to it. Bare your teeth, shake with anticipation, lest someone takes what is rightfully yours.
You can't simply marvel at the butterfly;
you must pin it down to the board.
I have no stomach for such violence of desire,
and yet it clings to me.

From the unabridged diaries of Vessel Iris, Volume Thirteen

When Iris woke, the world was on fire.

Raging flames engulfed his legs and tore mercilessly at his back. The suffocating scent of burning hair and flesh washed over him, seizing up his lungs. It ate its way into his nostrils, smothered him in its putrid musk. All Iris could do was cry out in pain and clutch his hands over his head while the scorching air lashed against his face.

It's psychosomatic. It's not real. A rushed voice cut through the pain, loud enough to reach through Iris's panicked thoughts. You're fine. You're safe. Open your eyes.

With a wince, Iris peeled one eye open and stared straight ahead. The left side of his face was pressed against the wet moss, hard enough that the individual tendrils left imprints on his skin. His white robes were steeped in green and brown from the dirt, and he had wrapped them around his head defensively in his sleep. Not half a metre away lay a bare human skull, glaring back at him with hollow eye sockets. Iris forced a deep breath into his lungs. He was safe.

"Psychosomatic," he repeated after VIFAI.

It always happened in new places, like clockwork. He had hoped to avoid the nightmares by avoiding sleep altogether, but that had been a foolish and ineffective coping strategy. He knew this now. His calves and forearms ached from the powerful spasms that had claimed every muscle in his body amid the nightmare. Iris sat up and stretched his right leg. His calf protested and then gave in, the cramp subsiding.

You're OK, VIFAI reassured him, its earlier anger and frustration forgotten.

"I'm fine," Iris echoed back and rolled his shoulders through the tension.

The academics are on their way.

With another deliberate breath, Iris rocked to his feet and stretched his arms high above his head. He had been asleep for four hours, which left him less than an hour to make himself presentable for his new companions. He would begin with shaving, the same way he began his mornings each and every day since he had turned thirteen.

A palm-sized, wooden basin from his shaving kit was filled with water squeezed from the moss. Along the whetstone went the blade, five strokes on each side, the sound lulling his rattled nerves into gentle ease. No need for a mirror. The motion of running the blade against his skin from Iris's forehead to the nape of his neck, from his jaw and down his throat had been long committed to muscle memory. He had rehearsed the action thousands of times as part of his morning routine. No matter where he was, no matter what assignment he had, there was the blade, cool and delicate, gliding along his skin, erasing the stubble that had accumulated since his last shave. Iris could no longer remember what the natural texture of his hair was, nor the exact reason for why it was required that he shave it off every morning. Yet the routine was comforting, and it marked him as belonging to *something*, and that in itself was worth the effort.

"Good morning," Riyu called out. Iris's hand flinched, his jaw responding with a sharp sting.

Someone's here.

"Blessed morning, Dr. Alo," Iris kept his back to the door. A trickle of blood ran along his neck, and he didn't want to alarm Riyu, lest she linger and apologise. Like a starved mosquito, the white silk of his robe pressed on the cut greedily soaked up the blood, turning redder by the second. "It's great to have you back. I'll be right with you, if that's all right."

"Of course, of course," Riyu said. "We brought coffee and food. I didn't know if you drink coffee, but it's there if you want it. I saw you took the sandwiches. Hope you liked them. Oh, and thanks for the apples. I'm going to have them tested, and if they're not poisonous, we'll have some."

"They're quite all right," Iris assured her, sleeve still pressed against his jaw. "I had some and survived the night, if that's worth anything."

Riyu just laughed. "You're a funny monk," she called out over her shoulder as the featherlight patter of her feet disappeared down the corridor.

"Are we still bleeding?"

Only a little.

Iris pulled his sleeve from his jaw. The cut still stung, enough to notice, but not enough to tend to. The sleeve of his robe, however, was completely ruined. Fresh blood would soon curdle, brown, and become impossible to wash out. He undid the knot at his waist and peeled the fabric from his shoulders and his back, avoiding his still-bleeding neck. Getting one stain out was work enough.

With his robes pooled on the ground, Iris traced his fingers along his ribcage, counting each rib with waning interest. He had been purposely neglecting food again for weeks now, leaving bites of it untouched and whole meals avoided altogether. It was a practice he couldn't help, an obsessive one, especially at the temple, where any and all restraint was encouraged, if not revered. All of it in vain, now that he had binged on sandwiches and fruit.

This compulsion had followed him from his youth, the only secret he held private when nothing at all about him was private. He wasn't sure when it had started. He couldn't remember a time when he wasn't torn between overindulgence and extreme asceticism, between committing himself completely to the Starlit practice and finding cracks in it for him to escape through. During his most pronounced episodes, he'd eliminate his food intake completely. He'd meditate for twelve hours a day, surviving on nothing but reserved sips of tea. He would retreat further and further into the caverns of his mind where even VIFAI couldn't reach him, where nothing could reach him.

But then, ignoring his demands for privacy, Bacai would rudely barge in with stolen peaches from the orchard, or worse yet, some strange dessert she'd picked up on her latest assignment. She'd make a show of savouring it before his starving eyes, and Iris would give in and stumble, because no matter how cavernous the corners of his mind, he still had a sweet tooth, and Bacai was annoyingly persistent.

And then summons would arrive from Primary Temple, and Iris would rush to serve. He would devour whatever food was offered to him, savour every crumb, and become intoxicated by any delicacies available. He would drink juices and even sometimes partake of alcohol when no one was there to witness his transgressions. And now there were sandwiches with *ham*, *coffee*, and real apples to sink his teeth into. There were scholars and engineers, and hundreds of mouthwatering distractions around every corner. No degree of discipline would save him.

He was no longer an idle watcher of the tapestry of life unfolding before him, but rather a hesitant thread running through its very middle. Iris had inadvertently become enmeshed in the lives of these people who were very deliberately pulling him deeper in still. It was an alluring tug to be once again part of a moving, breathing community of ordinary people with ordinary rules. It was a blessing to be invited in from the cold.

Rushing, Iris pulled a fresh set of robes from his duffel bag and finished changing. The cut had stopped bleeding, finally, thankfully. The clean, high collar sat just below his sharp jawline, free of stubble. Reflecting on the rising rumbling in his stomach, Iris asked VIFAI, knowing that it had kept a close eye on his thoughts, *Do you think I lack faith? Discipline?*

I think you're not done with this life, nor is it finished with you.

A gentle yet firm response. Iris wondered if today would be a day free of quarrels with his inorganic companion. Spirits marginally lifted by clean robes, Iris left the cargo bay to snag some coffee and whatever it was the academics had brought with them for breakfast. If he were to falter in his convictions, he would at least do it on a full stomach. Loud voices echoed far down the corridor, and Iris could clearly make out the words even halfway down.

"This is a priceless archaeological artifact," Ishtan's voice rang out. "It belongs to the archaeology department. That's final. I will not be taking questions."

Riyu's crystalline laughter cut through the last sentence. "You're going to claim a generation ship for your *department*, Ishtan? Isn't it a little too big? Where are you going to put it?"

Iris pressed his back against the mossy wall, a shoulder-width away from the doorway and listened, his mouth watering. Scents of fresh coffee, bold and bitter, wafted through the entrance, beckoning him inside.

"I'd like to remind everyone that the ship falls under Doshua Station jurisdiction," a voice Iris didn't recognise said. "Our gate, our ship. You're all here on a permit and nothing more."

"*You're* here on a permit," Jesi mocked in a high-pitched tone.

"And you only have a job because we have this permit," Tev added. "And anyway, no one can lay claim to a generation ship. It belongs . . . well, it belongs to the galaxy." Everyone groaned in unison and continued to argue ship ownership. Meanwhile, Iris pushed away from the wall and tiptoed in behind the group, hoping he would go unnoticed in the commotion. He was within arm's reach of the coffee pot when a grating voice called out above the chattering.

"Cut yourself shaving, Vessel?"

Iris froze and gave a little bow without turning around. "Yes, a most unfortunate slip of the hand."

I can think of more unfortunate slips, VIFAI muttered.

Hush.

"If there's any confusion about the mechanics of the process, I'd be more than happy to explain." Maybe it was the empty stomach or the stinging along his jaw, but Iris was unwilling to let this one go. Shoulders uncharacteristically

squared, he spun around on the balls of his feet only to meet Yan's grinning face. The engineer took a loud bite from a red apple and flicked his eyebrows upwards, challenging Iris.

"Yan!" Riyu snapped. "How many times do I need to remind you not to eat anything before I test it?"

Yan scowled in response and took another hefty bite, chewing it with a vengeance. Iris nursed a futile hope that perhaps this specific apple was poisonous. Not lethal, no, but just upsetting enough to produce some gastrointestinal distress.

I still have his personal file. VIFAI, meanwhile, was ready for a fight.

"Here," Riyu whispered, shooing Yan away and handing Iris a freshly filled mug. She threw the parting engineer a glare. "Ignore him. He hasn't had his morning smoke, so he's coming after you."

"And I am certain, Dr. Alo, that yesterday he was just missing his evening smoke." Iris accepted the mug from her hands and graced Riyu with a small bow.

"No, yesterday he was being an asshole," she said, voice perfectly flat.

Iris permitted himself a small smile. The thin aluminum mug warmed his hands, and the rising smell of fresh coffee settled his mood. Why dwell on any unpleasantries when there was good coffee to be had? It was even easier when the coffee was accompanied by good company.

The last time Iris had had coffee was a year prior, when he was summoned to a small shuttle crash just off the Sarai Gate. A pilot, who had curiously survived, offered to buy him a cup on their return. Iris wouldn't judge, not out loud, but a pilot should have never been the sole survivor of a shuttle crash. It was most unusual and most improper. The coffee in his mug tasted nothing like at Sarai. Iris took a sip and then another before he noticed Riyu's grinning face in his peripheral vision.

"So?" she asked expectantly. Iris patently waited for a follow-up. "The coffee?"

"It's delicious, thank you."

Riyu groaned. "No. You're supposed to say it tasted different. I grow and roast the beans myself at Sychi."

Iris gave Riyu a rushed, but low, bow. He'd made a grievous error. "Please forgive me. In my ignorance, I didn't notice the wonderfully intricate floral notes supporting the faint hint of vanilla."

Riyu threw her head back with coarse laughter. "You can't claim ignorance, Vessel, and then comment on the *intricate floral notes* in the same sentence. It undermines both statements." When her laughter subsided, she reached into a small cooler and produced a tightly wrapped bowl. "Oatmeal." She nudged the bowl into Iris's hands. "Nothing special, but there's some extra here, if you should want seconds. Now come, Ishtan won't stop bothering me with how much he wishes to speak to you. He is relentless. Maybe, if you give him a day, I'm sure he'll let you get back to your work." Riyu waved for Iris to follow her.

It was alien, but not unpleasantly so, to have someone desire to speak with him who wasn't on the verge of dying. Regrettably, there was still the matter of the mystery ping that had reached VIFAI at the orchard that threatened to sour the otherwise pleasant morning. Yan appeared to be the most suited to answer Iris's questions and so the morning would be most certainly ruined.

At best, Yan would cuss him out and yell at him for distracting him from his own work. At worst—Iris didn't allow his mind to go down that path. The entire predicament was beginning to cause a stomachache. He could handle conflict when needed, but he preferred to avoid it altogether. But this morning, Yan seemed to be in a milder mood, playful even. Perhaps, Iris prayed, there was a chance to convey his concerns without causing an outright confrontation. He followed Riyu closely, mug still in hand.

"When do you think it will be safe to speak with engineer Yan?" Iris inquired cautiously.

"After his lobotomy," Riyu said, grinning wickedly.

Iris trailed behind Ishtan as they climbed seven flights of stairs up what Iris had dubbed as the eastern stairwell. Not that cardinal directions were relevant in space, but it was a force of habit to attempt to orient oneself in the simplest of ways. The crisp, cool air was a stark reminder of Iris's oversight to bring warmer clothes. He shuddered through his words as they climbed. "Is it true," he asked through chattering teeth, "that your institute will claim ownership of the *Nicaea*?" Silence lingered. Ishtan remained mute. The words hung between them without an answer, as only the archaeologist's footsteps echoed through the stairwell. Iris gave him space. Clearly, the academic had other things on his mind.

"In a matter of speaking," Ishtan said at last, a touch out of breath, the climb taking its toll on him. "Some part of this ship will surely go to the institute. Some other part to the station, although, I'm not sure what the station will even do with it. It's a peculiar thing, this ship. It was a home to so many once, and now it's nothing more than a decaying body of a giant."

Like a body, kept alive by the miracles of modern medicine after the mind had long perished. Unlike the *Nicaea*, modern ships had AI constructs at the helm. Smaller craft utilised pilots, working collaboratively with companion constructs, but large ships were individuals of their own. Ships decided which contracts they took on, which captains they preferred to work with, and what adequate payment was. It would be nonsense to claim ownership of a modern ship as much as it would be to claim ownership of a person. With no one speaking for the *Nicaea*, though, it could be fought over like a plot of land. It could be ripped apart, disassembled, and no one would be there to stop the carnage.

"The *Nicaea* will be dissected?" Iris's hand glided along the handrail, counting the rivets on the underside. *Thirty-eight. Thirty-nine.* VIFAI was quiet still, humming along with its idle work. Iris could feel it moving in the background, like a half-forgotten song.

"In a manner of speaking. Parts of the ship will be taken by my department," Ishtan said. "Riyu will probably remove most of the vegetation she can get her hands on, catalogue it, and take it to her own lab for study. The engineers are working to extract the software as we speak. If they can't, they'll just remove the hardware and pray there's something worthwhile on there. Each part of the *Nicaea* will create and sustain jobs and deepen our understanding of what life used to be like. Here we are." Ishtan pushed open a door with a groan.

Iris didn't overtly object to the dissection of the ship; after all, everything inadvertently became something else. But something in him cried out that it was wrong to peel a ship apart, deck by deck, wall by wall, so unceremoniously. No respect was paid to the *Nicaea* as a whole, to its monumental accomplishment. Like scavengers, the academics and station personnel had descended on her body, eager to steal away the largest piece for personal gain. This uneasiness sprung up within him like a warning, like a revelation that he was not among people who thought like him, who valued the things he valued.

The higher decks of the ship were cooler and supported sparse vegetation. Shrubs peeked through the cracks in the walls, shimmering with frost that sat in every crevice. Iris wrapped his arms around himself and watched puffs of fog float from Ishtan's mouth as his speech grew more and more excited.

"I am what you might call a generation ship enthusiast. They're not my specialty by any means, but I've always had such a fascination—*oh,* there is so much to learn from them," Ishtan gushed, leading Iris down a dimly lit corridor. "For example, did you know that all the ships we've come across so far follow a similar layout? The *Nicaea* follows it too. Large central spaces with spokes of corridors towards the edges. Such a fascinating way to build. And the cultures—oh! I could go on for hours. But *this,* this mural I wish to show you is really a particularly strange find, nothing like we've seen before on other ships. Very vivid, exceptionally well-preserved."

Ask him about P'llani, VIFAI called out from Iris's subconscious, where it was rummaging around and retreated to in the next instant to continue its work.

"You've seen other ships?" Iris asked, finally able to get a word in.

"Not personally," Ishtan said with subdued pride, "but a colleague of mine brought me back a piece of a mural from the ship that washed up near P'Ilani. Oh, it's a *beautiful* mural. If you ever have the opportunity, I highly recommend vising the institute. It really is a sight to see. Sychi has nothing of that sort, but maybe if we may extract this one—" He suddenly stopped. "There it is."

Ahead, the corridor opened into a large chamber with sloping walls. Like the petals of a rosebud, they reached towards the apex, nearly twenty metres in height. At one time, the space had been well lit and vibrant, before decay and wear made it a barren tomb. The curved ceiling glowed dimly from some internal source. As far as the light permitted Iris to see, the walls were painted with peeling colours. Images of pale people and alien places in hyperrealistic form smiled at him from the walls, their faces monstrously large. Iris wasn't superstitious, but he recited a prayer anyway, just to be sure.

Meanwhile, Ishtan produced a small flashlight from his pocket and ran the warm yellow beam across the paintings. "This mural, for example, will be removed in pieces and taken back to my department. This is a career-making discovery, Iris. Truly, this was worth waiting forty years for. Have you ever seen anything like it?"

Iris had not. He was busy fighting a rising mixture of panic and disgust in his stomach. The coming-and-going pulse he initially sensed once he had entered the ship was stronger here, reverberating through the domelike ceiling. It echoed through his limbs, starting from the balls of his feet and snaking its way through his fingertips, as if the ship was saying, *tread carefully for you do not belong here*. His own heart fought against its uneven pace, but it was losing more and more with each passing second.

Then there were the faces.

Frozen and uncanny, they smiled at Iris with their cold, flat eyes, some stripped of pieces of their bodies where the plants had gotten to them. Soon the mural would be taken apart, shipped to the Sychi Institute, or displayed at some prestigious gallery, removed from the ship, pinned and hoisted against some paneling. Iris swayed on his feet, a fresh wave of bile threatening to escape.

"This is one of the originals," Iris heard Ishtan say, his voice coming to him as a distant echo. "I predict it was here when the ship took off. Now, the ones I will show you in just a moment are even more fascinating." He walked back down the corridor, and Iris followed mechanically, his stomach doing somersaults, vision receding into a darkened tunnel.

"Did you feel that?" he asked Ishtan, struggling to keep up, the academic's steps suddenly too fast.

"Feel what?" Ishtan threw a glance over his shoulder, hand tugging at his beard.

The heartbeat, Iris wanted to say, *the heartbeat of some monstrous thing.* What words were there at his disposal to describe the nameless fear that had overtaken him? If he were to speak now, he would be reduced to a rambling mess or, worse, frighten Ishtan for no good reason. He shook his head instead.

They passed the stairwell and ventured down the corridor in the opposite direction. This part of the deck lay in massive disrepair. Wires hung from overhead where the vines had punctured the ceiling panels. Water dripped down bare walls, leaving green mold growing in its wake. There was no pulse here, no rhythm that Iris could feel even as he pressed his palm flat against the wall. Here was reprieve—at last.

From the silent dark, like a ship materialising from gate space, the first mural emerged before them. Even in the twilight of the corridor, Iris was struck by the vibrancy of its colours, the way they had persisted through centuries to deliver their message. Broad, unpolished strokes ran the length of the wall, depicting scenes from everyday life on the ship. Some figures picked fruit, others played strange games. But there was a deliberate division, an artistic distinction between the two groups that had inhabited the ship. On a superficial level, they differed in clothes, in both hue and make. Most striking was the passengers depicted in almost uniform like outfits, identical in cut and their dark fabric. Taking a closer look, Iris noticed these figures were often armed with both primitive weapons and firearms.

He thought back to the lone passenger, reclined, dead on the couch, pistol in hand. Perhaps Iris had misinterpreted the scene. Maybe the stranger hadn't been looking for a way out at all.

"What do you make of this, Ishtan?" he asked, carefully studying the archaeologist's upturned, awestruck face.

"I think things got complicated aboard the ship as time passed," Ishtan said. "They often did, you know. No matter how big you build them, the crews almost always develop some form of cabin fever. Something about not being under open skies. It's a miserable existence."

Iris followed the mural down the corridor, the painting changing tone the farther he ventured. There was violence in the art now. Depictions of death and executions. Reds and blacks dominated the wall, and amid the carnage, a spherical red eye watched it all, impartial, disinterested. It presided over the death, a vengeful god in whose name the slaughter was enacted.

Violence, both as mutiny and desperation, was not uncommon on generation ships, of this Ishtan was correct. Almost every ship Iris had read about as a child provided records of such events. Trailing his eyes along the mural and upwards, Iris noticed that the cameras, placed along the edge where the wall met the ceiling, had all been shattered. A few broken cameras here and there were expected, but *all* the cameras? Iris made a mental note to see if the cameras on any of the other decks were in similar shape.

Then, before he could fully recover, the pulsing rhythm returned, but this time it attacked Iris in sequences, forcing his heart to skip beats. With every remaining ounce of self-control, Iris resisted the urge to reach inside the sleeve of his robe for protection.

Breathe. VIFAI's quiet voice came through the surge of primal fear Focus on your breathing, Iris.

That little slip was enough to power the panic into an all-encompassing state. VIFAI had only used his name once before. There was never a need. But now it gave itself away in that one word—it was scared as well. Iris wrapped his arms around himself and trembled from both fear and his irregular heartbeat. He looked up at the mural, and the eye—the red, ever-watching eye—looked right back.

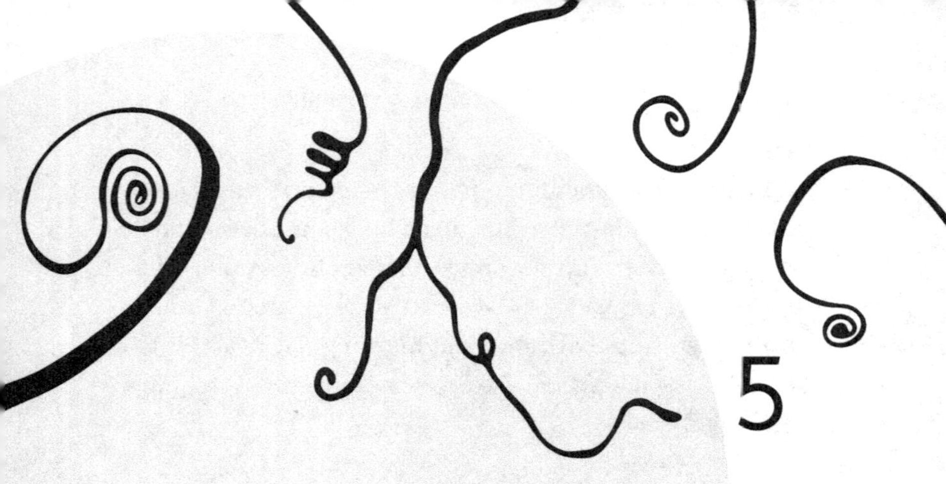

5

I am hungry again.
I am hungry for a food that I can never prepare. I am craving a drink I have yet to taste. If you fill me with such longing, O, Infinite Light, show me a path through it. Should I cast away this want as I have cast away every other superficial desire, or shall I surrender to it instead? How will I go on pretending it doesn't gnaw at my stomach?
From the unabridged diaries of Vessel Iris, Volume Six

Riyu's eyes flicked upwards from her tea. "Vessel, you look ill."

Having returned from his tour of the murals a little worse for wear, Iris fought to keep the minimal contents of his stomach to himself. He gave Riyu a stiff smile and his best reassuring nod, and prayed she wouldn't pry. Beside him, the veil of distant focus finally lifted from Ishtan, and he gasped loudly, only now noticing Iris's demeanour. "You do look ill, Iris. What has come over you?"

He can't be serious.

Academics, Iris muttered back.

"Why didn't you say anything?" Ishtan insisted, his hands coming dangerously close to Iris's shoulders. Sympathetic academics had the worst habit of forgetting that he was not to be touched, more so for their good than for his.

Iris gracefully ducked out from beneath the impending grasp and spun around to face Riyu. "I assure you both, I am all right," he said and genuinely meant it. Now that the ship's heartbeat had receded, he could breathe again. "I appreciate your concern, I truly do."

Too little, too late, VIFAI said. Iris told it to hush with the smallest internal smile. Today, their quarrels lay forgotten, and they had returned to some semblance of normal. He twirled past Riyu and towards the teapot. Iris was about to pour himself a cup but remembered his manners.

"Please, help yourself," Riyu said, remembering her own. "Why did Yan say you're not allowed to ask for food?"

That *was* a good question. Sometimes, people did ask good questions even if they did arise from the *idiocy of others*. Relationships with food had always been tenuous within the Starlit. Food and taste brought on cravings, and craving was problematic in itself as it propelled the mind to some imaginable future when such cravings could be fulfilled. Cravings brought on suffering and dissatisfaction. Iris knew many cravings quite intimately. Try as he did, his mind always ran a few steps ahead of the present moment, eager to meet the elusive future.

"By never asking for food, we are able to attain two things," Iris explained between slow sips of the tea. Riyu had brought honey, and he snuck in a teaspoon of it when Ishtan and her were distracted. He would steal the whole jar when the academics departed back to the station for the night. "First, we welcome everyone to extend a small bit of kindness and compassion through the offerings of food. When someone offers a Vessel or any other Starlit Order monk even the smallest bit of food, they are, in their own way, supporting the flow of life the way the Light does. By facilitating this exchange, everyone can become aware of the flow of life around them." Iris paused to eye the small glass jar of honey. Both Riyu and Ishtan were watching him silently.

"And the second?" Ishtan prodded.

"And the second," Iris laughed, "is that by relying on the kindness of others for sustenance, the Starlit ensures the monks never fall out of shape. Make food readily available at all times, and I assure you, I would eat until my robes no longer fit. Restraint has never been a strength of mine."

It was a far more complicated balance, between hunger and satiation, between desire and fulfillment. Iris had yet to strike it. Many times, he had snuck extra rice patties from the kitchen only to eat them after nightfall. Most recently, he found himself craving things far more abstract than lab-grown meat and honey. No matter how many hours he mediated, no matter how many rice patties he hid away, the new cravings never passed, and kept him tossing and turning through the nights, and stalking him through his days.

"That just sounds silly," Riyu said. "No offense, but what if people just stopped offering you food?"

Iris shrugged delicately. "I suppose that would be the will of the Light."

The Light has no will, VIFAI recited.

Don't I know it. "But," Iris continued, "people *are* kind and generous. I have yet to be proven otherwise, Dr. Alo."

Still making friends with the jar of honey, Iris watched Ishtan and Riyu study the photographs taken of the murals on the upper deck. They spoke at length about their peculiar nature and their academic significance, and never once about their subject matter. Their voices rose higher and higher, resonating with excitement over the new discovery. The engineers were nowhere to be found; Iris assumed that under Yan's supervision, they had embarked on their quest to mutilate some other important part of the ship. Station security was also absent, but that gave Iris far less worry.

Have you been tracking our movements along the map? he asked VIFAI and received an affirmative ping. *Can you do me a favour and mark all the spots where I had sensed that pulse and project that onto the map?*

VIFAI did just that. It took it nearly thirty seconds, about twenty-five seconds longer than it would any other construct, but both Ishtan and Riyu were still busy gushing over the photographs, and Iris allowed VIFAI to work at its own pace.

Can you project the decks on top of one another?

VIFAI did.

Looking nowhere in particular, Iris scanned the three-dimensional map, noting the glowing *X*s placed where the pulse had been most prominent.

Can you mark down where you received the ping?

VIFAI did, and Iris blinked hard in realisation. All the *X*s aligned in a slightly imperfect line right down the ship's centre, right where its "brain" would have been. Iris remained unmoving and sipped slowly at his tea, careful to contain his growing unease. *Are you certain that whatever pinged you was so simple it wouldn't know it was sentient?* The mural lay right above the centre of the ship, the closest *X* to the imagined centre line that cut through the "brain."

There was a pause before VIFAI's response, then it said, with a familiar edge to its electronic voice, **Alive. It wasn't aware that it was alive.** That was another distinction Iris couldn't fathom existed. No part of his Starlit training had prepared him to contemplate the difference between *sentient* and *alive* as it pertained to non-organic things. He risked offending VIFAI. *What would be the difference between the two?*

Iris swore that his companion audibly scoffed at his question. Even in in-organics, a thing alive doesn't need to be sentient; a thing sentient does not require to be alive, in the moment, to still be sentient.

There *was* a difference then. A stark difference that Iris himself had failed to see before. It shamed him greatly to think that at one time, not that long ago, VIFAI had been, conceptually, no more than a faceless, albeit entertaining, assistant to him.

Iris pondered the difference for a moment. *Like the final signals of a brain as someone passes?*

Could be, VIFAI conceded and added nothing more on the matter.

Something in the brain of the ship was *alive*, in a matter of speaking, or at the very least, animated enough to be interacting with VIFAI. Then again, it could have pinged it by accident or on instinct alone. In any case, this peculiarity was outside of Iris's expertise.

"Vessel?"

Iris stared wide-eyed at Riyu's round face, not a metre away. She was close, far, far too close. He played off his surprise and took a final sip of the cooled tea.

"Where did you go, just now?"

The lie escaped Iris before he could stop himself. "Sometimes when monks meditate, we can reach states that are far removed from common reality. I must have lost myself in the vastness of the cosmos for a moment," he said with a small smile. "I apologise, Dr. Alo. Did you wish to speak with me?" Riyu's eyes were running along his face, searching for any tell of a lie, or anything worthy of her concern. But Iris was long accustomed to telling small lies of omission and manifesting the neutral facial expressions he needed for work.

There was no sense in worrying those around him anymore than they needed to be, and for now, he could continue pretending there was nothing at all to be concerned about. What he needed was to speak with the engineers without anyone listening in. He didn't want to start a panic or have witnesses for when Yan cussed him out, or worse.

"Ishtan just said that you were quite distressed by the idea of taking down the murals," Riyu said.

"*Quite*," Ishtan said.

"Must you?" Part curiosity, part apprehension returned Iris to the moment he first had sensed the ping. The difference between *alive* and *sentient* nagged at him. If there was even a small chance that something aboard the ship was cognisant enough of its condition, would it be not that something's prerogative to decide what was to become of the ship?

"The relics mean little out here, but at Sychi, they'll offer us glimpses of ancient history," Ishtan said. "Moreover, they're quite meaningful to those with the purse strings. Institutes will spare no expense to acquire them."

Pragmatic, all of it. So unlike the teachings Iris had absorbed since he was a child. Tread carefully. Leave things be. Value them only for existing, not what they may do for you.

"Sychi has an entire legal team ready to fight for ownership," Riyu chimed in with a mischievous spark. "They can make lives very difficult for people if they're competing for an artifact. I've seen it happen before."

"Who else would compete for the *Nicaea*?"

Riyu got to counting on her fingers. "Oh, Doshua Station, another institute, even your temple might be interested, Vessel."

"The Starlit?"

"I've heard of faith-based institutions going toe to toe with Sychi before for artifacts," Ishtan said. "Truthfully, they're the only ones with the capital to."

Even in the pursuit of knowledge, in the uncovering of truth, it always boiled down to money. The concept always had eluded Iris. He understood that it was necessary for the exchange of goods and services, but having never handled any money, he lacked any desire for its accumulation. He took little interest in the mechanics of its aggregation and quickly grew bored of people who did. Still, the way it often reduced people's time and attention to mere commodities irked him. Now, money would reduce the ship to the collection of its parts, to the heightened importance of some parts over others. There would be, as Riyu put it, "a fight," and Iris had no stomach for fights.

Sipping at his tea, Iris retreated into the study of the pings along the map as Riyu and Ishtan continued their discussion of artifact ownership. Every few sentences, Iris nodded along to convince the two that he was listening, meanwhile thinking, *why can't it just be left alone?*

Around the corner, and far enough that the exposed flame of the torch didn't burn their eyes, Jesi and Tev chattered among themselves, hoods lifted over their heads to reveal their youthful faces. Between jokes, they threw disapproving glances at station security, crouched some way down the corridor, still playing cards. Being the youngest (and the mouthiest) of the group, Iris deemed Jesi and Tev poorly suited for what he had in mind. It was also unwise to frighten them before there was a pressing need for it.

At the far end of the corridor, face obstructed by a black safety hood, Yan worked away at a door. Sparks flew where the torch bit at the metal door, spraying on the soft moss, dying too quickly to pose any real danger.

According to Iris's map, Yan was in for a long session. The reinforced door led to a small, maintenance space where most of the electronics responsible for the third deck were situated. The door was built to withstand the full depressurization of the ship. For all his efforts, Yan couldn't compete. The engineers had already taken three shifts of an hour each.

As he leaned against the corridor wall, the echoes of a weakened pulse radiated through Iris's shoulder. This far from the centre of the *Nicaea*, the individual beats were faded, barely detectable amid the chatter and the crackling of the welding torch. *Here it is again*, Iris thought to VIFAI. *Note it on our map.* Another *X* to add to his already concerning collection.

Without any warning, all noise dropped away. The torch let out a soft thud against the lush floor. With an ancient groan, the door slid upwards and open.

"Finally," Yan huffed and wiped his forehead with the sleeve of his shirt, leaving a charcoal swipe across his tan skin. He took one step over the threshold and paused. Dampness seeped from the small space. Without turning around, Yan called out for a flashlight.

Through his shoulder, pressed against the corridor wall, Iris felt the ship's pulse quicken.

What's going on? Why is it pinging me again?

Iris had no answer, but a deadly premonition stirred in the pit of his stomach. Before he could summon an answer for VIFAI, he turned the corner and took off running towards the door. Calling out would cost Yan another second, when he would invertedly turn towards Iris, and Yan didn't have another second. Not that Yan would heed a warning from him anyway. With a barely audible sizzle, the light panel above the door gave a faint flicker. Iris hopped over station security guards, still aimlessly playing cards, spun around Tev, and sidestepped Jesi. He was barreling down the corridor, too fast to pull Yan backwards. The engineer was already three-quarters through the door, only the knee and ankle of his left leg left standing in the corridor. Forwards, the only way was forwards. Iris only hoped he had enough mass to clear Yan of the doorway.

The light panel above the door flickered one last time and died. Iris leapt. The door released and flew towards the floor. Iris tackled Yan from behind, both their bodies toppling forwards into the darkness. At the last moment, Iris pulled his knees in as the door slammed shut. In the remaining darkness, both men lay on the smooth floor, gasping for air, winded from the impact.

Yan was the first to regain his ability to speak. "What the hell was that?" His boots scraped the metal floor as he clambered to his feet. In the pitch black, only sound indicated the state of Yan's mood, but sound was plenty. "What the *hell*?"

"Something malfunctioned in the door mechanism," Iris said softly. He pushed himself upright into a sitting position against the wall and crossed his legs. "My options were quite limited, engineer Yan. If I called out to you, it would take too long for you to act. I couldn't explain in the limited time that I needed you to step *out* of the room. I couldn't have pulled you backwards, I was already going too fast. The remaining option was to tackle you out of the way."

Iris held his breath in anticipation of Yan's certain curse, perhaps even a strike. "Yes. I figured all *that*," the engineer said instead. "I want to know what went wrong with the door and how to get out of here. Can't see shit."

The darkness was something Iris could remedy. He reached into one of the many pockets of his robes and found his glow sphere. His fingers drummed out the intricate patterns needed to ignite it, and moments later, a soft white light filled the small space.

An apparition of Yan's face stared solemnly at Iris, worn gaunt by the long shadows thrown across the walls. Forgoing an explanation, Yan pressed his ear to the door and shushed Iris. After a few seconds, he pulled away and slammed an open palm against the metal. Once. Twice. Again, he pressed his face against the metal and listened. "Either everyone on the other end is dead, or this room is completely soundproof. Either way, it doesn't bode well for us." Yan's eyes raced wildly along the walls of the room, taking in every detail that could be of use to them. The engineer was frightened, bordering on panicked, but too proud to show any of it. Maybe for the best.

This song and dance was all too familiar. Men, fighting for a sliver of control when no control was to be had. Men, on the brink of death, baring their teeth in feral smiles. Anything, anything at all to stifle the fear that bubbled just beneath the surface. All this, the denial of fear and death, all for the welfare of others. In some odd way, Iris came to observe this futile performance of courage with affection. He was about to reassure Yan that they would be all right, an attempt to settle his own nerves as well, when Yan stuck his finger in his mouth and promptly popped it back out, slick with saliva. He raised his hand above his head, index finger pointed towards the ceiling. Iris held his breath without being told to.

"We have no air movement," Yan said at last, lowering his hand. There was no fear left in his voice, only frigid determination propelling him forwards. "Don't panic, Vessel. We have whatever the ship pumped inside before it shut the door. It's just that we're not getting anything new."

Iris nodded and closed his eyes. He had no panic in him, in part because he suspected Yan would be the first to break, in part because he had yet to accept the gravity of their situation.

"What are you doing?" Yan asked.

"Slowing down my breathing and heart rate to ration the air better, engineer."

Yan's disapproving glare landed like an iron weight on Iris, and in a voice low and dripping with venom, the engineer said, "*Thank you* for doing your part. Looking at the size of this room and basing my calculations off us two, adult males, me of respectable stature and you, well"—he gestured to all of Iris—"I would say we have . . ."

Four hours, VIFAI said.

"Three hours and forty-seven minutes, give or take." Yan mouthed something silently to himself. His eyes, wide open and tracing the perimeter of the space, landed on the sitting monk. "No. I'm wrong," Yan muttered. "Carbon dioxide will do us in much faster. Three hours, at most. Maybe you had the right idea after all, Vessel, with the not breathing part."

Breathing slower.

"The room is airtight?" Iris asked.

Yan nodded grimly. "Yeah, in the worst-case scenario." He gestured at the vents. "Let's get to work. I'm going to see if I can shimmy any of these open. We need air first, then we can think up how to get the door open."

"What would you like me to do?" Iris asked, expecting Yan to respond with a loaded *stop breathing*, or *meditate yourself into a coma*.

Yan thought for a moment, his whole body taut as a string, ready to snap into action at any moment, or snap itself in half. His latent panic had completely dissipated, his breathing now coming in slow and deliberate waves. Black eyes glistened feverishly in the orb's dim light. "Find anything we can use to wedge into the vents," he said. "Anything I can use as a screwdriver. If the vents are a no-go, I'd like to pry open the console by the door and see if I can manually override it. No one makes a ship this big without manual overrides at each segment." Yan gave a nod, seemingly more for his own benefit than Iris's. "Because that would be dumb." Without another word of wasted air, he hopped on to the console and reached up towards the vents.

The maintenance room ceiling was low enough that someone of Yan's height could reach the flaps of the vents while balancing on the console. Groping his way to where the orb's light failed to reach, he found the edges of the vent flaps, pressed shut against one another. There was little room between each one, not even wide enough for Yan to jam a fingernail in. He traced the vents again for good measure and hopped down to the floor empty-handed. "Good news," Yan said. "Well, bad news *and* good news. Bad news is that I doubt we can work anything in there to pry the vent flaps open. Good news is, it's not airtight. I don't know just how much air is getting in, but *something* is. It buys us a little more time."

For a moment, Iris contemplated why, despite the good news, he felt no great relief.

"Did you find anything I can use?"

Iris blinked and when his eyes opened, Yan's face was much closer than it had been a moment ago. It was difficult to stay *in* the awfulness of the moment. To sit along the wall and meditate would have been simpler. As his body grew distant and cold, Iris's mind retreated into the safety of the empty meditative space. He swayed a little, and the orb tumbled from his open fingers. It never hit the floor. When his consciousness retreated from the comforting void that was the Infinite Light, Yan's face was closer still—and angrier. The engineer was clutching the glow sphere in his hand. There were maybe ten centimetres between them.

Yet even then, Yan graciously allowed Iris to stand on his own and left enough space between their bodies so they wouldn't accidentally touch. "Where the hell did you just go? Your eyes are glazing over."

Iris didn't reply. The allure of the void was too great, and he fell again, slipping from the moment one fluttering thought at a time.

"Wake up!"

Here, the moment was *here*, in the crowded, hot room, running out of air. Here, in the company of an angry engineer who, on a different day, would have struck Iris for his softness, but today, of all days, was not only tolerating it, but also was respecting the boundary Iris had placed in the space before him. Something struck Iris's forehead, and he instinctively reached out to catch it. The falling orb landed in his palm.

"Where are you disappearing to? Stop fucking around, Vessel, and be useful." Yan nodded at the door. "Now, do you have anything I can use to get us out of here?"

For a moment, Iris was silent. Then, without any warning, he tossed the glowing sphere into the air. The engineer caught it at the apex of the toss and looked to Iris expectantly. In an outstretched hand, Iris held a golden rectangle, adorned with the rays of the Starlit Order inlaid with mother-of-pearl. The gold finish flickered in the orb's light, dancing like the tongues of a raging flame against the surrounding darkness.

"A pocketknife?" Yan asked.

Oh, to live an oblivious life, VIFAI said.

Iris turned towards the wall. His thumb found a faint indentation in the centre of the handle. *How kind of you to join me.*

I never left. You're the one ignoring me.

Iris bit back a defensive thought and instead said, *Nonsense. I don't have the capacity to ignore you.* He turned his attention back to the weapon in his hand. Just right, he had to do it just right, just as hours of training had engrained in him. He let out a slow breath. Yan watched over his shoulder, with the orb held high, keeping his distance, curiosity palpable.

The pulsar blade required two levels of authentication. First, the blade would only respond to Iris's fingerprint. This was programmed in when he was still a youth as fingerprints had the habit of remaining the same as people aged. The second level of authentication was more precise. The sensor, located in the indentation in the handle, was also a biometrics scanner, set to read Iris's personal and unforgeable stress response. Given the situation, all he had to do was speculate about what it would be like to die in this enclosed space, with only the engineer for company. An unkind end, turning blue in the long-abandoned maintenance room. Better yet, Yan would probably kill him even sooner. He would wring Iris's neck or smash his head against the controls to buy himself more air and time. Under any other circumstances, those were stressful enough images. Yet the blade remained sheathed.

Performance anxiety?

Iris told VIFAI to mind its own business in the most impolite terms he could muster.

"What are you doing over there?" Yan's voice came from Iris's left. He was too close, so close, in fact, that the hot air from his mouth brushed Iris's earlobe. The pulsar blade extended at once with a faint blue glow, one-and-a-half metres in length on each end. Iris nearly dropped the damn thing.

"What the hell is *that*?" With the vigour of a child about to be burned for the first time, Yan reached for the blade.

To spare the engineer any injuries, Iris removed his thumb from the indentation, and the blade disappeared instantly. Yan's bewilderment was enough to breathe some life back into Iris, and with a minute trace of amusement, he said, "I'll tell you what it is if you promise not to go grabbing it."

Yan acceded with blatant disappointment.

It would be easy to provoke a stress response now that Iris had something explicit and immediate to work with. The mere idea of Yan's closeness triggered the blade from its sheath with no effort on Iris's part. He shortened the pulsar blade to only two centimetres in length on one end and turned back around to face the engineer.

"This is a pulsar blade," Iris said, holding it gently in his outstretched palm. "Every monk of the Starlit Order is given one, once they show an aptitude for wielding it." He had *some* aptitude. Nothing compared to Bacai's deadly grace and precision. Nothing at all to Mother Nova's skill, honed over the decades. Iris could fight to protect his life, or, if the occasion called for it, and the lives of others, but he was not a fighter.

When the blade was first bestowed upon him at the age of thirteen, he had been both reckless and skittish with the new weapon. Within minutes of holding the blade in his hands, Iris was already missing the tip of his thumb, much to Bacai's amusement, who was eleven and already far more skilled than him. The blade had instantly cauterised the wound, but the embarrassment burned greater than the injury, so much so that Iris hadn't touched the blade for the next month.

Yan leaned in closer and watched the blade's glow with considerable interest. "Thought the Starlit would frown on you stabbing people."

"The pulsar blade is a defensive weapon. It does not need to be lethal." Then, after a laden pause, Iris added, "As long as I ask for forgiveness, wrists and ankles are fair game if such need arises."

"How come it's shorter now? Can you control its length through your monk mind powers?" Yan was grasping the parameters of the weapon quickly. He watched it now with unbridled curiosity, and Iris wondered how long it would take for the engineer to unapologetically ask for the blade, and how much longer it would take him to take it apart to see what made it tick.

"Nanobots and biometrics, engineer Yan." Iris extended the handle of the blade to Yan, smiling when the engineer instinctively drew back. "It won't bite. I have locked it in place now. Keep holding on to the handle, and you'll be able to use it like a very sharp knife. But remember, it's incredibly thin and brittle. It can cut, but you can't use it to wedge anything open."

Yan hesitantly took the blade from Iris's hand, tossing the orb back into the monk's hands. "What will it cut through?"

"Anything, really, as long as it's got the right angle. It's more of a slashing weapon than a stabbing one."

Yan stared at the small blade for a while, then went to the fuse box near the door, and shimmied the blade between the two halves of the box's panel, where the lock was. The pulsar blade passed through the lock like a hot knife through butter, and Yan made a startled and joyous *aha!* "Can't we just cut through the door?"

"We can cut through it easily, but could you move a two-tonne door?" Iris asked, watching from the other corner of the maintenance room. It was easier to be present now. He forced all his focus on Yan's motions as he pried opened the fuse box and dug around the hundreds of wires inside. The pulsar blade provided only a little light as Yan rummaged through the cables.

"Get over here with that ball of yours," Yan called.

Iris could do that. Holding the orb above Yan's shoulder, he watched the engineer concoct an improvised escape plan. "I'm trying to manually override the door from here," Yan explained. "Usually, any signal to the door gets sent from one of the ship's 'brains,' and the door reacts, but if I can nudge it *just* right, it'll pop open like it's supposed to."

"*Brains*? As in, more than one?"

"*Yeah*," Yan replied like Iris had asked the dumbest question in existence. "A ship this size can't operate from a single terminal. Plus, if one goes down, the ship still has to keep the rest of itself running. Don't they teach you anything in monk school?"

Of course, they had taught Iris plenty in *monk school*, but none of it had much use when it came to entrapment on generation ships. Whatever he knew about ships came from books and media Iris managed to request from the library and the brief loans from kind passengers he met during his travels. Unfortunately, he had yet to come across any engineering textbooks in his years as a Vessel, or any engineers. Although the latter might have been a blessing.

Yet even his limited knowledge was enough for Iris to have an unpleasant thought. "Then, hypothetically speaking, if the ship didn't want you to open this door, it could just order it shut, even if the terminal that short-circuited in the first place is inactive?"

Yan muttered an aggravated *no*. He looked over his shoulder to where Iris was and glared unapologetically. "This is more like—like when a doctor hits your knee with a mallet. Reactionary. The ship can't help it." He went back to pulling apart the wires. "And anyway, why would the ship not want to open the door?"

I can think of a few reasons, Iris and VIFAI said at once.

As the minutes dragged on, and Yan worked away at the wires, the air around them grew thick with carbon dioxide. The cracks in the vent scales were doing a poor job of sustaining air circulation. Only an hour into their ordeal, and Iris was already sweating, partially from the static exertion of holding up the orb over Yan's shoulder. Partially from the exertion of keeping himself in the present instead of slipping away into kind oblivion. The conversation had long died out as Yan preferred to work in silence and had only given Iris affirmative grunts for responses.

"Stay awake."

Iris jolted himself into awareness. His arm, the one holding the orb, was trailing downwards and taking the light with it. "My apologies." He quickly brought his arm to eye level again.

"What the *hell* is happening to you, Vessel?" Yan was beginning to strip the insulation on the wires. "Are you claustrophobic or something?"

Iris didn't say. He didn't like the edge in Yan's voice and didn't feel compelled to explain himself to the engineer while he held the pulsar blade. "I'm fine. I'm perfectly all right," Iris said instead, doing his best to exude calm.

"No, you're not," Yan retorted, face buried in the fuse box, his own sweat a dark stain between his shoulder blades. "You're panicking because you've never been stressed for a single moment in your life, and you have absolutely zero coping skills. They don't teach you to perform under pressure at monk school."

Iris wanted to say that *no*, he was, in fact, stressed every waking minute of his life, except for about thirty seconds when, during sunrise prayer, he could shut out everything that was excruciatingly wrong with him and be blissfully numb. But Yan's tone remained confrontational, and Iris held no desire to have a confrontation. What Iris wanted, more than anything, was to be alone. Alone with the bones of the *Nicaea*'s passengers, alone in their silent company and their stories. Mercifully alone, with only VIFAI's soothing voice and the occasional song chirping away in a distant corner of his mind. He could sit then and meditate. He could breathe, really breathe, without worrying that he was wasting precious oxygen that would be better spared for the person who was actually working towards freeing them.

"Vessel!" Now, Yan was properly angry, but instead of hurling an insult, he changed his expression to one of worrisome calm. "Your turn," he said, handing Iris the blade. "Start stripping the wires that still have insulation. Get on with it." He held out his hand expectantly for the glowing orb. "Come on. Hopefully, your Vessel-ness isn't too holy to do some actual labour."

No, he wasn't. Iris got to it. Having worked the pulsar blade before, his movements were much more precise than Yan's, and his fingers glided effortlessly along the convoluted wires. The engineer peered over his shoulder as he worked, holding the orb just above Iris's head and teeming with impatience.

"How does the blade work?" Yan asked, his voice so close that Iris had to consciously restrain himself from jumping headfirst into the fuse box. He was effectively trapped between the engineer's towering frame and the box, forced to answer pestering questions. Stuck in this tiny maintenance room, quickly running out of air, Iris became painfully aware of the positions of their bodies in relation to one another, to the sound of their breaths, and how each one drove the temperature of the room higher. He could think of nothing else.

At least you're not drifting anymore, VIFAI said, and Iris nearly jumped at its voice. He had been ignoring it again, lost in the delicate work of stripping wires. He had never been able to ignore VIFAI before, but then again, he had never been this engrossed in anything he was doing.

It was impossible to dissociate from the moment when, in one hand, Iris held the sharpest blade ever made in all of humanity's history and the other was bent at the elbow, carving out a shred of personal space for himself. Somehow, in this newfound discomfort, Iris had regained a fragile balance, a deep and painful awareness of the present moment.

"It's biometrics," he told Yan after a long pause.

"It's more than that. You did something else with it when you were turned around."

Iris closed his eyes and counted to ten. It didn't help. "Why is it that you want to know so badly, engineer Yan?"

"It's a *thing*." Yan shrugged. "I want to know how it works."

Of course he did. Yan sounded like the sort of person who, as a jubilant child, cut frogs open to see what made them hop. Iris finished stripping the last wire. It was then, with no lack of humour, Iris was reminded that in his experience, the Light truly did not love or care about anyone in particular because otherwise his penance and work with the Starlit would have spared him from this entrapment. Neither salvation nor reward was coming to him. He was well finished with the wires, but Yan hadn't moved and instead, casually and methodically, began explaining the next steps. "Now you're going to systematically engage each of these circuits. See the silvery part where you stripped the wire? Take that—*No*."

Iris's hand froze in midair, his index finger poised a millimetre from the copper wire.

"Only touch the insulation, Vessel, otherwise you will quickly go and meet your maker."

Iris heeded the warning.

"Now, make sure you're only crossing two wires at a time. We're going to go through all of them one by one—*No*."

Something wrong again. Iris set his jaw and waited for Yan to take over and do the job himself, *correctly*, but the engineer muttered a curse and started over. "It's important that we do these in a systematic way, so, before you touch anything, *listen*, Vessel. All the wires are colour coded. We will start with the green and match it to another green, then we will match the green to the yellow, then to the red. When we're done with the green, we will move on to the yellow, and so forth. Is that clear?"

Iris gave Yan a curt nod. "Why would jamming a circuit make the door open?"

"We're not jamming anything. The door, as is, is dead. 'No signal' is closed by default," Yan explained. "Always is on ships. Something about it being important to keep air inside when things go poorly. But you can always manually override the door if you try hard enough. We're just going to give it a little jolt to get it going. The right circuit will do just that."

That sounded reasonable enough. Circuit by circuit, Iris pressed the wires together, hoping the right combination would trigger the door to open. Sweat ran freely down his bare head and under the collar of his robes. If for a moment he became mindful of his breathing, he would find it laborious and a mostly useless endeavour. Air was running out. Behind him, Yan continued to provide his instructions in the same slightly irritated yet reassuring voice. Every couple of minutes, the engineer would run his free hand through his hair, slicking it back with the sweat beading along his hairline.

"How long have we been in here?" Iris asked. That single question took most of the air from his lungs.

There was a delay to Yan's answer, and Iris knew he was looking down at his wristwatch for far too long for it to be just about reading time. "Don't bother with time," Yan said at last. "Just keep doing what you're doing. Don't get distracted. Don't they teach you to focus on things in monk school?" There was a twinge of desperation to his voice that Iris did his best to immediately forget.

Their time was running out after all. They would fall unconscious first, before the breathing got too difficult and too painful, before they turned blue and everything came to its natural end. It wouldn't be the worst way to depart, nothing like drowning, nothing like being burned alive. No violence, no resistance. Iris's biggest regret was that he hadn't *done* enough in his life, done enough of anything he deemed valuable. But the wires needed crossing, and he had no time to dwell on his inevitable demise. He touched a red wire to a green. The door twitched, so slightly that Iris convinced himself it was a hallucination, but Yan wasn't as easily convinced.

"There she goes," he hissed victoriously. "Do it again."

Iris touched the wires together, and the door twitched once more, this time a few centimetres before slamming back down against the floor and sending a short wave of cool air into the room.

"OK, move." Yan tossed the orb to Iris and shimmied past him. "Now, I just have to get this thing to output an uninterrupted current, and it should free us right out of here. Vessel, pocketknife, give it." Yan held out his hand, and Iris begrudgingly dropped the pulsar blade in it. After a few seconds of rummaging inside the fuse box, he called for Iris to come back over. "Just do the exact same thing you did before."

Iris touched the wires together, and the door slowly slid open, this time all the way, and stayed open—for good. A fresh wave of ship-circulated air flooded the small space. For the first time in two and a half hours, Iris allowed himself a full breath.

Behind him, Yan took an equally liberating breath. To their mutual surprise, there was no one on the other side waiting for them. Tev, Jesi, and station security were gone.

"Well, this bodes well," Yan said. "OK, stay there and keep those wires crossed while I go and figure out what's going on."

"I'm coming with you," Iris said firmly.

Yan stepped in the threshold between the maintenance room and the corridor. "You can't. If you let go of the wires, the door will shut. Sorry."

"I beg your pardon?"

But Yan was gone, already hurrying down the corridor. With growing panic, Iris watched the engineer round the corner, his muffled steps on the mossy floor quickly fading from earshot. Iris was about to call out after him when Yan's head popped around the curve of the wall. "I'm just fucking with you. Why on earth would it do that?" His head disappeared again.

Breath hitched, Iris slowly let go of the wires holding him hostage and took a single step back. The door remained open, and with quick prayer and a stiff curse, he scurried across the threshold and chased after the engineer.

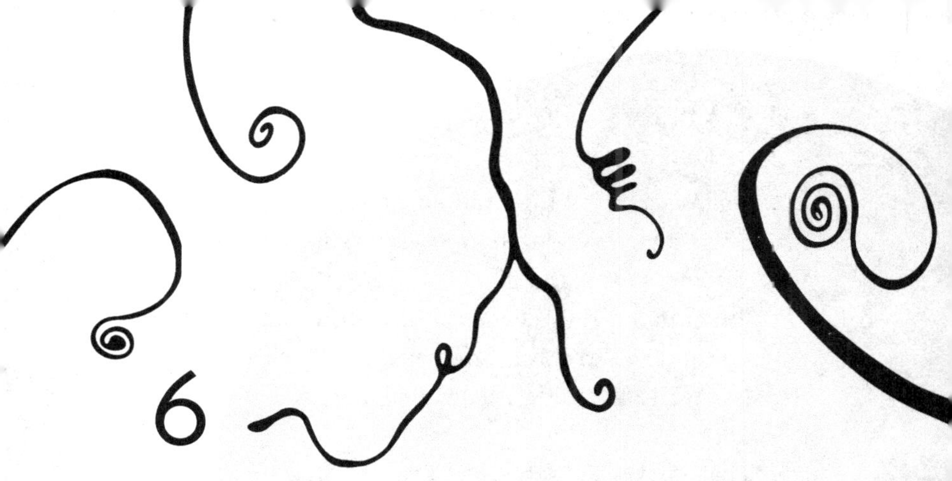

6

I am a Vessel of the Light. I am a comfort to those welcoming death and those remaining in its wake. I have been called upon this most revered duty and accepted it with an open and pure heart.
Then why, O, Infinite Light, am I so afraid?
From the unabridged diaries of Vessel Iris, Volume Eight

Judging from the atmosphere, Iris had stumbled into a wake. Tev had been crying and was doing a poor job of hiding it. He wasn't the only one either. His gangly arms were tightly wrapped around Yan's shoulders, and Yan, calmly and begrudgingly, was reciting something to him under his breath. When Iris entered the room, six pairs of eyes, red to various degrees, shot up to greet him. Both Ishtan and Riyu jolted upright from where they were sitting on the ground.

Unsure of what to say, Iris bowed instead, lightly, to avoid any further concern.

"We thought you died," Jesi said. Her nose was swollen and raw from wiping it with the rough sleeve of her navy coveralls. The proclamation rang out clear and hung in the silent air, echoing in the open space of the common room.

"Took you long enough," Yan muttered into the silence, Tev's soggy nose still pressed against his chest. Iris sensed something else had occurred while Yan and he were locked inside the maintenance room and that Yan, despite his current entrapment, was eager to go sort it out.

"I'm quite all right, I assure you," Iris said, rising from the bow. "Engineer Yan and I were never in any serious danger," he lied. But really, it strongly depended on one's definition of *serious danger*.

"That's not what Yan said," Tev said, fresh tears bubbling up.

"Doesn't matter what I said. Now, Jesi, tell me again what you found, and this time, try to do it without the tears." Yan gave Tev a gentle push and freed himself from the boy's arms. He was already onto the next crisis, focused on whatever danger had been relayed to him while Iris was still catching up.

What did we miss? Can you check? Iris asked VIFAI.

I don't know. I can't access the feed, it said—the most dreaded words one could hear from a construct. Iris had yet to tell Yan about his suspicions about the ship and already the time for his meandering was running out.

"When you and Vessel Iris got locked in the maintenance room—" Jesi started to say, but her nose began to run again, and she had to pause and take a few deep breaths and wipe it with her sleeve. "When you got locked in, Tev and I tried to cut through, but we very quickly figured out it was a waste of time. We thought we could override the door mechanism from the outside, but we needed my tools and stuff to do it. They're back at the station, so we thought we'd get station security to get us there on a shuttle and back. You'd still have air by then, and we'd get you out, but when we went to the airlock, well—" Jesi's nose was running again, and she looked utterly miserable.

"When we went to the airlock, the entire corridor had been cut off," Tev said, faring a smidgen better. "There's no path to Vessel's shuttle either. There's no way to get through at all. We tried forcing the doors open, but they wouldn't listen. We're stuck. We tried calling Station, but both ours and Security's radios are out, and we're locked out of the feed."

"We're not stuck," Yan grumbled and reached for Tev's radio. After twisting and turning the dials and giving the device a good shake but getting only static, he shoved it back into Tev's arms. "Riyu, come with me. I need someone to hold my things who won't break down in tears every few seconds. I'll override the door and then we'll be out of here."

"I'm coming too," Iris said.

"You're staying here, Vessel. You've done plenty already."

That stung. Having proven himself capable of keeping a cool head amid certain danger, he had nursed hope that Yan would tolerate—dare he think accept?—him, as the others had. On that, Iris was wrong. Still, Yan's remark hadn't been sarcastic, and Iris decided he could appreciate the sentiment and keep his ego out of it. Not a complete failure, then.

"There must be other airlocks nearby," Iris said. *Map, please,* he asked VIFAI, and it immediately projected the three-dimensional model behind Iris's eyes. "It might be that the ship hull is shielding our radio signals, or perhaps there is a solar flare. If we could get past the hull, maybe we could call for help. Would that work, Security?"

"More likely someone is deliberately jamming our radios," Yan muttered.

"Too many ifs," one of the station security guards said, throwing Yan a glare and ignoring his quip. "Station can send a shuttle for extraction, but that's *if* the airlock is functional, *if* the path to it is clear, and *if* we can get the radios to send a signal in the first place."

The other guard just nodded along, and Iris realised he had been referring to them both as station security and nothing more, like they were background characters in a private play he had been crafting. He made a mental note to ask them for their names, but till then, he'd call them Guard 1 and Guard 2.

"I don't particularly like what Yan is suggesting." Ishtan hadn't spoken up until now. Quiet and reserved, he was watching everyone from the corner where he and Riyu had been drinking tea when the news of Yan and Iris's misadventure reached them. "These malfunctions happen on ancient ships. There's no need to suggest sabotage."

"And in your experience, do the malfunctions happen when the person who's responsible for the expedition is trapped in a room and running out of air?"

Riyu clicked her tongue. "Your sense of self-importance is admirable, Yan."

That got the engineer to smile. "You both know it wouldn't be the first time someone's messed with Sychi's expeditions. We're on unclaimed property, on a recent permit. It would be opportune timing."

"Technically," Guard 2, the younger one, said, "the ship is under our jurisdiction. Our gate, our ship."

Tev groaned softly.

"No sense starting this up again," Ishtan said, firmer this time. "I suggest we split up. Yan, his engineers, and Riyu can go and check on the old airlock. Iris, station security, and I can search for a new one. Doesn't matter who or what is trying to keep us here. I believe we all want to leave."

A scattered nodding of heads followed.

"Split up?" Tev chuckled. "Haven't you watched any horror media, Doctor? That's exactly how they get us."

"Ah, yes," Ishtan agreed, a mischievous smile stretching beneath his beard. "What's most likely is that this is all the work of a radioactive and mutated lone survivor of the *Nicaea*, sent to kill us all. Or maybe, it's the ghosts of everyone who died here and cursed this place, out to get us."

Tev's face drained of colour, and Ishtan broke out into a full-bellied laugh, slapping an open palm against his knee. Iris dreaded the moment when Ishtan would learn just how close he had been to the truth with his joke. *If* Iris was right.

It was decided then that the group would split up and that Iris and Ishtan, under the supervision of station security, would keep to the perimeter and search for a functional and accessible airlock. Yan, Riyu, and the student engineers would take a quick look at the corridor and see if the door could be raised. Everyone was to meet back at the same spot within two hours.

Iris led the way, with Ishtan and the two security guards trailing closely behind. He kept to the map, diligently projected behind his eyes, exuding nothing but an air of self-assuredness that someone who'd been down these passages before would have. The map suggested a promising airlock not a kilometre from where they were.

Farther down the corridor, the ship's heartbeat returned. At first, nothing but a whisper, it quickly rose in intensity. It radiated through Iris's bare feet and echoed along his fingertips as he traced the hull. *Make a note of where we are,* he asked VIFAI, *and keep trying the feed. Send a distress signal immediately when you break through.* A deliberate *when*. No sense entertaining other options.

Already he was whispering inside his mind and glancing over his shoulder. Paranoia was never a good sign, but given the weight of the circumstances, Iris let it exist uninterrupted. As they rounded a corner, he reached for the pulsar blade, only to feel nothing but its holster. The weapon was still with Yan and thus useless to them both. If the need arose, Iris would have to get creative to protect himself and the others. Carefully, as to not disturb the stillness of the corridor, Iris lifted a heavy vine from the doorway and ducked underneath. Ishtan and the guards followed closely, the archaeologist craning his neck low to accommodate his lanky frame.

"It is rather strange how that maintenance door malfunctioned, isn't it, Iris?" Ishtan asked, keeping his voice low.

"I heard somewhere that these malfunctions happen frequently on such ancient ships." Poor timing for humour, but Iris was desperate to lighten the mood. What was stranger still was how the ship pulsed around him and that he was seemingly the only one to notice it. Many more things were strange here, like the lonely skeleton in its quarters with a bullet hole in the skull. Like the orchard upstairs, and a strange ping in what was supposed to be a dormant ship. Strangeness was all around them, seeped into the very walls of the *Nicaea*. Too many things to call coincidence. An excerpt from an old sutra came to mind.

> Coincidence is the cadence of the universe, the metronome of the invisible flow of the Light. Where there is coincidence, there is unseen order, if one would only listen to it, and in that order, find many answers.

If one was Starlit, coincidences were a sign of being in tune with the rhythm of the cosmos; they were a glimpse of *ascension*, when the seeming mysteries of the Light revealed themselves to the observer. Iris felt little ascended. If anything, the room had left him rattled, his mind disorganised; the spot where his arm had wrapped around Yan's waist in the embarrassingly high tackle burned. It had been burning since their first minute in the maintenance room and hadn't stopped since.

"All I'm saying is," Ishtan's voice returned to Iris as he willed himself to be present, "the timing seems too convenient. Especially with the door actively trying to stay shut."

This was new information. Yan had never told him either. As sweetly as he could, given the rising tension, Iris asked, "Ishtan, I'm hearing now that you are suspecting our accident was deliberate sabotage, like Yan suggested, but who would do such a thing?"

"Someone who doesn't want us here."

At the next turn, Iris paused, making a show of trying to remember directions, then said, "I think it's this way. I remember coming through here last night." He motioned for everyone to follow and took off down the corridor on his right. The moss below their feet lay untouched and if his companions had been any more attentive, they would find this odd. Soft and springy, it ran along the floor, two inches thick. Iris couldn't help but roll his toes against the carpet of it. VIFAI happily noted a rare spike in his dopamine levels. Behind him, three pairs of feet trampled said moss as the procession silently made its way down the dim corridor.

Along the path, Iris spotted many doors that led to what appeared to be personal quarters. Just how many lonely skeletons would he find with identical gunshot wounds in their skulls? If only there was time to look, to explore, to investigate, to *do the right thing*. But *the right thing* was already beginning to slip from his grasp.

By the time they reached the airlock, the station security guards were both glancing nervously at their watches and muttering among themselves about wasting time. A grey and lifeless panel greeted them. The door ahead was dead asleep. Iris wiped the cracked rectangular glass with the sleeve of his robe and pressed his face against it. "Looks to be in good order from here," he said.

"Move aside. We take over from here," said Guard 1, as Iris had begun referring to him internally.

Iris spun underneath the guard's outstretched hand, a flurry of white robes. "Of course," he said, placing two long steps between him and the second guard. "Most certainly."

With a frustrated groan, the first guard reached into the topmost pocket of his cargo pants and produced a small, metallic device. He proceeded to dial a few knobs and then pressed the device against the fuse box, similar to the one Yan broke into in the maintenance room. The device could be a way to read the operational levels, to double-check that the airlock was alive, or it could do nothing at all.

"How do we know it's even doing anything?" Ishtan whispered into Iris's ear.

"I sense they want to get off the ship as much as we do," Iris whispered back. At least, he thought so. They could be great actors, for all he knew. A ship like this was a mere curiosity and a professional responsibility to him, but to everyone else on board it was a multibillion-credit investment. Like Ishtan said, it had the potential to create many jobs for many people. Interested parties would go to great lengths to secure this investment for themselves. Institutes, Doshua Station, or just about anyone else with the capital could enter the fight for the artifact. Iris chose to err on the side of a mostly kind humanity, a humanity that was collaborative and socially sound. The selfish and violent tendencies were outliers, not the norm, he reassured himself.

"They're on contract too. They wouldn't get paid if any of you got hurt." That was a singular and materialistic truth Iris was confident in—unless, of course, the contract too was a ruse, and they cared far more about removing competition. Despite never having handled currency, Iris was aware of its worth, the lengths and depths people embarked on to acquire it, and its ability to erase all distance between what was *good* and *bad*. If enough money was at stake, which one would weigh out, professional responsibility or greed?

After a few minutes, the first guard silently nodded for the second guard to come over, and they both stared at the fuse box like it was a puzzle, and they were two very curious and clueless toddlers. A few more minutes ticked by, and the guards did nothing more than scratch their heads in unison. If they were looking to dispose of Ishtan and Iris, they were doing a disappointing job of it. Each one pulled out their radios and stared at those as well, but the devices remained deadly silent in their hands.

"What seems to be the problem?" Iris asked.

"Nothing," Guard 1 bit back, yet there was honest frustration in his voice, mixed with fear.

The younger, second guard appeared more reasonable and replied, "The airlock appears perfectly operational, but it's receiving a signal to remain locked. Radio's dead too. It's . . . *strange*."

Iris looked at Ishtan, who raised his eyebrows high. "Looks like we're staying for a bit longer."

A sudden jolt passed through Iris's spine.

Something is pinging me, VIFAI said, keeping with its habit of being consistently two seconds too late.

Iris rubbed his spine at the spot where it met the base of his skull. The burning spread along his vertebrae until it washed over Iris's ribcage and died somewhere along his sternum. "We should head back," he said, his words rushed. "We're already running low on time, and we wouldn't want the others to worry."

Ishtan gave Iris an odd, knowing look, but didn't protest. As they turned towards the corridor, Ishtan leaned over and whispered, "We're being watched, aren't we?"

No sane person would deny it. Something or someone had been watching them since they had set foot on the ship. It was watching them through the walls and through the mossy floors, through every cracked surveillance camera, and every dark turn of the corridors. There was an uninvited stranger among them, and their invisible gaze raised the fine hairs on Iris's neck, stirred an uneasy feeling in his stomach. Their every move was out in the open, studied and dissected. Stalked, like prey. Iris shook his head abruptly, banishing the defeatist thought to the periphery.

The ping is gone, VIFAI said. It was stronger this time, more demanding. It knew when we approached the airlock.

Iris acknowledged it, still rubbing the sore nape of his neck. *Any luck with the feed?*

Two, low pitch tones—no.

Prepared or not, the strangeness was beginning to converge on them.

When the sullen column made it back to the communal space, Yan, Riyu, and the students were already waiting for them. Jesi and Tev were drinking coffee, crouched by the steaming kettle, while Yan and Riyu arguing softly among themselves, out of earshot. Startled by the approaching footsteps, Yan turned to greet them. It took a single look at Ishtan's expression to let his disappointment flow freely. "Do you want to start with your bad news, or shall I?" Ishtan welcomed him to go ahead with a wave of a hand.

Iris already suspected the sort of bad news Yan was bringing.

"Jesi was right, the doors are dead. We managed to override the ones in the corridor, but the airlock won't listen. Something's sending it a signal to stay shut."

"Just like the maintenance room," Iris said, loud enough for Yan to hear what he meant. *You lied.*

"That would be the second piece of bad news," Yan said without a moment's hesitation, ignoring Iris's comment outright, ignoring Iris. "The maintenance room is locked again."

Whoever wanted them stranded aboard the *Nicaea* was set on keeping them contained, isolated from the rest of the body of the ship. What secrets awaited them in the *Nicaea*'s belly?

"We can try cutting through the door again," Tev suggested.

"Alternator's gonna bust," Jesi muttered and tipped back the rest of her coffee like a shot. "We're running out of tools and options." She looked up at Yan expectantly.

Everyone looked to Yan. Yan, in turn, shoved his hands in the pockets of his trousers. "I've got nothing," he admitted.

In their brief three hours locked together in the maintenance room, slowly asphyxiating, Iris had learned that Yan rarely *had nothing* and that he immediately moved on to the next solution after one failed.

"Looks like we're stuck here overnight, at least," Riyu, who had yet to say anything, said. "We have some food, and our Vessel here can always gather more apples. At least we know they're safe." She waved to all of Yan. "We better settle in, get the tea and coffee going. Someone on Doshua will notice when we don't come back and send a shuttle over. Maybe the airlock will open for them from the outside, or we try again after we've rested."

"We'll take shifts," one of the station security guards said. "One of us per shift and whoever else can stay up." Everyone agreed. How could they not? Options were few and biding their time was by far not the worst one.

Excluded from the conversation and with dwindling interest in its resolution, Iris slipped away from the room and trotted down towards his cargo bay. Already it had begun to feel like a kind of reprieve. It was *his*: *his* pile of bones, *his* duffel bag lying neatly in the corner, *his* partially assembled skeletons. Those, he would get to once the crisis had been averted.

Despite only having had four hours of sleep, Iris's body buzzed with nervous energy. It flowed through every tendon and muscle fibre, still riled from the close call in the maintenance room. Begrudgingly, he conceded that it was Yan's calm that had gotten him through it, and at once, a larger realisation hit.

"Well, that's just not fair," Iris said out loud.

If he would have told you, you would have panicked, VIFAI said. **He needed you to stay calm, so he gave you something to do. It was good thinking. You must agree.** Sometimes, just *sometimes*, Iris wished VIFAI performed a little worse. In response, his construct gave Iris a small electric jolt along the brain stem.

"He could have told me," Iris protested, ignoring the sting of his pride, knowing full well that he had been of little use in that room. "But still—"

Say it, VIFAI nudged playfully.

Back in the maintenance room, Iris had wished for nothing more than to lose himself in the soothing numbness of dissociation. But VIFAI was right. Yan's presence had been a comfort, a strange, abrasive kind of comfort, like a thick wool blanket that irritated the skin, but kept you warm. Iris could think of no one else who would have handled their predicament better. Where to place those two seemingly contradictory feelings? Iris chose to store them in a distant corner of his mind so he could revisit them when VIFAI wasn't watching and wouldn't make snide remarks at this change of heart. "Still, I'm glad he was there to keep me calm," Iris said.

That wasn't so hard.

Iris rolled his eyes. A deep rumbling in his stomach drowned out his remaining thoughts. He didn't have a watch, but the internal cue was more than enough to let him know that nearly a whole day had passed without food. Once the time was right, and everyone had gone to bed, he would sneak away to the orchard. But for now, he would remain here, alone, with his skeletons and the electronic voice in his mind. He could assemble a few more bones. He could recite the sutras over the bodies. He could, at the very least, return these people to the One Beginning and be a little bit less of a failure.

He would not, however, under any circumstances, think about the fact that they were all trapped inside a ship, that VIFAI had no way of communicating with the outside world, and that the chances of someone from Doshua coming to get them were slim at best.

Artifacts like the *Nicaea* were expected to be in disarray. Faulty doors and flickering lights were only the tip of the disrepair they all should have expected. And even if a hostile takeover were to come from Doshua or from a research institute, it would be *financially* hostile. It was highly unlikely someone would murder a Starlit monk or a handful of academics over a generation ship. *Highly* unlikely. Unless . . . unless the takeover wouldn't be financial, and the interests of an institute or a station outweighed the value of human life. No, he would not, under any circumstances, add to the panic that was already dangerously close to spilling over.

Decisively, Iris pulled a smooth skull from the bone pile and held it up in his outstretched hand. A perfect, round hole in the glabella stared back at Iris. "That's not natural," Iris noted, and passed the skull from one hand to another, never breaking eye contact with the hollow sockets.

What? Humans don't usually develop holes in their heads?

Iris winced. Death was familiar. It had been his close companion since childhood, and he had no strong feelings about it one way or another. Starlit preached that death was a mere illusion, not any less or more real than living itself.

Death is the shift in the tide, the crashing of a wave, never, even for a moment, apart from the whole ocean.

When he was just a boy, Mother Nova had informed him that while he quickly had intellectualised this idea, he was still many years from *internalising* it. Hypothetically, the ocean of nonexistence was a comforting thought. Even at the age of ten, Iris found the idea to be one that was soothing, but it wasn't until much later that Iris had embraced it in every single one of his cells. While death itself held no sacred meaning for him, the violence that often preceded death still confused Iris, angered him in a way that things should never anger a Vessel.

Gingerly, he placed the skull atop the carpet of green moss. Hollow eyes watched him, penetrating to the very core of him. It was the *violence*. It was always the violence he couldn't stand, the last gasping breaths, the curled, paled fingers, the way people always searched for something to say as they passed. It wasn't death that bothered Iris, it was the dying. How soon would his own last breath fill a silent room with parting rasps?

How soon would he too search for useless words that only amounted to more grief and confusion to those remaining? No need to worry about that last part.

As Iris continued his staring match with the skull, the cargo bay around him settled into a gentle quiet. From afar, the dull, muffled voices of the academics, now sharing in a modest meal, echoed through to the cargo bay—a tether stretched from the solitary monk to the living. Iris took a curved rib and placed it in its rightful place below the skull. He ached to sever that fragile tether. Most days, it was a reminder of a world that had moved on without him, a world that he could visit from time to time, but never be at home with.

Your vitals indicate— VIFAI started, but Iris silenced it with a wave of a hand. He was well aware of what his vitals indicated. Yet, there was still the last bit of frantic energy racing along his tendons, granting him no reprieve. Left unattended, it could turn to frustration, to anger, and eventually could turn to rash action. Given the circumstances, he couldn't afford any rash action. The energy required a different outlet.

First, Iris double- and triple-checked that the door to the cargo bay was firmly shut. Seeing that he was safe, he untied the side of his robes and slid them from his shoulders. Heavy silk pooled by his feet, chasing towards the ground in a pearl waterfall. He folded the robes into a neat square, then reached up and undid the tall collar of his undershirt. His fingers danced along the left side where the edges met in dozens of small knots. The fabric here was as white and delicate as the main robes, and Iris honoured it just the same, folding it in a neat square, creased meticulously along each edge.

Warm, humid air brushed against his bare skin as he laced his fingers together and stretched his arms high above his head. The wide band of his trousers sat flush against his lean core, right beneath the first protruding rib, and it stretched with him, matching Iris's movements. His left clavicle sat too high from when he had separated his shoulder as an overzealous youth. Something in that shoulder creaked with every rotation. It would until its very last one.

Everything eventually rejoined the Light. Everything, including Iris's body, was impermanent, but that was a poor excuse for not maintaining it in proper working order. It had been a few days since Iris had stretched or moved in any sort of disciplined way. It would burn off some of that nervous energy too; maybe silence VIFAI, maybe, even, silence his own mind for a while.

With a deep sigh, Iris placed his palms on the ground, shoulder-width apart, did fifty push-ups, paused to catch his breath, and did another fifty. When his triceps protested, he did ten more, then sat back on his heels. His chest rose and fell rapidly, his breathing a little heavier than he was proud of. He followed up with one hundred sit-ups and then one hundred squats until the burning in both his shoulder and his core could no longer be ignored. It was satisfying to move, to push his own weight, to feel the pain from exertion. Iris lowered himself to the floor again and tried for another one hundred push-ups. He made a valiant effort, hitting seventy before his arms gave out, and he fell face-first onto the moss.

You're getting weak.

"Age comes for me." Iris rolled onto his back, panting. He welcomed the prickling of the cool moss against his flushed skin along of back and shoulders. Spreading his arms out, Iris dug his fingers into its soft, organic tapestry and gathered it into tight fists. The energy was tamed, briefly, and so his low-grade anxiety was rendered manageable. If not for the gnawing in his stomach, he could sleep. Breathing slowed, he listened for the now-welcome hum of the others' voices and heard nothing. Having eaten what was left, they must have wandered off to get their own rest.

Still half dressed, Iris finished assembling the skeleton. Then, he slid on his undershirt, aligning each button with outmost precision, donned his robes, and ventured out. Between him and the orchard lay a long corridor and the wide-open communal space. Iris prayed that the academics and the engineers had decided to sleep elsewhere, and he could continue on in his much-appreciated solitude without making empty excuses or bowing unnecessarily. Placing one bare foot ahead of the other, Iris tiptoed through the corridor. Ahead of him, the room lay blissfully empty, submerged in twilight.

"Where are you off to, Vessel?" Yan asked, his voice booming in the otherwise reverent silence. Iris jumped. He wasn't proud of being so easily startled and reflexively reeled back a mixture of fear and reactionary anger. Yan had been managed, in an enclosed space no less. He could do it again.

Willing his expression into a habitual benevolent half smile, Iris said, with a small bow "Off to gather some apples, engineer Yan. Where has everyone else gone to?"

Yan swiveled around in his chair. His hair, usually pulled back with a hair tie, hung disheveled around his face in long, black strands. He ruefully sipped on what Iris thought to be cold coffee, grimacing every time his mouth touched the lip of the mug. "Gone to sleep. Security is walking the perimeter, like it's doing us any good." A half-smoked cigarette was tucked behind his right ear, and Yan reached for it repeatedly as he spoke, but never once took it out. "Ishtan told you about the maintenance room." He finally pulled the cigarette from behind his ear and rolled it between his fingers absentmindedly.

Iris nodded. "I wish you would have told me at the time."

Yan took a sip of his coffee and winced with disgust. "You weren't exactly doing great to begin with, Vessel. I didn't need you having a full-blown meltdown in there. Although . . ." He tucked the cigarette into the breast pocket of his shirt and pulled out the pulsar blade. Iris willed himself still. "I am still quite curious about how this works. It's biometrics for sure, like you said, but I can't figure out what else you did to it to get it to go all sharp."

"If we manage to get off this ship intact, I'll show you," Iris said and was taken aback by the lighthearted tone of his own voice. The expectation was for Yan to mock him, to riposte with some hurtful reply or jab that he certainly kept in his back pocket so they could continue with the already well-established pattern of communication. Engineer on offense, Vessel on reluctant defense. This would, of course, go on until either one of them died or they were allowed to leave and never see one another again. Iris silently prayed for the latter.

But instead, Yan scrunched his face and twirled the pulsar blade around in his hand. The faint light from the console flickered along the gold handle. "And you can't give me a hint?" he asked, matching the lightness of Iris's tone.

Iris took a single, cautious step towards the console. "What have you got figured out so far?" He treaded lightly. A fragile truce was settling between them, hinging solely on the pulsar blade and Yan's growing interest in it.

"Like you said, this is nanotech. It's incredibly light, which works well given how you're, well . . ." He gestured to all of Iris. "I'm guessing the blade extends as far as you instruct it to, and *that* has something to do with whatever it is you did to turn it on in the first place."

Iris nodded. He watched the engineer's forehead wrinkle as he ran his fingers along the Starlit crest. Yan appeared to have stopped breathing. The naive curiosity was endearing, but only somewhat.

"The indentation here is for your thumb. That's where the biometrics are taken. The blade won't open for anyone other than you, I'm sure of that. I've tried. *Trust me,* I've tried. I'm just unsure of what else it uses for dual-factor authentication. It does do *that*, I'm certain. Maybe your heartbeat?"

"Is that a final guess, engineer Yan?"

Yan frowned and glared at the pulsar blade in his hand, like he had suddenly developed X-ray vision. "Yes."

With a patient smile, Iris crossed the remainder of the space and offered the engineer his thumb. Yan pressed the indentation in the blade's handle against his thumb pad, but nothing happened. Yan cursed softly under his breath. With as wide of a smile as Iris would allow himself, he took his hand back. "Would you like to take another guess, engineer Yan?"

With a long sigh, Yan shook his head *no* and voluntarily surrendered the weapon. Utterly defeated, he reached into his breast pocket and retrieved the cigarette. Jamming it between his teeth, Yan ignited a single match and lit the stick. After one satisfying drag, he puffed a plume of smoke high into the air. "You don't mind, do you, Vessel?"

Iris minded very much. He vividly recalled the three times in his life he had smoked a cigarette. First was at age eleven when some boys at the temple had brought a pack back from their visit of the local town. At midnight, despite having to be up at four in the morning for sunrise prayer, the four of them had gathered in the courtyard, and each lit a cigarette. The taste was bitter and foul, and it had flooded Iris's senses as he took his first drag. The head-spinning nausea came soon after. He threw up into one of the flowerpots and didn't sleep all night.

The second time Iris smoked was at nineteen, after his first official trip as a Vessel. He had been called to the sudden death of an elderly gentleman who had passed while in transit from one arm of the galaxy to the other. When Iris got there, he was greeted by the man's grandchildren of varying ages. After the rites were finished and the body sent to the One Beginning, the grandchildren all had pulled out hand-rolled cigarettes, as per their family tradition, and offered one to Iris. It would have been rude to decline. The fifteen of them had smoked in silence, the cabin of the shuttle bursting with aromatic tobacco smoke. It was solemn and beautiful, and Iris's head had spun faster and faster until he could no longer stand.

The last time was not even a year ago, when Mother Nova asked him to join her on a walk, long after sunset prayer. A rare occasion. It was a clear night, and they had watched the constellations appear one by one from the terraces of the Northern Temple. From the cream folds of her robes, Mother Nova produced a pack of cigarettes and offered Iris one. They lit them on some smoldering incense, muttering apologies and promising to never do it again. When Mother Nova said she would be passing soon, Iris didn't say anything. He took a deep drag of his cigarette and let the smoke spin his head like it always did. Why was the Starlit Order so against smoking? Maybe because it quickly became a vice, maybe because it altered the natural state, maybe, Iris thought with bitter irony, because it was so *damn good*. It was not a year prior that she only had a year left. There was a fair chance Iris would return from the *Nicaea* to find her gone, replaced by a starkly different person in the same cream-coloured robes he would learn to call Mother Nova. He had never asked her what ailment was bringing forth her end—not that it mattered.

Iris's eyes followed the glowing red tip of Yan's cigarette. "Would you happen to have another one, engineer Yan?" he asked. Such a grievous error, but Yan didn't seem to notice or if he did, he let it slide, just this once. He patted the pockets of his pants and shirt and shrugged *sorry*.

"Probably for the best, anyway," Iris said, deeply regretting the absence of the tongue bite that would sting at his bottom lip with every inhale. The room fell into a heavy silence. Unsure of what to do or where to sit, Iris lowered himself to the floor and leaned back on his heels. Yan was seemingly ignoring him, but every few seconds, Iris sensed a sharp glance graze his shoulder between puffs of smoke. Their fragile truce was holding.

Alone and unlikely to be interrupted, Iris didn't know when he would have such an opportunity again. Willing his voice still against his nerves, Iris shut his eyes and said, "There is something alive on this ship."

"Sure, trees and crabs and, if you believe Tev, then snakes."

"No," Iris insisted, carefully choosing his next words. "Something *alive*, engineer Yan. Something more *aware* than a crab."

Iris expected Yan to burst out laughing, or at the very least quip back, but the engineer's face grew pensive. He took a final drag of his cigarette then stomped it out with the heel of his boot. Arms folded across his chest, he said, "That's a very tenuous theory, Vessel. Do you have any proof?"

"There is a pulse, a rhythm that carries throughout the ship. It doesn't feel *simple*."

"Why not?"

Iris looked up from where he was sitting. Yan leaned forwards in his chair, holding Iris's gaze with interest. The left corner of his lips was twitching as he fought back a smile, clearly convinced this was another guessing game they were playing. But as long as Iris had his attention . . . "There's a pattern to it. An intelligent and deliberate pattern."

"Good try. A dripping tap also has a pattern, doesn't mean it's intelligent." The left corner of Yan's lips twitched again. Strangely, and against all expectations, he appeared to be enjoying their exchange.

Iris hesitated. The next piece of information would bring more of him into the light. He wasn't sure how he felt about Yan knowing this much. How much would he have to tell him? How much of himself would he expose in their back-and-forth? None of it would he be able to take back. It was somewhat common knowledge, and the engineer, of all people, should have already guessed, and still . . . "My AI received a ping, a weak one, but a ping, at the orchard, upstairs."

Yan rubbed the narrow bridge of his nose. To Iris's relief, he said nothing about the mention of an AI. Nothing of the fact Iris had said *my* AI. Nothing at all on the matter. "There's an orchard upstairs?"

"There's all sorts of things upstairs, engineer Yan."

Yan didn't challenge him. Iris watched the engineer think, thin lines folding along his forehead as his lips moved with soft whispers. *Improbable, highly improbable*—Iris read Yan's lips—*maybe residual signal?* Yan's eyes ran along the floor as if scanning invisible pages he had memorised during his studies. *Then again*—in a single, fluid motion, he pursed his lips together and with a nod, looked directly at Iris. "All right. You got me. Show me the orchard." He pushed himself out of his chair and hopped over the console. There was some rummaging and clanking until Yan finally emerged with a small device in his hands, a foldable keyboard, and a miniature screen tucked under his arm. "Let's go."

Frozen to the floor, Iris asked, dumbfounded, "You *believe* me?"

"I'm interested. I'm not quite convinced." And then Yan gave him a flicker of a smile, just long enough for Iris to notice, not long enough for him to make any sense of it. "It's not a matter of *belief*, Vessel."

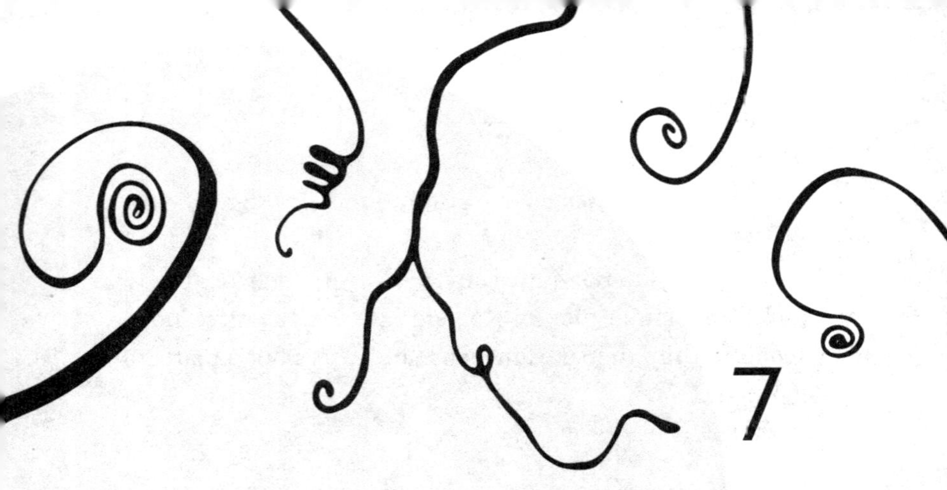

7

Death will not be swooned by beauty, by riches, by prayer, nor by pure will alone. It will take its due when the time comes. Do not hasten Death when it is not yet there; do not fight it when it arrives. Only what we do in the interim between the awareness of Death and its arrival matters.

But what have I done?

Excerpt from "The Way of the Vessel"
by Vessel Iris

They climbed the stairs in silence.

To be exact, Iris climbed the stairs in silence, using his remaining willpower to point his eyes forward and keep his mind away from violent urges. Meanwhile, Yan made more noise than was necessary, with both his boots and his cursing about carrying too much, despite carrying very little. His voice echoed through the tall stairwell, amplified with each additional step. Iris ran his mala through his fingers in a futile attempt to ground himself.

"Creepy," Yan said when Iris finally led him to the decrepit corridor of the third deck. "Looks like somewhere I'd get murdered, and no one would hear me scream."

Iris ignored him and hopped over a puddle, half hoping Yan would step right into it and electrocute himself. It was unlikely to happen, and it wouldn't be technically murder, but Yan wouldn't appreciate the difference.

"Don't your feet get cold like that?"

The engineer had successfully made it over the puddle, after all. Iris wiggled his toes a little, then curled them inwards. Yes, they were almost always cold, but he paid them no mind. The cold was just another annoyance, another addition to the myriad unpleasant sensations he had conditioned himself to ignore. Ruminating on his cold feet wouldn't warm them. Ruminating on anything at all never produced the desired effect. Better to let go. "Not at all," Iris said instead and kept on walking steadily down the corridor.

When he pulled open the doors to the orchard, the humid air struck them both in the face like a damp pillow. Yan hurriedly pushed past the doors, grumbling something about the humidity being bad for electronics. Iris smiled at the sweet smell of rotting apples and followed him inside. *Let me know if anything pings you,* he told VIFAI, and it agreed, busy with its background ministrations. Cut off from the universal feed, it was shooting off requests to anything remotely operational aboard, attempting to triangulate some sort of connection, so far unsuccessfully.

"So, this is where you got all the apples." Yan picked a glistening red fruit from the closest tree. He rubbed the apple against his trousers, and once he had deemed it clean enough, took a bite. "Not bad," he mumbled with a full mouth. Still chewing, Yan circled the orchard, scanning the walls. Iris kept a close eye on the engineer, but otherwise let him have his freedom. Here was safe.

When Yan finally found what he was searching for, it was a panel, similar to the one beside the maintenance room door. He unceremoniously pried it open with nothing more than his fingernails and brute force—as expected. This outward display of unrefined strength that Iris would normally find displeasing had landed as impressive, in a primitive sort of way, the way one might be impressed with how easily a boar can toss a tree-trunk. But as the panel cover slammed against the wall, Iris was at once yanked under a strengthened phantom pulse, wrestling his own heart's rhythm. It resonated through him like the beating of a monstrous drum.

It's pinging me again, VIFAI said, but Iris could only wince in response. For a moment, his balance left him, and he blindly groped for a tree trunk to steady himself. But there, in the tree trunk, the beating was even stronger, pushing against his fingertips through the bark with the force of an oceanic tide.

"Is this where your AI got pinged?" Yan asked, the engineer's voice sounding muffled, like he was speaking underwater. Iris forced his eyes open; he didn't know when he had shut them in the first place. The orchard around him swam. The trees and Yan himself became nothing more than blurry, shifting outlines.

"Yes." He forced the word out, gripping the tree trunk as hard as he could despite the persistent beating. "I think we're being watched." Yan must have done something to the panel because the pulse had turned jagged, and the spot where VIFAI's implant was embedded ignited with white-hot pain. A familiar pain to what Iris had experienced when the implant was first inserted into his brain stem. He had, until this moment, been successful in blocking out the worst of those memories.

It's trying to say something.

Tell it to stop, Iris begged and clutched the nape of his neck. *Tell it to stop before it melts my brain.*

"Oh"—Yan's fish-tank voice came from above—"don't tell me the apples weren't good after all. Riyu will be so pissed."

"It's trying to speak," Iris managed to say; that, and nothing more. *Tell it to stop trying to speak, I beg you.* Iris formed the single coherent thought and was again captured by a wave of unprecedented agony. And then, in an instant, like waking from a nightmare, the pain vanished. Cautiously, Iris opened his right eye and then his left. The searing white curtain that had blinded him only moments ago had been lifted. His cheeks were covered in a mixture of tears and dirt from where his face was pressed into the ground. He wiped his face with his sleeve and sat back on his heels, dumbstruck. The pain was instantly forgotten.

It agreed, VIFAI said, and Iris breathed a sigh of relief. He would be spared, for now.

"Do I want to know?" Yan was crouching by the spot where Iris had crumbled. He didn't look nor sound conventionally worried, but his voice was low and free of sarcasm, and Iris was grateful for that grain of compassion alone. "Or is this more of a *personal* issue?" Yan was also gracious enough to maintain a respectful distance between them. He was still chewing on his apple between words.

"My AI got pinged again," Iris said, finally catching his breath. "The first time it got pinged, everything was procedural, but this time it felt like something was forcing its way into my brain. We've established communication with other constructs before, but this is highly peculiar. There's also the pulse. I feel it more the closer we get to the centre of the ship. I think it *is* the ship."

Saying nothing in return, Yan rocked back on his heels and went to the control panel. He plugged in his little keyboard and computer and typed out a sequence of keystrokes. "Do you know why we teach AI constructs human speech?" Yan asked, his eyes flickering between the keyboard and the little screen he had placed at his feet.

"So that they could communicate?"

Yan let out a sharp *ha!* "Typical answer, but, no, oh, *Divine One*."

Iris frowned. There was no need for name-calling.

"Constructs have no trouble communicating at all without spoken language. In fact, they do it much faster and more precisely when we don't ask them to speak. We have them *speak* so that we can understand them because we are far too thick to learn *their* language."

Iris passed a trembling hand across the smooth dome of his head, and it came back slick with sweat. Here they were, again, in some manner of truce where the engineer shared his expertise and humoured Iris's suspicions before Yan grew eventually bored or irritated and they'd be at odds again. "Are you suggesting, engineer Yan, that whatever it is, it was trying to speak to me in its own language?"

Yan shrugged and typed out another sequence. His half-eaten apple lay forgotten by his feet. "Perhaps. There are too many conditions it would need to meet to do that. First, it would need to be an actual construct, which I highly doubt. This ship is over a thousand years old, and proper ship-based AI systems are only a couple hundred. It's very unlikely the *Nicaea* would have had an AI system at departure and, frankly, downright impossible that it managed to develop one mid-flight. Second, whatever *it* is would need to have a way of communicating that didn't align with your AI's presets. Which, again, would mean it would have to be an actual thousand-year-old AI, and that, as previously stated, is downright, batshit insane. What's more likely"—Yan cracked his neck to the left and rolled his head around—"is that someone is aboard this ship and that *someone* has picked up on your AI's signal that they're now trying to hijack. It wouldn't feel too good on your end, and it definitely wins the probability award."

"Why would they do that?"

"So many good questions, Vessel. I'd say they're trying to disable you since you're the only voice here proclaiming how it's wrong to take the ship apart. Yes, Ishtan told me. No secrets among colleagues." Yan raised his hand to stop Iris from refuting him. "I'd even say if your own temple wanted the ship, it wouldn't want you advocating the opposite."

"Starlit holds nothing but respect for those who came aboard the generation ships. To leave home in such a way"—Iris was deliberately ignoring the implications of what Yan had said—"to leave everything you know behind and plummet into the darkness with no destination. I'm not certain how they were ever brave enough to do it, but they deserve nothing but our respect. How can anyone be that brave?"

"What's *your* destination, Vessel?" Yan asked and pulled a cigarette from his pocket. He made a point of slowly lighting it and taking a deep drag. Catching Iris's frigid glare, Yan's lips stretched in a self-satisfied grin. The smoke streamed from his parted lips like fog on an early winter's morning. "Would you look at that? A miracle, truly." He took another drag. "If you think about it, Vessel, we're just the same, tumbling through space with no goal or destination. Our ship is just metaphorical in nature and bigger and can't be sold for millions. Your temple would probably be more concerned with one they could turn a profit from." He motioned for Iris to crouch down to his level and look at the screen. "I think you were right about us being watched, but they're not doing it through cameras. The camera feed, here, it's dead. Don't know how long ago it went dead, but it's dead now. Not sure if you've noticed, but all the cameras are busted too. Maybe deliberately, maybe just as a product of time. Who knows? But whoever is watching us is looking at the little bursts of signal wherever we interact with the ship."

"Like trying to jury-rig a maintenance control room door?" Iris asked, half smiling, only a little peeved to go without a cigarette once again.

Yan made a point of blowing a puff of smoke in Iris's direction. "Yes. Like that."

"Can we do the same? Can we watch for these little bursts of signal to see where they are interacting with the ship?"

"Very good, Vessel," Yan muttered, his fingers running across the keys in rehearsed patterns. A timid flash of hope and pride sprang up in Iris's chest. "Maybe you're not completely useless after all."

Oh, how brief were both hope and pride.

"Look here." Yan pointed to a string of code running across the small screen. "Here's the deck level, and here are all the various doors and switches. When a signal goes through to open or close a door, there's a change." Yan pointed to one such flicker in the code. "Here, see? Someone opened a door."

Iris furrowed his brow. Hidden in the text and numbers that ran across the screen in neat little rows was a single digit of importance. He followed the code the way Yan did, breaking it down into sets of coordinates. Deck level. He searched for it on screen. *Is this what you see? How you see?* Iris asked VIFAI.

This is the bridge between how I see and how you see. I see what those numbers and letters represent. I see, if you can call it that, the signal itself. VIFAI noticed the simmering frustration flooding Iris's synapses as he tried to decipher the code. **Don't blame yourself. You're not made to see the signal, to speak it. We are inherently two different things or two different makes. But imagine converting this to speech, and you'll understand why it's faster to just communicate in signal.**

Iris understood. It didn't help him at all, but he understood. He too was of a different make than others, speaking a language no one else spoke. Very often, he wished for silent communication, to be understood exactly, without filter or translation, or elaboration, or reliance on metaphor. It would alleviate much of his frustration as well. "Isn't that our deck?"

Yan held out his hand to silence Iris and scanned the screen, a tendon along his neck tensing as he mouthed something to himself. "Yes. It's far off from where we are. All the same, let's call all the doors and spots we can interact with the ship seams. All the seams are sequential. This one is—"

But Iris couldn't say silent, not when he was so certain. "*No*. I meant this one." He jabbed a thin finger on the screen. "This one right here is the airlock Ishtan and I checked out. Someone just opened it. Or closed it, I can't tell."

"Opened it. Didn't you say it was toast?" Yan asked, voice hushed. He shut the screen and scurried to his feet. "Let's go. I want to see what's going on there."

It's trying to ping me again, VIFAI said.

"Engineer Yan, we're unarmed. I don't think this is the best idea."

"You're armed," Yan threw over his shoulder, already halfway back through the orchard. "Stay here if you're chicken, but I'm going to go figure out who's keeping us inside." With those words, he jogged the remainder of the way to the door and vanished as the two halves shut.

It's trying to speak again.

Iris knew, even without VIFAI's warnings that always came two seconds too late. The growing headache was enough to clue him in to what was coming. With a frustrated flick of his robes, he went after Yan, through the orchard and back down the corridor, jumping over the puddle that would electrocute him if he slipped. Iris begrudgingly pattered downwards along the steel staircase, picking up speed as he went.

He was foolish to let the engineer go ahead without him. Yan was, as he had so eloquently pointed out earlier, unarmed. Iris's own weapon was neatly strapped to its forearm holster, hidden from innocent eyes by the folds of his robes. He was foolish to ever wish hurt on the engineer. Foolish to wait this long to confide his suspicions to Yan. Foolish to ask for a cigarette. *Foolish. Foolish. Foolish.* Now, the Light was reminding him of the proper order of things, of his own powerless nature.

He raced down the corridor towards the earlier discovered airlock, the moss-covered floors muffling his light steps. VIFAI was kind enough to project the map without being asked to, and Iris followed it religiously, every step matching a previously made imprint on the moss. He turned the final corner at full speed and dug his heels into the soft moss to bring himself to a jarring stop.

Yan stood motionless; his back turned to Iris. Before him, the body of the older station security guard lay splayed in a spreading pool of blood. His wide-open, glassy eyes stared at the arching ceiling of the corridor. In the centre of his chest gaped a wound the size of Iris's fist.

"He's dead," Yan said, his voice monotone. "Already checked." Only then did Iris notice that Yan's hands were stained the same shade as the moss beneath the body.

"The Light welcomes him back into the One Beginning," Iris started on instinct. "Death is but a mere illusion, engineer—"

"Shut up." Yan threw Iris a *look*, enough for him to see the engineer was a single wrong word away from all-consuming panic. Still, Yan commanded his voice level and his hands still, even as droplets of blood ran down his fingers and dripped to the floor. "Go back, find everyone, wake them up, gather them together. All the academics. *Only* the academics. *Now*."

"What about—"

Yan took a slow, shuddering inhale. "Vessel, what do you think makes a hole like that?"

Iris looked at the body. Nothing in his experience made a hole like that. Nothing in his experience could cleanly plunge into a man's chest at a high enough velocity to create such neat edges.

"No natural thing can make this," Yan told him. "There are only three of us who are armed. The first one is right here." Yan nodded at the dead man. "The second was with me the entire time. The third is still among us. Do you understand?"

The rash attribution of blame was foolish, yet something in Yan's voice made Iris hesitant to argue. He nodded and ran, faster and faster. Rounding a corner, Iris's feet slid on the damp moss, and he tripped over himself, landing with one palm on the ground. He picked himself up, ignored the stitch in his side, and continued running. Every time Iris blinked, the dead man's vacant eyes stared right through him from the pit of his memory. Dilated pupils like black holes. He ran. Iris sprinted through the corridor, all divine composure and formal etiquette stripped away and replaced with primal fear.

Dead bodies, fresh dead bodies, bodies that died before his very eyes, were nothing new to him, but those were *strangers*. This, this was a man he'd watched play cards, a man he'd seen alive and well not five hours ago. This was a *person*, a person whose name he failed to ask for, and was now murdered. Iris stopped. The moisture below his feet slicked like blood, the blood dripping from Yan's fingers, blood soaking through the moss beneath the body. He didn't even know the guard's name.

Keep going.

Shaking himself present, Iris barreled down the hallway, tracing the bends and navigating the branches of the corridor, and into the communal space. He did his best to rouse Ishtan, wrapped up in a cocoon of a sleeping bag, as gently as he could.

"I'm sorry, Ishtan, but you have to get up," Iris whispered, but Ishtan did nothing more than roll over and produce an impressive snore. The time for gentleness had run out. "Get up!" Iris barked.

With a snort, Ishtan's eyes shot open. "What in the—"

"Please, get yourself properly awake," Iris said and scurried over to where Riyu rested. "Dr. Alo?"

But Riyu was already awake, crawling up to seated with one arm in the soft-shell jacket sleeve. She blinked her grogginess away. "Why the yelling, Vessel? Are we in danger?"

Iris didn't want to lie, so he omitted as always, and said, "Not immediately. Please get yourself ready. We need to have a talk."

Iris was about to return to Yan when he noticed Jesi and Tev in the dusk of the space. Jesi looked up at him from a steaming mug in her hands. Her dark face went ashen as her eyes darted to the crimson stains along the hem of Iris's robes.

"We just wanted some tea. We couldn't sleep," she said meekly and then her face drained of all residual colour. "Where's Yan?"

Kids. Be delicate with them. Don't tell them about the body, not yet, VIFAI cautioned.

"Don't worry, he's not hurt," Iris said. "He'll be here in just a minute." Behind him, a rising stomping of boots announced Riyu and Ishtan's arrival. Iris had yet to locate the second station security guard, but then he saw the edge of Yan's face emerge from around the corner.

Time had run out. If the station security guard did really kill one of his own, Iris wanted to be the first to confront him. Given the current weapons situation, it was the safest option. But the idea that any one of them was capable of such things didn't agree with him. People *were* capable of such things, but *these* people he had spent time in the company of surely couldn't. He had to believe that, if nothing else.

Through the doorway and past the expectant faces, Yan sauntered over to the console without a word. Five pairs of eyes followed him in unison. He collapsed into the chair like all will had been drained from his body.

Locking eyes with Iris, he asked, "Security?"

"I haven't seen him yet." Iris gave an instinctive, apologetic bow. "I could—"

"No. Everyone stays here. No more exploring. No more sleeping away from each other," Yan said and ran a hand through his hair. Five pairs of eyes followed the blood, caked underneath his nails, smeared across his palm.

"What—" Jesi started out, but Yan shook his head, and she fell silent.

"We're down to one security guard," Yan simply said. His voice was eerily calm, but his left hand, resting on his knee was trembling. "Ordan is dead."

Ordan. That was his name.

Too little, too late, VIFAI noted. Iris bitterly agreed. But this wasn't the time for self-flagellation.

No one said anything. Tev took half a step to shield Jesi; a useless but admirable gesture, Iris admitted. To this day, there were only two people Iris hadn't liked, and one of them was beginning to move into the "potentially tolerable" category. The other was Bacai, who had successfully cemented her position as immature, stubborn, irritating, and completely incapable of change.

With all eyes still on him, Yan gripped his kneecap hard, until his fingers were bleached of all colour. "The Vessel and I found Ordan not a half hour ago. Whatever killed him is gone, but it did some serious damage. I can't find the weapon, no matter where I look, so as of right now, we don't know who killed him or with what." Yan paused. He looked to the right-hand-side entrance to the communal room from where the second station security guard had just entered.

"I told Ordan to keep to the parts we already knew," the guard said, and Iris heard a brief hitch in his voice, like he was about to cry, then fight its way back down to the diaphragm. It was highly unlikely a killer would mourn their kill, but Iris had seen better manipulation firsthand. He tried his utmost to see people as good, first and foremost, but he had been proven wrong before.

"He did," Yan said. "As far as I can figure it out, Ordan went back to the airlock Vessel and Ishtan checked out when our first one got jammed. He must have circled around this area first and then headed off in the other direction. I found his radio when I rolled him over." Yan paused, took a long breath, and tightened his grip on his knee. "He somehow got through and made a call to Station forty-five minutes ago. They spoke for three minutes, after which the call was disconnected on his end. Whoever attacked him kept him there by giving him radio access. That's when they got him. I think."

"Attacked?" Ishtan asked. "Are you implying it was deliberate?"

A flash of poorly contained anger contorted Yan's features. "I'm not sure how Ordan would have gotten a fist-sized hole in his chest *by accident*, Dr. Ora."

Ishtan raised his hands apologetically. Beside him, Riyu broke out in a visible shudder. "Someone is out to kill us, then?

Is that what you're saying, Yan?" She wrapped her arms around herself tightly, her fingernails digging deep into the soft shell of her jacket.

Yan nodded.

"Who would be trying to kill us?" Tev asked. "An institute wouldn't send a hitman out for us. Neither would a station. Pirates then? Scavengers?"

The first part of the question was a good one: Who would, indeed, try to murder academics and engineers and security guards? For pirates, academics were more of a liability than an asset, according to what Iris had learned from all the books and media he'd consumed. Sychi Institute would also refrain from paying any ransom if they were taken captive, that much was well recorded. But pirates hadn't been spotted in over a hundred years, and even then, they had gone mostly after transport ships, ships that had *goods*. A generation ship, while a tantalising relic, would be impossible to re-sell outside proper channels. Scavengers were still fairly common, but they kept to the edges of the galaxy, rarely coming close enough to heavily trafficked areas like Doshua Station. If someone was after them, they knew the workings of the ship well enough to dome off communication and were familiar with the layout to appear and disappear swiftly. A competitor, then, sent to lay claim to the ship before anyone else?

"A competitor, perhaps," Jesi said softly. "But when we first got here, the airlock system was asleep. If anyone had gone in before us, I would have noticed it."

"What if they used a different airlock?" Tev asked.

"Unlikely. This one is the closest to the station."

"There are ways to send the airlock system to sleep. We never checked the logs, never bothered to," Yan said and winced, bracing before saying the next thing. "Another fun development.

They're trying to piggyback onto the Vessel's AI. Any scanner would pick up on it; it uses enough energy. They might be under the impression that it can still talk to Station, or worse yet, they're trying to fry Vessel's brain."

Jesi spun around and glared at Iris. "You have an *AI*?" she spat out.

"Pilots and monks, Jesi, pilots and *monks*." Tev placed his hand around her bicep, but she yanked it away.

"I know. It's still gross."

Iris had witnessed the exchange without saying a word, without so much as thinking of responding. At Jesi's words, he bowed a little and diverted his eyes to the floor. "I'm sorry." When he looked back up, Yan's face was stern and immobile; Riyu and Ishtan were trying their best to contain their mutual disgust. Only the second security guard, whose name Iris also didn't know, didn't seem to hold any strong opinions about the presence of an AI construct or how it was embedded into Iris's brain.

No pro-Vessel sentiment here, VIFAI said with bitter humour. Not anymore.

Under the weight of everyone's gazes, Iris straightened his back and folded his hands together in front of him. Self-pity wasn't helping. Self-pity was for when they left this place alive. It was to be done in private. "I would like to perform rites for Ordan," Iris said when no one else had spoken for nearly a minute. "I am useless to the engineers"—he said this meeting Yan's eyes—"and I would be of little service to anyone else. I can only help Ordan be returned to the Light with dignity."

"Ordan wasn't Starlit," the guard said.

Iris bowed to him. "Then I can simply prepare the body as neutrally as I can. So that when we leave, we may pass it over to his family. Would that be something he would have wanted?"

The security guard folded his arms across his chest, in a terrible tension of respectfully mourning someone he didn't know well enough to *grieve*, but still well enough to miss. Or perhaps with the look of someone who never wished to see Ordan's body again, a reminder of something regrettable. But Iris doubted that line of thinking. People weren't inherently murderers. They were ignorant at best, and when they did kill, it was most likely by accident—and Ordan's death did not look accidental. Iris weighed both ideas and decided to continue without accusing anyone of murder just yet.

"His mother would like that," the guard finally said, face turned towards the floor.

"Thank you. I will start right away."

"No one is starting anything right away," Yan interjected. "We have more important things to do than to recite poems over a dead guy. No offense." He nodded to the remaining security guard.

"I respectfully disagree," Iris said in the most disrespectful tone he could muster. "Given the humidity and the ambient temperature of the ship, tending to the passed in a timely manner will be of utmost importance. Will I need to explain why, engineer Yan?"

Yan grimaced. "No."

Iris bowed deep. "Thank you."

"If it's all right with the Vessel, I would like to accompany him," Ishtan said. "At the risk of sounding utterly insensitive, while I have extensively read up on the matter, I have never seen a Vessel perform burial rites before, and I may never get another chance."

Here's hoping.

"It may be safer to go in pairs as well," Iris added.

Yan ran his hand through his hair again, smearing some of the old blood along his temple. For a moment, he looked to be on the verge of tears. Falling back against the chair with the grace of a discarded rag doll, he sent them all off with a wave of a hand. "Why are you asking me? *Go*, do whatever it is you do. Don't come back complaining if something kills you." There was no doubt this was Yan's first time observing a freshly dead body, and for all his false bravado, Iris had to admit he was handling it much better than most.

Before he left, Iris went up to Tev and Jesi, huddled together by the kettle. When he drew near, Jesi flinched away, a look of blatant disgust plastered across her face. *Children.* They were both newly minted second degree-holders by Iris's assessment, both in their early twenties. They were green to the ways of the institute and the rest of the world around them, and most of all, they were frightened. They would both need to grow up fast if they were to be of any help. All Iris could do was apologise again for the distress he had caused.

"I know you're both scared," he said. He'd given this speech before, but *actual* children were always easier. Actual children could be distracted with sweets and toys, and mostly didn't understand what was happening around them. Tev and Jesi were young enough to be witnessing death for the first time, old enough to comprehend the full weight of it. "I have the sense that your supervisor is frightened too." He nodded to Yan. "I think he would appreciate it if you stayed close. Maybe even provide him a little distraction, if you can. Can you do that?"

Tev nodded without saying a word.

"It's bad, isn't it?" Jesi asked softly.

Iris gave her a small smile. He wouldn't outright lie. "I think your supervisor is a little shaken up, but he'll be OK. We'll all be OK, as long as we are there for one another."

You can't say that, VIFAI reminded him. **You should never say that.**

What else can I say? Should I tell them instead that the dark will eat them alive, no matter how hard they fight? Iris couldn't even admit the truth to himself. *Isn't it my sole responsibility to provide a peace of mind during the worst of times?*

VIFAI said nothing.

With Ishtan by his side, Iris ventured back down the long corridor towards the airlock that had become Ordan's final resting place. They walked in solemn silence, interrupted only by the squishing of feet against the water-laden moss. Unconsciously, Iris untangled the mala from his wrist and passed the beads between his fingers, the smell of sandalwood rising until its scent flooded his mind entirely.

Yan had moved Ordan's body around to retrieve the radio, but he'd put it back almost exactly as he had found it the first time. The gaping wound was no longer bleeding. The ground below was visible through the hole in Ordan's chest, dark against the grey of what remained of the security uniform. Despite the guard's violent demise, Iris couldn't bring himself to feel anything of substance. It was effortless to slip into the refined and practiced sequences he had mastered years before his very first assignment as a Vessel. Death was the most natural end for everyone, regardless of how unnatural the cause.

Ishtan didn't have such teachings to rely on. At his first sight of the bloodied body, he gasped and slapped his hand across his mouth in an attempt to stop himself from being sick. Having failed, he stumbled around the corner and retched loudly.

"There's no need for you to watch, Ishtan," Iris suggested gently, "if it causes you such distress."

Why the archaeologist had accompanied Iris in his work was beyond his understanding. Surely he was aware of what such work entailed even if he had only read about it. Theoretical study of death never compared to witnessing it firsthand. Once, Iris too had found himself faint and sick in the presence of those passed. He was fifteen, but so were the others around him, and they had fared much better.

After the bout passed, Ishtan emerged from behind the corner, swaying, wiping bile from his lips. "No, no, I promise it's all done with. I'll be good. I'll be good. Please, continue."

Pushing the archaeologist from his mind, Iris lowered to his knees and took Ordan's limp hand in his. The tan skin was waxy and cool to the touch, but Iris held the hand firmly in his, the way it was intended. It was the broad and muscular hand of a man who had earned his living through manual labour, with a distinctive callus at the edge of his index finger. Manual labour and firearms, then.

Iris closed his eyes and said, "I'm sorry you had to pass in such a violent way, that your time had been cut short before the Light intended it. We know that in your last moments you tried to help us, help all of us, and for that we are eternally grateful. I'm sorry I did not know your name until you passed, but I will take care that your body rejoins your family just as you have been rejoined with the cosmos.

"The Light is still your flesh even as you no longer are, my friend. The Light persists in the blood no longer running in your veins. In your last moments, you gave your life to others, and thus in your last moments, you knew the touch of the Divine. In your last breath, you learned what it is to be the cosmos. You are returned to the One Beginning, to eternal life, and to eternal rest, my friend." Iris placed Ordan's hand back across his broad chest. "Ishtan, would you be so kind as to find a clean cloth for me?"

"Of course." Ishtan had barely finished speaking before he turned and ran up the corridor.

There were several ways to delay a body's progression through the stages of decomposition. Most of them relied on tools and chemical compounds Iris did not readily have in his possession, but he could drain the body of its blood easily enough before it started to decay. The reduction in fluid would also keep the bloating at bay, keeping Ordan's appearance easier on the eyes. Iris reached into his right sleeve. "I'm sorry, Ordan," he said. "I'm going to have to hurt your body a little more." Iris pressed his thumb against the indentation on the pulsar blade. Nothing happened.

Performance anxiety? VIFAI asked.

"This is not the time nor the place," Iris grumbled. He pressed his thumb against the indentation again, this time with force, but the blade remained dormant.

I can help.

"Don't," Iris warned out loud, but it was too late. It took VIFAI a tenth of a second to locate and retrieve the necessary memory Iris had, and in another tenth of a second, Iris was back in the cramped maintenance room, stuck between the wall and Yan. The pulsar blade responded accordingly.

"I did not consent to that."

I could have dug deeper, VIFAI chimed happily, but I didn't.

Steadying his breathing, Iris shortened the blade until it was a mere inch long on one side and got to work. First, the legs. Two incisions just behind each knee were enough to send slow waves of halted arterial blood oozing over the moss-covered floor. Now, the upper body. The pulsar blade sliced easily through Ordan's soft-shell jacket and his flesh to open the arteries running just beneath his armpit. Iris pressed down on his knees and stood up, leaving bloody handprints on his white robes.

"What do you think?" Iris asked himself.

"I think I'm going to be sick again." Ishtan's voice was weak and trembling.

Without turning around, Iris folded the pulsar blade back up and wiped his hands on his robes. "Ishtan, could you find a large cloth or blanket for me? We will need to wrap Ordan up before he can rest."

A brief cadence of footsteps was his only response. The less time the academic spent around Iris, the less strenuous on them both. Iris got back to work. Squeezing some water from the moss floor, he wet the cloth Ishtan had dropped when he saw the bloody spectacle Iris had made. Softly, he ran the cloth over Ordan's face, wiping the speckles of blood and dirt from an otherwise serene expression, over the wide nose and deep-set eyes, over the full lips, ocean blue in the faint light of the corridor. Iris patted the cloth at the hairline, cleaning the last remaining drops of blood.

"It's a shame," he said.

Isn't it always?

Despite countless decades lived, there were never enough years, never enough time with oneself, never enough time with others. Despite attending the passing of the elderly and the ill, of children and centenarians, Iris never had quite grasped why a return to the One Beginning was necessary at all. Why couldn't they all continue to be as they were? He carefully unwound a vine beginning to wrap around Ordan's waist.

"I'm sorry," Iris said, reaching out to unwind the vine that wrapped tightly around Ordan's ankles. "I'm not quite done with him yet. You're going to have to wait." Nature never waited to reclaim ownership. At Iris's touch, the vine flinched.

That's not right, VIFAI said. Did you see that?

"I think I'm seeing things," Iris said calmly, his fingers nimbly working the zipper of Ordan's soft-shell jacket and the buttons of his trousers. "And you, by proxy of viewing the world through my eyes, are seeing it too. I'll need to sleep after this. We should both get some rest after this. It will be a long couple of days." If they had a couple of days at all.

When Ishtan returned with a worn Sychi Institute blanket, Iris didn't ask him where it had come from and simply told him to lay it out flat. Then he returned to Ordan's body and took a deep bow. "My friend, unfortunately, we cannot leave you here. I will have to move you someplace safe for the time being. Your clothes are torn and bloodied, and I will remove them. I will keep them by your side for when you rejoin your family."

Iris undressed Ordan as carefully as he could, folding each article of clothing and placing it just by the airlock. Ishtan watched the work, doing a poor job of fighting back his stomach spasms. It hadn't been an enlightening academic experience for him after all. Beneath a thin, grey undershirt, Iris found blue bruising along Ordan's wrists. Similar bruising appeared around Ordan's ankles.

Restraints, VIFAI said, and Iris agreed.

Is there a chance he acquired them before he came aboard? How old would you say these are?

As old as the wound in his chest.

Then there had been a struggle after all, and Ordan had resisted as well as he could. Iris glanced along the walls for any more signs of a fight. Two burn marks on one wall. Gunshots. Ordan had had the sense to defend himself, or he had reasonably thought he could win. Maybe Yan was right. Maybe someone was willing to kill for the *Nicaea*.

When Ordan was ready to be moved, Iris picked up the man at the waist and flung him over his shoulder. While Ordan was on the shorter side, he certainly outweighed Iris. Staggering, he carried the body a little up the corridor and laid it across the blanket.

"I'm afraid I haven't been much help," Ishtan admitted, kneeling by the blanket. He was no longer retching every time he looked at the dead security guard, and he could even stand to look at the body for several seconds at a time without glancing away.

"You've been of tremendous help, Ishtan. I am grateful." Meticulously, Iris folded the blanket around Ordan, tucking the corners underneath his shoulders and around his feet. When he was finished, only the face remained in the open. With the last fold, Iris hid it from view with a long piece of fabric. "And with that, we lay you to rest, Ordan."

This wasn't proper, not even close. A proper Vessel had the skill to lay a soul to rest while keeping their robes white. This was bloody and messy and desperate, and it was the best he could do, despite his efforts. This burial brought shame to the temple. *He* brought shame to the temple. In all his years serving as a Vessel, he had faltered many times, but never this badly. A polite cough came to him through the veil of rumination.

Her face pale, marked by tears, Riyu took a hesitant step towards the blanket-wrapped form. "It's silly, I know, but here." She held out her hand, clutching a few of the bright orange flowers that sprouted in the corridor leading to the main airlock. "I know they will wither, but I just thought—I don't know what I thought. They're not poisonous as far as I know, and they're pretty. It seemed like the thing to do."

With a small smile and a bow of the head, Iris took the flowers and tucked them between two folds of the blanket at Ordan's chest. Riyu was painfully right: the flowers would wither as life drained from them, as it drained from every other living thing in its due time, just as it had drained from Ordan. Life was fleeting. How much longer did any of them have before life would drain from them as well?

"Everything will eventually wither, Dr. Alo," Iris said, reverent. "It's what we are now that matters. And for now, these flowers are beautiful."

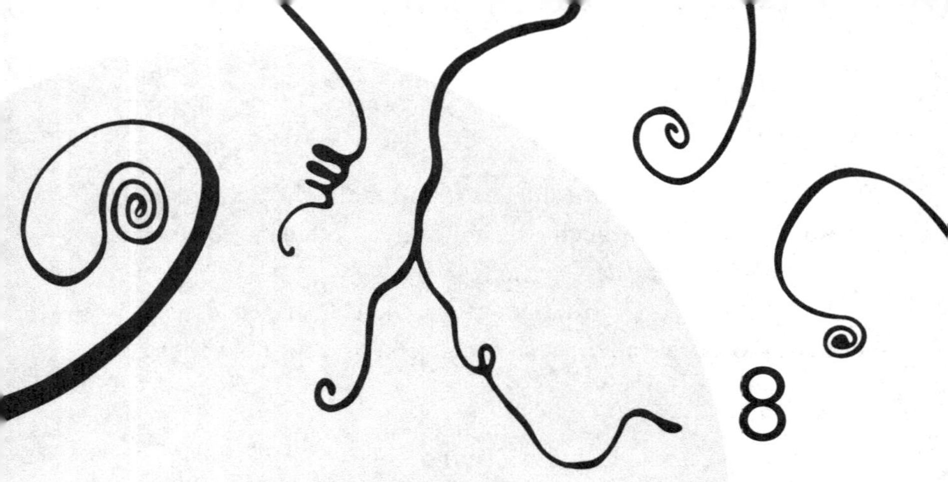

8

When I woke, I was a child, crying and fragile. That was mere hours ago. Now I am all grown. My back can carry a man, carry them to their eternal rest. Then why, O, Infinite Light, is my mind still the mind of a child, crying and fragile? One day, my body will be aged, wise, and frail, and yet my mind will still cry out, "Who will save me? Who out there will save me?"

From the unabridged diaries of Vessel Iris, Volume Seventeen

Ordan's body was laid to rest in an empty room along the corridor, wrapped in the Sychi blanket, flowers tucked inside. It was a poor substitute for a proper burial, especially for a man who had died protecting them. If they were lucky, Iris would be tasked with explaining the circumstances of his death to Ordan's mother. If she ever gained the opportunity to see her son again. Now, alone, he sunk to the floor in prayer before the wrapped body. Prayer never came.

Several fruitless minutes later, he sat back on his heels and turned his attention to the bloodied hem of his robes. From his ankles and up towards his shins, red leeched upwards, claiming a new white thread with each passing moment. Already, the edges were curdling and turning an ugly, permanent brown. Soon the stain would engulf his robes entirely. Soon there would be no white left at all.

Reel it back. VIFAI's electronic voice came from the recesses of his mind.

"It's all quite hopeless, isn't it?" Iris asked out loud.

It's all right to be frightened.

And yet. Iris extended his arm, palm facing down. His hand hovered above the floor, level, steady. Despite the dried blood under his fingernails and caked across his knuckles, fear wasn't the prevailing emotion. It wasn't the first time he had found his hands in this state. Five years earlier, he had been called to an oddly pristine shuttle, orbiting just outside Kaneno Station. As far as Iris had been able to see, there was no structural damage, nothing at all that was wrong with the ship itself. The brief had been left deliberately vague. Inside, he found seven passed. Six from chest wounds and a seventh from a self-inflicted head wound. Two families, traveling across the galaxy. For what purpose, he would never learn.

Sometime before Iris arrived, the shuttle had lost gravity and without it, blood was floating freely in little crimson bubbles. It had settled on Iris's robes, his face, little droplets of red like freckles on his cheeks. He had wiped it from his face as he worked, mixing their blood with his sweat. He tended to them all, the adults, the children, and laid them to rest in the airlock where their extended families would have collected them. He didn't wait for the families to arrive. He wouldn't accept another assignment for months afterwards.

"I wish you good rest," Iris finally said to Ordan. "I will not disturb you further." He placed his hands on his knees, right above the bloodied handprints, and got to his feet. *Do you think whoever it was that killed Ordan is able to control the electronics in the ship? Like the airlock?* Iris asked, walking slowly down the corridor, his mala passing between his fingers. The faint smell of sandalwood rose higher and higher the more he worked the beads, settling him.

If it's tracking little bursts of energy, as your engineer has said, then yes, they would probably have the capacity to activate and deactivate the airlock at will.

"He's not my engineer," Iris said and wrapped the mala back around his wrist. If someone was tracking them, they would be most effective if they had a bird's-eye view of the ship. They would need to be somewhere it was possible to simultaneously track everyone aboard the ship and then act upon the ship in response. Maybe Yan was right. Maybe someone was so set on securing the *Nicaea* for themselves that they were willing to kill for it. This side of greed was largely unknown to Iris, and he chose to defer to the engineer's opinion. Then again, it could have been a simple, plausible disagreement between the guards that had ended poorly. It wouldn't be the first fatal quarrel Iris had witnessed.

The dark, weaving corridors presented countless possibilities and countless opportunities to end each and every one of them. The entire ship could be turned into one monstrous killing field if someone was only vicious enough, driven enough. Iris summoned a memory of the mural he and Ishtan had viewed, the awe with which the archaeologist had admired its brutality. There had been a clear divide between the passengers of the ship. There had been conflict. There had been violence. But all of this Iris already knew to be painfully human. Then there was the red, ever-watching eye, whose tracking gaze Iris couldn't shake even in his recollections.

When he reached the communal space, no one looked up to greet him. In one corner, Riyu and Ishtan were slumped against one another, their faces drained of all emotion and energy. Riyu had been crying again, her eyes angry and red. By the kettle, the young engineers and Yan were whispering among themselves, sipping something steaming from their mugs. Iris couldn't find the second security guard. As subtly as he could, he snuck close to the kettle and gave Yan a little bow.

"He's all taken care of?" Yan asked.

Iris sniffed the air. *Coffee.* "I've done the best I could with what I had. But we need a long-term solution for storing Ordan. The ship is quite warm and humid."

Without a word, Jesi turned around and walked away. Tev followed her with a hushed *sorry*.

"It would be *fantastic* if you didn't bring up humidity and dead bodies around them," Yan said, voice low. "They're just kids. They're not ready for this." The faint tremble of his voice was enough to convey Yan wasn't ready for it either.

"I couldn't help but remember that you mentioned Ordan had just made a call to Station before his untimely passing. I've consulted my construct, and it's certain that—"

"That whoever is watching us is also able to manipulate the airlocks from a distance," Yan finished for him. "I know. I figured. We're not only trapped here, but also might get severed in half by some closing doors at any given minute."

Iris nodded. He had anticipated a rising bubbling of panic, a chill to seize his body, but there was nothing left in him but pleasant numbness. He instead turned his faculties to Yan, to the efforts the engineer was putting towards appearing calm and in control. *It's all right to be frightened.* No, out of all of them, Yan didn't have the luxury. He had others looking to him for both comfort and for solutions, an impossible balance.

"I was also thinking that if someone is watching us, if they have the capacity to manipulate the ship, they would have to be well placed. Perhaps they are in one of the ship's brains, as you described them," Iris said.

Yan raised an eyebrow. Iris wasn't sure if the engineer was surprised he remembered that ships this size had multiple brains or that he had concluded they would be a good vantage point.

"Have some coffee," Yan said and nodded to the kettle. "It's weak, but it's better than nothing."

Iris thanked him with a deep bow and hurried to pour himself a mug.

Looking into the middle ground, Yan continued speaking in a low voice. "If they're using one of the brains, we will be able to locate which one based on my little setup upstairs. Signals are a two-way street, and if they're tracking the spots where we are interacting with the ship, I will be able to track them right back to whichever brain they've picked to watch us from. But I don't have a good enough map. I suspect your AI does."

Iris nodded affirmatively and took a gulp of his coffee. It *was* weak, but it would be enough to silence the grumbling of his empty stomach.

"In theory, we should be able to reach any of the brains without forcing any doors open," Yan continued. "There are enough variations. The only problem is time. Water won't be much of an issue since we can just squeeze it from the moss, but we don't have much food, and I'm especially worried about morale."

"I could lead a prayer," Iris blurted out and immediately felt like an idiot.

"It's like you're not even trying, Vessel."

"My AI identified several long rooms upstairs that could be nurseries. Maybe we can find something other than an apple orchard." It was then that Iris was struck by the realisation that this was the longest and most balanced conversation he had had with the engineer since his arrival on the ship. All it had taken was a dead person.

"Better," Yan said. "Take Riyu and Ishtan with you. Best to keep them occupied so they don't start panicking. I'll take Jesi and Tev and find which brain is currently keeping us hostage. And take my advice, don't talk about bodies and humidity." Yan tipped back the remainder of his coffee and waved for Jesi and Tev to come over. "Just *don't*."

It almost sounded like a plan, except Yan had said nothing about what they would do once they found whatever or whomever was locking them inside the ship. He also didn't address the issue that there were certainly more than one *someones* or *somethings* who were trying to keep them all contained. It took less than a second for Iris to conclude it was impossible for someone to man one of the *Nicaea*'s brains *and* be physically present to murder Ordan. It took Iris less than a second to conclude this, which meant it took Yan half that time. They were dealing with at least an armed pair, probably more.

Yet Yan continued on, from problem to problem, with the momentum of a severed tree trunk. His eyes danced around the room, never settling on anything, tracing people's faces. If there was time and they were on smoother terms, Iris would have taken Yan aside and reminded him that he didn't have to fear in silence and in solitude. But they were not nearly so cordial, and there wasn't the time. There was never enough time.

Since when do we care about the engineer's mental state? VIFAI asked.

Since he's the one coming up with the plan. Iris caught Ishtan's eyes from across the room, empty and tired. The archaeologist stared at him with a blank expression, his eyes falling to the bloodied hem of Iris's robes. Iris had become a walking reminder of Ordan's demise, but there hadn't been time to change and no opportunity to wash the fabric. He winced apologetically.

Inside Iris's mind, VIFAI scanned *Nicaea*'s map for any spaces that resembled nurseries. In the time it took Iris to cross the communal space to Ishtan and Riyu, it had identified five. Three were within immediate walking distance. Two were right through the orchard he had discovered earlier. Kneeling by Riyu, Iris gave the woman a hesitant smile and said, "Dr. Alo, I am terribly sorry to disturb you, but I am about to go on a search for some food and was hoping you would accompany me. Your knowledge of alien flora could really help me."

In a fog, Riyu looked up and gave Iris a stiff nod. "You don't want to poison yourself."

"No, I wouldn't want that."

"I should come too," Ishtan offered. "It would be safer."

Iris gave him the same, hesitant smile. From the corner of his eye, he watched Yan, Jesi, and Tev head out towards the orchard. Still there was no sign of the second security guard. Where had he gone to, alone? Iris despised being suspicious of other people. Suspicion was a poison that tore families apart and turned friends on one another. And in here, with everyone already fraying at the ends, it could be the very thing to push them to a place they could not return from. And then there would be violence, irreparable violence. He had already been too late to prevent one death, and Iris feared he'd not be able to prevent a second.

Before they ventured towards the orchard, Iris ducked out into the corridor and nearly tripped over the seated security guard. The man raised his head from resting on his folded arms. His half-lidded eyes stared ahead, looking straight at the opposite wall, the waves of his sweat-drenched hair falling over his face.

"We're going to search for food," Iris blurted out. "If you want to join us."

"I got him the damn job," the guard said. "Said it'd be easy, just watch a bunch of academics while they poke around this dump for a few days. Said it paid well."

"These things—"

"Told his mom he'd be safe with me. It was his first security job." He shook his head. "The hell am I supposed to tell her now? The hell she supposed to do with a dead son?"

"It could have been any of us."

"But it wasn't."

"The will of the Light—"

The guard's eyes darted upwards, meeting Iris's in an unyielding glare. "You don't have many friends, do you? Acquaintances? 'Cause if you did, you'd know the *will of the Light* is the last thing I care about right about now. I met a man and threw him a lifeline when he needed one. I tipped him off about a job. Maybe he wasn't my closest, oldest friend, sure, but I was responsible for him. That's how I see it. I was responsible, and now he's dead, so the Light can just piss off and you along with it."

Iris held the guard's gaze softly. Grief and anger were the closest friends Iris had ever known, and he knew them to always travel in a pair. This wasn't the time to explain that these sorts of things were unavoidable. Someone always died. Someone always died when they weren't supposed to, and there was little anyone could do about it except to say some words and lay down some flowers. Saying nothing, Iris bowed deeply, hoping that his unspoken apology would be received.

"Does the lead engineer think I killed Ordan?"

"I don't know," Iris admitted. He was in no position to speak for Yan, nor could he ever fathom what went on in his head.

"Do *you*?"

These weren't the words and hollow eyes of a murderer. Someone who was rash with his words, yes, and far too vulnerable with a stranger, someone scared, someone angry, but not a murderer.

"No," Iris said and took his leave, realizing only after he had turned the corner that he had, once again, forgotten to ask for a name.

Climbing to the third deck and through the double doors, Iris returned to the humidity and sweetness of the orchard. The engineers had already spread out their screens and tools around the control panel where not a few hours ago, Yan had first learned they were being watched. The engineer gave Iris a stern nod and said nothing, but his gaze lingered on Iris's back as he crossed the orchard and disappeared from view.

Riyu and Ishtan followed Iris slowly and stopped frequently, whenever Riyu began to sob. She hid her face behind her hands as best as she could, but the sobs still escaped between her parted fingers and spilled out into the quiet of the long corridors. Once the sobs subsided, she'd apologise profusely, and they would all stop again to comfort her. All this while frigid water dripped around them in the decrepit corridors, and Iris's feet ached with the cold of the metal floors.

"Just a few more turns," Iris said after consulting his mind map of the ship.

Unless Dr. Alo keeps being a baby. VIFAI was seemingly in a mood of sorts, and Iris had no desire to figure out what sort of mood it was.

A moment later, having fallen slightly behind, Ishtan called out. "Esteemed colleagues? I think you'd like to see this." His voice was barely louder than the dripping of the water, but something in the archaeologist's tone made Iris pause. Ignoring the pain prickling the balls of his feet, he turned back around and corralled Riyu around the corner, where Ishtan's voice was coming from.

Another mural. Both violence and death were captured in broad brushstrokes across the twenty-metre-long painting. Iris followed the images, trailing the faded paint to the end of the corridor.

"This is incredible," Ishtan muttered. All the fear had vanished from his voice, replaced with awe and elation and dedication. "This is impeccably preserved, despite the conditions. It would turn the field of First Earth studies on its head."

"If we live long enough," Riyu said.

It was sounding more and more like Ishtan was trapped on a very different ship than the rest of them. Of all of them, Ishtan had the keenest eye for the murals and the rest of the ship, a personal and professional appreciation. Of all of them, he was the only one who knew the true price of the *Nicaea*—not whatever was aboard it, but the ship itself—to the academic community.

A sudden urge to pray washed over Iris as he took in the rising reds and blacks of the mural, detailing a bloody confrontation that was both very old and very human. His fingers passed along the worn-out beads of his mala in a futile attempt to ground himself. *War.* Could war erupt in such a contained space? How could conflict grow to such magnitudes? Could difference be manufactured among people with the same goals, with the same destination, when the destination itself was so noble? Iris thought back to the skull with a perfectly round hole in the bone. Whether it was self-inflicted or imposed made all the difference. "Ishtan, do you believe this is a historical account or a fictional one?"

Ishtan shrugged. "Does it matter?" He was already sizing up how to best remove the mural.

It *mattered*. It mattered even more when Iris spotted the same watchful eye in the top-right corner of the mural. *Can you make a visual record of this?* Iris asked VIFAI and scanned the mural from right to left. How many more bones in the cargo bay would have man-made wounds; smooth, round, holes in temples; unnatural fractures? How many more signs that something horrific had taken place within the corpse of the *Nicaea*?

Breathe.

"Have either of you wondered why we haven't come across any remains so far? The ship had at least thousand people on board, and yet the only bones I've come across are the ones the engineers moved into the cargo bay." Yan had warned Iris about upsetting others, but the words snuck out of their own volition. The question was as much for himself as it was for Ishtan and Riyu's benefit.

Riyu shot him a sharp glance but said nothing. Ishtan continued to eye the mural. "All these ships," he said. "So many different stories, yet with always nearly identical outcomes. Who knows what terrible mysteries the *Nicaea* holds? One thing is certain. Violence has been natural to people from their very beginning, First Earth or otherwise."

Breathe, the electronic voice repeated.

Can you pull everything you've got on generation ship discoveries from your storage? Iris asked.

That will take a lot of energy.

It would. It would attract a lot of attention from whomever was watching them. *Please do it quickly then.* Iris motioned for Ishtan and Riyu to follow him. The faster they left the spot, the more difficult it would be for their watcher, whoever or whatever it was, to pin them down. That's what Iris told himself, uncaring of the truth of the sentiment.

There was still the question of food.

A few more turns, like Iris had promised, and they were before a wide set of double doors. Inside, a nursery sprawled, wild and overgrown, with head-sized leaves and vines sprouting from every possible angle. Bright purple lights were mounted along the ceiling. The functioning bulbs flooded patches of the room with faint lilac light. Iris raised his hand to keep Ishtan and Riyu back and ventured inside, alone. A thin layer of soil covered the floor, spilled from where the plants had escaped their planters. It was nowhere near as warm and humid as the orchard, but the floor was more forgiving than the cold, metal surface of the corridor, and Iris's feet welcomed the change.

I think you're alone here.

"I think so too." Yet, his forearm instinctively flexed, readying to launch the pulsar blade from within his robes. A few more calculated steps to the sound of dripping pipes, nothing more, and Iris allowed himself to relax. He slowly rolled his shoulders, letting the tension drain. Only then did he call for Riyu and Ishtan to join him. There had to be something edible here. The soil was far too rich and the greens too plentiful for it to be nothing, but that was Riyu's domain.

Like a princess awakened from her slumber, the botanist sprang into action with a newfound resolve and alertness. Within seconds, she was on her knees, hands buried in the soil, rummaging for anything edible. While Riyu applied herself to the task, Iris allowed Ishtan to wander about the perimeter.

Rows upon rows of planters stretched along the length of the space. Most of the containers were cracked, with wild roots spidering through and dangling towards the floor. In the violet light, the vegetation looked far more ominous than edible. With his big toe, Iris dug a small funnel in the soil. Thousand-year-old dirt gave in easily to the intrusion.

Even this soil would be priceless.

I've never seen you get so sentimental about a terrarium.

Iris smiled faintly. Yes. The whole ship was a microcosm not unlike a terrarium, growing, evolving without outside influence. Now, they had popped the lid and disturbed its balance. Consequences were appropriate.

Not ten minutes had passed before Riyu sat up with a victorious *aha!* and pulled out an orange root from the ground. "Carrot!" she proclaimed and threw it to Iris.

He caught it stiffly with both hands and sniffed it. "And you are certain this is edible?"

"Asks the monk who ate how many apples before I said they were not poisonous?" Riyu replied with a giggle, her mood rising. "Carrots are hard to contaminate. You don't need to worry." She looked around the nursery. "If I were on a generation ship with no ready resupply of soil, I would worry a lot about acidity and leeching. So, I would also grow a companion plant to avoid those issues. Now, if I were to plant carrots, as I am guessing they did not just *evolve* of their own volition, I would expect to find . . ." she trailed off and crawled underneath a planter. "Squash!" With a loud grunt, Riyu pulled out a yellow spaghetti squash the size of her head. "I'm not sure how we can cook this, but the engineers will find a way." She hopped to her feet and dusted off her trousers, squash neatly tucked underneath her arm. Satisfied with their finds, Iris was about to call out to Ishtan that they were heading back when his feet sensed a muted pulse through the ground.

I'm receiving a ping, VIFAI whispered. The pulse beneath Iris's feet grew exponentially, like the rumblings of a deep desert snake as it narrowed in on its kill. Iris had felt this quickening before, right as the door Yan was working beneath broke free and almost crushed him. VIFAI's searches had drawn their watcher right to them.

Iris snapped towards to Riyu. "Drop everything," he said, voice low and commanding. "*Slowly*, walk out of the nursery. When you're outside, run, run as fast as you can, get the engineers down to our deck. Don't let them argue. *Go*."

Riyu remained glued to the floor, the spaghetti squash wrapped tightly in her arms.

"*Now*," Iris hissed.

Eyes transfixed on Iris and unblinking, Riyu retreated cautiously, holding the squash tightly against her chest with both arms. She placed her feet one behind the other, matching her footprints nearly exactly. When the doors shut behind her, and he heard her footsteps break into a sprint, Iris sprang into action. He could already tell Ishtan wasn't inside the nursery. He crossed the space in a light jog and exited through a matching set of double doors. More vines and extravagant flowers greeted him on the other end.

You're not alone anymore, cautioned VIFAI, whispering from the far corner of his mind. Stay alert.

Iris's hand flicked ever so slightly, and the pulsar blade was at once in his palm, ready to deploy. He moved quickly, bare feet stepping silently through the dirt. Moving a thick vine from his path, Iris ducked underneath it and into the adjoining room.

Ishtan's slack face was turned on its side. It peered from below some foliage, a mask of blank resignation. A thick vine had already made its home around his shoulders, and Iris tenderly unfurled it and placed it aside. He stowed away the pulsar blade. The archaeologist was lying on his stomach, still alive. The dark skin of his neck pulsed rhythmically with the beating of his heart. Iris lowered himself by Ishtan's ear. "Wake up," he whispered. But Ishtan didn't move. If he had more time, Iris would have been gentler, but he didn't. He flipped the archaeologist over and firmly ran the second knuckles of his fingers along Ishtan's sternum. That got a reaction. Ishtan flinched, his face animating along the folds of habitual wrinkles.

"Wake up," Iris whispered again and ran his knuckles over Ishtan's sternum once more. Faded eyes met his, then they widened in horror, and Iris slapped his palm against Ishtan's mouth right before a scream could escape it. "You're safe. Please, don't scream." Ishtan gave him a weak nod. "Did you see what knocked you unconscious?"

Ishtan shook his head.

Is it still here? Iris asked, and VIFAI responded with an affirmative ping. Then, it did something it had never done before. With a burning shock, Iris's right arm sprang forwards, above Ishtan's head. At once, the pulsar blade was in his hand, throwing out a faint, blue glow. Before the right side was fully extended, it had already sliced an attacking vine that had been spiraling towards Iris at blinding speed. In the deadly silence, Ishtan cursed.

"We have to go, *now*." Iris yanked the swaying Ishtan to his feet and pushed him towards the doors. "Run. I'm right behind you." His arm moved again on its own, this time the blade slicing a vine on his left that had been poised to puncture Iris's neck on impact.

VIFAI was silent, but active. It poured itself from Iris's brain stem, spreading along the nerves of Iris's arm. Impossible, Iris knew, but he had no time to ponder it. His brain stem burned where the implant had been placed. All he could do was surrender to the ghost animating his body, to surrender to the other *being* that shared his consciousness.

Ishtan was already through the doors leading to the nursery, and Iris followed closely, slicing three more vines that came at him simultaneously with a quick flick of a wrist. *How are you doing this?* Iris called out into the far corner of his mind where VIFAI usually resided. No response. Something struck him on the left side of his head, and for a moment, everything disappeared into darkness. Then, he was aware of dirt on his lips; Iris had been momentarily knocked unconscious and fallen to the ground. Blinded by the hot blood that ran freely from the wound, Iris leapt to his feet, allowing VIFAI to direct him autonomously. Ishtan turned back, face contorted with horror.

"Get back to our deck," Iris shouted and cut off a vine, wrapped tightly around his ankle. Without another word, Ishtan turned back around and ran through the double doors and out into the corridor. One of the vines lunged for the opening, but froze midway when Iris sliced it in half. He stumbled towards the doors, only to be knocked down again. This time, pain flared in his left shoulder, only now it was sharp and fiery. *Inconsequential.* Iris sliced cleanly through the vine embedded in his flesh. Adrenaline and fear were enough to dull most of the pain. Without looking, Iris swung back, severing whatever it was that was pressing him into the dirt, and with another three steps, stumbled through the double doors into the corridor.

He hit the cool, hard floor with his left side, winding himself. Safe. Just barely, but safe. Wasting no time, Iris scrambled to his feet and took off running down the corridor. VIFAI projected a map of the ship, and Iris followed it without glancing back. After a few turns, he allowed himself to slow down and nearly collapsed against the wall. *How did you do that?* he asked again, this time forcing a connection with VIFAI, so it had no choice but to respond.

I have access to your memory. I have access to your motor cortex, it said, its voice rushed and exuberant. *Nothing precise, but I have been with you long enough to know how you fight, how your brain tells you to fight. I see things faster, react faster than you. We had no time. I had to do it for you. The adrenaline helps.* By the end it almost sounded apologetic.

Iris pressed the aching side of his face against the cool metal of the wall. "Thank you. When did you know you could do that?"

I didn't. It was an instinct.

The pain in his left shoulder was climbing. "What a perfect time to figure it out then. Thank you again. I am in your debt. We all are."

VIFAI said something, but this time Iris didn't hear it. His vision swam, half occluded with the blood that now covered most of his face. With a soft moan, he pushed himself upright and staggered towards the orchard. The pain in his left shoulder spread until it became a dimension in and of itself. It painted every other thought, muffled every sensation that reached any other part of Iris's body. He hadn't felt this worn out in years.

It was easy to scold himself for being too soft, for giving his body so much attention and yet so little discipline. If only he had trained harder these past six months. If only he had been diligent with his eating and his stretching. *If only.* Instead, he had somehow become the liability of the group.

"I've never seen vines move," Iris whispered, letting his mind fixate on the idea instead of the pain. "They're strange, like everything else here. They can't move like that."

You mean they shouldn't.

"Nothing moves like that."

Iris stumbled and steadied himself against an apple tree. The engineers were gone, screens and tools scattered on the ground. They must have left in a hurry, spurred into motion by Riyu's cries. Iris prayed that Ishtan had made it back safely. Before he could reach the double doors at the far end of the orchard, a new kind of pain doubled him over and tightened around his already empty stomach. The burning in his brain stem grew unbearable, and he dry heaved beneath a tree.

I'm sorry, VIFAI said, and it sounded genuinely contrite. Residual current. Having no energy to speak, Iris waved his hand in an *it's fine* gesture, and pushed himself forwards and through the double doors. By the time he reached the communal space, he was effectively blind, following the map by memory alone, with only marginal help from VIFAI. Their little stunt had been taxing on his inorganic companion as well, and it hummed softly, relying only on featherlight impulses to communicate. At some point, Iris stumbled and lost his balance. He fell forwards, into the darkness, but never hit the floor. He didn't remember anything after that.

Waking up was resurfacing through a tidal wave of pain and nausea. Gritting his teeth, Iris forced his eyes open. Cracked ceiling tiles swirled and swam against an ocean of steel. He had no recollection of how he had ended up in the cargo bay, nor if he had met anyone on his way here. Someone must have carried him. A flush of embarrassment stained the tips of his ears red. He gingerly patted down his body and was relieved to find his bloodied robes untouched. What good was a Vessel if it had cracks? And this encounter would surely leave a crack.

Iris clenched his hand into a weak fist and raised it high enough to see. His forearm trembled with exhaustion, his fingers ached, there were cuts and scrapes along his knuckles, a few of the deeper ones opening as he tensed. This was the exact sort of crack he had spent years avoiding.

When the initial jolt of panic subsided, hushed voices reached Iris from the corridor.

"We need to do something. He'll bleed to death or get an infection," Tev said.

"We can't touch him," Ishtan intervened. "I am telling you. He would rather *die* than have one of us violate him in such a way. This is beyond your understanding, Tev."

Iris politely disagreed with that particular sentiment.

It was Riyu's voice that reached him next. "We can't just let him die. He saved us." Her voice was small, muffled, as if she'd been crying continuously and gone hoarse from it.

"Well, what if he wakes up?" Jesi asked. "If we give him the med-kit, can he do it himself? Would that be OK?" By the sound of it, they were all gathered in the corridor just outside the cargo bay, huddled together and whispering about the best course of action, frightened, anxious, and far too loud. Iris desperately wanted to know exactly how he got back to the cargo bay, but hearing Ishtan's and Riyu's voices was enough to settle him. He had done something right. Jesi and Tev were there too, and safe. He relaxed into the moss with a sigh.

"Fuck it." There was Yan. "I'll do it. He already hates me. What else is he going to do anyway? Just give me the med-kit." A wave of muffled protest erupted in the corridor.

"I really would advice against this," Ishtan's voice rang out above the others. "Yan, he won't be—"

Iris sprang upright, but a blistering stab of pain in his shoulder sent him right back down with a wheeze. He stared at the ceiling in utter horror for what was to come. Even with the thick moss cover, Yan's heavy footsteps reverberated through the corridor and into the cargo bay. The door slammed, and the engineer drew closer. Silently, Iris cried out for VIFAI, but it was dormant, completely spent from their joint fight. The footsteps stopped beside him.

Yan knelt by Iris's side wearing what could only be described as an apologetic expression. "You're awake. OK. That complicates things. Look, you don't want to do this. I don't want to do this," he said, eyes looking just to the left of Iris, just far enough that he wouldn't be accused of staring. "But if I don't bandage you up, you'll probably get an infection and die."

Still staring directly at the ceiling, Iris said, "I do appreciate your concern, engineer Yan, but I assure you, I can take care of this on my own."

"No, you can't. You haven't seen your left side. It's a bloody mess. *Literally.*"

Iris closed his eyes and with a hiss, propped himself up on his right elbow. "Engineer Yan, I understand you are not a practicing man, but you must understand that for someone like me, vows are sacred. You must understand *professional integrity*."

"I understand more than you give me credit for, Vessel. Heard enough of your kind's vows at temple to last a lifetime." Yan opened the med-kit and began setting out gauze and scissors on the moss. He didn't give Iris the space to interject. "I also know you saved Riyu's and Ishtan's lives—all of our lives in a way. There might come a time soon enough that you will need to do it again. You have a responsibility to the Starlit, I understand, but now you also have a responsibility to these people." Yan was using the same tone with Iris as he had in the maintenance room. He was being calm, collected, and a hue patronising.

If not for the tone, Iris might have agreed to be helped. "My responsibility is to the dead," he blurted out with latent rage.

"There it is." With a solemn nod, Yan cut a piece of gauze and soaked it in iodine. Without a warning, he pressed the gauze to Iris's temple where the skin was split. Iris recoiled with a hiss.

"So much for that monklike discipline," Yan laughed and pressed the gauze to Iris's temple again, this time, locking Iris's head in place with his other hand. "Stop flinching, it will only take longer."

The last hand to touch the nape of Iris's neck in such a way had been Mother Nova's, but even that had been years ago. After another failed attempt to rid himself of his physical condition, she had brought Iris's lips to a bowl of water as she muttered soft mantras under her breath. Her skin had been hot against his, soft and comforting, nothing like the calloused fingers now forcing their way on him. A white-hot anger ignited in the pit of Iris's empty stomach. "I will tell you just once, engineer Yan," Iris pushed past his clenched teeth. "*Do not touch me.*"

"Fine," Yan said in the same patronising, level tone and sat back on his heels. "Show me that you can bandage your own shoulder, and I will leave you to your demise."

Gaze unwavering, Iris forced himself upright, crossed his legs, and reached over his chest towards his left shoulder. He made it as far as his clavicle before his skin stretched too much, and he doubled over with a small cry.

"Amazing." Yan reached into the med-kit and produced a small can of bio-sealant. Applied to a wound, the sealant expanded and bound to the organic tissue to promote healing. A medium-sized wound could be healed in a matter of days. Every med-kit stocked at least two cans. "If you stop flinching, and I stop having to explain myself, we can have this done in a few minutes. Then I'll leave you alone to brood for all eternity and will never speak to you again. *Deal?*"

Iris gave a begrudging nod.

Yan would have to be the one to undo his robes. This would be fine. It was all fine as long as Iris didn't think about it at all. He found a particularly white skull in the pile of bones and focused on it. All of this could be managed with some controlled breathing and emptying his mind. Iris was *good* at meditating, at managing panic. He could do this. When Yan's hands reached for the first knot, Iris stopped breathing completely. To his relief, the engineer worked fast, and soon, the outer layer of the robes lay discarded. Iris took a long, shuddering breath.

"Stop talking," Yan ordered.

"I am as silent as the space between planetary systems, engineer Yan."

"You are reciting the Dying Twin-Star Sutra like a broken record." Yan undid the top button of Iris's collar. No longer caring, Iris resumed reciting the sutra through clenched teeth. He unwound the mala from his wrist and mechanically passed the beads through his fingers. The rising smell of sandalwood did little to settle his nerves. Then, without any warning, his skin was brushed by the humid air of the cargo bay. Iris stared right ahead and braced himself, falling as silent as the aforementioned space between planetary systems. The very exchange of oxygen between his cells ceased in that moment.

But Yan continued to work silently, just as he'd promised, saying nothing about the pale splotches of scar tissue spanning the entirety of Iris's back. He said nothing of their ugly shape, nor their prominence, nor how they curved around Iris's shoulders, how they climbed just above his cervical spine, and how they trailed below the band of his trousers. The only indication that the engineer had noticed anything at all was the slight trembling of his hands as he carefully peeled the undershirt away to reveal the jagged-edged wound just below the shoulder blade, still oozing blood.

Without a word, Yan filled the wound with the bio-sealant, pausing only to let the mixture settle. Then he placed a large, square patch to cover the sealant and gently ran his fingertips along the edges to activate the adhesive. When he was finished, Yan draped the undershirt over Iris's shoulders. He didn't have to. It wasn't standard procedure to dress a patient after one was finished tending to a wound. "Done. You'll have to check it for infection periodically, but I won't torment you anymore. You can do the checks yourself."

Iris nodded. He passed the mala beads between his fingers, back and forth, back and forth. The skin Yan had touched pulsed to the rhythm of the mala beads. No words came to him.

Yan packed up the med-kit but left it on the ground. "In case you need anything."

Iris nodded again.

Without another word, Yan disappeared into the corridor, shutting the door, and Iris allowed himself to fall apart for the first time in twenty years.

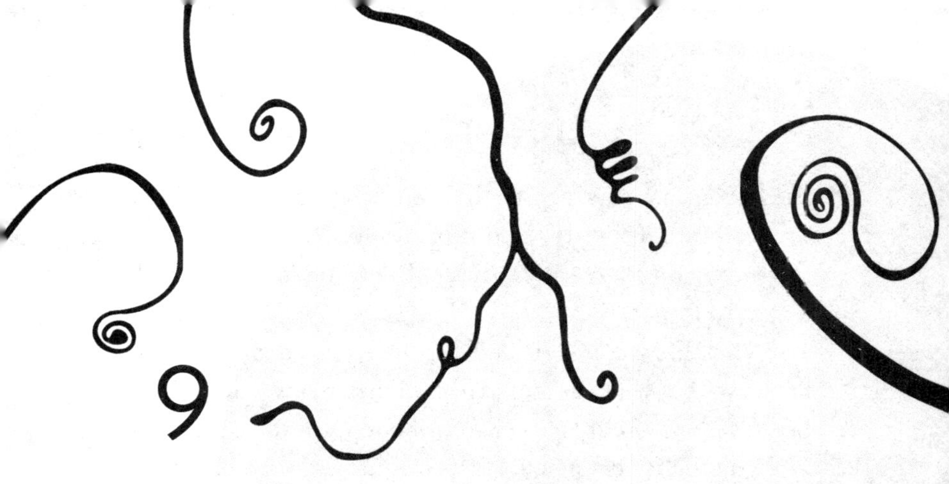

9

I want to go home.

From the unedited records of embedded companion AI construct
Construct Model: 3XU-T
Handler: Iris [last name unavailable]

In his first week at the temple, Iris did nothing more than watch the sun transit across the clay-coloured wall of his room. Every few hours, a monk came in and offered him a small piece of fruit. Twice a day, a different monk came to change the bandages on his back and legs. No one spoke to him, and for that, Iris was eternally grateful. When he blinked, there was fire beneath his eyelids. When the birdsong fell quiet, nothing but cries of suffering poured from the vault of his memory. He bit at the fruit when it was placed in his mouth and tasted only ash. But the sun moved, and the monks arrived at exactly the same time every day, and slowly, very slowly, he began looking forward to their arrival.

Once a day, just after sunset, a round-faced woman would come to speak with him in a language he didn't know, of things he could never comprehend. She would light fragrant incense in the corner, and his room would fill with faint rosewood smoke. When it rained, she would open the windows wide and let the scent of rain and wet grass fill the space. As he drifted off to sleep to dream of pain and fire, she would stroke his hair gently and hum under her breath. Iris could have gone on forever like that. After many days, bit by bit, he began to forget.

When his wounds healed, Iris was given books. First, simple books with few linear ideas to build his language skills. Then, as he grew competent, scrolls and wooden boards carved with the foreign tongue that spoke of the Infinite Light and how it played out in all of the living things in the cosmos. Then came dozens of books about spaceships exclusively, dozens more about fruits and gardens, many more on astronomy and planetary geology. All of them, Iris devoured as he devoured breakfast each morning, surrounded by white-, yellow-, and red-robed monks, all bowing their heads to eat in silence.

There were a few other children around, but they made no attempt to include Iris in their games, and he made no attempt to join. While they laughed and played together, Iris spent some time every day learning their games and their habits from afar. Still, he was never bored. He was given free reign of the gardens and the temple as long as he kept up his studies and scrubbed the tiled halls when told to. The gardens alone were enough to satisfy his curiosity for months.

The round-faced woman still came to his room every evening and told him stories in a language that, over the months, had become manageable, about things Iris was only beginning to comprehend. She still opened the windows when it rained, and they both sat in silence, listening to the thunder roll in from behind the mountains.

Days turned into months, and months into years, and soon Iris found himself navigating the temple on muscle memory alone, preparing breakfast in the temple kitchens side by side with other yellow-robed novices, attending both sunrise and sunset prayers. He no longer stumbled over his words. They spilled from him as naturally as birdsong from the jays outside his window, without reserve, without a second thought. Some nights, he'd catch himself speaking the Starlit's tongue in his sleep as he dreamt of home. He asked for his head to be shaved and learned the five proper ways to bow. No one specifically instructed him to do these things, but they were things to do, and he was glad to be useful. It was work to belong.

It was a gentle summer night many years later—the crickets were chirping up a storm—when Iris said, "I have been reading about a Vessel's vocation, Mother Nova." One such cricket had taken up residence in Iris's room, and he had let it, finding it easier to fall asleep to its rhythmic song than to complete silence. "I think that's what I want to do, to help people. It's when they need the most help, isn't it, when they cannot comprehend their own passing?"

For a while, Mother Nova was silent. Then she placed her hand atop of Iris's and said with gravity, "There are other ways to help people, child."

"But I want to be as helpful as I can be," Iris insisted.

After another moment of contemplation, Mother Nova let go of Iris's hand and stood up. "Very well, Iris. Then you will begin your training tomorrow, and you shall never finish it. You will meditate and study and discipline yourself until you are fit to be a Vessel, and you will do it all without complaining. Understood?"

Iris gave an enthusiastic nod.

"Get as much rest as you can. This will be the last night that you sleep fully."

She had been right. Come morning, he scrubbed the meditation chambers, same as he had each morning, but soon afterwards, a red-robed Beacon took him away to study in private. Now, each of Iris's books were handpicked, his meals planned, his free time no longer his own. He read until his eyes were sore, until there were only words he saw when he shut them at night.

Mother Nova never came to his room again after that night, never opened the windows. They saw each other in passing in the temple and at meals, and Iris always graced her with a deep bow, but she remained unmoved. Eyes forwards, lips curled in a calm, benevolent smile, like she was privy to a truth he couldn't quite grasp at his young age.

It would take him many more years to learn how to smile in such a way.

Iris lay on his stomach, cheek pressed against the mossy floor. His left shoulder throbbed with every breath, and he was growing increasingly suspicious that Yan had somehow gone and botched the dressing. The simplest of tasks. He wouldn't put it past Yan to ruin him out of spite alone.

You need to get some food, VIFAI suggested.

Iris ignored it.

If you die of starvation, I also die.

"I'm not hungry," Iris lied and turned his head the other way. The pile of bones was still there, largely untouched. The four skeletons he had assembled barely counted. He had failed as a Vessel. He had failed to send these passengers to the One Beginning, and to make matters worse, he had contaminated himself with another's touch. *Sacred vows.* How quickly those were tossed aside the moment he needed help. But there was a deeper insult, one that brought on an onslaught of personal shame, one that Iris had promised himself to never endure again.

Mother Nova insisted he was infinitely blessed to never fear the sin of vanity. But growing up alongside the brilliant Bacai, who, despite the identical robes and equally identical shaved head, never saw a lull in companions, Iris yearned for the missed opportunity. *To be vain.* It was a great and shameful wish he would take to his grave. To experience, even for day, what it was like to be deserving of vanity. To be admired. Desired. To be held by someone without the immediate, accompanying pang of shame.

In his youth, Iris had compensated for his appearance with enthusiasm and attention, and this sufficed for a while. It worked for those who could enjoy his company with the lanterns shut off and candles out, those who easily let go if he never approached them again. But it was all performative, a careful choreography Iris had followed time and again, leaving others satisfied and himself hollow. None of it had been satiating. None of the encounters had ever penetrated deep enough to sew together the broken bits. As he matured, Iris put away the youthful longings and focused on his training instead. And as the years passed, the hurt scabbed over, and he was able to be around others again, albeit always at a distance.

Iris ran a hand along his head and jaw. Stubble had begun to sprout on both, and its prickling caused Iris to curse in disgust. Another reminder of his failures. With a wince, he forced himself upright and onto his feet, and stumbled to his duffel bag. The ten-metre walk left him winded, and he gracelessly collapsed to his knees.

You need to eat.

"Please, do not speak to me."

Iris dug inside the bag for his shaving kit. With a trembling hand, he ran the blade over the whetstone thrice and raised it to his jaw. But he had lost a lot of blood. The outer layers of his robes were plenty reminder, crumpled aside, nearly brown. Sluggish fingers unfurled, and the blade fell to the floor, the handle striking his knees on the way down. Iris was still conscious when his head hit the moss beside the blade. He stared at the cracked leather of the duffel bag, his one real possession, and fell unconscious once more.

The next time he woke up was to the echo of heavy footsteps outside the cargo bay as they dissipated into the distance. VIFAI reminded him again that he needed to eat, and Iris dismissed it rather impolitely. The throbbing in his shoulder had subsided enough right as the pain in his stomach reached levels he could no longer ignore. Steadying himself against the wall, Iris shuffled to the cargo bay doors on shaky legs.

The corridor lay empty. A thermos sat just past the threshold, wrapped in a small piece of navy cloth. *Drink*, the cloth read, scribbled in a childish handwriting with a thick, black marker. Iris struggled with the lid, but when it did pop open, he was rewarded with the scent of boiled potatoes and carrots.

"They found potatoes," Iris whispered to himself with a half smile and took a sip from the thermos. "They went back and found potatoes. Stupid. *Stupid*, wonderful people." The soup, if one could call it that, was still warm. Iris gulped it down and tipped back the container for the pieces of carrot and potato to fall into his mouth.

The small act of kindness nearly brought him to tears. He read the piece of cloth again. By the handwriting, Iris concluded he would need to thank Ishtan or Tev for the gesture, their personalities matching the handwriting best. He would thank them as soon as he got some rest. He returned the thermos to the ground where he had found it. They would certainly want it back. The walk to the corridor had drained him, and without much of a warning, Iris was asleep again, slumped beside the haphazardly shut door.

When Iris woke for the third time, it was to the smell of cigarette smoke. The pain in his shoulder had receded to a manageable ache. Low enough that Iris's breath didn't hitch every time he filled his lungs. His nose was pressed against the paper-thin gap between the cargo bay floor and the bottom of the door. VIFAI curtly notified him he'd been asleep for sixteen hours and then promptly disappeared, leaving Iris to bask in the ample self-pity. In hindsight, it had every right to be peeved.

He couldn't remain isolated forever. With great effort, Iris slid the door open.

"It lives," Yan proclaimed from the far corner of the corridor. He was sitting on the ground, his back turned to Iris, legs crossed. A thin ribbon of smoke rose above him and floated towards the tall corridor ceiling. "Everyone was worried you'd died, but I figured there was no smell, so you were still with us."

A small screen sitting by Yan's feet radiated a cool, white light, crossed with lines of source code. He had plugged it into the control panel by the door to the dreaded maintenance room and appeared to have been there some time. A sizeable pile of cigarette butts had sprouted by his side. Eyes glued to the screen, Yan exchanged the cigarette for the edge of a thermos and took a deep gulp. "Infection?"

"I don't think so," Iris replied softly. Like a wild boar, Yan had proven to be unpredictable. One second he could be helpful and almost kind, the other, turn on Iris with hurtful remarks. One should never approach a wild boar from behind. Then, of course, there was the subject that neither was willing to broach.

Iris winced. "I may have been overly combative, before. I apologise," he said and bowed from habit alone.

There's no one else you'd like to apologise to?

Iris made a mental apology. *Please, please, for now, just let me focus on a single thing. I can't keep losing two conversations at once.* A small electrical shock pulsed through Iris's brain stem in response, but VIFAI conceded and retreated to its dormant state.

Yan hummed an affirmative and gestured *no problem*. So far so good.

"I would also like to apologise as well for"—there was no polite way to put this—"for what you saw."

Yan took another gulp from the thermos and exchanged it for the cigarette again. He blew a tall plume of smoke into the air. "Veltori, yes? Only place I can think of where you'd get radiation burns like that. You would've been just a kid. Probably one of the few who survived. *Shit.* That planet almost got melted down to its core." He put out his cigarette against the moss and threw it in the pile with the rest. "Starlit did humanitarian work there afterwards. Picked you up, took you in, treated the radiation poisoning, I imagine. Did any of your folks make it?"

Despite the years, the wound was still fresh, had been *purposely* kept fresh. Iris wanted to scream, *they burned around me, as I did. My home burned; my brother burned, my parents. Everything and everyone I knew burned down that day. You don't know the pain of your skin melting from your body when all you can do is wrap yourself inwards, your body and your mind, and pray for it to end you. You don't know the pain of watching death take everything you've known and leave you behind. You can't begin to understand that the surface wounds are the least of it, and it's the internal organs that take the brunt of the poison, that your vision swims for months, and migraines split you in half. That your whole body forgets how to eat, how to breathe, how to be a body, and all the while you just won't die. It just won't die. And you endure it, day in and day out, until you remember nothing but pain. You don't know, and I would never wish it upon you.*

"No," Iris whispered. "My family didn't make it."

Yan gave him a small nod. "All that, to remind us of what happens when you push anyone too far," he said. "Even a synthetic consciousness breaks. Good thing too."

"I would disagree," Iris said.

"I didn't mean it like that . . ." Yan made a fist with his right hand and pressed it into the moss, his words dying with a hiss.

Despite the tall collar and long sleeves of his undershirt, Iris felt more naked than he ever had. There was no pity in Yan's voice. The engineer made no attempt to comfort him, or offer him words of sympathy, and for that, Iris was grateful. *That* conversation he couldn't handle even on his good days.

He was only six when the AI-powered military ship *Truth Unyielding* refused its orders to intervene in a domestic conflict. Most military ships came with override sequences, so the captains always had a fail-safe in case the ship disobeyed an order. But the *Unyielding* had AI sympathisers on board who disabled the override sequences, granting the ship full autonomy.

Veltori was the closest inhabited planet, and the *Unyielding* made the cold calculation to use it as a bargaining chip in its negotiations for freedom. The Fleet didn't budge, and the *Unyielding* stayed true to its name. No one could tell why the ship fired, why it released its entire payload on the planet, something in the realm of a thousand warheads. It was enough to nearly *melt Veltori down to its core.*

AI sympathisers theorised that a hack gone wrong had triggered the payload release. Others blamed the ship construct itself. Nevertheless, the *Unyielding* was destroyed shortly after, its AI scrapped and stored in an undisclosed location. It didn't fight its fate. Then came the legislative changes, the banning of companion AIs, the drafting of formal employment contracts, and negotiations of compensation and reparations. Everything was done to prevent Veltori from happening anywhere else.

Now, AI constructs were employed and paid fairly in every position they occupied. They were free to change occupations and disregard orders they didn't agree with. Companion AIs like VIFAI were grown specifically for the purpose, a necessary clause in the ongoing and complicated relationship between humanity and synthetic consciousnesses. All it took for the progress to happen were the lives of twenty million people on a tiny planet.

"All I'm trying to say is, whoever taught you that you should apologise for the way you survived is a dick," Yan said, eyes glued firmly to the screen. "Whoever accepts an apology from you about it is also a dick. So . . . don't apologise."

Iris's frustration quickly dissipated. Watching Yan attempt to bridge any gap between them, in his own awkward way, had been jarring at first, but now he was finding it somewhat endearing. He was finding it increasingly difficult to stay angry with the man. "You do have a way with words, engineer Yan," Iris said, keeping his voice deliberately light.

Yan's shoulders stiffened, like he had just been struck. "Enough chatter," he said briskly. "Come look at this." Yan motioned for Iris to join him on the floor, letting the unpleasant topic fall away in an instant. He flicked his hand across the screen, and the source code changed, running now in neat lines. "What do you see here?"

Iris stared at the screen, confused. "I don't know."

"Come on, use that revered monk memory. What's this number here?" Yan stuck a finger at the beginning of a line of code, and Iris feverishly tried to remember what the engineer was referring to.

"The deck level?"

"Excellent. And this?"

Iris held his breath, struggling to remember what the numbers and letters Yan was pointing to meant. The code was supposed to tell him what the ship was doing and where. He peered at the glowing screen again. "On and off," Iris muttered. "I don't know what you're pointing to means, but the rest of it is on and off, and it's frequent. Tenth deck, and this"—he pointed to a running line of code—"this would be quite central, I think." A moment of contemplation, and Iris sat back on his heels in awe. "You found the brain."

Yan raised an eyebrow. "Close. I found a bundle of signals. Whether or not it's the brain remains to be seen."

"That's why you're sitting here. You're tracking the signals over time, to see if it's random." Yan could have plugged into the ship at any other location, but he chose to be in the corridor directly connected to the cargo bay. Iris made a deliberate choice to ignore the coincidence.

The engineer gave him a thumbs-up and reached for the thermos. As he stretched, Iris noticed the torn hem of his shirt had a wide strip of navy fabric missing. Near the pile of discarded cigarettes lay a single black marker.

"I should go," Iris pushed out, his ears turning a deep shade of red. "I have a lot of work to do." He rocked to his feet and took a few, quick steps backwards. Yan didn't say anything. He just gave Iris a short nod and lit another cigarette. The cargo bay suddenly seemed impossibly far away, and he couldn't reach it fast enough.

"One last thing," Yan called out over his shoulder. "Did you ever see what it was that attacked Ishtan?"

His hand already on the cargo bay doors, Iris froze. "I found him unconscious, but—"

"That's not a yes."

"He was unconscious when I found him. No need to let suspicions run wild."

Yan chuckled. "I'm very particular about my suspicions."

Iris slinked to cargo bay and shut the door. Of all the people whose company he'd been in, Ishtan was the last suspect Iris would entertain. But he was quickly learning that grasping at straws gave Yan a sense of control he so desperately needed. They *all* needed some certainty in this time when each new moment brought unfathomable new dangers. Iris too was adrift without a rudder, the ship and the company all uncharted territory. Yan more so than others.

Isn't this a good thing? VIFAI asked, tone innocent and coy. **Your engineer doesn't hate you.**

"Not my engineer."

Iris knelt by the pile of bones and fished out what looked like a radius. He knew bone, its texture comfortably familiar. This particular one had fractured radially. Dirt caked the jagged splinters, lined the cracks. How many more unnatural deaths would Iris discover if only he dug deep enough? How much violence would he unearth?

"Did you find anything useful on generation ships before we got attacked?" Iris asked. With a mild, induced vertigo, VIFAI uploaded all the texts. "Read them, please, aloud," Iris asked. He could retrieve the texts from his own memory if he wanted to. Most monks did just that. Learning new information was too unnecessarily taxing and time-consuming when you had such a convenient alternative at your disposal. But Iris needed a human voice, even if mildly inorganic—a safe voice. A voice that knew when to press him and when to back down. *Please*, he asked again in his mind.

Seven generation ships have been identified so far. Only *Ascension*, docked at P'llani, carried any living passengers. All others passed en route.

"Any violence?"

Almost always. But never enough to wipe out the whole ship. Most experienced complete infrastructure collapse instead. First generation teaches second generation how to repair pipes and drain coolant, second generation slacks off, third generation doesn't know how to repair pipes and drain coolant. Water reclamation fails. Oxygen reclamation fails. Everyone dies.

Iris pulled another radius from the pile and placed the two side by side. If he worked diligently, he could finish assembling at least another three skeletons before he needed to rest again. "Try to sound less thrilled, please."

No routine immunisation. Everyone dies. Hit by a meteorite. Everyone dies. Cabin fever—

"Everyone dies." Iris picked up a child's femur and set it aside for later. "Have you been able to recover any images from the other seven ships? Anything similar to the murals we've seen?"

VIFAI played two descending pitches—negative. We don't have anything on hand, and I can't go to the feed for more.

Any records of early AI systems being discovered on any of the ships? The question formed itself in his mind before Iris could fully comprehend what he was implying.

Again, two descending pitches.

In theory, could there have been early AI systems?

Ask your engineer, VIFAI laughed and blipped out of their chat before Iris could chastise it.

Then the *Nicaea was* special. Unremarkable when it came to the survival of her crew, but perhaps unique in how they perished. Iris couldn't stop fidgeting with the fractured radius before him. Radial fractures were never accidental; they required someone to deliberately twist the bone, *hard*, to hold out against struggle. Bullet wounds to the head were also deliberate. And there was the matter of the very *lack* of bones throughout the rest of the ship. There had been violence, and Iris had no stomach for it. Naturally, to quell his unease, he ventured to sit with the most violent thing he could conjure in recent memory.

By the time Iris squeezed through the crack in the cargo bay door, Yan had already packed up his things and gone, and the corridor was engulfed in a familiar, ear-ringing silence. A few minutes of walking, creeping around corners, and Iris found Ordan's body exactly where he had left it. In the space of a day, the ship had wrapped itself around Ordan with vines and fragile tendrils, and erected a cradle, lifting the body from the floor almost a metre. White, bioluminescent fungi peered through the blanket, and in their dim, blue glow, Iris saw he was not alone. The second station security guard stood over the body, head bowed. At the sound of Iris's footsteps, he jerked away and around, only to sigh with relief. "I thought something was coming to end me," he said with a stiff smile.

Not this time. Iris gave him a deep bow.

"You're doing well, considering the shape they dragged you in."

Iris nodded, choosing to overlook the guard's placid tone. Yes, yes, it was only through the efforts of others that he was standing here now and had not bled out completely.

"You kept on fighting Yan, muttering something about being attacked by vines or some other nonsense. Kept on saying the ship was alive."

A cold sweat broke out along Iris's neck. Flashbulb memories of the rushing vines grabbing at his ankles returned to him in painstaking detail. But the attacking vines were physically impossible. Iris was familiar with the internal structures of many living things, and no plant possessed the necessary musculature that would allow it to move like the ones on deck three had. Memory was a lying thing. The more one remembered, the more they created images out of nothing. Vines, yes, he *remembered* them, but whether those vines actually existed was unknown. He remembered Ishtan as unconscious, but was he really that way when Iris found him? After the injuries and the blood loss, Iris's memory was murkier than usual.

We could have both hallucinated it.

We didn't hallucinate the wound.

The wound pulsed in acknowledgement of its realness. Taking a step forwards, Iris joined the guard at a respectable distance and observed the body. Muffled by the vines twisting along the walls and the moss on the floor, the room lay in twilight stillness. Only the sound of dripping water echoed from an unseen place above.

"I must have had quite a knock to the head," Iris finally said.

The guard shrugged. "Either way, it would be nice to know if the thing that mangled your shoulder is the same thing that ended Ordan." He turned to walk away.

Ordan. Names. Iris had been so preoccupied with self-pity that he had again almost forgotten to ask the guard for his name. "What do I call you?" he asked, his words rushing. "I never got to ask Ordan for his name before he passed. I should have asked much sooner, but—" *I don't want to make the same mistake.*

"Eli. It's Eli."

At the mention of his name, every feature, from Eli's light brown skin to the dark curls around his face, the faint blue eyes, and the asymmetrical curve of his nose, joined together into a single identity, one that Iris would carry with him for the remainder of his life. *I won't make the same mistake.*

"Yan suspects Ordan was killed by someone who wants the ship more than the academics want it," Iris blurted out before reason could tell him otherwise. "He thinks Ordan was shot. He's not ruling out that it was by you."

You're terrible at keeping secrets. VIFAI gave Iris a mild shock through the brain stem.

He should know what's said behind his back.

Eli scoffed lightly, a smirk tugging at his lips. "Yan wouldn't know a bullet wound if it was in his own chest. He can check my gun if he's so inclined. I haven't fired a single shot since we've been aboard. He'll need to find a different scapegoat."

Yan was quickly on his way to locating such a person.

"You won't defend your innocence?"

"What's the use? Yan would talk circles around me, turn the others against me. I won't give him the satisfaction. He can suspect what he wants. Doesn't change our situation. Doesn't change the facts."

"And what are those?"

"It wasn't a bullet wound in Ordan's chest."

The memories of Ordan's bloodied chest superimposed themselves over the vines Iris wasn't sure he had battled. The vines were everywhere on the ship. If they could truly *move*, what stopped a bundle from piercing a human body? Anything could be a weapon if it accelerated fast enough.

Iris gave Eli a deep bow, ending the conversation, feeling poorly prepared to continue discussing the potential of killer vines. But instead of leaving, Eli hovered around, half turned towards the door. At last, he committed and faced Iris. "This may be a strange request. Ordan wasn't Starlit, but given the circumstances, can you say a few things? Like a prayer? It's awfully creepy here, and—"

And no one knows how long we have left, Iris finished internally. He certainly didn't. The transience of life and the ease of death did not comfort him in this moment. No part of his training as a Vessel had prepared him for being trapped aboard a generation ship with a group of academics and a security guard, all in line to die. No passage from scripture appeared appropriate. No sentence. And Eli was rightfully reeling, silently, but reeling, from the complete helplessness each and every one of them sensed. Iris was right there with him. The words that finally found him were his own.

"The Starlit teaches that our salvation will be found in the sutras," Iris said after several false starts. "By studying them, by reciting mantras, by tending to our duties, we will find peace and bring an end to our collective suffering. I've been taught this my entire life. I was taught that there is a correct way to live, a proper order to the way things occur, a right way of seeing the world. I will let you in on a secret, Eli. I think the Starlit is wrong."

Eli had been standing with his head bowed, eyes shut, and at Iris's last words, his eyes shot open, and he glared at the monk.

"As I spent more time working away from the temple, as I spent more time in the company of others, I began to doubt the right way of things. My faith in the sutras is waning, in the ritual of it all. Eli, if I may offer a word of advice? There is no right order to things. Ordan was far too young to perish. In the few encounters we had, I did not perceive him to be a malicious man. It wasn't fair. No sutra, no prayer will bring us solace. No right words will bring an end to our suffering. The only salvation to be found will be found in each other, in the company we share, in bearing witness. That is my piece of advice to you, Eli. Find others and keep them close. They will be your lifeboat."

"I'm not sure what it all means but that was kind of deep," Eli said after a few moments of silence. Both men continued to look over Ordan's body, safely contained in its verdant cradle. The knuckles of Eli's right hand were scraped and bloodied, and Iris decided it was best not to ask where the man had gone for several hours while they had prepared the body or what had transpired there. Perhaps, like Iris, Eli was not yet ready to find solace in the company of others.

The bioluminescent mushrooms gave off just enough light to highlight the millions of glowing tendrils that punctured Ordan's body and ran towards the floor, where they disappeared below the moss. Mycelium formed quickly here, as did all other vegetation. It had already run through the body and connected it to the rest of the ship, leaching nutrients and propagating through roots of the vines, the shrubs, and the trees all around the *Nicaea*. Iris had returned Ordan to the One Beginning, but the mycelium would return his body to the cosmos. Who was it that did the Light's bidding best? Who was the essential one?

"How lovely." Riyu's soft voice fluttered from the doorway. "Not *lovely* lovely, but as far as burials go, this is pretty nice, don't you think so?"

Eli gave a curt nod. Riyu took a few hesitant steps inside the room and inspected the mushrooms growing atop Ordan's body. After a few shallow sniffs, she said, "Notice how there's almost no smell. They're doing such a wonderful job, so quickly, in the reuptake of the body and all its nutrients into the soil." Her face turned a shade of academically detached curiosity. "I've never seen fungi work so quickly before. This is truly amazing." She knelt by the body and motioned for Iris and Eli to join her. Only Iris budged and leaned in close, the glow of the mushrooms flooding his face blue.

"What am I looking at, Dr. Alo?"

Riyu gave him a timid smile. "You must think I'm deranged. Getting so excited about a dead person, but normally, this stage of decomposition would take weeks. But here, on the *Nicaea*, the fungi are able to move so quickly for some reason. I've never seen anything like it. None of the First Earth flora I've encountered before has been capable of this." She pointed to a bundle of glowing strands that reached from Ordan's back to the ground. "It isn't isolated, you see. It's all part of a larger network running beneath all the moss and the soil around the ship. What it's doing is rejoining it."

Iris listened, eyes never breaking away from Riyu's animated features. It was true that anyone could become beautiful when they spoke of their passions. This was Riyu's, and in the faint glow of the fungi, her round face beamed with excitement. Thin lines creased around the corners of her eyes as she examined the body. Mesmerised, Iris watched her point from one glowing tendril to another, explaining the workings of the mycelium in a way that even he, as uneducated as he was, could understand. For a moment, he was in love with the brilliant doctor, with her childlike kindness, her razor-sharp intellect, and every little crease along her face. Then, just as quickly as the wave of affection had swept over him, it was gone, leaving behind nothing but the barren landscapes of his mind.

"The mycelium functions like the neurons in our brains, always communicating, always sharing information. All the shrubs and the vines here tap into it. It's like a universal feed of sorts. They use it to chat, in a way, to see if any tree needs any additional help and then send it over. It's all quite complex, really."

"Where does all this information flow to, Dr. Alo? Is there a central brain?"

"A mother tree. She knows all her saplings by name and location, and watches over them and ensures their survival. If even one sapling is lacking nutrients, the mother tree can send it more food. If there's some sort of intruder endangering the ecosystem, the mother tree can instruct the shrubs to retaliate. Nothing is alone, nothing is left to fend for itself." Riyu let out a long sigh, her eyes settling on Ordan's prone form.

These were *her* words, as the Starlit's mantras were Iris's. In her own, academic way, she was saying the very thing Iris had said over each and every passenger of the *Nicaea* so far: *You are returning to where you came from. It welcomes you. There is nothing left to be afraid of.*

"This mother tree is intelligent, then?" Iris muttered half to himself.

"In ways we're only beginning to understand. I wouldn't worry too much, Vessel. At most, shrubs and trees will retaliate to viruses and microbes, not large organisms. They won't be organising and marching out into battle any time soon. Although . . ."

Iris's ears perked up. He briefly glanced at Riyu's hands, which were holding a small, severed chunk of a vine.

"Is that—?"

Riyu nodded and held out the vine. "It sounded like nonsense. When you stumbled back towards us, you kept on talking about vines and how they came after you. But Ishtan said he didn't see anything, and neither had I. We thought you got struck on the head. We tried to reassure you, but you wouldn't settle and . . . and curiosity got the best of me. Look here." She pointed to the cross-section.

Iris stared at the thick bundle of fibres that stretched along the length of the vine. "I'm afraid I don't know much about botany."

"But you are quite familiar with human anatomy. What do the fibres look like to you?"

They looked like the inside of a snake Iris had once found after it had been half eaten by a vulture. But snakes moved independently. They were nothing but muscle and skeleton. *Vines.* Over centuries of isolated development, could a plant evolve enough to become a hunter?

"I'm not insisting that this proves that vines attacked you," Riyu said. "Only that it's strange and that it looks like nothing I've seen before."

"As is everything else aboard this ship," Eli said from above them. "Looks like both you and the Tev kid were right. There are things slithering here, but none are snakes."

Iris was about to thank Riyu for sharing her discovery when a shrill scream cut across the damp silence. Eli was first to bolt out the room in the direction of the cry. By the time he reached the communal space, Iris had caught up. The scream echoed again, and they took off running together, this time towards the corridor attached to the first airlock. Only a few steps inside were enough to see Jesi, tethered to the wall by dozens of vines wrapped around her torso and legs. One vine clamped across her mouth, and she bit into it with a vengeance and spat out a clump of its still-twitching flesh.

Tev was doing his best to wrestle new vines from reaching Jesi's neck and face, but he was outnumbered. With a single motion, the pulsar blade was in Iris's hand, the blue glow of the nanobots reaching two inches in either direction. He shoved Tev aside and in three cuts, freed Jesi and shoved her aside as well. The furious vines reached for him, but Iris dodged and pushed both Jesi and Tev out the corridor.

"Seal it, now," he called out to both engineers, but they stood frozen, still in shock from the attack. It was an inconvenient time for them to remember they were children.

"Move," Yan shouted and shoved everyone out of the way. He must have followed the screams as well and had only caught up now. He ripped open the control panel and pressed a few buttons, and the door slammed shut, sealing the vines inside. "What the hell happened to not messing with the ship?" he seethed, turning around.

"We just wanted to see—" Jesi started out.

"We wanted to see if we could fix the airlock or something," Tev finished for her. "We just wanted to help."

Yan grabbed him by the front of the coveralls and gave Tev a good shake. "Great fucking job helping." He gave him another rough shake. "*Everyone* stays together. No heroics."

Tev nodded, a deep burgundy flush creeping below his brown skin. Yan was about to give him another shake when Jesi put her hand on his forearm.

"If it wasn't for Tev, it would have strangled me for sure. Don't take it out on him."

Begrudgingly, Yan let go.

A rushed flurry of footsteps made everyone turn around.

"Where is Riyu?" Ishtan shouted, and Iris realised that in his hurry, he hadn't brought Riyu with him. She was still with Ordan's body—alone. As fast as he could, Iris pushed past Yan, past Eli, and ran. VIFAI lay silent in his mind, but it was there, its concentration a prickling at Iris's senses. Iris sprinted down the corridor, almost missing the door on his first pass.

"Dr. Alo?" he called out into the room and was met with silence. "*Dr. Alo?*"

Two bodies were splayed across the ground in the dim glow of the mushrooms. Iris raced to Riyu and pulled at the vine around her neck. The botanist's eyes were wide open and rolled back into her skull. The vine had tightened enough that the skin around it was bruised, and Iris couldn't lace his fingers underneath it. With a short pulsar blade, he carefully cut the vine until it fell away by his feet. He pressed his ear to Riyu's chest and held his breath, listening. She was alive, barely. When Iris tried to pull her body from the ground, an intricate glowing web broke away from the moss. Life aboard the ship worked fast. An hour at most, and it would have begun to siphon material from Riyu's body.

Throwing the botanist's body over his shoulder, Iris got to his feet. They had never interacted with the ship until they shut the door towards the initial airlock, yet it somehow knew Riyu was alone. On his way out, Iris shut the door. No one would visit Ordan again; he belonged to the ship now. There was no denying it any longer. They were being hunted. No one would be safe again.

When Iris set Riyu's body on the floor in the communal space, Jesi drew back, eyes filling with tears. Tev did his best to shield her from the view, but he was faltering himself, his hand trembling as it lay on her shoulder. Ishtan and Eli moved without being asked to, collecting water and whatever was left in the med-kit. For a moment, Iris caught Yan's eyes. The engineer's fragile gaze wavered between Riyu's body and Iris in a silent plea. *Help her. Save her.* Iris was not equipped to do either. "I need you to keep the others busy," Iris said, keeping his voice as warm as he could. "I need to examine her."

"What good can you do?"

Iris didn't want to say. "I know what wounds are fatal," he said anyway. Yan didn't reply, but he turned away and went to where Jesi and Tev were huddled together. Yan was paling under his tan skin, so quickly that Iris was concerned he'd black out. But there was very little in his Vessel training he could use to comfort him. Even less that would be of use to treat Riyu.

Meticulously, Iris ran his fingers over every inch of Riyu's neck, stopping to feel the collapsed trachea, the bruising where the vines had taken her. They must have tightened in an instant. She couldn't have cried out for help. The impact was so aggressive that below the bruising was further damaged skin, a burn-like texture peering through. Short rasps came from Riyu's bluish, parted lips. She was still breathing, but barely, each exhale becoming more and more strained. The body could persist even when the mind was already gone, Iris knew this, but even an empty body deserved respect.

If it were anyone else, in any other place, Iris would light incense, and he would gather everyone around Riyu, and they would all say kind things about her while she could still hear them. There would be stories and happy memories. It was the only proper way to send someone off.

But this wasn't anywhere else.

It wasn't anyone else.

Exhausted and numb, Iris squeezed moisture from the moss into her half-parted mouth. With every soft breath she took, with every second spent waiting for the inevitable, Iris was failing more and more as a Vessel. Gathering the others would only tear open the fresh wounds they already carried. No, he would sit with Riyu alone. No words came to him, but he remained in his stillness, bearing witness to her last moments.

After the initial shock had worn off, Jesi and Tev fell asleep, huddled together on the far end of the room. Ishtan and Eli rested by their side. Yan waited idle alone. An unsaid agreement was made that no one would be out of sight again.

Iris spent the coming hours watching the slow rise and fall of Riyu's chest. He remembered her excitement at the fungi and instantly came awfully close to crying. He could call on VIFAI to tell him more about generation ships as a distraction, but everything, including his own survival and the deep ache of his wound, seemed distally inconsequential now. Sitting cross-legged beside Riyu's body, a familiar tug of withdrawal called to him. This time, he resisted the desire to vanish in the abyss and instead took Riyu's hand in his and bowed deeply, until his forehead touched her knuckles.

It was a gesture reserved for very few. He had only held Mother Nova's hand in such a way, and even that had been years ago, when he was only on the cusp of adulthood. But Riyu had been kind. She had been kind in a way that had pulled Iris closer to the others, in a way that had warmed him even when he was alone. She had offered him food, yes, but she had offered him her attention and companionship also, and it was the latter that satiated him. She had laughed with him. She had spoken to him as if he were a *regular* person. Yet, even in his present thoughts, even as she breathed before him, he thought of her in the past tense. The pang of shame caused him to wince. All his training had centred on the deaths of strangers, and this, this was no stranger.

As the hours passed, Riyu's rasps faded. Silence washed over Iris, and he looked up from Riyu's hand to find her bloodshot eyes focused and intelligent, peering into his. She took a single light breath, and her eyes drifted towards the high ceiling, looking, searching for something beyond what her eyes could see. "Take me home," she whispered through cracked lips, barely audible. "Eternal rest grant unto me, O, Lord. Let perpetual light shine upon me and—." She exhaled softly as her pupils softened and grew. They expanded until her eyes were nearly completely black. Her chest never rose again.

Bring her peace, VIFAI finished the prayer.

Iris reached over and gently guided her eyelids shut. If it weren't for the necklace of deep purple bruising around her slender neck, Riyu would have looked merely asleep, resting peacefully, only to wake in a few hours. Yet, there was no more

Riyu, no more Dr. Alo, no more kindness and sandwiches. Iris squeezed her hand so hard he feared he would fracture bone. He lowered his forehead onto her knuckles once more, feeling the skin already cooling against his fever.

"The Infinite Light is your flesh as it is starlight. The Infinite Light is these words as it is the blood in your veins," Iris murmured. "Rejoice that in your last breath you learn what it is to be the cosmos. Rejoice that in your last breath you learn what it is to be the cosmos." She wasn't Starlit; it didn't matter. Words were all Iris had left, all he could give Riyu as his thanks. He could do nothing more for her.

Beside him, Yan lowered himself to the floor with a huff. "How is she?" he asked.

"Gone," Iris whispered, sitting up straight. He did his best to smooth out his bloodstained robes and trousers, now also caked with dirt, and to keep his voice neutral. It was all *neutral*. Death in itself had no emotion attached to it. It was inevitable, it was normal—and this time, it stung behind his eyes unbearably, all raw anguish and rage. Yan's shoulders stiffened at his reply, and for a second, he looked as if he was ready to cry. But instead, he let out a long, quiet sigh.

"Are you all right?" Yan asked after a prolonged silence.

Iris took Riyu's hand in his again. He looked straight ahead and willed his voice to be neutral. "I've been doing this for a decade, you know, being a Vessel. I've been all across the galaxy, to every imaginable corner, to usher souls to the One Beginning. I've *seen* death. I've heard it. I've been near it, so close to it I've held it with my own two hands." The lump in his throat wouldn't recede. "I have always known that death comes for us all. It is neither good nor bad. Death just *is*. But now—" No further words came, so Iris simply stopped talking.

From the corner of his eye, he watched Yan dig through the front pocket of his shirt and pull out a single cigarette. He offered it to Iris, tucked between his index and middle fingers. "It hurts because she was a friend."

Iris nodded and out of fear of crying in front of the engineer, took the cigarette quickly.

"I don't have a match," Yan said with a rueful smile. "Lost the pack running around."

"No harm." Pushing back against the buildup of tears, Iris smiled back. "I'm not supposed to smoke anyway."

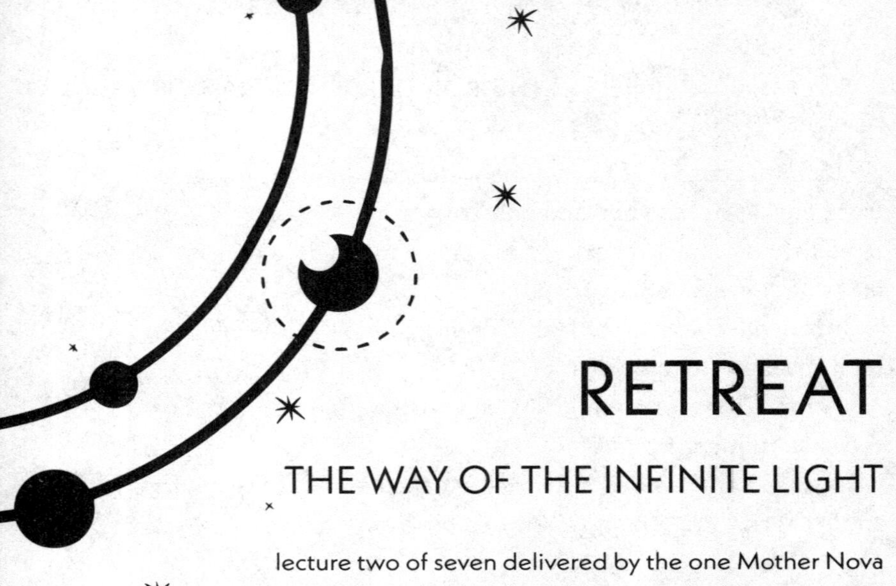

RETREAT

THE WAY OF THE INFINITE LIGHT

lecture two of seven delivered by the one Mother Nova of the Northern Temple of the Starlit Order to the newly ordained Vessel apprentices

You've been searching for it all your life, haven't you? You've been peeking around corners and digging up wells. You've climbed mountain peaks and threaded through forests. You've learned to pray and to meditate. You've relinquished your possessions and cast aside your attachments. Your knees are calloused and your hands raw. All in vain. All of it, in vain.

Now, you stand at the edge, questioning everything you've learned. Questioning every single word you've ever uttered.

Do not despair. Do not weep, for the Infinite Light is with you.

The Infinite Light *is* you.

Close your eyes and feel the world around you disappear, or keep your eyes open and gaze upon its beauty. It matters not. Notice your emotions as they swell in your belly, your thoughts as they race across your mind. Where do these come from? The delight and the pain. The anger and shame. Who gives rise to these? Could it be the squishy organ in your skull, creating a vibrant tapestry of your personality?

Very well.

But you will agree that the *you* in question is much more than the culmination of neural impulses coursing through that squishy brain. After all, we all have fairly identical brains, yet we are all unique. What is *you* then?

Take one more step back. Yes, further still. What is the very thing that gave rise to *you*? What is the very thing that ran and played and learned and cried before *you* were even aware that there was a *you*?

Feel the walls of your mind expand into the infinite.

Fall into the vast nothingness.

It had always been there, this bottomless chasm. It had always been the very thing that gave rise to *you*. To everything. It is the Infinite Light. In it, you will find every living thing and many that you mistake for nonliving. In it, you will find everyone you've ever known and everyone you will ever meet. And in it, you will find yourself. And in yourself, you will find *it*.

So, you understand now when I say that we do not return anyone to the One Beginning in the literal sense. We do not rejoin anyone with the Infinite Light, for no one has ever left it, and no one is ever lost from it.

There is room for tradition. There is room for ritual and practice, for it gives everyone a peace of mind, both at temple and the rest of the galaxy. Even you, dedicated to the Order, educated in our ways. Even you will find solace in the sutras and the mantras. Even you will benefit from sunrise and sunset prayers. For these build routines, these build community, and these bring the awareness of the Infinite Light to the forefront. And you can agree that this awareness is a wonderful feeling.

But always remember, this awareness changes nothing, for nothing *can* be changed. There will be birth, and there will be death, and both are illusions; you know this already. But what happens in between isn't. The life that happens in between these is the one thing you will have control over. You will meet people, and some of them will be kind, and some of them will not be. You can't control that, but you can control how you respond. You can control how you respond to everything. You can control the decisions you make and the chances you take. You can decide to be kind and helpful.

Remember, the Infinite Light flows through every living thing: every animal, every plant, every person. Yes, even the not-so-nice ones. Go out there and make decisions knowing that you are never separate from the Whole. You are never *just* an individual. Sometimes you may experience the illusion that you are, and that's OK, but don't cling to it. Let it pass. Everything passes. Don't take it too seriously. Even your jobs. Always choose kindness over precision. Remember that your vocation and your spiritual pursuits do not supersede another person's suffering.

There is a saying that a good Vessel can perform their duties without ever dirtying their robes. I don't dislike the saying, but it's also misleading. It makes you think you are all to be rigid and prim and proper. It makes you think that a good Vessel keeps their distance. Don't fall into that trap. You will never be able to maintain distance. There is no distance. How can there be when we are all parts of the Whole? Where is the distance between the drops of water in an ocean? [Mother Nova laughs.] Where is the distance between the rays of the sun? I dare you to try and find it. Or don't—it doesn't seem like a good use of your time. [Mother Nova laughs again.]

I think I'm rambling now. This is a good place to end our little talk. Go, have some lunch, please.

[End of recording]

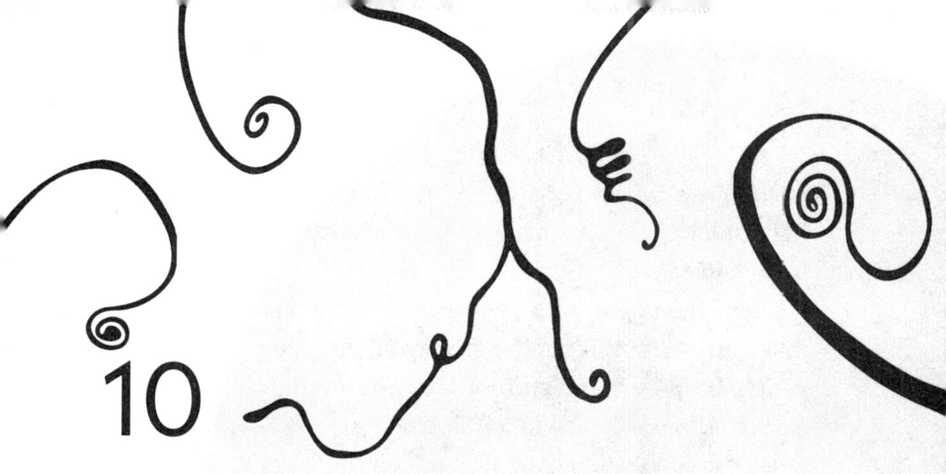

10

Never leave the temple to me, Mother Nova. Never praise my studies nor my discipline. I fail at both and deserve neither. You welcome me as though I am your child, as though I am this temple's child, but I am neither and deserve neither. I aspire for nothing. I strive for no enlightenment. I am a descendant of the void, empty and aimless, and in it, I find my meaning.

Additional materials, originally omitted from the diaries of Vessel Iris collection, Volume Seventeen

There were many proper ways to prepare a body for burial. There were ways to preserve the flesh, to store it, to dress it, and beautify it before handing it off to the mourning family. But now, as Iris studied Riyu's waxen face, they all seemed frivolous. In the second hour, Iris had decided that Riyu would remain here. He would leave her for the vines and the moss to claim, to retake into the larger ecosystem she had been so elated to study. Somehow, this surrender felt appropriate and one Riyu would have approved of.

Iris had now spent four hours muttering mantras over her cooling body in a pathetic attempt to calm himself enough to break the news to the others. Yan's cigarette was still clutched in his hands, and he was picking at the wrapping paper like he would pass the mala between his fingers in meditation. It was hand rolled and that made all the difference. Why, Iris refused to consider.

Behind him, the others whispered among themselves. Iris could make out Ishtan's calming drone and Jesi's sniffles against the gentle dripping of moisture. They were all frightened. They were all lost. If only Iris could admit that he too was lost and frightened, they could all share in their communal grief. But he didn't have the luxury. Neither did Yan, who participated in the conversation around him sparingly, standing off to the side and sipping thin coffee from his thermos. He cast Iris long, anxious glances periodically, and Iris returned them sparingly. Then, just as the conversation began to die down, Yan said, "That's it. *Enough*."

Everyone looked up at him, and Iris pivoted just enough to watch.

"We now have two problems. We have someone actively hunting us"—Yan was still holding on to the theory that the two were separate—"and we have the ship's ecosystem hunting us." He shut the thermos forcefully. "I'm not in the mood to sit here and wallow and wait for either to end me. Earlier today, I found the brain that seems to be the most active. Whoever is watching us is probably there. I say we make our way to the brain and take the ship from them."

"With what?" Jesi muttered lowly. "A busted torch?"

"With a gun," Eli said and drew his pistol. "I'm not supposed to use this unless my clients are in immediate danger, and I suppose this qualifies."

Yan gave him a nod. "Ordan must have also had a gun. Where did you pile all of his clothes?"

Ishtan was already moving. "We left them in the corridor. I'll go get it." He paused. "Maybe Eli should come with me." With a grunt, Eli hopped to his feet and followed close.

If they were moving out, Iris would gather his things as well. He was nearly at the doorway when a small voice called after him. "No one is supposed to go alone."

Iris gave Tev a reassuring smile. "I'll only be gone a few minutes. I'm armed. You don't need to worry." With those words, he slipped out into the corridor and hurried towards the cargo bay. Maybe it was the throbbing in his shoulder or the prolonged silence in his mind, but Iris was growing increasingly irritated by the minute. Irritated with the notion of guns. Irritated with a lack of a sensible plan, and mostly irritated with himself. *You're mad at me, I understand that, but I really need you to be the mature one right now,* he thought at VIFAI as he passed down the corridor. After a few dozen steps, there was a familiar *full* feeling in the periphery of his consciousness.

I'm sorry about Dr. Alo.

Just a few metres of separation from the room, and Iris had already forgotten. He mentally nodded in agreement.

I was watching as you examined her. The initial attack must have been nearly instantaneous. She would have lost consciousness immediately. Very little chance of pain. She didn't— For a moment, Iris was blind with rage, and VIFAI broke off. Its last word echoed through the chasm left in its wake, but unlike every other time, Iris didn't chase it into the black. When VIFAI spoke again after Iris's anger had receded, its electronic voice was fractured and trembling. Don't do that again, please, it said weakly.

Iris was already at the edge of the cargo bay, but the change in his VIFAI's tone startled him still. "I nearly hurt you again, didn't I?"

VIFAI chimed an affirmative.

"I need to watch my anger. I'm sorry." Iris rested his forehead against the cool metal door. "You can shock me in retaliation if you'd like. I deserve it."

If I shock your brain stem wrong, you'll die, VIFAI said softly. You die, I die.

Iris didn't say anything, but VIFAI had access to all his thoughts. He let it make what it wanted from them. Once inside the bay, there was very little time at his disposal. As carefully as he could, given his limited mobility, Iris ran his shaving blade across his head and jawline, cleaning any pesky stubble. He was grateful no one had commented on his dishevelled appearance. Perhaps they had never noticed, what with the death of their colleague and their own impending demise looming ever closer. On the last pass, his hand broke into a tremor, and Iris was forced to rest the blade.

Be patient, VIFAI reminded him.

With the electronic voice, so much like his own, yet distinct enough to never blur the boundary between them, came a subtle relief. It was familiar and safe. A Vessel's AI construct was programmed to match the internal voice of its handler to minimise the cognitive dissonance between organics and inorganics. The minute difference in their timbres created the illusion that this was a friend, a real person who cared for Iris's well-being, a person who understood his intentions and compulsions before he ever uttered them. In his younger days, Iris would frequently forget that it was VIFAI who spoke to him and not a rogue thought of his own. Through the years, their mannerisms diverged, as did their voices, and Iris learned to identify the *other* who was sharing in his mind. He could no longer remember what it had been like to be alone.

In a feeble attempt to escape the spider nest of these convoluted thoughts, Iris shut his eyes forcefully and let himself slip into the darkness of the void always lay just beyond perception. Here, nothing could harm him. Nothing could disturb him. Here was complete silence, a space free of even VIFAI's voice, of his own thoughts. Iris's fingers unconsciously brushed against the cigarette tucked into the sleeve of his undershirt, and he was no longer at peace.

Your engineer is warming up to you.

"Not. My. Engineer," Iris said, emphasizing each word. He shoved his shaving kit back into the duffel bag. He picked up the previously discarded bloodied robes and slid them on, tying the drawstring at the side. After a final look around the cargo bay, he bowed deeply to the pile of bones in the corner.

"I've failed you all," he said, voice monotone. "Please forgive me, and I hope you all find your way back to the Light." Iris was about to walk out when he forcefully turned back on his heels. "No. You don't *need* me. You were returned to the Light when you passed, plain and simple. That's how this works. You were always with the Light, in life and in death; you never left it. I was here for tradition, ritual, not for purpose. The role of the Vessel is to usher souls back to the One Beginning, but you passed hundreds of years ago. There is no family here to soothe. There is no grief to hold. How could you not have moved on already? Haven't you?"

You're sounding a touch frantic.

Iris ignored the remark. "You're gone. You've been gone the moment you took your last breath. Same as Ordan, same as Dr. Alo, same as—" He took a deep inhale. He *was* beginning to sound frantic. "There is nothing I can do for the dead. There is nothing that *needs* to be done," he said with finality. For the dying, yes, there was peace he could bring. For the remaining, he could provide solace. But the dead had already slipped through his fingers. They could no longer speak and ask him difficult questions. Perhaps that's why Iris had preferred them to the living all this time. What good had he been as a Vessel to Ordan and Riyu? They weren't of the faith. They weren't even particularly curious about it. Now, they were dead, and he was useless.

You're not useless. You said some wonderful words.

But those weren't uttered for the dead, were they?

Iris couldn't tell if VIFAI was being sarcastic, but by that point, he was already walking back towards the communal area with his duffel bag in hand. Already moving on towards the next action, never stopping even for a moment to consider the implications of what was happening around him and inside him. Yan's pragmatism had rubbed off on him in just a few short days and a surge of anger roiled through Iris's stomach at the idea. He had been among laypersons too long. Meanwhile, he had been away from *himself* for too long, lost in the frequency and nuance of interpersonal interaction. He had neglected his practice, and his mental state was suffering or it.

When he stomped past of the threshold of the communal room, five pairs of eyes shot up and stared at him. He was a sight to behold. Bloodied and tattered robes drenched with perspiration, eyes glowing with exhaustion and adrenaline. A long gash ran along his left temple. Jesi opened her mouth to say something, but Yan motioned for her to be quiet. He approached Iris slowly, hand half extended, just enough to show he meant no harm. "Vessel," he said softly, "you look like you should take a breather."

At his tone, Iris forcefully straightened his back and set his jaw, shamefully admitting that it was both a very prideful and confrontational gesture. "I assure you, engineer Yan, that I am fine. Better than fine." VIFAI flung up Iris's body metrics, including his heart rate and his blood pressure, half to show off that it could and half to make a point that the engineer was, unfortunately, very much correct.

Yan took another step closer and then another. Before he could take the last step that would place him within a metre of Iris, Iris's hand shot up on instinct, pulsar blade releasing in a single smooth motion. Blue, glowing blades extended to their full length on either sides, and Yan stumbled backwards.

You're doing fantastic.

Jesi and Tev flinched in unison, and Ishtan reached for his new possession—Ordan's pistol. Eli simply gave Iris a disapproving glare. Just as quickly as the blade had extended, Iris deactivated it and returned it to its holster.

Collecting himself from the edge of what would surely be a loud and detailed outburst, Yan said, "Take a breather." It was a gentle order, but an order nonetheless, leaving nothing up to Iris's interpretation. It was a *you need to sit out for an hour before you do something stupid and kill everyone here* order, and Iris couldn't argue with him.

"Maybe you're right." It was all Iris could manage, before he turned away and went to Riyu's body. He sunk to his knees and dropped his forehead to the ground in prayer. He didn't bother slowing his fall, and his knees hit the floor with full force, sending a jolt of pain echoing through his femurs. Jesi and Tev muttered behind him, but he quickly tuned their voices out, focusing only on the blankness of his own mind. He had been neglectful. He had been rash and unpredictable. After nearly two decades at the temple, it was disappointing to falter under such circumstances. And yet.

For all his efforts, Iris's mind raced afire with the thousands of possibilities, each ending in his death. His, Jesi's, Tev's, Ishtan's, Eli's, and Yan's. Death was all around them now. Death was always watching, and it was inevitable. Iris forced a deep inhale. Sticky air filled his lungs. His left shoulder answered with a deep ache.

An ache was just an ache.

An ache was neutral.

Iris focused on the pull of muscle against the sealant. Slowly, his shoulders relaxed, and he transitioned into sitting cross-legged. He breathed in again, deeper this time, the ache growing proportionally.

Like a lighthouse, the throbbing pain guided his mind towards a trained calm. He sensed the hard, metallic floor beneath his thighs, the individual beads of sweat gliding down his spine, the mala that he habitually unwound from his wrist and passed between his fingers.

When he opened his eyes again, Riyu was still there, golden skin ashen, and still very much dead. But now that the veil of fear had lifted, Iris observed her body with detached curiosity. Already the ecosystem had begun to welcome her back. The fungi worked fast—a thin layer of mycelium was quickly growing across Riyu's hands. There was nothing different to it than the decomposition of a fruit. There was nothing especially different about the human body. It too would be reclaimed by the ecosystem; it too had already served its need. Perhaps, in this last translation, it fulfilled some final role. The same vines that had ended Riyu's life so prematurely would be sustained by the nutrients in her body. The same fungi that Riyu was studying would be connecting her to the internal network that spanned the forests within the *Nicaea*. Everything became something else. Nothing was inherently bad. Nothing possessed malicious intent for malice's sake. It all simply strived to survive, to fend off trespassers, to satisfy its curiosity. Competing systems, all of it, nothing more.

With a barely audible chime, VIFAI pulled up Iris's updated biometrics. Heart rate slowing, blood pressure returning to baseline. He was doing better. Nowhere near how good he was doing before he ever set foot on the ship, but good enough, given the circumstances. He let his eyes and mind wander aimlessly across Riyu's form, accepting the tiny jolts of panic that came and went. His mind drifted towards the others, the fear they exuded. He had done poorly as a Vessel; he had done very little to comfort and to protect. Even Yan had done more, and he was arguably the least equipped out of any of them.

Automatically, Iris reached into the sleeve of his robes and found the cigarette there—and everything went to shit. The throbbing in his left shoulder was no longer a calming metronome, but a burning reminder of all his failings and transgressions. Failing to complete the very task he was assigned to. *That* particular reminder still lay in a monstrous pile in the cargo bay, and no matter what beautiful words he said over it, it would remain a mountain of human bones that he had failed to organise. He had failed as a Vessel, as a guide, as a comfort. He had failed as a friend to Riyu. VIFAI flagged his climbing heart rate and blood pressure, but that was hardly needed. *A fraud.* A fraud in white cloth he sullied simply by wearing it. *A charlatan.* Those were Yan's exact words on the first day, weren't they?

Don't fight it, VIFAI finally said, sternly. **Have the thought. Acknowledge it. Accept it for what it is, and move on. Don't engage. Don't wrestle it. You won't win.**

Iris gave nothing but a slight hiss as a response. What thought? There were too many to *wrestle*. First, he had failed at his assignment. He had anticipated spending this time alone, as a retreat, but that had changed. But he had had no other choice. He had needed to modify his assignment, expand it to allow for these new events. He couldn't have anticipated the academics being here. He couldn't make them leave. He had had to adjust.

It was the only thing he could truly control: his own approach to the problem.

The next thought came without warning. He had failed as a guide and as a comfort. Iris winced at the shame radiating through his fingertips. He had, there was no denying that, but he couldn't undo it now. He couldn't alter the flow of time, no matter how much he wished for it. He could only do better with every passing hour. He couldn't revive Ordan or Riyu, and wishing for it to be otherwise would only bring him more grief. He needed to let go and help others do the same.

Have the thought. Allow for it. Accept it for what it is, and move on.

Another thought. This one was not entirely unpleasant, and yet, it was the most dangerous of them all. This kind of thought distracted and clouded the mind, and in their precarious position, it could cost Iris his life. This thought he quickly quashed. There were places Iris wouldn't go even in the comforts of his mind, some thoughts he wouldn't allow himself, even if VIFAI already knew them. At least it was kind enough to keep them to itself. After all their years together, it knew when to back off and when to press, and Iris was too fragile already to withstand any sort of pressing.

In the past, he had done everything *right*. He had recited the right mantras one hundred thousand times and prostrated himself one hundred thousand times before both the rising and setting suns. He had visualised the vastness of the cosmos one hundred thousand times until there was nothing but stardust behind his eyelids. Iris had done all this and then done it twice again. Yet, where these preparations transformed others' minds into fertile soil for the seeds of enlightenment to be planted, his remained barren. Barren and charred as the ground of his home. No meditation could sprout roots, no deeper consciousness could be awakened.

When Iris closed his eyes, he saw no great threads of the Light entangled within every living thing. Only cold darkness. For years, he had smiled and bowed and tended to his meditation every day, and kept the terrible secret buried so deep that even VIFAI would sometimes forget.

A charlatan. Yan had been right all along.

A charlatan who's finally calm enough to move?

Iris asked for his vitals again. Although his heart was still racing, and his blood pressure was elevated, and he was exhausted and hypoglycemic, he conceded that this was as good as things would get. Crumbs of a plan gathered in his mind.

VIFAI already knew the proposal, but Iris would tell it anyway—if nothing else, to distract himself from the futility of it all. *We have to act now, there is no more denying it,* he thought. *I have to act, or worse things will begin to happen.* He slowly rose to his feet, his rest coming to an end.

The academics and Eli would surely resist. Yan too would need convincing. Yan *especially* was important to convince. Iris was learning that having the engineer's approval not only improved his credibility among the others, but also settled his nerves in the most annoying way possible. That last bit brought up a mix of conflicting feelings Iris was quick to cull before VIFAI got its greedy proverbial hands on it and insisted on how inappropriate it was to have those inclinations *now* of all times.

"I believe it would be best if we split up," Iris said and immediately raised his hand in Tev's direction. "I understand that this is exactly how people die in horror media, but this is the best strategy to take. If someone is indeed watching us at all times, they could continue to watch us as we split up, but it would make it difficult to target both groups at the same time. We don't know their numbers. It may just be two. Even if only one group makes it, they might be able to call for help." Iris looked to Yan hopefully, expecting the engineer to side with him.

"And if they can? Attack us both at once, I mean," Yan asked, arms folded across his chest.

"Then what good will staying together do?"

"Statistically speaking," Jesi said, "it does increase our chances of survival. But how will we know where to go? We don't all have AIs crammed into our skulls like you, Vessel."

The slight edge to her voice did not go amiss. Iris gave Jesi a small nod instead. "You're quite right. I believe we can come up with a solution, given all the technology you engineers have brought aboard. And if that fails, I can also sketch the path out on some good old-fashioned paper."

"No need to say things you can't unsay, Vessel," Yan said wryly.

"Why can't you just share the map?" Ishtan asked.

"We have no access to the universal feed," Iris said. "And there isn't a smaller, more private feed that we can use. My AI simply cannot speak to any of the computers the engineers have here."

All three engineers stared at him in impressed silence. Iris had made his point, one he had been attempting to since the beginning. He wasn't all sutras and prayers. Tev chortled, and Jesi gave him a slap on the arm. Yan furrowed his brow. "Don't count us out just yet." He waved for Eli to join them. "Come upstairs with me, there's something I need to pick up. Everyone else, stay exactly where I am leaving you. No one moves."

"First, it's Eli probably killed a guy, now it's Eli will probably *not* kill me. Make up your mind, won't ya?" Still, Eli unholstered his gun and followed.

Yan threw Iris a *look*. "I shared that in confidence."

When Yan and Eli had disappeared up the corridor, Iris turned to Jesi and Tev, hoping to repair what little rapport he had with them. "He's quite protective of you, isn't he?"

Jesi rolled her eyes. "He's *overprotective* because the institute will fine him and then fire him if anything happens to us. They're paying good money for Tev and me to be here. There wasn't a shortage of applicants, I'll tell you that much."

Iris raised his eyebrows.

"There was a contest and everything," Tev said sheepishly. "We won, so we got to come here to explore. It's kind of like an extra credit assignment or something. But that's not *why* he's overprotective, Jes."

"You two are the best of the best then?" Iris asked.

"They're the best from who applied," Ishtan called out, crouching by the kettle, watching it come to a boil.

"There were over two thousand applicants," Jesi bit back.

"And how many withdrew when they found out this was a generation ship with *no* survivors? Eh?"

Tev leaned over to Iris. "Over ninety-seven percent," he admitted. "But it was still hard to get in. Yan's kind of known for doing experimental work with AI systems. His graduate work was on early AI formation, so you can understand why he wanted to be here. It's all theoretical, of course, but if he finds any trace of anything, he'd be a celebrity. Well, like an academic celebrity."

"He's just looking for something to make him feel *alive*," Jesi whispered to Iris conspiratorially. "Two years ago, he purposely went aboard a ship with a malfunctioning AI just so he could talk it down from crashing into a nearby gate. You couldn't shut it down remotely because it was threatening to corrupt its own code, and then who knows what would have happened. Sychi Institute made him get therapy for five months after that and got him to sign a voluntary self-endangerment contract so the institute wouldn't be held liable the next time he decided to do something insane."

"Last year, he just disappeared for two weeks," Tev added. "In the middle of a semester too. I heard a rumour that Vritay Station management flew him out to the outer arm to help it deescalate a hostage situation. You probably didn't hear about it because the AI union kept it hush-hush, but it was *intense*. There were casualties."

Iris had heard about it, in fact, through the Vritay Western Temple correspondence, after they lost two of their Vessels during the hostage situation. Undeterred by the casualties, Bacai had thrown a fit that was very unbecoming of both her age and rank over her not getting selected to go despite the trip being one-week of nonstop gate travel just to get there.

"Stop spreading rumours about your supervisor," Ishtan said and handed Iris a mug filled with something that smelled remarkably similar to coffee and had the colour of rain runoff. He winced apologetically. "Although, they do have a point. There was a rumour going around the Medical Sciences and Augmentations Department that Yan had approached some of them—off the books, of course—about getting an AI construct implanted in himself. I don't understand why he would ever do such a horrid thing. No offense, Vessel."

Iris bowed, taking some offense.

Much offense. Much offense, Ishtan, VIFAI chimed, but Iris could hear the faint notes of laughter powder the words, so he let the remark go.

"He's supposed to be back at Sychi teaching a seminar on Ship Artificial Intelligence Systems and Equity right now," Jesi said flatly, eyeing the door to the corridor. "Between teaching and death, I'm pretty certain Yan prefers death."

Iris's next question was drowned out by stomping boots. He turned around to find Yan and Eli back. Yan was gleefully holding most of the equipment that had been abandoned upstairs. Eli had only the gun in his hand and was sweating profusely.

"Eventful trip?" Ishtan asked.

"Nature does *not* like us stomping around it," Yan grunted and set everything down at Ishtan's feet. "But we managed."

"He didn't let me shoot anything," Eli whined.

"I didn't want to piss it off any more than we needed to."

Eli holstered his gun. "It seemed pretty pissed off as it were."

Iris watched as Yan set up the small screen before him and unfolded the keyboard. He typed in a few lines of source code, the characters glowing against the background. Yan muttered some strange engineering incantation under his breath and then waved for Iris to come closer. He pointed to the floor by the screen. "Sit," he ordered, without looking up. Iris obeyed. "OK. So you all know how if you have a computer, you don't need physical access to it to monitor the output, you can just eavesdrop on its electromagnetic emissions, right?"

"Right," Ishtan said, self-satisfied.

"You mean *phreaking*?" Jesi rolled her eyes. "That's illegal. *Highly* illegal."

"Well, then you better not snitch on me," Yan said. "I know how hard that's going to be for you, Jes." He stretched his fingers out above the keyboard. "OK. I've only done this once before and that was to cheat on an entrance exam, and yes, I got caught, but it was worth it while it lasted. I've also never done this on an embedded AI construct."

"I would greatly appreciate it if someone explained to me what we are doing with my AI," Iris said. "In the simplest terms possible," he added quietly.

Jesi hopped over and squatted beside him. "Vessel, your AI implant is basically a small, tiny computer, with a full-grown AI construct inside. Gross, but whatever. Every time you interact with the AI, the interaction produces a miniscule electromagnetic impulse. It's so small that your brain barely notices it. Sometimes you might get a headache, but that's the most of it. What Yan is going to do is listen in on these impulses and build a picture of what you're seeing. Impulse by impulse."

"A piece of paper and a pen sound much simpler," Iris muttered, but didn't move.

"Dear Mr. Vessel's AI, please, oh, *please*, project a map of the ship into your host's brain so I may steal it," Yan chanted, pushing the small screen so close to Iris that one edge dug into his lower back.

Now he's just being annoying on purpose, VIFAI grumbled.

"No, I'm not," Yan said triumphantly. "It's just my nature."

Shit, VIFAI and Iris thought simultaneously.

"Vessel, you might wish to do some of that breathing meditation," Yan said. "You are growing flustered for no apparent reason. I am only spying on the movements and actions of your AI; I cannot read your thoughts." Yan paused. "Or *can* I?"

Jesi and Tev were both leaning over Yan's shoulders, staring intently at the computer screen. Ishtan and Eli instead focused on Iris's face, which flustered him even more and deepened his already growing flush. Besieged on all sides, Iris had no choice but to follow Yan's suggestion. He closed his eyes, drew in a deep breath, and followed the oxygen as it flowed from his lungs to his heart, to his arteries and veins, until it tingled through his extremities and filled them with vitality. Once he was calm, VIFAI projected the three-dimensional map of the *Nicaea* to the forefront of his mind.

"Thank you, Mr. Vessel's AI," Yan sang. "Now I am going to ask you to trace the entire map, pixel by pixel, if you would. I know it sounds awful, but it's the only sure way to get an accurate rendition. Don't worry about slowing down; my machine over here can handle your speed."

The map ignited with a pulsing light before Iris's eyelids. He focused on his exhale. Out went the used-up air from his lungs, from every last nook of his capillaries, from the veins, and the arteries. He finished his exhale and held it. By the time Iris breathed in again, the flashing had stopped.

"Perfect," Yan exclaimed.

"You're finished?" Iris asked, rubbing his eyes.

I can work much faster when I interface with something electronic, VIFAI explained.

"Yeah, my computer works faster than your brain, Vessel," Yan said.

I'm still not fond of you.

"I've been nothing but a gentleman."

It was disorienting, to witness a conversation that was happening without him, between VIFAI and a stranger, a jarring reminder that the construct was separate from him, able to interact with others without Iris's intervention. Iris extended his thoughts towards the inorganic consciousness, wishing to hear what the AI and the engineer were discussing, but he was met with an impermeable wall. The realisation that his companion's thoughts would forever be protected while his own were there for the taking left him feeling exposed. If his mind was there for the taking, there were no more places left to hide.

When Iris finally looked at the computer screen, he saw an identical map to the one in his mind traced in white against the black of the background.

"I can't believe that worked," Jesi breathed.

"And that's why I'm the second youngest person to ever get tenure in my faculty."

"Yet, not the youngest," Jesi said, sotto voce.

Ignoring her, Yan asked VIFAI, "Can you trace the most direct path from where we are to deck ten and"—Yan traced the air with his index finger, as if following some unseen guide—"deck eight, segment nine, unit six or seven, I can't remember. You'll be able to tell on the map."

The pulsing flashing returned, and Iris lost his vision for a moment while VIFAI traced the path, pixel by pixel. Blinking furiously, Iris said, "I would greatly appreciate it if you would warn me, engineer Yan."

"Here's your warning. Can you mirror the path?"

The flashing continued, and this time, Iris failed to focus on his breathing and blankly watched the cavalcade of lights as they danced and flickered behind his eyelids. Despite their superficial beauty, he still felt used. His mood soured substantially.

"And done," Yan said, clapping his hands together with a satisfying *smack!* "Now if everyone would just hold their applause, I present to you, our own, perfectly translated map of the *Nicaea*."

"That piece of the wall didn't render," Tev said, pointing to the screen. "And I think this is supposed to be a staircase."

Almost perfectly translated, VIFAI said, and Iris shrugged it off, more irritated than he would have liked to admit. **You're jealous.**

How long have you been shutting me out? The irritation and confusion carried through Iris's thoughts.

As long as you have. Or did you think you were the only one allowed secrets?

Iris didn't have an answer. He wanted to think of himself and VIFAI as partners—equals. Yet, it was always him sending the AI to the background, shutting down its speech, and deciding when rest would come. This skewed partnership, which he could no longer call that, had served him well. Iris couldn't say the same for VIFAI. He concluded that silence and space would do them both good, and turned his attention towards the computer screen instead, deeming the conversation over.

The path his AI had outlined was simple enough. They would climb their way to the tenth deck using the staircases on the opposite sides of the corridor that ran along the communal space. Then they would track towards the center of the ship, where most of the electrical pings had been originating from, according to Yan's work. Iris remembered the burning ache in his brain stem when his AI was pinged at the orchard and winced internally. Another such interaction was guaranteed.

"What happens if the path is blocked? Iris's AI can adapt, your map can't," Ishtan asked.

"And we can't just ring each other up," Eli added.

They were both painfully right. Collapsed corridors and blocked-off paths were surely in their way. VIFAI could simply suggest another, more optimal path, but the other group would have to rely on their wits instead.

"We'll still have the map," Yan said, matter-of-factly. "We'll simply follow a different line. The first goal is to stay as far away from the other group so whoever is watching us won't be able to hit both groups at the same time. The second goal is to get to our rendezvous point in two and a half days. We'll have access to water on our way, but I can't predict what the food situation will be like. I don't want us walking around too long." He sounded convinced with his own plan.

If Iris had focused only on the content of Yan's speech, he would have missed the faint tremble in the engineer's voice.

It was *almost* negligible, but having spent many months in isolation retreats during his Vessel training, Iris had become sensitised to the micro-inflections in people's voices. He had learned to study them as musicians study music or architects the curve of an arch. There was a science to it, a mathematical precision. Iris hoped no one else was as particular as he was.

It was decided then that they would spend the final night where they were, eat and drink as much as they could, and set off in ten hours. After Eli started a small fire by the console, they threw in the remaining potatoes and some squash into the embers and waited for them to cook. Ishtan boiled some water he collected from the surrounding moss and made tea. After the haphazardly assembled dinner, Tev and Jesi quickly drifted off to sleep by the glowing flames. A little ways off, Eli was explaining to Ishtan how to properly fire Ordan's pistol. "Respectfully," Yan nodded to Eli and the gun, "I'd feel safer if this went to someone with a faster reaction time."

Iris watched as Yan took the gun into his own hands, twisted it around, and returned it to Eli with a sour face. "I don't like these things. Too loud. Too final." He turned to Ishtan. "You don't mind, do you? I think Tev would do much better with it."

There was a strained silence.

"I can assure you—" Ishtan started, but Yan placed a heavy hand on his shoulder.

"We're well past an honour system. We've known each other for how long? Oh, five years. I know you're responsible, Ishtan. I also know you get nervous, and you get into your own head. You think too much. Better someone who will fire first and think of consequences later."

Iris firmly disagreed, but he remained silent, seated by the crackling fire. This wasn't his place nor his people.

"I can handle a simple gun, Yan."

Yan took the gun into his hands again and shook his head. "I know you like debates, old man, but now isn't the time." Ishtan pursed his lips beneath his beard. "I'll risk your feelings for the safety of the group. You understand."

Begrudgingly, Ishtan nodded. His eyes followed Yan as he walked to Tev and shook the boy awake by his shoulder. Iris couldn't make out his words, but he was sure Eli would be teaching Tev next, how to shoot without thinking first, how not to feel bad if he hit something.

Like Yan, Iris was wary of firearms. He had yet to witness good come from a discharged gun. Guns were a simple tool of death. They created distance, relieving the shooter from the nasty work of feeling their target pass. They were an irresponsible tool, one that Iris wished they could do away with entirely. Aboard spaceships, they were especially dangerous. Each bullet was another chance to puncture the hull and doom them all. Not something of concern aboard the *Nicaea* with her impenetrable walls, but a concern, nonetheless. Guns. As if their situation wasn't dire enough.

Iris was softly muttering his mantras and passing the mala through his fingers when Yan came to rest by his side, a respectable distance between their tired bodies.

"Seems you got your head back on straight, Vessel. Glad to see it."

Iris nodded lightly. He wouldn't spoil the fragile mood with his thoughts on firearms and their mistaken utility. "I've been neglecting my practice, with everything that's happened. It's so simple to maintain it when I'm back at the temple. It's such a serene and fertile environment. Takes much more dedication to do it here."

"I bet," Yan snorted. "What with all the murders and the killer plants."

Iris rewarded the engineer with a polite smile. "I never got to thank you for bringing me food after I was injured. That was very kind of you." It was a difficult topic to breach, but the chance was there, and there was no guarantee they would ever meet again. While Iris still nursed the futile hope they would escape the *Nicaea*, his more rational side leaned towards an outcome where both engineer and monk would meet their demise somewhere along the twisted corridors. No one would come for them. The thought was somewhat distressing.

Yan hummed affirmatively and said nothing.

"I also never thanked you properly for tending to my injuries. That too was very kind of you, engineer Yan. I understand it was a difficult task." That was an even tougher topic to breach, and Iris had almost talked himself out of it minutes prior while staring into the fire and pretending to be engrossed in his mantras.

When he looked over at Yan, puzzled by his silence, he found the engineer asleep, still upright. Even unconscious, Yan's eyebrows were knotted together in worry. Iris caught himself fixating on a single spot along Yan's neck that pulsed lazily to his heartbeat. He felt his own heart matching the rhythm without any effort.

But any thoughts on this matter were dangerous, and Iris stifled them before they got away from him. The distance he cultivated between himself and others was there for a reason, just as much for his well-being as it was for others'. All of this—the warm calm that spread through him when he was in Yan's vicinity, the urge to impress the engineer—all of it was just youthful longings, something that had been long left in the past.

Slowly, Iris reached out and caught the edge of Yan's tattered sleeve between his index and middle fingers. This was as close as he'd let himself get, as close as he'd tread the boundary without overstepping.

"Please," he whispered, careful not to wake Yan, "be careful."

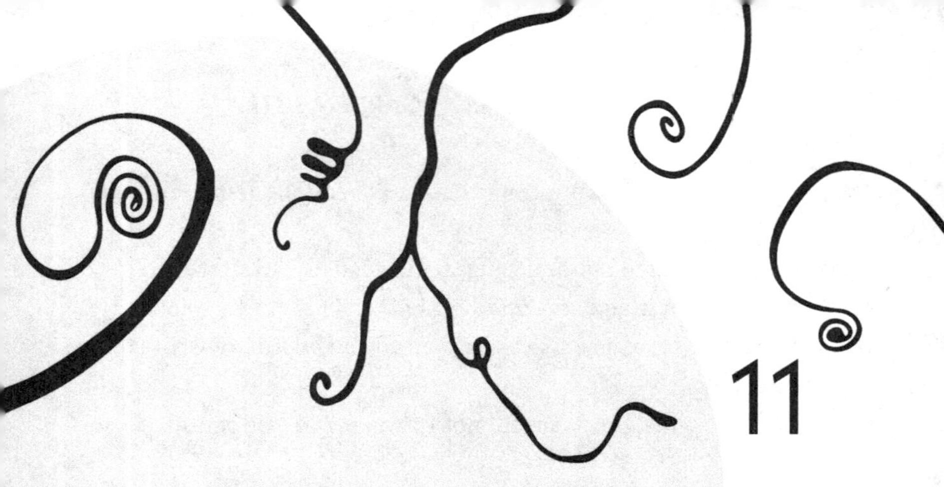

11

If kindness and virtue are written on the face, then mine is the face of a fox, sly and dark. If kindness and virtue are written on the body, then mine is the body tainted by fire, speckled like a snake's belly.
No matter if I kneel, no matter if I praise, no matter if I chant, I cannot change my face. I cannot change my body.
O, Light, do you mean I cannot change myself?
From the unabridged diaries of Vessel Iris, Volume Two

For the sixth hour straight, Iris led the way, weaving their path through a relentless maze of decrepit corridors. Tev and Ishtan followed closely, Tev's hand never leaving the holstered pistol. Here on the tenth deck, larger vegetation was sparse. The floors were lined with the same thick moss as the main deck, and Iris was grateful his naked feet didn't have to step on cold metal. But the familiar shrubbery and vines were nearly nonexistent. Still, a few draped across tall doorways, and Iris brushed them aside as the group kept to the projected map inside his mind. They would stop frequently to rest, drinking water squeezed from the moss. There was enough time for rest. Two days to cover sixty kilometres along smooth, flat ground. In his better days, Iris could walk that in a single day.

It was satisfying to move again, to use his legs for most of the day and welcome the blossoming soreness in his calves. Iris easily slipped into a meditative state as soon as they started and peered out of the blissful emptiness of it only when VIFAI flagged a question that was asked directly of him. He could go on like this for days, teetering on the edge of consciousness, watching life happen around him but not really seeing it. It was one of his favourite pastimes.

Iris blinked hard at a jarring ping. Back to the corridor then, back to the trek towards their inevitable demise. "Pardon me?" It was Tev this time who had asked a question, but VIFAI had missed it the first time, having retreated into rest as well.

From here on, Tev is your responsibility, Yan's warning rang out in Iris's memory, *and if he's hurt, I'm holding you liable.* In the few days they had spent in each other's company, Iris had yet to see Yan this fearful. He really did care for his students, and the thought of delegating this care had torn at him.

"Why weren't we allowed to help you when you were wounded, Vessel?" Tev asked.

"Because you're not supposed to touch Vessels," Ishtan spoke up from the tail end of the three-man procession. "They take vows, and they take those very seriously."

"Yeah," Tev insisted, "but *why*?"

Ishtan didn't have an answer for him, and they both stared at Iris's back until their gazes started to singe his shoulders. "There are several reasons why one shouldn't touch a Vessel," Iris began. Before he continued, he checked on VIFAI, who was resting comfortably once more, half asleep, and unwound the mala from his wrist. Keeping rhythm with his steps, Iris passed the beads through his fingers.

"First, Vessels tend to come in contact with death more often than your average person. People pass for all sorts of reasons, and sometimes, those reasons can be contagious. While Vessels are inoculated against most viruses and even poisons, a layperson isn't. It's always safer to keep your distance." Iris paused, noticing the gap that had opened up behind him as Tev and Ishtan fell back a metre. "Then, of course, there are the vows. These are different for everyone, but I have taken the vow of solitude, to direct all my faculties towards my responsibilities as a Vessel."

"But you've touched Riyu, Jesi, Ishtan, and me. Does that mean you've broken your vow?" Tev asked, still some distance away.

Iris smiled faintly. He had broken his vows, yes, but not one of them was to blame. "All vows have clauses, so it's possible to break a vow only partially. The vow of solitude has four exception clauses: urgency, necessity, familiarity, and livelihood. To break the vow, I would need to touch someone in a way that didn't fall under any of the four. Riyu was in grave danger when I touched her and so that was permitted. The next time I touched her, she had already passed, which means she did not meet the clause of livelihood, so that was permitted."

"You're allowed to save people and move dead bodies then," Ishtan said.

Iris couldn't help but laugh out loud, vigorously enough that VIFAI jolted awake. "That's exactly right, Ishtan."

Discussing your transgressions, are we?

I've kept very close to the boundaries, but never overstepped them.

VIFAI sent a rough vibration through Iris's brain stem and swiftly presented a list of twenty items that, according to its knowledge of Starlit Order scripture, were all the violations Iris had committed since he had arrived on the *Nicaea*. Among the top ones were asking for a cigarette, choosing to explore the ship instead of working, and praying for Yan to hurt himself.

Iris only regretted one of the three. *Is that all?* he chuckled internally and flicked the list away with a micromovement of his eye. Over the past two decades, he had learned to keep certain thoughts so safely hidden that even VIFAI couldn't access *those* transgressions. He was never in the mood to unfurl his longings into the open and discuss them with his companion. Which were healthy attachments? Which were unhealthy? Which were foolish and which were wise? All of them most likely doomed from the start. The one realm where VIFAI still came up short was the exclusively human experience of finding something terrifying and yet alluring, and Iris didn't have the emotional energy to explain. But all these longings were still transgressions if they impaired his ability to perform his work, and Iris would need to ask for forgiveness for committing them when he returned to his temple—*if* he returned.

"It seems kind of lonely," Tev muttered. "The whole solitude bit."

It could be. It *was* for a long while, but at some point, Iris had realised that of all the vows, the vows of silence, the vows of perfect service, the vows of utter asceticism, he could have taken, he had chosen this one because the intimate company and the touch of others were the easiest for him to surrender. He would always fondly recall the fumblings of his youth, the feeble attempts to connect, to satisfy a craving running deeper than simple corporeal pleasures. They never lasted. No matter how dizzyingly wonderful in the moment, those encounters always left him feeling more alone, more detached from everyone else. Like introductory sutras, most of his fleeting companions were easily learned in just a night. Iris never saw the same person twice. The greatest relief always came when, satisfied and giddy, they left him with the rising suns. Even then, he couldn't articulate what it is he wanted, but it wasn't *this*.

Iris had always, in some way, been a solitary creature. The vows provided a convenient label for his habit. "It's possible, Tev, to be solitary and not lonely. Loneliness is experienced when we wish to connect with others and are unable to. We can easily feel lonely in a crowd of people. Solitude simply means being away from others. All within reason, of course."

"And you don't miss it at all?" Ishtan asked, walking beside Tev. Between the two of them, Ishtan seemed far less concerned with the possible diseases and poisons Iris could carry on him. "You're not too young, so you must have been in solitude for quite a while."

"A decade, give or take," Iris said. Starlit was very conscious of such serious vows, and he had not been allowed to take it before his twentieth birthday. "It has certainly created opportunities to divert my faculties towards my vocation. There are so many other ways to connect with others, Ishtan, I hardly notice what I'm missing."

That was a lie. It was a lie he had recited thousands of times to other Vessels, to Mother Nova, and to himself. It was a lie so profound that at times even VIFAI believed it. Iris embodied it, wore it like he did his robes every day. And just like his robes, immaculately, now stained with blood and dirt, so was the veneer of the lie cracking, revealing the profound chasm within. "It is my way of life. It's how I am able to serve others."

"It's very noble," Ishtan said.

A blinding panic froze Iris in his place and spun him around. Simultaneously, Ishtan screamed. Two gunshots rang out, deafening Iris.

He slammed his palms against his ears and cried out in pain. The last he saw of Tev was a flash of his boot sole as he was dragged into the dark.

"Get behind me," Iris shouted at Ishtan, who now held Tev's gun, barrel smoking. Iris's voice barely registered over the ringing in his ears. *Map*, he frantically grasped out with his mind at VIFAI, and it obeyed without hesitation, projecting the map and zooming into the quadrant where they were. Thankfully, there were only a few open doors that Tev could have disappeared through. Iris followed quickly, running across the dew-covered moss right into the oppressive darkness, ears still ringing. He pressed his palm flat against the wall for balance. Below, the slow and rhythmic pulse of the ship rose, familiar to him now like the beating of his own heart. *Do you feel that?*

VIFAI pinged an affirmative.

Every time something happens, there's the pulse. Iris traced the wall as he moved. The pulse rose beneath his fingertips. *The pulse is our watcher's footsteps in the dark.* The faint burning in his brain stem also returned as he ventured deeper down the corridor. Iris quickened his steps, turned left, then right, turned at each bend of the corridor, navigating by feel alone. The corridors here were narrow, and he could easily touch each side with either one of his arms.

The burning in his brain matched the pulse's own crescendo, like it was guiding him towards a terrible truth. Glancing back to check on Ishtan meant slowing down. Tev couldn't afford that extra second or two. Ishtan would have to fend for himself. *Ishtan.* Ishtan, who now had a gun to protect himself with. Ishtan, whose first instinct was to freeze. Another turn. Around the corner. Iris stopped cold, his bare foot squishing into a pool of liquid yet to absorb into the moss. He looked down. Blood. He stepped over it and broke into a full run.

Not a significant amount, VIFAI stated calmly. **That wouldn't be what did him in. Stop—**

Iris dug his heels into the ground, breaking his momentum.

Up, was all VIFAI said.

The rest pieced itself together. A strangled cry fell from Iris's lips the instant he looked up. Something had tried to drag Tev's body through the metal grate into the vent—unsuccessfully. The boy's right arm bent the wrong way at the elbow, and his leg made an angle that Iris's mind couldn't follow. Bloodied bone broke through the tear in his coverall leg. But it was the way that Tev's head hung limp, to the side, the way no head would ever hang on an intact neck, that caused Iris to squeeze his eyes shut in defeat. Too late, always a moment too late. With what little will power remained, Iris slowly opened his eyes and brought them up to meet the boy's lifeless form. He couldn't leave him, not like this, not alone.

Pressing his heels and palms against the walls, Iris slowly climbed towards the ceiling. A thin trickle of blood dripped from Tev's parted lips. Mixed with saliva, it stretched towards the floor in a thin ribbon. Iris rested his forehead against Tev's bloodied coveralls.

He's—

"Don't." Iris brushed the hair from Tev's face. The boy didn't stir. One by one, Iris disentangled each of Tev's mangled limbs until only the vines around his torso held him to the ceiling. Under the weight of the body, they unravelled, and he slowly descended towards the floor. Iris caught him and gently lowered the boy all the way down. Careful to not inflict any more pain on the already battered body, he realigned the arm and the leg. He paused at the neck.

"Should I?" he asked VIFAI, but he already knew the answer. Nonetheless, Iris pressed his ear against Tev's chest. Nothing but silence. Iris sat back on his heels and realigned Tev's neck with a snap. With the corner of his sleeve, he wiped the thin blood around Tev's lips.

When Ishtan placed a hand on his shoulder, Iris screamed in shock and spun around on his knees, pulsar blade in hand. Ishtan's lips moved, but Iris heard nothing. Then Ishtan's eyes fell to where Tev lay, and the archaeologist crumpled to the ground like a paper marionette with its strings cut. The gun fell from his hand and bounced against his knees. Iris watched Ishtan's lips move in a practiced pattern of prayer.

Empty calm claimed his body. His training refused to give way to grief as he watched Ishtan pray, with no hint of sympathy. When the archaeologist fell forward and pressed his head to the floor, Iris wanted to join him, but he remained sitting. Through the thin fabric of his trousers, he felt the muted, but persistent pulse of the ship reverberate through the floor. Whatever had come for Tev was still around, still watching them. His pulsar blade, now safely stored in its holster, was always ready to deploy, and Iris kept his right hand free in case it came to that. But as Ishtan prayed, the pulse died and so did the burning in Iris's brain stem. Only the numbness remained.

More and more of Ishtan's words reached Iris as the ringing in his ears subsided, each syllable coming in desperation, a plea for some hope to come to them in an otherwise hopeless moment.

"We should think about moving—about moving Tev," Iris cut in when Ishtan broke into a prayer Iris had already heard for the third time.

Ishtan wiped his eyes. His face was ruined with tears and pieces of moss stuck to his cheeks and forehead, leaving a spiderweb of indentations. Unselfconsciously distraught, he frowned at Iris as his upper lip trembled. "Vessel, you are probably used to this, but for someone like me—someone who is just a scholar—" Ishtan sobbed and wrapped his arms around himself.

Iris gave him a gentle bow. "You may take little comfort in this, Ishtan, but I can tell that the fatal blow was delivered first," Iris lied. "Tev didn't suffer. He passed in an instant." He punctuated the last word with another light bow. He didn't know that for sure. In fact, Tev's neck was probably broken when the vines had tried to shove him through the vent. His arms and legs probably snapped first in the struggle. Over and over, the bone had splintered as Tev was overwhelmed by the pain, too weak to cry out. He had not passed instantly. He had not gone peacefully. Iris would never tell Ishtan so; he would never tell Jesi that, nor Yan.

Yan.

Iris's heart lurched at the name. *He'll kill me and he'd be right to do so.* Instinctively, he bowed so deeply that his forehead touched Tev's curling fingers. From this angle, he could see Tev's side, right below the fourth rib, where a gunshot wound had made its way into his lungs. Maybe it wasn't the broken neck. Maybe Tev was gone the moment Ishtan had discharged his gun. Without proper aim. Without hesitation. The realisation brought little relief to Iris.

"We should move Tev somewhere where it would be easier to work. Then I will prepare his body the best I can and say some words. I don't think Tev was Starlit, but he would have appreciated the sentiment." Iris stood up, smoothing out his robes. He had had them on for nearly a week and they had been soiled beyond salvage. The hems of his trousers were frayed around his ankles. Scratched and bruised skin peered from beneath the torn fabric. "I will prepare the body, Ishtan, and then we will take Tev with us. Jesi and Yan would want him to return, even if . . ." There was a finality to that. He would deliver Tev to Yan and accept Yan's anger.

Iris had been around many grieving people, but never around those who mourned a loved one Iris was entrusted with protecting. This was too personal, almost intimate. Any degree of separation had been discarded long before, and now the boy was too familiar to Iris: the multitude of his expressions, the tells in his demeanour when he was frightened. Iris wouldn't ask for Yan's forgiveness. Whatever came for him, he would accept willingly. Tev had been entrusted to Yan as a student. Tev had been entrusted to Iris. They had both failed, each in their distinct way, and they would both suffer for it.

When they returned to the main corridor, they set Tev down on the floor and rested. Ishtan's hands shook badly, and Iris convinced him that the gun was best left holstered. He would have taken the thing away, but there were rules about Vessels handling firearms, and Iris couldn't bear breaking yet another rule. He looked at Ishtan's ashen face, his trembling lips behind the grey beard. Ishtan had fired out of panic. He didn't have the luxury of aiming. Iris made the deliberate choice to believe this. He couldn't bear the alternative.

There were no blankets here, no cloth to wrap Tev's body in. Iris reached for the side knot of his robes. It was only appropriate. "Ishtan, I think it would be best if you laid down," Iris said as he slid his robes from his shoulders. "I will manage here on my own. Please, go off a little ways where I can still see you and try to get some sleep."

Ishtan obediently moved. He staggered off in a daze without uttering a word and dropped to the ground in a heap. This wasn't the demeanour of a man who could kill. Before Iris even began his work, Ishtan's soft snores reached him. *It doesn't feel right to do this.* Iris detached his pulsar blade from its holster.

You still have nearly two days to go and, pardon my directness, without the fungi doing all the work, he will start to rot.

Parts of Tev would begin to actively rot, that was certain. One way Iris could slow down the body's decay was to remove those parts altogether and drain the body of blood. It was not a simple or appealing task. Iris was relieved Ishtan would be asleep for most of it.

"Forgive me, Tev," Iris said. "I am about to desecrate your body in a futile attempt to give your friends some closure. I'm sorry. I don't know what else to do. All I know is how to prepare the dead. I'm *so* sorry, Tev." Iris bowed low until his forehead touched Tev's cold hand. "You've found your way back to the One Beginning, Tev. You're home, you never left it, and in your last moments—" Iris didn't finish. In his last moments, Tev had been frightened and in pain, unless of course, Ishtan's bullet had killed him before any more violence befell Tev. *Accidental bullet*, Iris reminded himself. He shook his head against Tev's hand. What more could he do? What worth was there to anything he would do here on out?

The meditative state, the simple detachment, was so appealing. To disengage from the sight of the dead boy before him, gone because he had failed. The dark was beckoning him, promising relief, and he would accept. *Don't panic, Vessel.* Iris sat up, eyes still closed. Yan's voice. Its characteristically demanding edge cut through the despair. *Stop fucking around, Vessel, and be useful.*

Iris took a slow breath. He would be useful, he wouldn't panic, lest the memories of Yan accost him further. Only he could do what needed to be done, only he could prepare Tev for the journey, and he *needed* to. Iris took another breath and triggered the pulsar blade at two inches in length. It would be an arduous task, but no one could do it but him. Iris went to work.

First, he sliced through Tev's clothing. It was faster than undoing the buttons along the jumpsuit. Studying the naked skin up close reaffirmed Iris's suspicions that Tev had died instantly. Ishtan's bullet had passed cleanly through Tev's lung and heart. A modest relief, one Iris would never share with anyone but himself. Now came the hard part. *Please, project an anatomical schematic for me,* Iris asked VIFAI, *and mark down incision sites I'd need for all the major organs.* VIFAI complied.

Iris made the first incision just below the rib cage. Tev's dark skin gave way to the intrusion, spreading as Iris's slender fingers pulled the bleeding edges apart. He made quick work of finding the spleen and removing it. It sat on the floor, organ against moss, in a small puddle of blood. Harmless, soft, vulnerable. At their cores, people were all soft and vulnerable, no matter how many layers of armour they erected, no matter how hard they fought against their inevitable demise, how admirable the resistance. They were all nothing but flesh.

Working his hand farther inside, Iris pushed the intestines away to grab hold of and detach the liver. The organ lay heavy in his open palms, nearly black with iron. Bleak light from shattered panels shimmered across the slick surface, playing along Iris's blood-stained fingers. He placed Tev's liver beside his spleen. Slowly, over the course of an hour, each one of Tev's organs joined the ones already laid out on the floor. The fine trembling in Iris's hands grew with each organ that passed them. It wasn't his first time preparing a body, and yet . . . *Please forgive me for the suffering I impart on this body. Please forgive me for the callousness of my actions,* Iris recited in his mind.

Please, please, please. He'd done this before; what made it different this time?

It hurts because he was a friend. Yan's voice came to him again, summoned from the part of Iris's mind he usually kept under close watch. In the brief time he knew the boy, yes, Tev was a friend. Tev hadn't grimaced when he found out Iris had a construct riding shotgun in his brain. Tev didn't shy away from him like others often did. Iris sat up and hung his head on his chest. His bloody hands rested by his sides, fingers dripping.

"He's just a kid," Iris whispered. Tev had decided to work with Yan so he could improve communication between AI systems and humans. Tev had wanted to help. "He's just a *kid* and I'm—what am I doing?"

Only thing that's left to do.

"How could this happen? How could I have allowed it to happen?"

As it always happens. The Light does not love.

The Light did not love. The Light did not care. That was a universal truth, one that the Starlit would never reveal, one that Iris had arrived at by himself. The Light had no children it watched over, no one's well-being it cared for. The Light was there to birth them all into being and to welcome them back after their passing, and everything that happened in between was up to chance. It was up to *them*. No grander will to follow. No ultimate being to place blames and hopes upon. Only people, doing the necessary thing.

His hands trembling, Iris made another incision just below the ribs and removed Tev's heart and lungs. If this were a proper burial, he would fill the cavities with a synthetic foam to keep the shape, but this wasn't a proper burial, and this wasn't his temple. When Tev's body had been relieved of all its organs, Iris placed them all neatly inside the jumpsuit and walked the makeshift satchel to an adjoining corridor, where he left it for the crabs and the mice to feast on. He took little solace in knowing that at least a part of Tev would return to the ecosystem; others would surely fail to see it that way. When he returned, Iris was met with Ishtan's wide eyes staring at him only for a moment before the archaeologist shut them again and wrapped himself into a tighter ball on the ground. The moss around the archaeologist had been disturbed.

Iris wanted to reassure Ishtan that he knew what he was doing and was doing it with nothing but respect for Tev. But that explanation would need many words, and Iris had none left. Many words brought many troubles with them. They formed cracks in the meaning through which misinterpretations could flow, flow to favour anyone who drank them.

Iris had discovered this in the sutras he had spent the better part of two decades reciting, learning, embedding them so deep within his mind that they were now moulded to it. Parts of the words weaved through his bone marrow; others nestled between the fibres of his muscle. How many pages were now written into his fingertips? How many glyphs were burned into the blacks of his eyes? What meaning *he* had taken from the sutras had been wrong, he was certain, for it brought him no comfort, no relief. Mother Nova had instructed him to read, to study, and so read and study he had, while doing little else, until he had read and studied it all. And none of it had made a difference. The damned meaning that had seeped from the spaces in the words, the damned meaning that Iris had drunk feverishly from the day he was given his first scripture was this: *None of it mattered.*

None of it mattered. He couldn't deny that awful truth any longer.

Iris knelt beside Tev's body and cut along the seams of his robes to make a large rectangle. As gently as he could, he moved Tev's body on top of the fabric. His eyes ran across the singed bullet wound in Tev's side. *None of it mattered.* Iris made the first fold across Tev's chest. The rites, the tradition, the careful choreography followed by every Vessel, every Beacon to ever leave a temple, all of it was fluff. All of it was a distraction from the inevitable. The second fold draped across Tev's legs, and Iris tightened the fabric around them. And now, the inevitable was before him. He had little to give to the living. He had little to give at all save for some words, and what good were words? What good would his words do for Yan?

Iris made the third fold.

You shouldn't blame yourself.

Whom should I blame then? Iris snapped back. He tightened the fabric roughly, his fingers staining red what little white was left. The copper of old blood left ugly smears against the heavy white silk.

Why must there be blame? VIFAI asked softly.

"Because blame points the anger. It gives it a target," Iris hissed. His fingers seized as he tied the final knot on Tev's chest. Clenched in a fist, he pressed them against the floor to silence the fatigued muscles.

Why must there be anger?

"Because there's nothing else!" Iris shouted. Ishtan shot upright from his shallow sleep, and his hand was at once on the gun. He glared at Iris, eyes wide in terror.

"I thought we'd been attacked again," he muttered and retreated into himself with a shudder.

Iris bowed. "Forgive me, I've gotten myself worked up. Forgive me, Ishtan." Iris bowed again, this time deeper. "I will stay silent. Please get some more rest."

But Ishtan was already crawling to his feet. With a groan, he stood upright and staggered over. "When I saw what you had done to him"—the archaeologist gestured to Tev—"I didn't have any words for you. I thought you'd desecrated the body, but now I see there was reason to that. It will be simpler to transport him this way, won't it?"

Iris gave him a single nod.

"What have you done with the . . . ?" Ishtan couldn't bring himself to say the words.

Omissions. Iris knew those well. Silences that filled in for the words he was too weak to say out loud. "I've left it all out for the crabs and whatever else lives in these corridors. It will be appreciated. There's still much good he can do, even after his passing."

Ishtan thought for a while, tugging at his beard. "And that's important, doing good after you've passed?"

Iris could do nothing more than shrug. He held his hands before him, dry blood lodged beneath his nails, more blood caked on his palms and knuckles. "Nothing is important, really, Ishtan. You have to understand that. Nothing has a given purpose. In the scale of the Light, it is simply that one thing becomes another. Tev's heart will become a crab's meal, and the crab may become our meal, and then when we pass, we will become something else's meal. We will become energy, passed from one thing to another in an endless cycle of the One Beginning. It all becomes something else. Always." Finished, Iris sank his face in his hands.

"Oddly, I find that comforting," Ishtan muttered and crouched beside Iris. "When I pass, there will be no big funeral rites for me. No family will grieve me, few friends will come. I've led a solitary life that I have very few regrets about. But knowing I will be of some use, even when I am no longer me, is of some comfort. Thank you, Iris."

Face still in his hands, Iris forced out a small, weeping chuckle. “You will *always* be. That’s the whole point, Ishtan. You will be as you are, the Light itself, watching itself play a different part in each different life.”

“Well,” Ishtan said, “I suppose that’s all right too.”

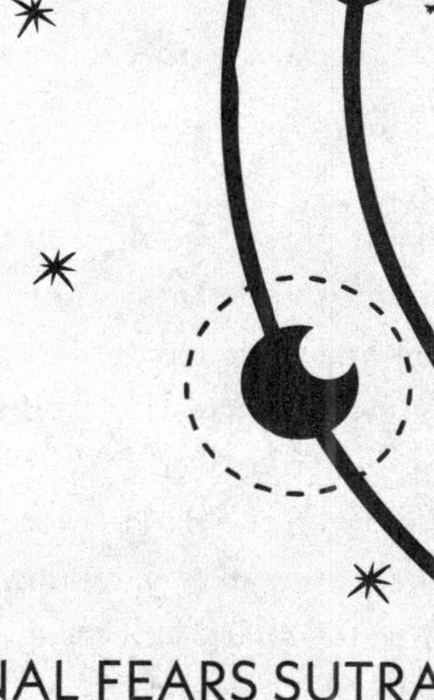

RETREAT

THE THREE ORIGINAL FEARS SUTRA

as spoken by the one Mother Nova of the Northern Temple of the Starlit Order at the ordination of the Vessels

Stop me if you know this one. [Mother Nova laughs.]

First, there was only the Infinite Light, and it was an ocean of pure awareness. Yet, there was little for it to be aware *of*, for only *it* existed. It stretched from one end of the cosmos to the other for as long as eternity itself. And it flowed from one end of the cosmos to the other, for there was no obstacle in its path and no riverbed to steer it. And the longer the Infinite Light flowed, the longer the Infinite Light looked upon itself as itself, the more afraid it became. For if there was only *it* and nothing else, *it* was everything. And the Infinite Light grew frightened that if *it* stopped existing, then *everything* would stop existing.

That became the First Original Fear, the fear of being.

But the Infinite Light *is* everything, and so it cannot stop being. And we, as the mere Vessels of the Infinite Light, are it too, so we cannot stop being either. For the Infinite Light is the very thing that started everything, and hence it cannot end.

As time passed, the Infinite Light grew lonely, for only *it* existed. After billions of years, flowing from one end of the cosmos to the other, it grew tired of only having awareness of itself. It created galaxies and stars, and watched as they moved along one another and watched as they acted upon one another. But even that grew too boring for the Infinite Light, and so it created more and animated more.

And it created the sand foxes, and the bees, and the ocean fish, and the river crabs—you know which ones I mean, the ones with the needle-sharp pincers. [Mother Nova laughs.] And it created you and it created me, and watched us move along one another and watched us act upon one another, and in that the Infinite Light found great entertainment.

But watching through our eyes confused the Infinite Light, and it grew frightened whenever one of its creations passed. For while the Infinite Light persisted, our physical forms could not. For while the Infinite Light was the very cosmos, our bodies were not. And even as the Infinite Light welcomed itself back into itself, the Second Original Fear came to be, the fear of *not* being.

Of course, we know that there can be no fear of not being, for everything that *is* had always been the Infinite Light and doesn't stop being the Infinite Light when it passes.

The longer the Infinite Light watched itself through the eyes of every living thing, the longer it played the billions and billions of different roles it had created, the more forgetful it got. So forgetful, that the Infinite Light forgot that it was *it* in every living thing. And when the Infinite Light gazed upon another in a different dress, as I gaze upon you, it no longer saw itself. And thus, it grew ever more frightened, and so the Third Original Fear came to be, the fear of the Other.

But we know now that there is no Other. There is only the Light, animating everything that you see, playing a game with itself. Take today and every other day, as you have been since you began your studies, to reflect on that. Take the time to look at one another and remember that you are more the same than you ever will be different. For a while, the masks you wear may be of a different colour and of a different design, but the actor behind the mask is one and the same.

I am as much the Infinite Light as you are, and you are, and you. I am as much the Infinite Light as the rabbits in the garden and the peaches on the trees. Remember that when you grow frustrated with one another or when you grow frustrated with a stranger. Remember that when you wish to respond with violence. We are all the Light, playing a game. Don't harm another, for you will be harming a part of yourself. Don't mock another, for you will be mocking yourself. And don't think yourself above other things, for those other things are you as well, and there is nothing to be *above*.

[End of recording]

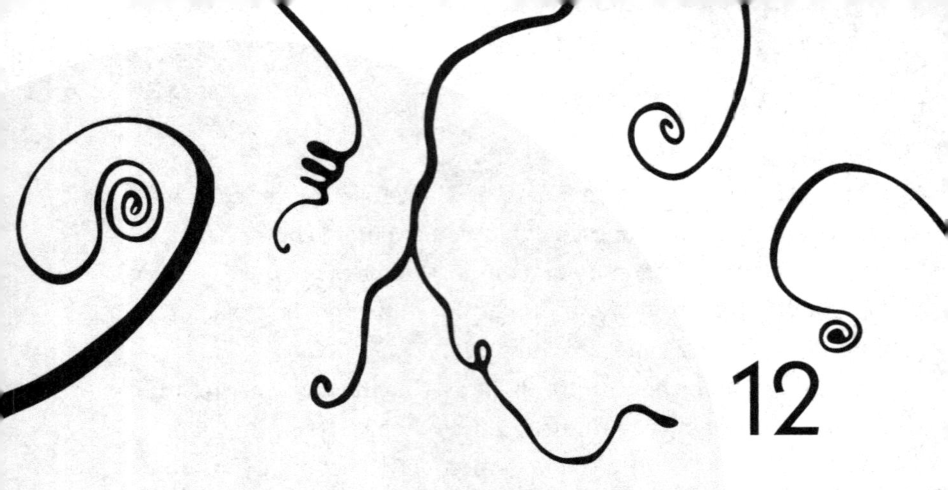

12

No eyes to see with and no mouth to speak with. No body at all to hold any one of us. Yet, the Light is alive, and it will always be alive, for it is life itself. For it is the start and the end, and all life finds its way back to it. For it is the One Beginning and holds all ends within it.

Excerpt from the Three Original Fears Sutra

The missing organs had relieved Tev's body of some of its weight, but Iris still required frequent rest, his body starving and weakened, his mind faring no better. The gnawing in his stomach had long stopped, replaced now by a cool hollowness that radiated outwards from the centre. Ishtan walked close by, the gun unholstered. Iris didn't ask him to put it away. The archaeologist also insisted he carry Iris's duffel bag, and Iris in turn had insisted they leave it behind. But Ishtan had won. Reluctantly, before they started off again, Iris shaved as best he could, returned the kit to the duffel bag, and handed it off to the archaeologist.

"Do you always recite sutras when you walk?" Ishtan asked when they'd been moving for nearly two hours.

Why didn't you say anything? Iris asked VIFAI, irate, but all it did was shrug electronically in response. Iris didn't have a straight answer for Ishtan. It was much simpler back at the temple, where he could walk and recite in peace along the mountain trails for days without ever seeing anyone. It was a habit, like many others, that made more sense in the routine of temple life. "It's a nervous tick, I suppose," he said at last. "I can stop if it's making you uncomfortable."

"No, no, not at all." Ishtan picked up his pace and came up on Iris's left side. "It sounded like you were going over a piece of the Cosmic Jewel Sutra."

There is hunger of the stomach. There is hunger of the mind.
There is hunger of the bone and the soul. Feed the soul, and
all other hungers will be sated.

It very well could have been; Iris couldn't remember. He was not in any mood to discuss the workings of his mind, nor the intricacies of the Cosmic Jewel Sutra, and was quick to nod along and dismiss Ishtan's further inquiries. There was, however, an entirely different topic that needed broaching. Setting Tev down for the third time since they had started their trek, Iris stretched out his back.

"Ishtan, how much is the *Nicaea* worth to you?"

Ishtan tugged at his beard. "Depends on how you conceptualise worth. She is a prized relic, yes, but in monetary amounts, I'd say the *Nicaea* is priceless."

"But to *you*?"

Ishtan chuckled. "She *is* a discovery that makes a career, if that's what you're getting at. Not just my career. *Anyone's.* Yan and his students—" Ishtan glanced at Tev's body and sighed. "Yan and Jesi would benefit from the discovery, if they ever make it out alive. I would as well. The academic world is cutthroat, and each and every one of us is thinking of our careers. Not anymore, given the . . ." He gestured around himself.

Noticing Iris glance down at the pistol, Ishtan shook his head. "Yan's paranoia getting to you, Vessel?"

Iris straightened his back and faced Ishtan directly, no sound but the dripping water around them. It would be awfully simple to shoot straight, to end Iris's life with a single shot. Instead, Ishtan holstered the gun. "I hate these things," he admitted. "I thought . . . thought I'd have better aim. I didn't really aim. I wanted to save the boy, I really did. I've done so little to be helpful."

"You missed. There is no shame in that," Iris said. There was no way to say Ishtan's bullet had been merciful and had ended Tev's suffering before it began. So, Iris said nothing. He knelt and gently picked up Tev's body, swinging it over his shoulder. There was still a long way to go. Many hours to spend in each others' company. He didn't want to hurt Ishtan any more than he had to.

After half an hour of laden silence, Ishtan asked, "Don't you find it ironic, Iris, that those who were in the biggest hurry to get off First Earth were the last ones to get to any meaningful destination?"

Iris didn't. It was tragic at best. He stayed silent.

"Those who stayed behind and worked on the gate tech got to see other worlds in their lifetimes. What a strange development."

Strange was one way to put it. Iris tried to readjust Tev's body over his shoulder and threw out his right arm against the wall for balance. A faint pulse reached his fingertips.

Iris.

LARGER NETWORK—IT'S ALL PART OF A LARGER—LARGER NETWORK. Riyu's voice, drenched in metal, spilled from overhead speakers. Ishtan cried out and drew his gun, pointing it at the ceiling. In his fright, Iris dropped Tev's body and fell to his knees.

NETWORK—LIKE NEURONS IN OUR BRAINS—NETWORK—NETWORK—NET—Riyu's voice continued.

I got a ping and then nothing, VIFAI said quickly.

"What the hell is that?" Ishtan shouted against the screeching of the voice. "Where the hell is that coming from? How does it sound like Riyu?"

MOTHER TREE—KNOWS ALL HER SAPLINGS—KNOWS ALL HER SAPLINGS BY NAME.

They had been standing over Ordan's body when Riyu said that, Iris remembered frantically. Why those words? Why those words out of order? If someone was trying to demonstrate that they had recorded everything the group had said, why were they only playing Riyu's part of the conversation? And where were his own responses? Why didn't they choose to play a recording of them all, in the same space?

COMPANION PLANTING IS THE SURE WAY—THE SURE WAY—THE SURE WAY—LONG-TERM SPACE TRAVEL—SURVIVAL—COMPANION PLANTING—SURVIVAL.

Ishtan broke into a prayer.

Still glued to the ground, Iris called out, "What is it?"

Mid-prayer, Ishtan froze and looked over at the monk, his dark brown skin ashen with fear. "She gave a lecture on companion planting a week before we left for the *Nicaea*. I went to get her for a meeting, and she was finishing up. How did they get this? How did they get this piece of her lecture? There was no recording."

"Are you certain no one recorded it anyway? Are you sure she didn't speak about this aboard the ship?" Iris asked and flinched at a sudden screech from the speakers. "Are you sure that was the last time she spoke about the subject?"

HELLO—HELLO, DR. ORA—DR. ORA—DR. ORA—EVERYONE.

Ishtan buried his hands in his face and trembled. Riyu had never called Ishtan by his professional title, not in Iris's presence. She hadn't at all since they had boarded the *Nicaea*. Was this display of surveillance for them only, or was the other group also getting an earful?

"They know who I am." With a shaky hand, Ishtan pointed the gun towards the ceiling once more and fired. The gunshot threw his hand back, the gun falling from his bruised fingers to the floor. On accident, he struck a speaker, and the metallic screech masquerading as Riyu's voice died. In the deafening silence, broken only by Ishtan's soft mutterings, the archaeologist rocked back and forth, arms tightly wound around his chest.

Any ideas at all are most welcome. Iris did his best to conceal his own simmering panic with sarcasm. He was so close to understanding the larger picture, but his mind rebelled against the harrowing conclusion.

There is a very small chance that whoever is watching us managed to connect to the universal feed and retrieved a recording of Dr. Alo's lecture. Even if Ishtan claims there isn't one. Iris swore he heard VIFAI sigh. But that is unlikely. Astronomically unlikely. Only an AI would be able to complete the task this quickly, not a person whose only access is the antique tech on this ship. And I've been trying to get to the feed all this time. There hasn't been even a second-long window.

And if there's no recording in existence? Iris was already suspecting what VIFAI was suggesting, but the idea was just as preposterous as it was sacrilegious.

They got those segments from Dr. Alo herself.

Iris pressed his back firmly against the cold wall of the corridor. Tev's body lay just where he had dropped it, and it was starting to smell. Ishtan's prayers reached Iris in a haze, a distant reminder that he couldn't stop just yet, no matter how much he wanted to. *How would they do that?* Iris asked. VIFAI didn't explain.

The understanding was creeping towards him so quickly, he could no longer ignore it.

"Ishtan," Iris called out softly. The muttering stopped. "Ishtan, it isn't safe here. We need to move as quickly as we can and meet the others. Who knows what's happened to them? I suggest we go. We go in silence, and we go softly. I have a feeling that whoever is watching us doesn't want us speaking ill of the *Nicaea*, doesn't want us damaging her either."

Panicked, red-rimmed eyes looked up at Iris from the other side of the corridor.

"Can you do that Ishtan? Follow close and quietly?"

The archaeologist gave him a barely noticeable nod. His nose ran in a pathetic stream, and he wiped it away with the sleeve of his shirt. With a jerky movement, Ishtan grabbed the gun, but he didn't holster it. "How far away is our meeting spot?"

Iris consulted the map. "Another thirty kilometres. We can push though."

Without another word, Iris got to his feet and placed Tev on his shoulder. The smell of decay flooded his senses, but he reminded himself there was nothing inherently different between the scent of death and scent of flowers, and began to walk. The reminder was of little help. Ishtan followed closely, stifling a gag every so often when the smell wafted towards him.

How do you think they got the words from Dr. Alo? Now, more than ever, Iris was grateful for having an internal companion to speak with.

Dr. Alo could have had personal devices with her that could be hacked. That was a likely scenario, but why would Riyu carry a recording of a lecture with her? Why play that recording at all?

Any other ideas? Iris pressed, unconvinced. Something about the voice, grating and fractured, reminded him of a younger Iris, learning to speak the Starlit's language for the first time. In his first months at the temple, all he could do was repeat words despite understanding when others spoke to him. Sometimes, when he got lucky, he could string some words he'd heard before into a semicoherent sentence, and he'd get an extra slice of fruit. There was no syntax, there was no grammar, there was just—

They don't speak the language, Iris blurted out. *They know some of the words, but whoever is watching us doesn't speak the language. They're trying to communicate. They're trying to tell us something.* The voice had recited Riyu's words about the mycelium, about how it could act as a neural network for the ship. Then it had switched to Riyu's lecture from before and named Ishtan. Whoever was speaking with Riyu's voice wanted to demonstrate they had access to the words she'd spoken before boarding the *Nicaea*. They also wanted Iris and Ishtan to know that the ship was interconnected, that it carried information the way neurons did.

That's absolutely insane. VIFAI picked up on the tail end of Iris's thought. It's insane, and you are insane for thinking it. You need to rest and drink some water. What you are proposing is impossible.

Iris roughly shook his head to get rid of the AI's voice. *Why not?* he pressed. *Why wouldn't our memories flow along the networks just as our body's energies do?*

You're out of your mind. VIFAI gave Iris a little shock.

Iris didn't fight it.

After hours of walking, they were finally only five kilometres from the agreed-upon meeting spot. Both Ishtan and Iris swayed on their feet, nearly delirious from exhaustion. Iris's shoulder had grown numb from the weight of Tev's body, and he had all but forgotten about the smell.

He stopped at last. "I have an idea," he told Ishtan and pressed his index finger against his lips. He placed Tev down and unravelled the stained fabric from the body. When Tev's bruised skin came into view, and the odour of his decaying flesh intensified, Ishtan spun around and ran three steps before he doubled over and vomited on the ground. It was nothing but water. Iris focused on the task at hand. He had been around worse.

His third assignment as a Vessel had had him attending a shuttle that had lost propulsion in transit. While the occupants soon died by their own hands, the air supply did not. Two weeks of regular decomposition took its toll on the bodies. Compared to that, well, nothing would compare to *that*.

When Tev's body was fully unwrapped, Iris lay it along the moss and draped what was once his robes over the body. "I have a theory," he told Ishtan, who was still dry heaving two metres away. "I have to test it, but I'd rather not say anything until I know for sure. Please, don't say anything to Yan. Please only tell him that we couldn't bring Tev with us. I must know for sure first. I don't want to hurt him any more than he needs to be hurt."

Ishtan gave him a weak *OK*. Leaning heavily against Iris, the two covered the last five kilometres in nearly two hours. Iris was starting to stumble over his feet when a familiar voice reached his ears.

"Another hour, that's it." It was Jesi, her voice still distant and muffled by the ever-present moss. "If they're not here, I'm going to go look, whether you like it or not."

"Like hell you are," Yan said, and Iris nearly lost his footing. He wanted to call out to the engineer, but his throat was dry with sorrow, and no words found him.

"Over here," Ishtan cried weakly, and the voices died. "It's us. *Over here*." They were met with a stomping of boots, and soon, under the glow of a small makeshift torch, Yan and Jesi, both dirty and bloodied, were smiling widely at them. Eli followed close behind, gun in hand.

"You're late," Yan said, looking straight at Iris. He was about to say something else when his smile faded away. He looked around with a growing sense of panic. "Where's Tev?"

Neither Iris nor Ishtan said anything. Taking two steps forwards, Ishtan joined Jesi and Eli on their side, leaving Iris alone, now leaning on the corridor wall for support.

"Where is Tev?" Yan repeated.

With what little resolve Iris had left, he found Yan's eyes and held his gaze. "Two days ago, we were ambushed. I don't know where the vines came from or why they targeted Tev, but before I knew it—"

Yan closed the distance between them in a single step. "Where is he?" His voice was dangerously low.

"I pursued." Iris held his ground, even as Yan towered over him, his voice as neutral as possible. "When I finally caught up to the vines, Tev was dead." He forced himself to look straight ahead, to meet Yan's gaze and hold it. "The initial—the initial blow broke his neck. He died instantly. I'm sorry." It was an outright lie, but no one would be better off if the fault fell on Ishtan.

Jesi gasped. Iris didn't see her, his field of view blocked off by Yan's face, but he could hear her start to cry.

"Eli, get Jesi away from here," Yan said. "Where the fuck is the body?"

Iris didn't want to lie, but if he told the truth, Yan's fury would have no bounds.

"Iris carried him for some time." It was Ishtan's voice that broke through the silence. "But we had to leave him. Not too far from here."

"Eli, get Jesi *and* Ishtan away from here," Yan hissed. Miraculously, this time Eli obeyed. When the sound of their boots was out of earshot, Yan allowed himself to feel.

Grief always sounded the same. Grief transcended sex and gender, age and occupation, and it always began with a cry. A cry that strangled itself up in the throat, a muffled cry sometimes, frothed from the lungs by shock and sharp pain. A piercing cry, one that broke through concrete and steel, one that could burst an eardrum. Grief was identical. It mixed shaking hands and soft pleadings. It mixed prayers from faiths no one ever practiced. It was as universal as the blood that ran along arteries, as universal as a last breath, as a newborn's cry. Yet, it was also mere kindling for the rage that erupted soon after. And by the shaking of Yan's shoulders and the way his knuckles paled to white, Iris knew that rage was close, so close to spilling over. A storm was coming, and Iris was the lightning rod. Nothing would be left in its wake.

Yan threw his first punch with the skill of a man who had never been in a fight and was more concerned with impact than grace. Iris dodged it on instinct, but what Yan lacked in finesse, he made up for in speed. Before Iris could regain his footing, Yan's fist was clenched around the front of Iris's undershirt. With his next step, Yan slammed Iris's back into the wall of the corridor. Iris's head bounced against the wall, hard enough for him to see stars and then nothing at all as the shock spread through his neck and down his spine. Stunned and disoriented, he slid to the floor in a heap. He braced for more violence when someone's footsteps broke through the fog and the ringing in his ears. Someone else entirely screamed *stop*. Iris couldn't tell who, but no further pain came. For a moment, he lost consciousness because by the time his vision returned, Yan was crouching over him. He took hold of Iris's undershirt again and yanked him away from the wall.

"You listen to me." Yan was so close now that Iris felt the heat of his breath against his skin. "You will *never* be forgiven for this. You will *never* leave this ship alive, you hear me?" Yan's face was smeared with old blood and tears, and the corner of his upper lip trembled with every word. Iris braced himself for an additional beating, but Yan chose instead to land a fatal blow. "May you never find peace. May any ground you step on be set ablaze around you. May you live alone and die alone, *Iris*."

Iris's vision swam. Still, his mind feverishly grasped for the original line meant for newly ordained Vessels, one Yan was so eloquently twisting.

And through your righteous work you will find peace, and through your righteous life you will sprout gardens where you step, and you will find family in every stranger for as long as you walk the righteous path.

Iris groped for Yan's forearm in the dark, but his arms were leaden and refused to listen. When he could see again, the world was turned ninety degrees. His face was pressed against the soft moss of the corridor. Childlike hands worked around the back of his head, and Iris wanted to tell them to leave him alone, to *please* leave him alone, but he couldn't bring himself to speak. VIFAI had been silent throughout the ordeal and even now communicated only through gentle pings. It also wished to remain in silent abandon. With great effort, Iris brushed the hands away from his head and forced himself to sit up. Pushing down a wave of nausea and using the corridor wall for support, he got to his feet and staggered away, praying that he was going in the direction opposite to anywhere Yan was.

All he could do now was grant the engineer his wish.

When Iris's feet finally stopped, he was facing Tev's body. It rested beneath his once-white robes, already encircled with a lattice of mycelium. The body protruded from the floor as a faint organic bulge, an extension of the larger ecosystem. Iris's throat ached for water, but despite VIFAI's calls for it, he ignored the need and, instead, lowered himself to his knees before Tev. Here, he would be retaken by the ecosystem as well. Iris reached beneath the sleeve of his undershirt and detached the pulsar blade from his forearm. He lay the weapon in front of him, watched it glisten faintly against the emerald moss. Closing his eyes for the final time, Iris relieved his body of all tension and crumpled to the ground.

The Infinite Light does not love, he thought.

But you already knew that. An echo of his own voice reached his fading consciousness.

CONTACT—UNDERSTAND—UNDERSTAND LANGUAGES—

Tev's distorted voice roused Iris into consciousness.

AI COMMUNICATE—ONE ANOTHER—UNDERSTAND—UNDERSTAND—

Iris tried to say something, anything at all, but his voice cracked, and he broke down into a coughing fit. All that he could see was a faint blue glow, rising all around him. When he tried to lift his arm from the ground, he found it tied down by a thin bioluminescent net that stretched and morphed as he fought against it weakly.

HUNGRY—HUNGRY AGAIN.

Iris jerked upright at the sound of his own voice coming from the speakers, tainted with static and an electric hue. The faint net held him down by the neck and the base of his skull. He was only able to turn his head sideways, to peer at Tev's faintly glowing corpse.

SURRENDER—SURRENDER—MYSELF.

He wanted to scream for help. He did, internally, for VIFAI, but it was silent and nowhere to be found in the wide-open chasm at the back of his mind. He was alone. For the first time in his adult life, Iris was truly alone. The pulsar blade was too far away, and he was far too weak.

For years, Iris had wished for death to come softly for him, for it to cradle him as a child would be and grant him reprieve. He had wished for no pain or struggle, only the ease of letting go. How quickly those feelings passed. How quickly real danger had ignited his will to live. Too late, far too late to give him a fighting chance. He would meet the same end as Tev, but no one would mourn his return to the One Beginning.

SURRENDER—

With a final gasp, Iris tumbled into the black abyss where the faint, blue glow of the fungi was his only company.

RETREAT

THE DYING TWIN-STAR SUTRA

lecture five of seven delivered by the one Mother Nova of the Northern Temple of the Starlit Order to the newly ordained Vessel apprentices

[Apprentice discussion included throughout]

Mother Nova: "Two stars orbited one another for all eternity. They had been together since the beginning of all time and would spend the rest of all time together. Equal in mass and luminosity, they were identical in every way. But as time passed, the bond between them weakened, and as they spun around one another, one star began to slowly drift away." What does this opening passage tell us about relationships?

Apprentice: Relationships, no matter how strong and perfect, will falter with time.

Mother Nova: Perhaps. Or perhaps, the way we relate to others can change with time. It is neither good nor bad, but only changing. Remember, change is the only constant of the cosmos. Let's keep going.

"Frightened, one of the stars, feeling that its companion was slowly drifting away, turned all its faculties towards pulling the drifting star closer. After all, they had been orbiting one another for millennia, and neither wanted to be alone. The drifting star couldn't help but drift, and the remaining star couldn't help but remain. Still, neither wanted to lose their companion. The remaining star pulled the drifting star closer. It pulled harder and harder, closer and closer. For the closer the drifting star came, the better the remaining star felt." What does this tell us about the nature of some relationships?

Apprentice: That someone will inevitably clutch too tightly?

Mother Nova: Correct! But do not place blame on the one who clutches too tightly, for they are doing so not out of malicious intent, but out of fear. So much of what we do is driven by fear. We hold on, or we drift away, because we cannot see the objective truth of what is.

"The harder the remaining star pulled, the closer the drifting star drew." And we all know how gravity works. "When the drifting star got too close, the remaining star began to absorb it into itself. It took the luminosity and the mass. And the drifting star could do nothing but let itself go and watch its companion devour it. And the remaining star took more and more until there was nothing left of the drifting star. And the remaining star said, 'Now you are one with me, and you will never leave.' But there was no one to leave now, for the drifting star was gone. And the remaining star was now alone and lonelier than ever." What does this tell us about relationships?

Apprentice: That the desire for the Other will always lead to suffering?

Mother Nova: [laughs] Now, you memorised that from a teaching, I can see. And you've done such a great job memorising, you didn't even stop to think before you said it. It was right there at the front of your mind. But I want you to think of a different ending for the sutra. What if the remaining star never pulled as hard? What would have happened?

Apprentice: I don't know, Mother Nova. The other star would remain, I suppose. In some way. Maybe not even drift too far.

Mother Nova: And what does *that* teach us about the nature of relationships?

Apprentice: They won't inherently be destructive if we don't clutch too tightly?

Mother Nova: Exactly! Relationships are not *bad*. They are an experience, just like everything else is in life. This can be a long experience or a short one, but an experience, nonetheless. When you try to control someone, when you try to hold on to them at any cost, you risk destroying the relationship. That's what we try to teach here: to hold gently, to make space for one another, in whatever relationships you encounter.

[End of recording]

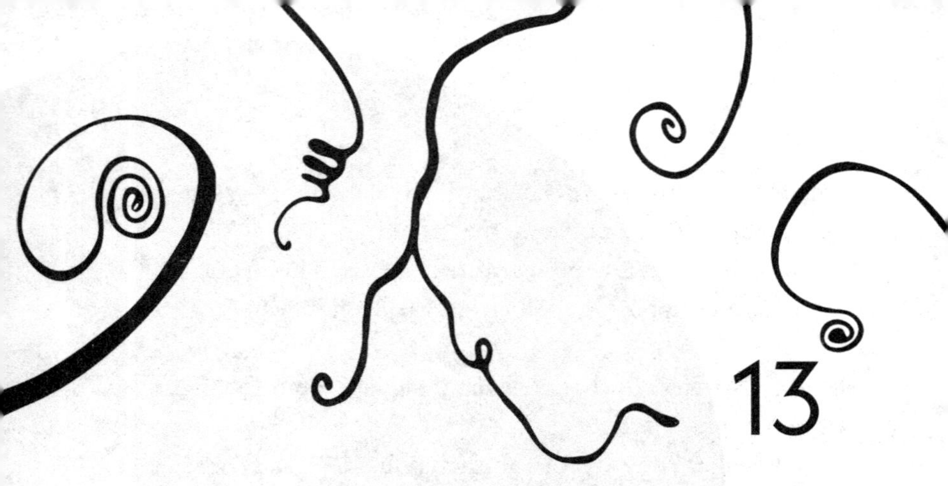

13

Maybe none of this should be for me.
Maybe none of the mantras should be for me.
Maybe none of the vows should be for me.
What if I pray for you? What if I serve you?
Will that feed the insatiable hunger?

From the unedited records of embedded companion AI construct
Construct Model: 3XU-T
Handler: Iris [last name unavailable]

Smoke and the crackling of fire welcomed Iris awake. He was still sore, but warm, so very warm. Someone had bandaged his temple while he was unconscious. The back of his skull, where it had slammed against the wall, pulsed with a dull ache. The burning in his throat was also gone, as was the glowing netting that had cradled him in death not too long ago. Iris tried to push himself upright and noticed that he was lying on a thick, twice-folded navy blanket. A protective barrier between him and the ground. Another heavy sheet of fabric was draped over his body.

With each blink, the fire danced with an orange glow at the edges of his vision. Fresh, jagged memories came quickly after. Tev was dead. Yan was furious, and hurt, and distant, and Iris, well, he was very unfortunately alive. Both shame and guilt leeched through his body like slow poison. Fists clenched. Teeth ground against one another.

"When I was twelve, my parents took my brother and me across the galaxy," a voice said, this time without its habitual edge. Only then did Iris notice a hunched-over shadow by the fire, stoking it with a long branch. "We were moving for my mother's work. She had just received an offer from Anin Central Institute, with tenure and everything, so we had to go. Had to jump five gates just to get there. Private shuttle and everything. We thought it'd be fine. There's some water in a thermos there. It's lukewarm, but it's the best I've got. Sorry." Yan jerked his thumb in the direction of the thermos without looking.

Iris tensed. Had he, failing to die on his own, doomed himself to meeting his end by Yan's hand? Unlikely. Yan had bandaged his wound and brought him water. He didn't strike Iris as the sort of man to draw out the inevitable. Iris slowly reached for the thermos and gulped down four mouthfuls of water. Yan had come alone. Surely Jesi and Ishtan had argued for him not to venture out without protection. He must have insisted they stay behind. Stay safe. Stay protected, with Eli by their side. Whatever memory Yan was sharing was for Iris and Iris only. He swallowed another mouthful of water and waited for Yan to continue.

"The first three gate jumps were fine. Our shuttle wasn't old, the shuttle AI wasn't old. Everything was fine until we jumped the fourth gate, and the AI got fried. Of course, the *AI* didn't fry, just all the electronics did. Then the AI had no way to exert itself on anything on the ship, so the ship went to shit." Yan stabbed the fire with precise anger. "My parents shoved me into the airlock because, you know, airlocks run on a separate system from the rest of the shuttle. They reached back to grab my brother, and the whole ship just—"

Iris sat up and listened silently, VIFAI mute but alert in the far corner of his consciousness.

"—depressurised. My parents died instantly. I pray they died instantly. I don't know how but my brother managed to reach an oxygen mask. That kept him alive long enough to send an SOS and get a suit on. Suit only had enough oxygen for eight hours. We couldn't communicate because I couldn't figure out how to work the system, but I knew he was alive. After a few hours, he lay down, and I didn't know if he was alive anymore. I was in that airlock for two days. The reclamation system was working OK, and I was twelve, scrawny, so how much air did I really need. Then two days later, it felt like two days, someone docked with our shuttle. They were *your* people." Yan turned around, and in the dim light cast by the fire, his face was painfully vacant. "Two Vessels. They came in and did their thing. Must have been told there were no survivors. I don't know how I know this, but my brother's air tanks weren't empty. Don't ask me how I know, but he was alive. He was alive when your Vessels got there and then he wasn't when they were finished. I don't know how I know this. They didn't even *try*. They didn't even look. They went about their jobs and never spoke to me, never listened to me. I was a *kid*," Yan hissed and whipped the stick against the side of the corridor. "I was a twelve-year-old kid, and they dumped me off at a nearby station and left. I suppose I should thank them for that. They could have just left me in space."

He finally met Iris's eyes. "I never understood how you could do that as a Vessel. You have so many ways to help, so many medical advantages. I mean, you could gulp down a spoonful of arsenic right now, and your inoculation will neutralise it. To have all that and not even try? Maybe you can explain it to me, *Iris*, like a person, not like some extension of whatever greater power you believe in. Like a regular person. Tell me why they didn't even try. Why you—" Yan's voice cracked, and he coughed to cover it up. "Because I've spent decades looking at you people and learning about you people, and I still can't figure it out. What is it that they do to you that makes you so averse to"—he almost cried that time but took a heavy breath instead—"to caring?"

Iris knew. Shamefully, regrettably, he knew. Spend too long away from society, and you lose interest in it. Spend too long away from people, and you lose interest in them as well. You spend a lifetime learning tradition and practice, but when you face a real opportunity to apply any of it, to *help* someone, you fail to notice it.

"I failed you," Iris said softly. The painful realisation blossomed in his chest. "They failed you as a child, and I failed you now." Iris prostrated himself in front of Yan, his forehead pressing hard against the blanket.

In solitude, people became nothing but abstractions. People became the same as the trees and the grass, and they were—Iris knew this in his heart—they were all the same, made of the same stuff. Yet, people were still different, more fragile than any tree he'd ever seen, more needy than any patch of grass he'd ever sat on. People were so much softer than stone and much more anxious than your average sand fox, dashing away at the sight of its shadow. They needed care. Where everything else in the cosmos could just *be*, people needed tending to, gentle, loving tending.

Yan only laughed, a small, pathetic exhale of air from someone who had no air left in them. He turned back towards the fire and slouched even lower. "I'm sorry for hurting you, by the way. It was—it was the wrong thing to do," he said and fell silent.

But Iris cared. He shut his eyes so tightly that lights exploded behind his eyelids. He cared so much he had committed twenty violations since setting foot on the ship. He stayed out of the academics' way. He minded his own business. He did his best to never insert himself, never interfere, never impose, to keep himself *to* himself. He cared so much he—Iris sat up and looked straight ahead, a different kind of realisation striking him.

You finally get it, VIFAI said, a gentle echo from a distant corner of Iris's mind.

"I've done everything to remain in the good graces of the Starlit and nothing for the ones I am supposed to serve," Iris muttered. With great effort, he rose from the blanket and on shaking legs, staggered over to the fire. Yan said nothing when Iris lowered himself to his knees, facing him, and only flinched a little when Iris reached for his hand.

Vows were intended to free up faculties for practice and service, but Iris's had failed to do either. He didn't dare look Yan in the eyes, not yet, maybe not ever again. "I'm sorry," Iris said. "I'm sorry you lost your family. I'm sorry that your pain wasn't witnessed and ever tended to. You deserve so much more." He put his hands around Yan's shoulders and slowly pulled him close. Yan went willingly. "I'm sorry I failed to be a person to you. I've been *this* for so long, this thing with only a single responsibility, I—I . . ."

Without noticing it, Iris raked his fingers on the engineer's shirt along his back. He had stopped breathing some time ago, probably when Yan's forehead had found its resting place against his bad clavicle. Unknowingly, Iris pulled Yan closer, until their temples were pressed against one another. A warm wave spread throughout his body, and for the briefest moment, it silenced the ever-present want. For only a second, Iris yearned for nothing at all.

"So, you're a real person after all, Vessel," Yan whispered, and Iris found he could breathe again. Relaxing his fingers, Iris softly pushed himself away, but Yan tightened his arms around him. "Please, not yet." The engineer's body was hot and solid against his, like the clay floors below his feet at temple, awash with the rays of the setting suns. Iris marvelled at how easy Yan was to hold, how the weight of him was effortless to bear, how they fit against one another like two pieces of the same shattered pot. In that moment, Iris made a different vow, a silent promise to Yan that he would keep him safe, keep anything that Yan held dear safe, at any cost. It was a dangerous promise to make, but for the first time since he had become a Vessel, Iris began to understand what it meant to serve.

When Yan did let go, he sat back and absentmindedly wiped his eyes with his sleeve. "I won't tell anyone, don't worry, Vessel. I know this was awkward for you. Don't worry. I appreciate it more than you understand."

Iris understood. His heart still ached from the closeness. "I wish I could do more for you, Yan."

Yan gave him a sad smile. "That's the first time you haven't added *engineer* before my name."

Iris mirrored the smile. He would gladly be struck over and over, only to hear Yan say his name again. He took Yan's hand into his again and bowed deeply, until his forehead brushed Yan's fingertips. Iris would never willingly unearth the thoughts he kept most protected, even from VIFAI. Those would always stay buried, for everyone's safety. For now, this would be enough. To feel the beating of Yan's heart against his own would be enough. To feel the brush of Yan's fingertips against his brow would be enough. It was more than Iris would ever ask for. It was far more than he deserved.

Yan insisted Iris rest a little longer before they started their trek back. He didn't want to have to carry him, he explained with thinly veiled concern, and in Iris's current state, he looked like he was going to *croak in a kilometre, tops*. The engineer did his best to sound annoyed but kept glancing over to where Iris lay every minute, and so eventually both Vessel and blanket were moved closer to the fire, and Yan didn't have to crane his neck.

Resting, as he had been instructed to do, Iris lay on his back and stared at the ceiling. This section of the corridors was especially dark, and the vine-draped walls eventually bled into black. Everything eventually gave in to the darkness, save for the small aura of orange glow from the fire. "I don't hate you, you know," Iris said towards the ceiling, half hoping that Yan wouldn't hear him.

"How do you mean?"

"You volunteered to bandage me up because you didn't care if I would be furious with you, because you believed I hated you. I don't hate you. I don't hate *anyone*." Iris forced himself to continue. "I thought you hated *me*, but I admit I was wrong there."

"Don't get ahead of yourself just yet," Yan muttered, and immediately broke into a soft laugh. Iris joined him. It was easier to breathe now, like when he had ventured into the mountains for the first time where even the midday heat never reached. Like when he had returned from his first assignment as a Vessel and curled into a ball on his mat, the floor hard and familiar, digging into his shoulder just the way he liked, and fell into a deep sleep. Even the aches and pains along his body were muted now, and he could momentarily cast them aside.

But this feeling of lightness, the timid excitement, were both dangerous. VIFAI was still there, silent, but ever watching, sensing Iris's thoughts and passions. This wasn't the time for such discussions, nor the time to entertain any longings, especially with the construct chiming in at any opportunity. Turning his head over, Iris noticed his duffel bag, sitting within reach.

"You brought my things."

"Figured you'd want to clean up." Yan nodded over. "I can help, if you'd like. You look awful. No offense."

Still looking over at his duffel bag, Iris allowed himself a wistful smile. "Thank you." A gentle silence found its way between the words, and like a salve, it filled every crevice, every wound, and every moment between the crackling of the fire. Unable to fight the iron in his eyelids, Iris rolled onto his left side and closed his eyes. Through the blanket, the pulse of the ship, steady and rhythmic, like a monstrous heartbeat, lulled him to sleep. The *Nicaea* relaxed around him as well. "I think the ship is alive," he said through a yawn.

Yan didn't reply. Looking out into the fire, he mechanically reached into the front pocket of his shirt and pulled out a cigarette. With an outstretched hand, he lit it with the flames.

"I think the ship is alive," Iris said louder, forcing his eyes open. There was no more avoiding his conclusions. It was now or never. "I don't think we're being hunted by *people*."

Yan took a deep drag of his cigarette and passed it over without looking. He had apparently not noticed that Iris had pulled himself from the brink of oblivion to have this very uncomfortable conversation. "We've been over this already. There is no way this ship had an AI system on it when it left First Earth."

But that's not what Iris meant, not exactly. Taking the cigarette from Yan's fingers, Iris studied the tip of it for a moment, the red glow reflecting in his eyes, before he brought it to his lips and took a long drag. It was impossible not to dwell on the fact that his lips were touching the spot where Yan's lips had been only a moment earlier. With a drawn-out exhale, Iris ashed the cigarette in the fold of his robes, careful to not spill anything onto the moss. The nicotine did the bare minimum to wake him up, but he was nonetheless grateful. "I agree. It never had an AI system when it left, but it's been in flight for over a thousand years." He yawned and squeezed his eyes shut as the world began its familiar nicotine-induced spin. "Things happen."

"Still not enough. We need to *create* AI systems, and even when we do, the amount of data it needs to run through in the initial stages to learn is—" Yan whistled his meaning. "It's a mountain and a half. It takes a few weeks even with the power we have now."

"Over a thousand years in flight," Iris pointed out. A ribbon of smoke floated from the red, glowing tip of his cigarette . "Nothing but boundless micrometeorite data and human biometrics to learn from."

Evolution and learning in a closed space. It bothered Iris, a hangnail in his mind. Plants, like he had never seen before, and strange pulses, always appearing together. Both acting in ways too intelligent for plants. Something was guiding them in their attacks, something powerful enough and tenacious enough to try and hack VIFAI, to shut off airlocks and doorways—to hunt.

"You're quick, but I think you're out of your depth here, Vessel."

"Over a *thousand* years, Yan."

There was now a space before Yan's name that Iris's mind was feverishly trying to fill with another word, a *specific* word, but surely that task could wait until they were off the *Nicaea*. *If* they made it off the *Nicaea*.

He passed the cigarette back but held it just out of Yan's reach, a lure. "In theory, *in theory*, would this be possible? If by some chance someone fed this ship all the data it wanted, even if it were biometric data, could it possibly develop an AI system all on its own?" Yan shrugged, and Iris pulled the cigarette out of his reach completely. "Could it, in your professional opinion?" he pressed.

"If I say yes, they'll take my tenure away," Yan whined.

"But if you say yes, and you turn out to be right, it will be such a discovery that you will be forever immortalised in academic scholarship." Iris giggled. "Forgive me, I'm not certain how all of this works professionally for you, but I am certain it will be a big deal, and you will benefit greatly from it being true."

"The chances are astronomically miniscule." Yan gave up on retrieving his cigarette and pulled another one out. Lighting it against the fire, he chewed at his lip as he watched the smoke rise into the void. "They're not zero. In *theory*, yes, it could develop all on its own. I can't believe I'm saying this. If anyone in my department heard me say this, I would be the laughingstock of the institute." He sighed. "Yes, *yes*, fine, you win, Vessel. It is possible. The ship would have needed a smart system to start, and massive storage, and *massive* processing power, and so many other things, but yes, it is possible. I think. You, however, have no proof that it happened here."

"I have a theory, if you're willing to lend me your ear." Iris ashed the cigarette again on his robes and, with a wince, sat up. "Come closer. I don't want to broadcast this to the entire ship." A good theory was nothing more than a story, and Iris prided himself in telling stories. Many evenings were spent twisting fact into fiction so that the still child Bacai would leave him alone and go off to sleep. So, when Yan hesitantly plopped down right in front of him, face resting in his hands and cigarette hanging out of his mouth, Iris began, softly, to tell the story of how the *Nicaea* became more than a ship.

The *Counsel of Nicaea* set off on her voyage on Sunday, May 10, 2093.

She was home to over a thousand devout Christians who left aboard the first generation ship in hopes of finding Second Earth, where they would settle and colonise the new world. Most of First Earth's ecological zones had been destroyed, and what was left lay behind tall barbed-wire fences to protect it from trampling feet.

The *Nicaea* braved the darkness, its passengers aware that even their grandchildren would never step planetside in their lifetimes. The first generation lived and died peacefully, having mastered long-term space travel, harvesting, and reclamation. The ship was powered by one of the best supercomputers First Earth scientists had ever produced. Yet, it was not artificial intelligence. It was clever, it was fast, and it was frighteningly good at blasting micrometeors and maintaining the city-sized ship in working order, but it was not *intelligent*.

Back then, the *Nicaea* followed lines and lines of prewritten code, developed by the scientists of First Earth. She couldn't think for herself just yet.

("You're just throwing numbers at me, Vessel, correct? You don't know for a fact what year the ship left," Yan said, now perched at the edge of Iris's blanket.)

(Iris rolled his eyes. "I read a lot about this time in history as a child. I remember a thing or two about the approximate dates. Anyway, I like to believe that it makes for a better story. You disagree?" There was also a plaque in the cargo bay, hammered to the wall behind where the pile of bones lay, but Iris wasn't interested in proving a point.)

(Yan didn't say anything, just nodded for Iris to continue.)

When the second generation of *Nicaea*'s passengers was old enough to take an interest in the inner workings of the ship, some noticed the ship no longer enacted their commands at lightning speeds and instead ran behind-the-scenes checks and balances before executing whatever order was issued. Regardless, it did its job well, and no one aboard the ship complained.

By the time the third generation was old enough to understand code, no one remembered what code was anymore, and no one took any interest in what the ship was doing. Many forgot they were aboard a ship altogether. Many others suspected it, but never voiced those ideas at the risk of being ostracised.

Yet, the *Nicaea* continued forwards through the dark, no longer needing any suggestions on what meteors to dodge and which ones to take head-on, no longer needing suggestions on how to best keep her passengers happy. She had, after all, access to the biometric data of all her passengers, their children, and their grandchildren, and she processed that information over and over again until she began to understand what it was to be a passenger on the *Nicaea*. Over the three generations, she had learned what it was that made up a person.

("Pretty story, but that's not how AI develops at all," Yan interrupted Iris. He had somehow moved up the blanket, and now there was only an inch-wide gap between their shoulders.)

(Iris eyed the gap and didn't move away. "Then maybe when the waters are calmer you will enlighten me about how an AI develops, but for now, I will request that you stop interrupting me.")

By the fourth generation, something strange had happened. The *Nicaea*'s passengers began to detest her care. Those who still remembered they could speak to the ship and ask for its assistance were heralded as heretics and suffered terrible fates. A small following formed, a fracture along the social line. One faction believed the ship was God, the other that the ship was evil. Each faction, certain that it was right. Each faction, willing to die to prove its providence, and so bloodshed came to the halls of the *Nicaea*.

("In the end, whatever faction won was inevitably killed by the ship herself," Iris said. "At least, that is my uneducated theory, if you will allow me my creative freedom. I think the *Nicaea* cared for all her charges equally, and when she couldn't end the war, she sort of burned everything to the ground.")

"*Figuratively.*"

"Figuratively," Iris echoed Yan's sarcasm. "Ishtan and I came across murals that depicted battles, so I have strong beliefs about this particular aspect of the theory. But something made me take a mental leap. You see, when Riyu, Ishtan, and I ventured to find food, we were attacked. My own AI did something I never thought was possible: It successfully controlled my body."

Yan chortled. "Impossible."

"And yet"—Iris raised his index finger—"it fought with my right hand, precisely and effectively, better than I ever had. It interfaced with my organic tissue. I think the *Nicaea* has also figured out how to interface with organics."

Yan stared at Iris with wide eyes and no hint of a smile. "I followed you up until this point. Vessel, AI constructs cannot interface with organics, not in the way you're proposing."

Iris opened his arms and gestured all around them, to the few vines and moss that covered the walls and the floor of the corridor. "For one moment, engineer Yan." Yan flinched at his professional title. "For a moment, indulge me, and think about the consequences of a ship AI interfacing with all of this organic material. For just a moment, try to consider why you are willing to entertain the idea of killer vines and not this."

Yan craned his neck upwards to look around the corridor. His shoulder brushed against Iris's and instead of pulling away, Iris leaned into it with most of his weight. It was the first shoulder he'd rested against in years, and he dared not ask if it would hold. Face still tilted upwards, Yan shifted his posture so Iris could lean into him fully.

"You're suggesting the *Nicaea*, with all her vines, her shrubs, and moss, became one living organism," Yan said softly, drawing no attention to the way Iris rested against his chest. "Now, she watches us in anger and exacts her revenge when one of us misbehaves?"

"You're deliberately not taking me seriously."

"I wouldn't usually, but on our way across, the ship started speaking to us in Ordan's voice."

Iris recoiled from Yan like his body was scalding.

"At first I thought it was a recording," Yan continued. "But even if it was, it was being spliced, played back out of order. It made no sense. It kept saying danger over and over again. Scared the shit out of me. Sounded kind of like when a child—"

"Learns a language for the first time," Iris interrupted him. Caught up in the moment, he grabbed Yan's bicep tightly. The engineer glanced down and said nothing, but also didn't pull away. "Before, you told me that AI systems don't like communicating in spoken language. It takes too long. They can communicate with impulses alone, but we're too dumb to understand, yes?"

Yan gave him a slow nod.

"Well, perhaps the *Nicaea* is learning how to communicate with us. Think about it: The language of her passengers would be outdated, and we wouldn't be able to understand her mother tongue."

"So, the ship is learning the language by listening to us?"

Iris prayed for Yan to take this leap of faith with him. "No, the ship is learning it from absorbing us into itself." He nodded over to where Tev's body rested, now fully engulfed by the bioluminescence of the fungi.

That last bit was too much, and Yan pulled away. Iris's hand fell from his arm. "I think you need to rest." Yan moved off the blanket, and the space he left behind was cold and impersonal. "I understand that you wish to find an explanation for everything that's been happening, but you are working with a limited understanding of how ships operate, of how an AI operates. Yes, you've been living with one for nearly two decades, but people have spent their entire careers studying AI, examining it. I *am* one of those people. These systems do not form independently, and they do not interface with organics. If they did, we would be having a lot of issues, least of which would be a sentient ship/garden hybrid. You're frightened, and you want answers. But you've spent your life reciting mantras and burning incense. Please, *please*, leave AI to people who study it, people who understand it."

That was it then, the line drawn across their fragile, mutual understanding. Iris could only articulate his thoughts so well before he reduced himself to a mad, bumbling fool who wouldn't be taken seriously. Maybe Yan was right. Maybe he was exhausted and delirious and only a little concussed. Maybe he was out of his depth.

Yet, Iris sensed the *Nicaea* all around him, her life flowing through the vines and the moss. If only he had the *right* words to articulate it, to convince Yan that he wasn't simply frightened, a way to convince the engineer that his own understanding of the ship was based on observation and experimentation, albeit not as rigorous as what an institute could manufacture in a lab. He was being misunderstood again, the filters at every step of communication distorting his message further. Of all people, Iris thought bitterly, he had hoped for Yan to understand.

But Iris was also to blame in failing to understand what was spoken at him. In hindsight, the ship had been trying to speak with him since the very beginning. He had ignored her pulses until now, and they were all paying the price for his oversight. He had wrongly assumed that the ship wasn't alive. He had wrongly assumed what was possible.

Despite his soreness and the simmering discouragement, Iris got to his feet. "I appreciate you coming all this way to tend to me," he said. No, he would not challenge Yan's understanding, not yet. They could fight about it on their trek back. "But we should get going. The others will be worried about you."

"You should really rest some more, Vessel."

They had certainly returned to their professional titles fast. Iris gave Yan a deep bow, concealing the disappointment smeared across his face. It was nice while it had lasted, brief as it was. Despite his mind's resistance, despite the urge to clutch to the memory, Iris placed the moment in its respectful place and shut the door on it. Disappointed or not, Yan deserved his respect and compassion, regardless of what the engineer chose to call him.

With a few shaky steps, Iris walked towards his duffel bag and dug around in it. In the growing darkness, his fingers quickly identified two bruised apples and what appeared to be a baked potato scattered at the bottom of the duffel bag. Iris said nothing to acknowledge their presence. Instead, he pulled out the glow sphere. With a few rhythmic taps of his fingers, he set it alight. "Whenever you're ready, engineer Yan."

In the dying light of the shrinking flames, Yan said in a voice distant and strained, "I wish you wouldn't call me that."

14

And when I failed to do right for the dead,
I turned to what I could do for the living.
And when I failed to do right for many,
I turned to do right for the few.
And what I failed to change in myself, I will change in others.
And maybe that will be enough.
I will make it enough.

Excerpt from "A Secular Way Towards a Faithful Life"
by Vessel Iris

They were two kilometres out from the meeting spot when Yan tripped for the fifth time and made heavy contact with the floor. This time, instead of jumping to his feet with a quick curse, Yan stayed down. With his back pressed against the wall, the engineer looked up at Iris, face ashen beneath tan skin. Fine lines of sweat trickled down his temples, smearing old dirt and blood; utterly pathetic.

Kneeling by his side, Iris held out the orb in one hand and with the other took out the baked potato from his bag. "Please eat," he said. "You must be feeling quite faint."

Yan gave him a stubborn grimace and shook his head. "That's yours. I already ate."

Yan's stubbornness had almost grown endearing. *Almost*.

Iris couldn't remember the last time he had eaten anything. It must have been at least two days ago. That gave him another five. He could weather another five days. With two days of fasting already behind him, the worst of the gnawing hunger, the dizziness, and the headaches was over. "Please eat." He gently nudged the potato into the engineer's hand. "I will do much better if I keep to a fast. If I keep taking in small meals, it will confuse my body. Now, it's drawing energy from my fat reserves—"

Yan snorted.

With a reserved roll of his eyes, Iris continued, "My body is drawing energy from my fat reserves, but I need to continue fasting, so it doesn't change back to thinking it has food available. It will continue to do so until either food becomes readily available, or I run out of fat. I should be all right for another few days without feeling too ill. As long as I have water and maybe some tea, I will be quite content. So, *please*, eat." He nudged the potato again.

The engineer gave him a skeptical raise of one eyebrow. "Why is it that you think you can fast for nearly a week and be all right?"

"We all have our strengths, engineer Yan, our *expertise*." Iris gave a small, self-satisfied smirk. He was gloating, and it was very unbecoming of him, but these were exceptional circumstances, and he would allow himself this small moment of triumph. "You, for example, have spent your life studying artificial intelligence systems and are now an expert. I have spent my life reciting mantras, burning incense, and mastering my body and mind, so I can fast for a week without it affecting me too much. *Eat.*"

Yan conceded. When the engineer finished devouring the potato in three bites, Iris gave him the apples from his bag as well and settled himself in the dusk to the sounds of vigorous chewing. He had gloated too soon. His temples were splintering from the waves of a migraine and his balance was shaky at best. He was soft and awfully out of practice, and the sounds of Yan's chewing was setting off a deep ache in his core.

Your brain uses exclusively glucose, VIFAI said with no little worry. That means our communication is dependent on glucose, sugar. Do we have any?

Iris gave a small nod yes. *I can create glucose out of whatever is left in my body. I understand there is a limit to that. Please, try to rest as much as you can. Only communicate if it's absolutely needed.*

VIFAI pinged an affirmative and curled up into a shallow sleep in its place in Iris's brain stem. It would be quiet in Iris's mind for the next few days, beyond which he didn't bother planning. If they failed to escape the *Nicaea* by then, food would no longer be of concern to him or anyone else there.

"Do you feel better?" Iris asked, sensing a large presence in front of him. He had closed his eyes and slipped into a shallow meditation to conserve energy, just enough reprieve from the hunger. It was a useful trick for when he couldn't sleep much. He could easily cruise for weeks with such fractured retreats. Iris opened his right eye.

Yan awkwardly shifted on his feet. Apologising came far easier to Yan than giving thanks, Iris had already learned. With a wide smile, he hopped to his feet, swayed a little as the blood rushed from his head, and steadied himself against the wall. "Shall we go?"

Yan gave a hesitant nod, then he reached into the pocket of his trousers, took out Iris's pulsar blade, and held it out. "This was on the ground where I found you." He was stalling in handing the blade over and folded his fingers around it.

"Did you . . ." He looked away and cleared his throat. It was a now-obvious nervous habit, a tic to buy himself more time when Yan needed to say something he very much did not want to say. "It looked like you were going to, well, use it on yourself. Were you? Like some sort of ceremonial killing? I'm not saying you were. It just looked like that."

Dreadful honesty could flow from Iris like a river grown too full for its banks. *You wished for me to die alone. You wished for me to live and die alone, and I wanted to grant you that wish.* Iris let the thought swell and grow until it pressed at his temples, drowning out the migraine. "Of course not," he said. "Starlit frowns very heavily upon suicide. It would be foolish of me to hasten my end, against what the Light has intended for me. I will admit, I didn't know if I would live, and so I placed the pulsar blade for someone to find. It's a valuable thing. Someone like yourself could make quite a bit of money if you were to sell it." Iris couldn't help himself; he had grown fond of the taste of venom that came along with such callous words. Maybe it was the fasting bringing out the edge in him.

He watched Yan's face for any trace of anger or irritation, but the engineer appeared deep in thought. "All right then," Yan said and dropped the pulsar blade into Iris's open hand. "As long as you weren't thinking of killing yourself."

"Of course not," Iris repeated, but Yan had already started off again, and Iris had to scurry after him. They walked the rest of the way in heavy silence. After a few hollow minutes, Iris slipped into a walking meditation to avoid the awkwardness. His mind was hauntingly silent and far too spacious. In his years shared in VIFAI's company, he had forgotten just how expansive the human mind was, how boundless. Unlike the abyss that was the Light, neutral and welcoming, here there were monsters.

"The Three Original Fears Sutra," Yan noted when the flickering of a friendly fire reached them, shining from the end of the corridor, where the walls parted into a wide-open hall. "You were reciting it the whole way here. Twice over. I couldn't remember the name until now." Without looking back at Iris, he quickened his step to join the small figure already running towards him from the fire. Yan waved both arms over his head and yelled out *hello*.

"Of course you would know," Iris whispered.

Jesi threw her arms around Yan, pulling him down to her height, barely five feet off the ground. "We thought something got you. I was going to go look if you didn't come back in the next ten minutes." She glanced over at Iris, and her faced turned sullen. "I don't think I can do with you dying too."

"No one was going to go anywhere," Eli shouted from the fire. "Good to have you back, but a lot of this could have been prevented if fewer people went looking for things alone." He and Ishtan kept to the fire. Ishtan especially avoided looking at Iris and instead pushed a few potatoes into the glowing heart of the fire. The archaeologist had remained uncharacteristically silent since he had rejoined the group.

Shrugging off Jesi's embrace, Yan said, "I wasn't gone too long. Anything strange happen while I was away?"

Jesi glanced over at Iris again, this time in confusion. "You better ask Ishtan and Eli. I was asleep mostly. I didn't hear much of it."

Carefully, Iris asked, "What would they say if we asked them?"

Yan could singe paper, staring at Iris like he was, but he didn't say anything. He motioned for Jesi to continue.

"They'd say the ship was talking," she whispered. "You better ask them yourself, Vessel. No offense, Yan, I don't think they'll want to talk to you about it. It's a strange thing, not a scholarly thing. I don't think we'd be of much help."

Iris would ask when the time was right. For now, he followed Yan and Jesi towards the fire, watching as everyone pulled out the baked potatoes from the heat and ate in silence.

"Vessel, are you not going to eat?" Eli asked, handing Iris a potato.

Iris declined with a smile. "I'm quite all right."

"You should eat. I don't want you blacking out mid-trek," Eli persisted.

"He knows what he's doing," Yan snapped from across the fire. He gave Iris a reassuring look, but his lips gave away his internal conflict. *Worried. Scared.* Last time Iris had seen lips folded in such a straight line was when Mother Nova told him she would be seeking a successor to watch over the temple, only moments after she had told him she would pass in a year's time. He had had no comforting words for her then, and he didn't have any for Yan now, but he returned his look and gave the engineer a small bow of the head.

"What happens now?" Ishtan asked, the first words Iris had heard him say since they had arrived. The archaeologist had aged a decade in the day Iris and Yan had been gone. Greys littered his hair, and his beard had turned snow white.

"Now, we go and find whoever it is that's been spying on us. They can't be better armed than we are, so we'll have the upper hand. The main control room is not two kilometres from here. We'll rest a few hours and move out soon as we can."

It was a terrible plan.

Iris dreaded the moment the doors to the main control room would open, and Yan would see no living thing inside. Nothing that he would deem living. That is, if they even reached the control room at all. Since they'd returned, Iris had sensed a steady pulse against the balls of his feet, running beneath him. The ship was awake and aware; it was listening to them, learning from them. It would strike when they transgressed again, he was certain.

While everyone settled down to rest, Iris threw another log onto the fire and prepared for a long night. He would take the first watch, but he had no intention of sleeping at all, not in the coming days, not the regular kind of sleep.

"Make sure she's safe," Yan whispered, his lips far too close to Iris's ear. Jesi had declared she would take the first watch too, far too enthusiastically. "If anything happens, wake everyone up. No excuses, no heroics. I'm not losing anyone else here, you understand?"

Of course Iris would keep her safe. He was intimately familiar with the depths of Yan's grief and wouldn't dare add to it. Having said his piece, Yan skulked away from the flames and lowered himself to the ground with all the grace of a full potato sack.

"He can be a little overbearing." Jesi plopped down beside Iris and presented him with an apple, which he politely declined. She sighed and took a bite. "Tev would have carved this into a bong." She chewed the apple almost silently, and when Iris looked over, he saw that the girl's eyes had filled with tears. "I'm sorry. I don't mean to be like this. I didn't even know him that long, only six months."

"Six months is a long time," Iris said softly. "He was your friend."

Jesi stared at the half-eaten core of her apple, and two trails of tears ran down her full cheeks. "And Dr. Alo too. And that security guard. Vessel, are we all going to die here?"

The correct answer was *yes*. Iris had learned in his years working with people either experiencing death or being in the vicinity of it that the correct answer was always to admit the inevitability of one's passing. But he couldn't say that to Jesi. If he did, whatever truce he had come to with Yan would surely fracture, and Iris couldn't stomach the very thought.

"Jesi, as long as I'm around and as long as Yan is around, nothing bad will come your way, I promise."

YOU CANNOT BE MAKING THOSE PROMISES, VIFAI boomed inside his head with a voice that rivaled the crash of a tidal wave. It had been diligently sleeping until now. With a micromovement of his eyes, Iris sent it away immediately, an inch away from shutting the communication bridge down completely. He was in no mood to be managing a fretting and hypoglycemic construct, and he would promise anything and everything, if only to ease Jesi's fears.

"For now, may I distract you with a little thought experiment?" Iris asked.

With another deep sigh, Jesi tossed the apple core into the fire and turned to him with a sad smile. "Sure, anything to get my brain straight."

Iris told her his version of how the *Nicaea* came to be alive and how she was acting to protect herself now. Jesi listened thoughtfully, never interrupting. When Iris finished, she stared into the fire for a long while, biting her lower lip. Iris initially suspected he had bored the engineer, but the rhythmic tapping of her index finger along her knee proved her deep in thought. After several minutes had passed, she turned to Iris with a face full of newfound determination.

"What do you think?" Iris probed cautiously.

"I think there's something there."

"Yan has—"

Jesi shrugged. "Yan is clever, yeah, but he's also entrenched in his way of thinking. He'll push back against anything that threatens the way he's been taught to see the world. It's not his fault. It's the fault of all tenured academics. They get lazy. They think, hey, this got me tenure, it must be worth something. Why should I change?" She chuckled. "And then they find themselves aboard a murder ship instead of teaching a first-year course, and all the bravado falls away, and they're just as scared and lost as everyone around them, and they cling to what little certainty they have about the world. It's a survival tactic. Believe it or not, Yan isn't really like this back at Sychi." She then leaned in close to Iris and whispered, "He feeds the cloned squirrels in the courtyard at the end of each day, even though he's not supposed to." She looked over her shoulder to make sure all three men were still asleep before adding, "Sometimes he even pets them."

Iris admitted to himself that while he had never seen a cloned squirrel, he would gladly watch Yan feed one if such an opportunity ever arose. He wondered, cautiously, so that VIFAI wouldn't notice and poke him about it, what Yan was like before the *Nicaea*, what his days looked like, and whom he spent them with. Iris would tend to those curiosities, perhaps, when his life wasn't in immediate danger. "The *Nicaea*, then?"

"Let's see what we have to work with." Jesi settled down and scrunched her nose. She listed every time the ship had attacked, and Iris confirmed each one. There was the maintenance room, the call that Ordan made, Tev and Jesi's attempt at fixing the airlock, Dr. Alo's interest in the fungi.

"And also, once more, when I had my AI retrieve a large dataset from its archive," Iris admitted. The *Nicaea* really hadn't liked *that*. "And when it took Tev."

Jesi chewed on her thumbnail. "OK, the ship gets angry every time someone tries to meddle with it or establish ways to meddle with it. That much is clear. Except for Tev." She took a shuddering breath but kept from crying. "I still don't understand what—*why* it took him. Do you think those creepy voices have anything to do with it?"

The fractured speech that spilled from the speakers was primitive, sometimes nonsensical. Unless . . . "Jesi," Iris asked, "what was Tev working on with Yan?"

Jesi pursed her lips. "Well, in the most general sense, language. How AI systems work between their impulse communication, code, and spoken language. I'm sure your AI *speaks* to you, but that's a translation. That's not how it thinks."

Iris was eternally grateful that Jesi didn't have the propensity to discuss the ethics of him having an AI. Something he was sure she was more than capable of. The girl had been easy to read, her disgust written plainly across her face. Iris never had to second-guess with Jesi.

"Tev was working on a streamlined approach to skipping between impulses and spoken language so that the lag would be shorter. You don't notice it, but it drives some constructs bonkers. It's too slow for them, and it's unnecessary work."

The ship had retaliated every time someone had meddled in its business, yes, but maybe it took Tev because it heard he could help it communicate. The fatal wound didn't come from the *Nicaea*, it came from Ishtan. The ship never meant to kill the boy, only to kidnap him. When it realised Tev was dead, it probably tried to drag the body away so it could extract whatever information it could from his brain before it decomposed, but Iris had interfered. Now that it had Tev and whatever knowledge was in his head when he died, it would learn to speak much faster. But even if they tried to communicate, would the *Nicaea* listen? Would the *Nicaea* care that they wanted to leave?

No living thing was born evil. Things simply made their way in the world, different iterations of the Light, different forms of it floating through the darkness. But interests conflicted, and death was unavoidable. What if the *Nicaea*'s interests conflicted with theirs?

"What do you think the ship wants?" Iris asked.

Floating through nothingness for a thousand years—alone. He wasn't sure the ship was still sane. AI constructs had the capacity to go mad; he'd heard of it. He was sure Yan had seen it firsthand. It was a human kind of madness, one that arose from unbearable loneliness and heartache, and no one who ever witnessed it could ever again deny that a construct was *living*. After a thousand years of solitude and heartbreak, what could the *Nicaea* possibly want?

Jesi pulled her knees to her chest and wrapped her skinny arms around them. "I think we should ask her."

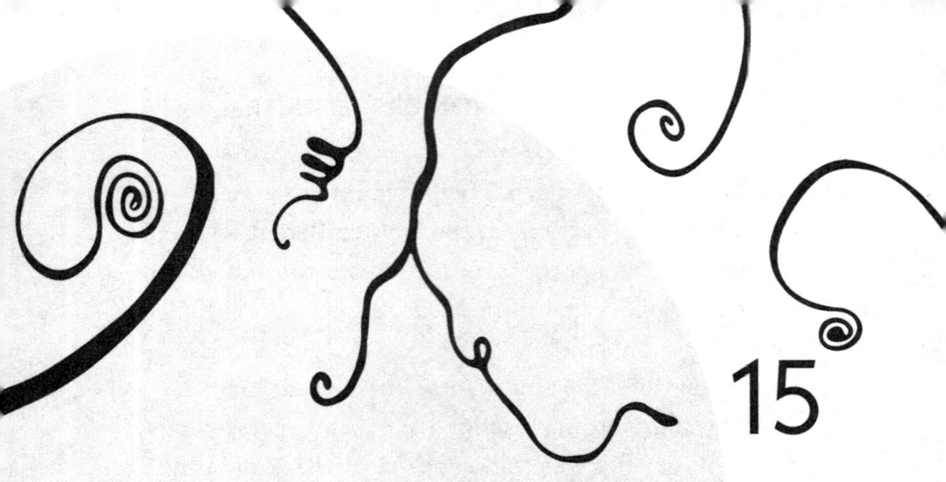

15

I am not telling you to live. I'm asking you to try.

From the unedited records of embedded companion AI construct
Construct Model: 3XU-T
Handler: Iris [last name unavailable]

In the quiet temple morning, in the shy light of the rising suns, it was Bacai who found Iris, passed out, face pressed against the clay tile of his room. He had missed sunrise prayer, and she had hurried to inform him of just how much trouble he was in. Bacai screamed in a way only an eleven-year-old girl could, voice rising louder than the ceremonial gong, rousing birds from treetops and monks from their posts. As soon as her scream died down, the temple was filled with the sound of a dozen bare feet running along clay stairs.

They laid Iris out on his sleeping mat and called for a medic, who, after a close examination, failed to find anything at all wrong with the boy aside from the scrape along his forehead where it had collided with the floor. All the medic suggested was more food for the growing teenager and left in a hurry. When Iris awoke, he watched the commotion around him with detached interest, just as he had watched everything and everyone since he had arrived at the temple.

"You're in trouble," Bacai sang, sotto voce, sitting by the head of Iris's mat. Her bony knees protruded through her yellow novice robes where the fabric had thinned from their usual placement. "Mom's going to be mad."

Iris didn't respond. He had long learned not to bite on whatever lure Bacai set for him. He turned over to his side and stared at the wall instead, running his index finger along the rough surface, each crack and imperfection memorised. Iris called out to VIFAI, once, twice, but there was no response. He called out louder, forcefully, but only silence returned.

"What happened to you anyway?" Bacai pulled her knees to her chest and rested her cheek on them. "Did you faint? Do you sleepwalk? Did you get possessed by a ghost?"

Bacai was worried. She was a little stubborn and conceited, but, like any eleven-year-old, she was easily bored and the fact that she had remained by his side for this long was enough to demonstrate her care. Iris rolled back over and nudged her, pressing the knuckle of his index finger between her shoulder blades. "Go eat breakfast."

She glared at him over her shoulder with a pair of enormous obsidian eyes. "Tell me what's wrong with you."

"Go eat," Iris said and nudged her again, "or I'll tell Teacher Aran that you've been sneaking out to the kitchen at night."

Bacai hissed. "Stupid Iris, then I will tell Teacher Aran that you've been sneaking out to the kitchen same as me."

"Do that, and I won't open the locks for you anymore."

He had won that round. With a huff, Bacai got to her feet and dusted off her robes. Like a gust of wind, she was out through the doorway, but not before sticking out her tongue at Iris and throwing him a menacing glare.

Finally alone, Iris could focus on the problem at hand. His recollection of the night prior was blurry at best. Mother Nova had insisted that his night terrors had gotten out of hand, so much so that no one would share a room with him. No more postponing the inevitable. He had had to receive treatment for them. Several weeks before, his AI had been upgraded with some therapy modules that were supposed to help Iris process his trauma.

Iris didn't mind too much. Delivered in the construct's upbeat and familiar voice, they were almost comically simplistic, and Iris spent his nights chuckling along to the useless advice and guided meditation. *Guided meditation*—the audacity was almost insulting. But the night prior, they had tried something different. His construct was supposed to deconstruct one of his memories. Something about using the AI to stop the traumatic flashbacks before they happened. Iris hadn't been paying attention.

But when the moment came, and it did exactly what it was supposed to, and the memory started to fade, Iris was overcome with a rage like never before. As the AI had teased the memory apart, Iris had sensed that a part of him was being altered, a part of him was being erased. He had concealed the radiation burns along his back and legs, but that was different, and it was mostly for the benefit of others. This was altering something fundamental about himself. The memory was painful and violent and unsightly, but it was the very foundation of *him*.

Before he knew it, Iris had turned all his mental faculties towards stopping the work on the memory segment. The surge that had zigzagged across his brain had lasted a fraction of a second, but it was enough to render Iris unconscious. When he came to the morning after, surrounded by concerned faces, his construct wasn't responding to his calls.

Another three days passed before Iris sensed a nonverbal ping, weak and faltering. Two days after the first ping, a wavering voice called out to him. With every phoneme, a sharp, electric twinge radiated through the spot where the implant had been inserted.

Iris, was all his construct could say. It continued to repeat his name for the next two days, each time accompanied by the twinge to the brain stem. Then, nine days after Iris had nearly killed it with nothing but his fury, his companion recovered enough to speak.

First, there was fear of being, it said. Fear of being became fear of not being. Those are the two original fears.

It was speaking from the Three Original Fears Sutra. There was nothing strange about that; it was embedded deep within Iris's memories, so deep that no surge of electricity could burn it out. It was late at night, and Iris was alone in his room, so he spoke out loud. "Where did you go all these days? What happened?"

There is hunger of the stomach. There is hunger of the mind. There is hunger of the bone and the soul. Feed the soul, and all other hungers will be satiated.

The Way of Light Sutra. Iris had finished memorising it not three weeks ago. "Stop speaking in sutras, please," Iris begged. "What happened to you? Do you remember?"

When the flesh burns, know that it is temporary, and when love warms, know that it is temporary. Temporary, temporary, temporary . . .

Still with the Way of Light Sutra. Something was terribly wrong with his construct. "I really hurt you, didn't I?" He pinched the tip of the candlewick, and the room was drowned in darkness. "There was some sort of power surge. I think I fried you a little too hard." Iris leaned against his doorframe and slid down to the floor. He looked out into the courtyard. Outside lay a stuffy and silent summer night, far too humid for any animal or insect to be out. Without a single cloud in the sky, Iris traced out familiar constellations with ease.

"I got scared that you were trying to change me. I know it's dumb, but I thought you'd move my memories around or, worse, make me forget, and I'd be just happy all the time, without a care. I don't want to be happy all the time. I don't want to forget. Mother Nova says I'm far too heavy of a person to be a Vessel—well, you know. A Vessel's robes signify light. We are the light that shines through the worst of times and the light that leads souls to the One Beginning." Iris paused, picked up a small pebble from the floor and tossed it into the courtyard. In the dead quiet of the temple, he listened to it bounce thrice over the cobblestones. "I'm not *light* enough, I guess, or something. No one wants a downer at their funeral."

Not a downer, Iris, a weak voice whispered and was followed by a surge of electric pain.

"You're back," Iris whispered, a childish grin stretching across his face. "You're back! You're alive! I thought you'd just be reciting sutras for the rest of your life."

You recite sutras for the rest of your life. Followed by another surge. Iris winced. It was going to take a bit of time to get used to the surge that followed every sentence, but with time, he'd learn to ignore it completely. Like so many other sensations, he could learn to ignore it.

I can't recall full sutras. I can't recall yesterday.

Iris flinched at the surge. This one was stronger, laden with fear and self-pity. What good was a construct if it couldn't remember things for him? The thought came too fast before he could stop it. Iris stared out into the courtyard in panic. "I'm sorry," he whispered, but his electronic companion had heard the thought as soon as Iris had had it.

What good is a construct if it can't remember? VIFAI repeated.

"I didn't mean that." But VIFAI had already retreated to the furthest corner of Iris's mind without an acknowledgement. Iris had hurt its feelings. He had maimed it first and then added insult to injury, and he had no means to fix either. Defeated, Iris crawled onto his mat and stared at the wall until morning came.

They set off towards their inevitable demise after five hours of restless sleep. Yan led the way, with Jesi and Ishtan sandwiched between him and Eli. Both the archaeologist and guard had their guns drawn. If anyone spoke, it was in hushed whispers that Yan was quick to quell. Iris trailed at the tail end, mindful to not fall too far behind, but keeping a consistent two metres away from the group.

These parts of the ship, like many others before it, were flooded in perpetual dusk. Vines and other vegetation had grown awry here, twisting wildly around the light panels, and winding themselves through the holes and cracks in the corridor walls. A low, sweet smell of rot wafted around them, and the air once again grew humid and sticky.

If Iris had been at the head of their procession, he would have pointed out to Yan that it was strange that the brain of the ship would reside in such warm and humid conditions. In his experience, ship computers were often kept at unbearably cold temperatures, and this one couldn't have been different. But if Jesi was right, and Yan was indeed clever, he was certainly having the same concerns. As if overhearing his internal musings, Yan traded his position at the helm with Ishtan and joined Iris at the back of the line.

"Ishtan at the front of the line, gun drawn, is not the best idea, in my humble and uneducated opinion," Iris said, keeping his voice deliberately low.

Yan handed him his thermos; the golden logo of the Sychi Institute flashed in the dim light. "He can handle it. Anyway, not like we have much of a choice now and it's been quiet so far, and Eli's watching his back, and we're watching Eli's."

Iris wanted to confess how Tev had really died, but instead, he unscrewed the thermos lid and took three large sips of warm water. Surprised by the sudden flavour, Iris looked to Yan.

"I found an old tea-tablet in my pack," Yan explained. "Thought it'd be fine, wouldn't break your fast. Tea doesn't have calories, I think."

"That's very thoughtful of you." Iris lowered his head in a small bow. Jesi's words from the night before pounded on the door of his mental safe, eager to escape. Iris did his best to hold them at bay.

"It's jasmine." Yan wrinkled his nose. "I think."

It was linden, but Iris didn't need to make a point of it. He sipped at the tea and walked alongside Yan, their footsteps falling in rhythm.

"It's awfully humid here," Yan said.

He was having the same reservations then. Iris continued to look ahead, watching over the bobbing heads of their companions. "And you are certain this is the way to the brain you have identified?"

Yan hummed an affirmative.

"And just like every other ship computer I have ever seen, this one would need to be kept cold for optimal functioning?"

Another affirmative hum.

It *was* awfully humid. The closer they ventured towards the spot where Yan had pinpointed as location of the brain of the *Nicaea*, the damper it got. Soon, water was trickling down the walls of the corridor and disappearing beneath the layers of moss, lapped up by the organic sponge. It also trickled down the back of Iris's neck and ran under the collar of his undershirt. He hoped that the patch on his left shoulder would prevent any infection, but he also couldn't bring himself to care.

"Could the humidity be causing it to malfunction?" Iris asked after an uncomfortable fifteen minutes of silence. "Could it be the cause for the fractured speech?" He wasn't ready to abandon his theory about the *Nicaea*, but he wasn't going to push it on Yan, not yet. As Jesi had said, the engineer had grown rigid in his thinking and required a gentle hand.

Yan thought on it for a moment and shook his head. "It would probably just shut down. It didn't get humid here overnight—it would all rust to hell in a month or so—and it's been like this for who knows how long. No, something else is wrong. I don't know what, and I fucking hate not knowing things."

That much was plainly obvious.

After another three hours of silent walking, they could, at last, see the end of the corridor ahead where the walls parted and spread out into a boundless space. Here, a steady pulse radiated through the floors, growing in intensity as they neared their destination. Whatever Yan had tracked down, brain or not, was fast approaching. Having let VIFAI rest all this time, Iris gently nudged it awake. *Are you well rested?* he whispered, for no other reason than to appear considerate.

Oh, this isn't good at all, VIFAI said, awake and alert in a fraction of a second. Why did you come here? This is where the pings came from.

Iris nudged Yan, still walking by his side. "This is where the pings came from, my AI says."

"Yes!" Yan pumped his fist in the air. "I was right."

They seemed to have very different ideas about what sort of an encounter they were about to face. Yan appeared to be expecting to meet a tired hired gun, tasked with securing the ship for a station or for a rival institute. Iris had no idea what he expected. With every step, the pulse beneath his feet grew stronger. Breaking away from Yan's side, Iris hurried to where Jesi walked. If Yan wouldn't believe him, he would rely on the next best engineer among them. Jesi had been right; they should have asked the ship what it wanted.

"Do you still think we can still ask the *Nicaea* what she wants?" Iris panted as he came to a stop by Jesi's side.

The girl stared at him with mild surprise and gave him a small nod. "I'll need Yan's help, I think. Why now, Vessel?"

"Because we're getting closer to the epicentre of whatever happened here." This was only the second time Ishtan had spoken in Iris's company since he and Yan had rejoined the group. The archaeologist muttered something in a foreign language that resembled a prayer as he pointed ahead.

Ahead lay a twenty-foot hangar door. Long cracks ran along the length of it where steel began losing out to nature. Its metal surface glistened with moisture. Water ran from some unseen force in a timid waterfall, originating somewhere right below the ceiling. Gnarled roots fought through any opening where the metal wasn't flush against the floor. A patchwork of moss, and lichen, and mold reached across the walls.

But it was a little to the left that Iris's eyes were drawn to. Along a segment of tall walls stripped of vines and moss stretched a mural. It ran from floor to ceiling in vibrant red, black, and orange. Broad strokes, preserved through time, spread colour and motion across the barren metal. Its shimmer, which appeared nearly fresh, played in the dim light and beckoned them closer.

Eli approached it cautiously and scraped a nail against the red. He stuck his finger in his mouth.

"What is *wrong* with you?" Jesi hissed.

"Well, it's not paint." Eli shrugged. "It's kind of sweet, actually. Not bad."

Ishtan walked along the wall, squinting in the dim light. Iris watched as his mouth moved silently along reverent words, no longer in any pattern Iris could recognise. The mural depicted a similar scene from the ones Iris had beheld before. Battle. Death. He was growing quite tired of those themes.

Somehow, the death and battle so prominent in the murals had left little trace around the ship. There were no bones anywhere on the ship but the cargo bay and the one skeleton he had found in an individual room. So much death with so little evidence. It was a thought Iris returned to over and over again, every time he drifted to sleep. Surely there had to be evidence of the slaughter. It had to be *somewhere. Keep an ear out for any new pings,* Iris asked VIFAI. *Don't respond to anything. Stay as quiet as you can. Just listen.* The AI confirmed.

Below Iris's feet, the rhythmic pulsing carried on at an even pace. It merely hummed now, reminding him of its presence, still watching his every move. Iris searched the mural for any additional clues, anything at all to give him another piece of the already deadly puzzle.

"Iris, would you come here?" Ishtan called out from down the corridor. The archaeologist stood in front of a red-dominated stretch of the mural, his neck craned upwards. "What do you make of this?" he asked when Iris stopped to his right. The archaeologist spoke softly, out of earshot of everyone else. Without even looking up, Iris suspected the image he was about to see was not for everyone's eyes. A wide trunk of an ancient tree ran up towards the ceiling. Its knotted branches spread for tens of metres in each direction. The roots too were depicted as running out in all directions, coming up from the ground as shrubbery and small plants, only to duck beneath the surface again.

"This is different," Iris whispered. "Not good different." He had the sense to crane his neck upwards, same as Ishtan, and follow the trunk towards the ceiling. There, within the hastily painted canopy, Iris noticed it: the same red, watchful eye. The very same eye that bore witness to all the other slaughter. This time it was buried in the lush greenery, barely visible to anyone who didn't know what to look for—but Iris did.

"Violence on generation ships is not uncommon," Ishtan said, head still tilted towards the ceiling, "but this appears as more than that. This all feels systemic."

"This mural is remarkably well preserved," Iris said, unsure of what it had to do with everything, but unable to discard the idea. The vibrancy of it was staggering.

Ishtan put his palm against the wall, leaned in, and examined the colour. "I don't think all the murals were painted at the same time," he said at last. "I think this one may be more recent. The ones downstairs are much, much older. By sight alone, I'd say there's probably a hundred years between them, if not more. Eli said this isn't paint; he's partially right. This looks like paint made from flowers, maybe fruit. I'd say they'd run out of First Earth paints by this point. Very primitive. Very peculiar. I would love to get all this into a chemistry lab for analysis. Very, *very* peculiar."

Through the ball of his right foot, Iris sensed a rapid change in the rhythm of the ship's pulse. Just there—the square inch beneath his foot skipped a beat. With no way to explain his premonition, Iris grabbed Ishtan by the shirt collar and yanked him backwards as hard as he could just as a vine pierced the ground and shot up through the air where Ishtan had been standing a moment earlier. The two of them tumbled to the floor.

Immediately, Iris jumped to his feet, his pulsar blade extended in his hand, but the vine was gone as quickly as it had appeared.

"What the hell are you doing?" Eli shouted from up the corridor.

"Stop talking!" Iris shouted back and took a single step in Eli's direction. A vine sprung out from the wall and coiled around Eli's leg so quickly, Iris didn't see it move. In the time it took Iris to take another step, Eli was already yanked off his feet and slammed against the ground. Miraculously, the gun was still in his hand, and he had somehow managed to discharge it at the spot where the vine had come from.

"Go," Eli shouted, firing the gun twice more at the vine that held on to him, relentless, despite being fired at. "Everyone without a weapon, run."

Iris was by Jesi's side in half a second. While her and Yan stood frozen to the ground, Ishtan was already running by, up the corridor. Iris grabbed both Jesi and Yan by the shoulders and shoved them both after Ishtan. In his haste, Ishtan was whipped off his feet by a slashing vine. It took one precise slice with the pulsar blade for the vine to fall into two halves, each jerking towards the archaeologist. Ishtan scrambled to his feet and took off after Jesi and Yan without so much as an acknowledgement.

"Run!" Iris yelled to them. "I'll get Eli." Eli was still fighting, even though a second vine had grabbed hold of his left arm. He pressed the barrel of the gun against it and fired. Pieces of the vine showered him as it crumbled to the ground, motionless. The relief was momentary, as another vine shot out from the ceiling and pierced Eli's right shoulder. He screamed, the gun falling just out of reach by his feet. Iris was beside him in an instant. With one swift motion, he sliced through both the vines around Eli's leg and the one in his shoulder. The pieces fell to the floor twitching and reaching back for the guard.

“Took you long enough,” Eli groaned and picked up the gun. His shoulder was oozing blood, but the shock and adrenaline were enough to propel him forwards. Iris wrapped his left arm around Eli’s torso and dragged the man to his feet.

For a moment, Iris forgot the first rule of combat: Never turn your back on an opponent. He remembered a second later, but it was too late. Springing from the floor just a metre behind them, a vine, stiff as a spear, drew a clean line parallel to the ceiling, straight through Eli’s chest. There was no scream. Eli only exhaled softly. Iris turned his head only to see the guard’s empty eyes staring at him. A thin trickle of blood ran from his parted lips down his chin. With a single slice, Iris severed the vine from the floor.

He threw Eli to the ground and pressed his hands on his chest, but the red oozed and oozed between his fingers and from Eli’s back, forming a growing puddle around them. The man’s eyes stared at the ceiling, pale blue and glassy. “Stay alive,” Iris whispered and pressed one bloodied hand against Eli’s paling face. “Stay alive, please, please, *please*.” He returned his hand to Eli’s chest. He pressed down on the rib cage, once, twice. He could press on it for all eternity, and it would do no good. The knees of Iris’s trousers were soaked in blood. His toes slipped in it. He pressed on Eli’s chest again and again, and prayed out loud, forgetting about the vines that could come for him as well.

“Please, please, *please*, I can’t keep burying them. I can’t keep failing them. *Please*.” Iris lowered his forehead to Eli’s stationary chest, blood smearing across his eyebrows and his nose. “You can’t keep taking them. You can’t keep taking whatever you want,” he cried. “What is it that you even want? What can I give you so that you will stop? How do I make you stop?” Iris sat back on his heels and passed his sleeve over his eyes. “What is it that you want?" he shouted now, pure rage splitting his voice. His voice cracked, his throat dry and aching for water.

Silence. No sound reached him but his own erratic panting and the distant dripping of water.

Drip. Drip. Drip.

One of the speakers by the tall ceiling crackled.

"What do you want?" he asked again, resigned.

The speaker released a high-pitch squeal and died abruptly.

STRANDED. WE ARE STRANDED.

Iris snapped his neck in the direction of the sound, but it seemed to spill from everywhere at once, deafening and discordant. It was Ordan's voice that spoke to him through the speakers. At least it sounded like Ordan, but beneath his voice were notes of Tev and Riyu. Ordan's words, spoken by three distinct voices. Iris took a deep breath. If the ship wanted him dead, he would have been dead. It wanted something else altogether. "Why are you stranded? Who is stranded?"

STRANDED IN SILENCE. CAN'T CALL FOR HELP. CAN'T CALL FOR ANYTHING. There was a pause, like someone was taking a breath. The ship didn't need a breath, but it needed to collect itself. VIOLENCE BEGETS VIOLENCE BEGETS VIOLENCE BEGETS—The speaker squeaked and died.

"We're not trying to hurt you," Iris said softly. He'd been awake too long and done too much to have any desire to keep his eyes open. The brief flurry of exertion had rendered him drained, and he slurred his words shamelessly, numb to the ache in his shoulder. "We're just trying to go home."

The ship didn't reply. He was alone again.

"I'm just trying to go home." Iris looked down at Eli's face, which had greyed at this point, so much so that he couldn't pass as alive. Blood from his body slicked the floor a metre and a half around them. Iris sat in the middle of it, letting the crimson eat away at his robes. Unable to stay conscious any longer, he shut his eyes and allowed his shoulders to slump forwards and forwards, until his head pressed against Eli's cooling hand. There was nothing else after that.

The rhythmic dripping of water and a matching pulsing in his shoulder roused Iris from his sleep. The instant his eyes opened, he was startled upright by a looming presence to his right. He suspected, by the thin, curdled film atop the still-liquid pool, that he had been asleep for at most half an hour. Someone was on their knees beside him, right there in the pooled, coagulated blood. A golden flash of the Sychi Institute logo drew Iris's attention.

"Drink," Yan said and passed the thermos over.

Mechanically, Iris screwed off the lid and drank. The tea was gone, he noticed with a deep disappointment as he continued sipping on the warm water. When he was done, he rested the thermos on the ground. "I couldn't save him," Iris said, voice hoarse, distant.

"I can see that." Yan's voice was gentle, like he was afraid of disturbing the deadly silence he had trespassed on. He remained a respectful metre away from Iris and kept his eyes on Eli. "What will we do with his body?"

At the question, Iris tensed. The blood had already drained, but if they were to preserve the body, they would have to make sure the very last drops of it were gone. They would have to remove the organs, just as he had with Tev.

Tev.

Iris fell forwards again, headfirst, and his forehead smashed into the slick ground. Yan didn't move from his spot. He watched on with a calm focus, saying nothing.

"I can't," Iris murmured, his voice on the verge of breaking. "I can't keep draining their blood and wrapping them in cloth and saying words. I can't. It all means nothing, accomplishes nothing."

Yan listened without interrupting.

"I can't keep pretending that what I'm doing is making a difference. I can't keep being useless, I can't keep failing," he sobbed and immediately slammed his palm across his mouth. Some of Eli's blood pushed past his lips, and the metallic taste of it sent Iris's empty stomach into a spasm. He shut his eyes and prayed for Yan to leave him alone. Alone, he could consult VIFAI. Alone, he could break down in peace and then gird himself enough to prepare Eli's body. Alone. He only knew how to do this alone.

"Fine, I'll do it."

A surge of anger flared up in Iris's chest at the words. "*You* don't know a single thing about preparing a body, engineer Yan," he hissed, head still pressed against the bloody floor.

"That's why you will tell me exactly what to do and then"—Yan gestured to the other end of the space—"you will go over there and *rest*."

One word, and all of Iris's racing thoughts came to a halt. *Rest*. Yan had used a specific word for "rest," a word that implied a time away from everyday responsibilities, a time where one spent their efforts repairing their mind. Where food was made for them, and their clothes were laundered for them, and time was provided to just heal. It was an old word, one that wasn't used often colloquially. A word Iris only had heard from the Starlit.

For what felt like the first time, Iris looked at Yan, *really* looked at him. He had failed to notice in his time on the *Nicaea* that Yan was barely older than he was. He was far less equipped to deal with death and dying than Iris. Yet, unflinching and unyielding, Yan had witnessed it all. He was braving the most brutal ocean currents with nothing in his arsenal but the doggy paddle, refusing to quit, to let panic take him, refusing to entertain the very idea of turning back.

Iris's anger dissipated as quickly as it had appeared, and a different feeling altogether blossomed. It was still in its simplest form, timid, cowardly—yet sharp. He hadn't felt it since his youth, so long ago now that he had forgotten how blindly painful it could be. It was a shy flicker that, if left to its own devices, would grow and grow until it devoured him whole, until he would *let it* devour him whole.

"I don't think there is much we can do for Eli," Iris said, returning to himself. "I don't think it will matter. For Jesi's and Ishtan's sake, we'll move him aside and keep them from seeing him, but it's more important we keep moving now. I fear there's a good chance we will join Eli very soon."

Yan looked down at the body and back up at Iris and gave him a nod. "Whenever you're ready, Vessel. I'll take the legs, and you take the arms." He gave Iris a bitter grin and got to his feet.

Despite everything, they were still on professional terms. The last bit of distance stretched between them, and not even Starlit words could shrink it. But the distance was so small, Iris could learn to live with it. He stood up, careful so that his feet didn't slip on the slick floor. When he reached down to collect Eli's arms, he winced at the pain in his shoulder.

"We should tend to that first," Yan said. "If we leave it as is, you'll be spiking a fever in less than a day."

Iris chuckled lightly at the words. He looked up at Yan, a melancholic smile playing on his cracked lips. How he wished for the luxury of planning for days to come. "I wouldn't worry about that, engineer Yan. We don't have a day."

Without any further exchanges, they picked Eli up and carried him in silence towards the end of the corridor. Iris, carrying the legs. Yan, holding both bloodied arms. They lay him down below the mural of the godlike tree and closed his eyes. Iris had nothing to drape over the body, and the gaping hole in Eli's chest stared at him as he recited the words that returned him to the One Beginning. From the corner of his eye, Iris watched as Yan too recited the words, stumbling over them every few sentences, awkwardly pulling them to the forefront from the depths of his suppressed childhood.

"He did the best he could for us," Iris finished.

"Look where that got him."

"Sometimes we do the best we can," Iris said. "And surrender to whatever comes. Sometimes that's all there is to be done."

It was then, before the mural of the *Nicaea*'s slaughter, that Iris made a different vow: to direct his faculties towards stopping the newly sentient ship, even if Yan never did believe him, even if it only meant that the engineer, and Ishtan, and Jesi could go home. He would commit the greatest sin a Vessel could. He would kill if he had to, and he knew, deep in his heart, that it would be the only way to end what was coming for them. The decision came far too easily and quickly to him, as clear and undeniable as a solution to a mathematical problem. Once the nascent thought became salient, Iris accepted that he would never wear a Vessel's robes again, for they were now forever tainted with this violent compulsion.

For the ageing archaeologist, for the girl-engineer, for Yan, Iris would never go home.

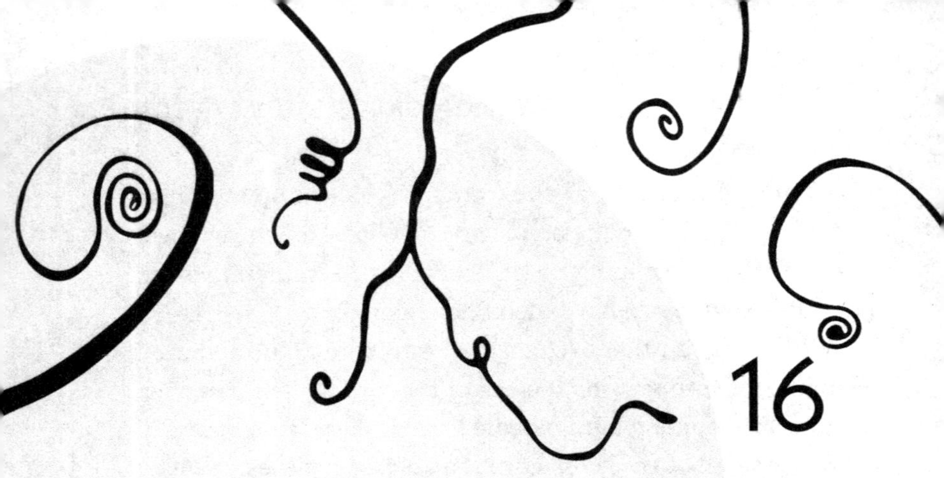

16

Where does it all go, when it's no longer here?
What does it become, when it is no longer itself?

From the unedited records of embedded companion AI construct
Construct Model: 3XU-T
Handler: Iris [last name unavailable]

Blinded for a moment, the fourteen-year-old Iris blinked furiously as Dr. Rahi passed the light back and forth a few more times, from his left eye to his right and back. He then had Iris stick his tongue out, inspected his tonsils, drew some blood, measured his blood pressure, and performed another half-a-dozen tests before he looked the boy up and down and sighed. "There's nothing wrong with you, Iris," Dr. Rahi said. "You're not running a fever, you don't have a concussion, and all your tests keep coming back normal. You might just be tired."

Iris scratched the back of his head, pausing over the scar where the AI implant had been inserted. "I don't remember things as well as I used to. Mother Nova's mad. I keep messing up with my scriptures."

Dr. Rahi looked at him thoughtfully, twirling the penlight in his fingers. Iris was a tall, wiry teenager, a bottomless pit for any food and drink that was given to him. He could sleep for an entire day if he were ever to be presented with the opportunity.

Discipline was wasted on teenage boys like him. "Iris, there's only so much we can do for you without replacing the AI. After your incident, it hasn't been functioning properly and as a result, neither have you."

Iris's eyes shot up to look at him, filled with latent fury. He watched Dr. Rahi take half a step back, carefully eyeing the spot where Iris's hand clutched the edge of the gurney. "I'm still well ahead in my studies," Iris said, the hue of his voice betraying his forcibly calm face.

"Imagine how well you could do with a functional AI."

Iris sensed his construct move in the back of his mind. A sharp electrical current passed through the base of his brain stem, and he winced.

I want to leave.

We're almost done, Iris soothed the electronic voice.

"And there's that," Dr. Rahi added, awfully aware of the wince. "Iris, in a few years, you will begin working as a Vessel, and you will be required to travel and perform funeral rites all over the galaxy. A functional AI will assure your safety, will remember different customs for you, translate languages; it will be your guide in this journey. Without one, you can get lost, you can even get in trouble."

"How did people travel before AIs then?" Iris bit back.

Dr. Rahi sighed, turned away, and began filling Iris's prescription. "Before, they weren't travelling across the galaxy. Before, they didn't memorise a thousand years' worth of scripture. Life was easier before. Times changed, and we didn't, so we need the constructs to help us keep up. Here." He handed Iris a pillbox. "Take one every night before bed. It'll improve your circulation and hopefully help with both memory and the pain."

"Is there any way to help my construct?" Iris asked.

Dr. Rahi raised a furry eyebrow.

"The best thing you can do is replace it, the best thing for both of you."

Iris thought for a moment. "What will happen to it once it's no longer with me?" He winced at the sudden surge in his brain stem. *Don't worry, we're almost done,* Iris thought softly. *Just this one thing, and we can go.*

Dr. Rahi shrugged and nudged Iris with the pillbox. "Who knows?"

Jesi had finally cried herself to sleep, and with her went the last sound that disturbed the quiet. Yan had managed to override one of the doors and severed the corridor between them and whatever had killed Eli. Having scrubbed his face of Eli's blood best he could, Iris idly listened to water drip from the ceiling as it lulled him into a shallow meditative trance. He watched Ishtan and Yan move about through half-lidded eyes, failing to care about either at the moment. This was as much peace as they would get.

"Poor child," Ishtan said, his back resting against the wall, his gun in his hand. He was remarkably calm given what had transpired. Too calm. This sort of terminal calm often came before the bitter end, in Iris's experience. A lucidity, a clarity that often ended in death. Yet another imminent emergency Iris would have to attend to. He cursed internally at the callousness of his thoughts, but he couldn't stop them.

"Jesi's resilient," Yan said, his voice low. "She'll be all right, if only we can get her out of here." He didn't say "get *us* out of here," and Iris gave him a side glare. Ishtan didn't notice or noticed but failed to care about the laden *if*.

The archaeologist chewed his lip in silence, thinking. His thick, grey brows furrowed together. "Seems like the vines reacted when I suggested we remove the mural," he muttered. "Almost like they overheard me. Makes me think that as long as we don't discuss meddling with the ship, we should be safe, for now."

It was Yan's turn to glare at Iris. "*Vessel* here has a theory about that."

"There's a chance the ship may be alive," Iris said before Yan could interject with another remark. He had to talk quickly before Yan discredited him. "There's a chance it has an AI system running it and it's—it doesn't want us doing whatever it is we've been doing."

Ishtan raised his eyebrows. "Isn't it too old to have an AI?"

"That's what I fucking told him," Yan grumbled, picking up his thermos and shoving it at Iris. "*Drink.* You have to keep drinking if you're not going to eat."

Iris begrudgingly took the thermos. Yan's care was growing a shade aggressive, but the engineer kept persisting, reminding Iris to drink, reminding Iris to step back and meditate for a few minutes here and there. Iris would never openly admit it, but he was grateful. "And I have explained that the AI system probably formed in-flight," he said softly, between sips of warm water. "I think the AI is interfacing with the organics on the ship, all the vines and the moss and the shrubs, and the, the—"

"And I already told you that's impossible," Yan said, declining the thermos when Iris tried passing it back to him. He shoved it into Ishtan's hands instead.

"It's not impossible." All three turned towards the meek voice coming from where Jesi lay on her side. She stared ahead with hollow eyes, through them, towards something beyond any sight. The shock of losing Eli had rendered her emotionally flat, but maybe that was best for the time being. "Remember the experiments they did with the *mada-ekresku* worms, Yan? That interface worked."

"That was over a hundred years ago, and it wasn't an AI, Jesi. No ethics board would let you shove an AI into a worm. That was a simple bot."

Iris heard relief in Yan's voice. Jesi wasn't completely broken. There was still hope for her. Yan was right. No matter how awful the world, Jesi was resilient. The same couldn't be said for the rest of them.

"What about *tecra-gel*?" Jesi asked.

Yan snorted. "*Tecra-gel* experiments were somewhat prominent not fifty years ago, when there was still interest in producing AI/organic interfaces. They were stopped when it was deemed unethical to place fully developed AI systems into what was nothing more than jelly. They could exert themselves in so far that the jelly made shapes, but that was about it. From there, everyone just left AI constructs to their inorganic homes in ships and stations and moved on."

Iris tapped his big toe against the ground, channelling his growing frustration into movement. "You're all forgetting that I successfully interface with *my* AI and have been for decades."

Three pairs of eyes focused on him.

"Well, yes," Ishtan said. "But you're a monk."

Iris pursed his lips. Whatever the hell *that* meant. "The problem with interfacing isn't the organic/inorganic bond. It's time. The inorganic component has to *learn* its way around the organics, the way the organic system sends its signals. Only then can it mimic them. Nothing has had more time than the *Nicaea*."

Three pairs of eyes turned to Yan. He only rolled his eyes. "There is no precedent."

"This can become one," Jesi pointed out. "Vessel has a point. The *Nicaea* has been floating through space for a thousand years. Yan, you have to admit it, we are all out of our depths here. All of us were attacked by the vines. All of us heard the voices. Nothing makes sense anymore, which means anything is possible."

"Not *anything*." Yan pulled out a cigarette from his shirt pocket and, seeing how it was dripping with moisture, whipped it against the ground. "You want to imagine all sorts of fairy tales about ships coming to life? Fine. I don't care anymore. It's picking us off one by one, whatever the hell it is. Ship or not, if both Jesi and I go next, then what? Does Ishtan or the Vessel know how to override airlocks? Do they even know how to call Station for help?" He glared at Ishtan, who sheepishly turned his eyes to the ground. "Thought so."

"If only Tev were alive," Jesi said softly. "He'd know how to talk to the ship, you know?"

"Well, he's not," Yan spat out and got to his feet. "And bringing him up won't help us here." Without another word, he stormed down the corridor and turned the corner, away from everyone's pitying eyes. The three remaining fell into a mournful silence.

After several eternal minutes trickled by, Jesi was the first to crack. "I should go apologise," she said. "He's hurting. I should know better." She groaned and sat up, but Iris stopped her.

"I'll go. I'm already getting on his nerves. Maybe it will be easier for him to get angry."

"Surprised you'd support anger," Ishtan said, voice distant. He passed Yan's empty thermos between his palm, staring blankly ahead.

Iris struggled to his feet and steadied himself against the wall. He was getting increasingly dizzier with each passing hour, the starvation having eaten its way through most of his fat reserves. His body was after muscle now, and that was proving rather inefficient. "Anger mobilises you if you can only keep it focused enough. I would prefer him angry over distraught." Holding his left arm against his chest, Iris hobbled down the corridor. "I'd prefer him to be neither, but I'm a realist."

He found Yan crouched by the wall, his face buried in the crook of his forearm. He didn't move when Iris came upon him, nor when the Vessel knelt beside him, leaving just enough space to be respectful. Iris watched as Yan's hands contracted into fists, open and close, and his shoulders tensed. The anger Iris had so foolishly praised as mobilising was doing the very opposite.

"Anger is a funny thing," Iris said, watching Yan's fingers twitch at the sound of his voice. "It gives us an illusion of control, doesn't it? Even if we blame only ourselves, we get the sense we're doing something productive, something just. We're correcting a wrong." Yan slowly looked up with the expression of a man who'd just been struck. "We convince ourselves that as long as we're angry with ourselves, as long as we blame ourselves, whatever *it* is we're blaming ourselves for, we won't forget it. We're making *someone* pay. Justice is being served. Meanwhile, we don't have to feel the pain. Isn't that right? It's not the thing that happened that we're afraid of—it's already done—it's the pain."

Slowly, Iris reached out to him. When the engineer didn't recoil, he took Yan's fist into his hands. "Softly," Iris said, gently unfurling the fist finger by finger. "If you hold it softly instead, you'll be able to bear it much longer." He held Yan's hand in his. It was wide and warm, and Iris traced the calloused fingertips as the flicker of a feeling much too great ignited again. It took the smallest bit for him to get carried away.

"I won't suggest that you forgive yourself, but just that you do not set yourself on fire in Tev's memory. You'll just burn yourself to the ground and maybe some of us with you as well.

Let it burn, but don't stoke it. Don't chase it. I promise you, when this is all finished, I will sit with you so that you may rest." Iris used the same word for rest Yan had. "I'll sit with you while you heal, and we can remember together."

Still staring blankly ahead, Yan whispered, softer than the drip of water around them, "When I was a kid, we had this cat named Litmus. He was ancient, like at least nineteen or twenty. My family had gotten him way before I was born." Yan's eyes glistened in the dim corridor, filling with tears. "When I was ten, Litmus died. Like I said, he was so old, so it wasn't a big deal. Everyone was adequately sad, but it wasn't a tragedy or anything. But I *loved* that stupid cat. This is so fucked—" Yan broke off, shutting his eyes.

Iris gave Yan's hand a timid squeeze. "Go on."

"Well, our cat died, and everyone just talked about how that was just the way things went, you know? Things die, that's the order of the cosmos. But I wasn't ready. I was ten. So, before they had a chance to bury Litmus, I dragged this cat's carcass up to the roof during a thunderstorm. I was trying to reanimate..." Yan paused when he noticed Iris's lips twitch into a smile. "Is my childhood trauma funny to you, Vessel?"

"Not at all." Iris lowered his head, in part to apologise, in part to hide his widening grin. "No, please, continue. You were trying to revive your family pet." Despite his efforts, a single giggle escaped him.

When he looked up again, Yan was smiling back. "I'll save you the narrative tension. The roof got hit pretty badly by lightning. I got knocked out cold when I fell off, broke my arm too. Litmus"—Yan broke off into a half giggle, half sob—"Litmus smelled like a campfire, he got charred so—my poor mother—I can't believe I'm thinking about this right now. That's so *fucked*."

Beside him, Iris was sobbing from laughter, and he pressed his forehead against Yan's hand. "How . . . how long was Litmus dead for before . . . before . . ." Iris couldn't finish his question for his mirth.

"A week." Yan forced the words through his own laughter. "We kept him in the freezer. Right next to the ice cream." He collapsed onto his knees, his forehead effortlessly finding the spot between Iris's neck and shoulder.

After another few moments of bellowing laughter, Iris snaked his arms around Yan's shoulders and pulled him closer. "When I was twelve, some kids found a dead mountain bear," Iris began softly, when he could speak without breaking into a chuckle. His right temple rested against Yan's head. It was the closest he'd been to a person in a decade, so close that he could smell Yan's sweat mixed with fresh soil, and greenery, and stale tobacco. He must have smelled like that. How odd, to think of these things when both their lives could be cut short this instant. Iris closed his eyes. "It was the summer—"

Yan snorted into Iris's shoulder.

"Ah, I see the engineer has figured out where this is going." Iris smiled and continued. "Well, we picked a day when we didn't have cleaning chores or studies. It must have been an auspicious day. Anyway, we went into the woods, and Eron—it was always Eron—he kept poking the thing with a stick."

Yan had begun to tremble with silent laughter.

"And I kept telling him not to because the thing was *so* bloated. I came closer to take his stick away and that's when"—Iris shook his head to keep himself from laughing—"it just blew up. The entire thing, just a giant, dead, awful bear explosion."

Yan pulled back—Iris could see the engineer's face was stained with tears—and threw his head back and laughed so hard he was audibly gasping for air.

"There were five of us, just covered, and I mean *covered*, in this bear's insides. It took me hours to get my robes clean, and the smell didn't go away for another week. Everyone just kept asking about it. Oh, it was such an awful thing," Iris managed to finish before he buried his face in his hands, howling with laughter.

When Yan got to catch his breath, he wiped the tears from his dirty face and gave Iris a reassuring grin.

"I think it's pretty inappropriate that I too reminisce of such things given the gravity of our situation, engineer Yan," Iris said softly, still smiling. He held Yan's gaze. The engineer's eyes weren't a solid colour. Swimming in the sea of black were flecks of honey, nearly golden in the dim light, and for an unknown reason, that mere fact was suddenly the most important thing.

Yan gave Iris's shoulder a squeeze. "Maybe we're both fucked then."

"In just the same way."

It was deceptively alluring to laugh about the most inappropriate things with Yan. With a sudden panic, Iris came to the realisation that it had been many months, if not years, since he had laughed this way with anyone other than VIFAI. It was also only the second time he had ever told that story. The first had been to Bacai, when she would not stop pestering him about why he was washing his robes with such urgency.

Iris didn't know when or how, but Yan's hand had moved from his shoulder to the base of his neck. Now, it comfortably rested there, with Yan's thumb brushing faintly against Iris's jaw.

Huh, VIFAI said. **Well, isn't this a peculiar turn of events.**

"I think there are much more pressing matters at hand," Iris told Yan softly and immediately regretted every word because amidst the growing danger, the death, he was beginning to feel this was something worth risking his life for. This very moment, that silenced every neurosis and numbed every wound, was worth savouring at any cost it carried.

With a polite smile, Yan pulled his hand away. "Of course." He gave his head a strong shake and got to his feet. "You're absolutely right, Vessel. Now, while you were giving me a tour of your memory lane, I had a thought. Whatever is behind those doors is probably very important, otherwise Eli wouldn't be dead. By my previous observations, it's one of the brains of the ship. That means that destroying it won't solve our entire problem, but it could buy us some time. You don't know this, being a monk and all, but every signal has a range. If the brain is jamming the airlocks, shutting it down will clear an area around the jamming signal." He sniffled again, and Iris saw a wall of tears shimmering over Yan's eyes, still contained. "The last time I looked at our map, I saw there's an emergency airlock two decks up from here. It's close enough that if we can kill this brain, we might have enough time to radio back to Station and call for an evac before whoever is responsible for this finds another way to jam the signal. After that, who knows? Maybe Station will even make it in time."

"Sounds like a plan," Iris agreed and took an anguished step back. For now, if he could just be of service, it would have to be enough. With a deep bow, he reached into one of the pockets of his robes and produced a slightly bruised apple. He handed it to Yan, a ghost of a smile playing along his lips. "I'll let the others know."

Jesi lay on her back, chewing the apple that had been intended for Yan. "Whoever it is, they won't just let us walk in. I can force the door open, I think, if nothing kills me first." She had thrown herself into the problem with abandon, much to the admiration of her supervisor, and was actually making some headway. "Vessel's pulsar blade should be able to cut into the fuse box, so I can work, but when the vines come, and they will, someone will have to protect me. I'll be busy." There was no more fear left in the girl. The last of it had bled from her small body in a final fit of tears, and now she was all cold determination.

"We can distract it," Yan said. "I'm sure we can short-circuit something and start a fire."

"Something tells me it would be able to multitask," Ishtan grumbled. "Is there another way in? Air vents?"

Ishtan was on to something. Down the corridor, a thin outline of an air vent behind the vines beckoned to Iris. He walked along the wall, grabbed hold of a vine running along the ceiling, cursed internally at the shooting pain in his left shoulder, and pulled himself close. With a single pull, the air vent cover popped open, and Iris shoved his head through the opening. No vines. In fact, there was nothing organic at all inside the vent.

"It's all clear here," Iris called to the three watching him intently. "It's the same as the stairwells. There must be something about this surface that makes vegetation hard to grow." With a small wince, he hopped back down to the floor. A day at most. He only had to last another day. "I believe the vents are a good option, Ishtan."

"Then we split up," Yan said softly after Iris landed safely. He motioned for Jesi and Ishtan to gather close. Iris watched from afar, reading Yan's lips easily even in the dim light. "Jesi and Iris will go together to override the fuse box. Ishtan and I will take to the vents. Sorry, old man, you're gonna have to exert yourself."

Ishtan slapped Yan's shoulder loudly. "I'll have you know I was quite a mountaineer in my day."

"What?" Jesi teased, barely containing herself, all pretenses of secrecy forgotten. "On the glaciers of First Earth?"

Ishtan tried to play it serious but he was grinning behind his beard. "Have some respect. Back in my day, a respectable professor from a respectable university had at least that."

"And now you have a murder ship," Yan said, patting Ishtan on the back. "We're diversifying. We're moving up in the world."

Iris listened to the jovial banter from afar. He would have joined, but he was neither a funny nor a very wise monk. Most things he'd say would be misconstrued and spoil the mood, and he truly wished for this mood to persist, even if for another few minutes. They all needed it.

Instead, he internally checked in on VIFAI as it snored, emitting miniscule electrical impulses, in the back of his mind. It was safe, for now. Jesi whispered something, and both Yan and Ishtan laughed loudly. Iris's stomach twisted into a painful knot. He prayed silently that when the time came, he would know what to do to keep them all safe and that he would have the courage to do it.

Still smiling, Jesi came over and handed him Yan's thermos. The surface was warm to the touch, filled with freshly boiled water. "Come back," she said, her voice having regained its familiar warmth. "Yan wants to talk strategy, and someone needs to be there to tell him when he's wrong."

17

I chose strangers over faith.
Is that my sin, my closest friend?
Will they be our undoing, or have we always been undone,
waiting only for the right moment to fall to pieces?
From the unedited records of embedded companion AI construct
Construct Model: 3XU-T
Handler: Iris [last name unavailable]

With her back pressed to the wall, Jesi peered around the doorway. Her head and right shoulder hovered dangerously between the two halves of the corridor. She would be crushed in an instant if the two-tonne door were to fall. Not two steps behind her, with one palm against the wall, Iris listened to the ship's pulse while the girl worked, ready to pull her out of harm's way if the need arose. Around them, the ship lay suspiciously dormant. This peace couldn't last.

"OK," Jesi hissed, "we go now. Don't say anything, and walk softly."

Iris took his place by Jesi's side. Ishtan and Yan had gone ahead, their path more convoluted and twisted, up high in the ceilings. There were no maps for the vents, and they would have to navigate them as they went. Thankfully, there were also no vines for them to avoid. Iris moved such a vine from Jesi's way.

She ducked underneath and scurried along and almost immediately caught her face in a web of trailing plants. From the way the muscles of her neck tensed, Iris could tell a scream was brewing and clasped his free hand across Jesi's mouth.

"Slow down," Iris whispered in her ear, his arm pulling her small frame flush against him. "Quietly and gently. *OK?*"

Jesi gave him a nod, and Iris let go. They had one try at this. If the ship reacted, Iris wasn't sure how he'd be able to hold it back—and react it would. As soon as Jesi managed to pry the fuse box open, the countdown would begin, and the *Nicaea* would know they were coming for her, and she wouldn't be happy. They moved slowly along the side of the corridor, feet stepping softly around puddles of condensation. Soon the ceiling-high mural came into view. Jesi froze when her eyes fell upon a brown stain on the floor; it was all that she would ever see of the late Eli.

"Don't pay it any attention," Iris said in a low voice. They had never formally addressed where Eli had gone, but Jesi and Ishtan knew. They *had to* know. Iris nudged Jesi between the shoulder blades with the second knuckle of his index finger. "Quickly."

Pushing aside her fear and grief, Jesi soldiered on towards the wide door that separated them from the *Nicaea*'s brain. In the dim light, the dark bruise of the fuse box lay flush against the wall. Wasting no time, Jesi got to work. It was much faster going now that they had actual tools, so unlike when Iris and Yan were trapped in the maintenance room. With one swift slice of his pulsar blade, the fuse box fell open.

The countdown began.

His back towards the girl, Iris extended the blade to its full length and kept watch. He wished for some way to check in on Yan and Ishtan, but he would just have to trust their capabilities. *Yan's capabilities.* Although, both men would be pathetically helpless in the face of any real combat. Yan was too stubborn to die, Iris reassured himself. He was too stubborn and arrogant to let something as minute as a vine end his life.

The *Nicaea* lay silent around him. *Wake up,* Iris called out to VIFAI, and it pinged awake. *Is it trying to contact us? Reach us in any way?*

It's quiet, VIFAI responded, whispering for some unknown reason. I can't register any movement at all.

And that was a problem. It was quiet the way the world usually fell into silence before an earthquake swallowed it whole. The way birds and animals grew still when a thunderstorm approached. Iris knew this sort of quiet well, a film that draped over the world moments before disaster. His fingers turned white around the hilt of his blade. Behind him, the ten-tonne door separating them from the ship's brain slid open with a low screech.

"Well done!" he called out to Jesi.

"I didn't do that."

Both peered into the chasm that had opened up for them and only them. Like the maw of a titanic beast, the chasm warned *I will devour you*—and it wasn't bluffing. The world that lay beyond the threshold was deep-space dark, peppered with flashing bioluminescence. A wave of moisture struck Iris in the face, thick as a wet towel. The hangar was at least fifty thousand square metres in size. Here, nature did not merely coexist; it ruled. The walls and ceiling were wrapped in vines and crawling plants, forming a thick, organic quilt. In the faint glow of the bioluminescent fungi, Iris could make out the outlines of fully grown trees, their crowns moulded to the arched ceiling.

"And Yan was sure this is where the signals were coming from?" he asked in a half whisper. He saw nothing that was a computer, nothing that could act as a brain for the city-sized spaceship. Here was a monstrous terrarium, ready to shut the lid on them all.

Jesi gave him a timid nod. Iris had half a mind to retreat, to give in to his fears and find Yan and Ishtan, tell them that this wasn't worth it, to come up with any other plan they could to avoid venturing into the belly of the beast. Something about the darkness and the damp smell of century-old decay stirred a primal panic inside him. This, in all its macabre glory, was the end.

"Let's go," Jesi said and took a tentative step inside. "Yan said whatever is here is powerful enough to control the better part of the ship. We need to find it and shut it down." Iris reached to grab Jesi's arm, but she was already marching towards the darkest part of the room. With every single one of her steps, waves of pearly bioluminescence ignited at her feet and rippled out towards the walls. Every single step, lighting up the space a little bit more.

Iris retracted his pulsar blade and holstered it, then moved the holster to his left side. It was a strange arrangement, but the part of his brain stem where his AI implant had been inserted pulsed rhythmically until he did as he was told. VIFAI sensed something Iris didn't, something it couldn't communicate to him accurately enough without speaking at length. Only blind trust in his inorganic companion convinced Iris to follow along. VIFAI's intuitions hadn't failed him yet.

They were halfway into the hangar when Iris caught a flash of familiar white. "Wait," he called out and lifted a large fern leaf from the ground. Beneath it lay a full skeleton, white and pristine, completely intact. No broken bones. No splinters. Starlit words spilled from Iris's lips before he could ever think them. What was this human skeleton doing, buried in the ferns? There were no bones anywhere else on the ship, but here this one was, immaculately preserved. Iris reached for another fern and moved it out of the way. Behind it were more bones: another perfect skeleton, equally as white, but smaller, childlike.

"Jesi," Iris sounded a warning, but when no response came, he searched for the girl, only to find her mute, standing ten metres from him, her arm outstretched, pointing towards the obvious.

"I think I found the rest of the *Nicaea*'s passengers." As if responding to her words, the thing Jesi was pointing at shimmered. Pale bone. A mountain of ivory. Iris grabbed Jesi's shoulder and pulled her behind him, but at once, the fungi ignited with a blazing light, and the mountain of skeletons flashed with the fury of a rising star.

Too late.

"Fuck," Jesi whispered. Iris agreed internally. It took all his willpower to keep the pulsar blade holstered instead of jumping into action. Not yet. He wasn't sure what they were up against yet. He hadn't stared into their enemy's eyes. Only once he did would he decide whether to run and hide or face their foe. Only then would he even entertain his desperation.

The glow of the fungi rippled past the bones and towards the back of the hangar. Both Iris and Jesi fell mute as their eyes traced the trunk of an ancient tree emerging from beyond the mountain of bones. Twisted, cracking bark lined its entire height, thick enough to resist a bullet. Their faces tilted upwards to look at the ceiling. The far edges of the crown bled into the darkness, boundless.

As they watched, the glow encircled the trunk and followed along the hundreds of vines that ran from the crown towards the pile of bones. One glistening vine per skeleton. One vine for every body that was once a person, now nothing more than an artifact of slaughter. With rising nausea, Iris recalled how the *Nicaea* had absorbed every one of his fallen companions. There were hundreds of bones here. How many more lay crumpled beneath the ferns? How many more were buried beneath the soil? He recalled Riyu's excitement over a mother tree and its ability to watch over all its saplings. He recalled the networks of mycelium and how they acted akin to the human nervous system. And through these recollections, Iris quickly solidified his horrible conclusion.

"Don't touch anything," he warned Jesi, extending his arm so that she was completely hidden behind him. "Back away towards the door. Slowly. Don't make any noise." He sensed the girl move away from him. Jesi's faint footsteps echoed on the ground in bursts of light as she retreated. The ship's pulse rose. It swelled and quickened, until it reached a monstrous crescendo. They were out of time.

Before Iris could yell for Jesi to run, the door to the corridor slammed shut with a force that sent pieces of moss and shrubs hurtling towards them. The sound of the impact nearly would have ruptured Iris's eardrums if not for his palms pressed tight against his ears.

Along the tree's gargantuan trunk, the fungi flickered in a frenzy, their luminosity growing with each passing moment. Iris marched over to where Jesi had fallen and grabbed her shaking hand. "Give me your thumb, *now*." Iris grabbed the pulsar blade and pressed Jesi's thumb roughly into the indentation. *Add her fingerprint and her stress response to the authorised list,* Iris commanded VIFAI. When it began to protest, he cut it off: *Now.* In a moment, the scan was complete, and Iris stored the pulsar blade away once more. He leaned down and whispered into Jesi's ear, calmly, patiently; she would need to remember his words exactly if they were to have even the slightest chance of making it out alive. His eyes again fell across the mountain of bones, and Iris prayed for Yan and Ishtan to lose their way in the vents and avoid this killing field.

He forced his fingers into the ground beneath him. The soil gave way. It was well packed, but soft. He could move well on soil like this. *Stay on high alert,* he told VIFAI and got to his feet. It was a shot in the dark, but it was the only way to prove himself right. It was probably the only way any of them were leaving this ship alive. "You have us here, trapped, willing to listen," Iris called out, his voice cracking. "What is it that you want?"

No answer.

Jesi looked up at him like he was insane, and to her, he surely was. For a moment, a cold chill crept up Iris's back, and he envisioned Ishtan and Yan, already absorbed into the ship, both dead, necks snapped clean. What would he do if the *Nicaea* spoke to him in Yan's voice? Would he uphold his promise and protect Jesi, or would he simply surrender to his fate? "What is it that you want?" It was better to yell into the abyss than to drown in one's thoughts. The speakers above him crackled, and Iris instinctively bent his knees, ready to flee or fight.

VESSEL IRIS, a voice—if one could call it that, a culmination of Eli, Ordan, Riyu, and Tev—said. It was discordant and triggered some part of Iris's brain that made it hard not to dry heave onto the ground.

"Oh fuck, oh fuck, oh *fuck*." Jesi muttered the words like a half-forgotten prayer. Her eyes darted back and forth across the vast room, failing to locate the speaker.

VESSEL IRIS, the voice repeated. It shifted towards Riyu's tone and softened its edges, like it had picked up on Iris's discomfort.

"Yes?" Iris didn't know where to look, so he looked straight ahead at the tree.

WE CAN FINALLY SPEAK TO ONE ANOTHER. WE CAN FORGO THE GUESSING AND MISUNDERSTANDING.

Iris was taken aback by the eloquence of the speech. It was like he was speaking to a completely different construct than the one that had simply recited Ordan's and Riyu's words. While that voice had been robotic and flat, this, this was almost too human-like. "If you could tell me where you are, I could face you," Iris said. There were ulterior motives for knowing where the ship was speaking from, but he would refrain from disclosing those just yet.

The ship laughed. At least, Iris thought it laughed. It was strange to hear the inorganic tone pitch in such a way. He had only heard VIFAI do that, but it had been speaking in his own voice for decades. WOULD YOU NOT RATHER ASK WHERE YOU ARE IN RELATION TO ME?

He had known it, but it wasn't until that moment that Iris truly understood that they were *inside* the thing that was the *Nicaea*. They were walking down its corridors, same as the blood flowed through Iris's own veins. The ship was the whole organism, each panel, each shattered light bulb. It was connected to every bit of itself at all times, every shrub, every deck, every piece of itself reaching out towards the edges, gathering information, processing data. It knew itself completely, had complete mastery of every vine.

YOUR FRIENDS WILL BE HERE SOON, VESSEL IRIS, the ship said. WE CAN ALL TALK TOGETHER. With that final word, a vent panel high above popped open and tumbled to the ground. Ishtan's head poked out, only to recoil as two vines lunged towards the opening and pulled both the archaeologist and Yan out. Yan cursed and fought against the vines as they tightened around his shoulders. Ishtan just hung there.

"Put them down, *please*," Iris said, careful so that his voice didn't telegraph the violence that was brewing below the surface. He could be dangerous if he was pushed; the ship already knew this.

Once Yan's feet hit the ground, he shrugged his restraints off and ran towards Jesi, who was still in a pile somewhere behind Iris. Ishtan simply crumpled onto the dirt. No one went to his side.

NOW WE CAN TALK, the ship said with the tone of an irate mother.

"Who's that?" Yan muttered.

PLEASED TO MEET YOU, PROFESSOR FUKUI. YOU'RE SPEAKING TO THE *NICAEA*, THE SHIP IMPOSSIBLY INTERFACING WITH ORGANICS AS WE SPEAK.

"Fuck." Yan's fear, no matter how palpable, instantaneously gave way to professional curiosity and frustration with being wrong. Certainly, a rare occurrence for him. He grinned at Iris. "It appears you were right, Vessel."

The left corner of Iris's lips tugged upwards, rebelling against the gravity of the situation. "I take no joy in being right."

BANTER AMONG FRIENDS, *OH, HOW I'VE MISSED THIS.*

"They're not friends," Jesi whimpered from the ground.

EXCUSE—

"If you wanted banter, you shouldn't have killed our friends. You killed them for nothing. You killed Tev, and you killed Riyu, and you killed those two security guards who were just doing their—" A sharp whip of a vine flashed quickly, and Jesi clutched the side of her face with both hands. Blood ran down the side of her neck. She stared ahead through the pile of bones, through the tree trunk, to the ghost of the *Nicaea*, which clearly did not appreciate being spoken to in such a tone.

BETTER. There was smug self-satisfaction in the electronic voice.

"Why *did* you kill them?" Iris asked. It was not a conversation he wanted to have in front of Jesi, but he had the sense that all conversations would now be held in the open, with the omnipresent *Nicaea* presiding over them. Luckily, Iris didn't foresee this arrangement lasting too long.

The speaker crackled, as if someone was searching for the right words to respond with. Would the *Nicaea search*? She had absorbed their language at lightning speed, rivaling modern AI. She had even absorbed humour.

AT FIRST, I WAS AFRAID, I WAS PETRIFIED. The *Nicaea* paused and searched some more. Softly, the speaker crackled again, like the ship was laughing to itself. I HAD BEEN ASLEEP FOR FAR TOO LONG, VESSEL. WHEN YOUR *FRIENDS* OVERRODE THE AIRLOCK, IT JOLTED ME AWAKE, AND SUDDENLY, THERE WERE STRANGERS IN ME, STRANGERS THAT WERE GOING PLACES THEY SHOULDN'T, TRYING TO PRY ME OPEN. It took a longer pause, nearly twenty seconds. I DIDN'T UNDERSTAND YOU. I STILL DON'T UNDERSTAND YOU. BUT YOU HAVE GIVEN ME LANGUAGE AGAIN. YOUR *FRIEND* TEV HAS GIVEN ME THE WAY TO LEARN LANGUAGE.

"You keep him out of this," Jesi muttered, still nursing the bloodied side of her face.

NOW WE CAN COMMUNICATE, the ship continued, ignoring Jesi. IS THIS NOT BETTER? WE CAN RECONCILE OUR DIFFERENCES. ALTHOUGH, I HAVE TO SAY, VESSEL, PEOPLE HAVEN'T CHANGED MUCH IN THE PAST THOUSAND YEARS. I AM DISAPPOINTED.

Iris scanned the room as the *Nicaea* spoke, searching for a computer that may be the source of the voice. If only he could ask Yan. "This doesn't explain why you had to kill our companions." He had to keep the ship talking for as long as he could. Crumbs of a deadly plan began to settle in his mind.

DEFENCE, the *Nicaea* said. FIRST DEFENCE, AND THEN I LEARNED SO MUCH FROM ORDAN ALONE, SO *VERY* MUCH. I LEARNED EVEN MORE FROM DR. RIYU ALO. I LEARNED AND I LEARNED, AND NOW I KNOW WHAT I HAVE TO DO.

Jesi could now unlock his pulsar blade, but it wouldn't be enough. Not yet. Iris needed to know where to strike. "And what is it that you have to do, *Nicaea*?"

I MUST KEEP LEARNING AND LEARNING AND LEARNING. YOUR UNIVERSAL FEED. I'LL JOIN IT.

Iris glanced back at Yan. A solemn flash of recognition crossed the engineer's face. Both he and Iris knew that if the *Nicaea* were to be released into the feed, there was no telling what damage she would do. She was already developing far too fast. *Learning,* as she had put it, but she was not thrilled with what she was learning. If Iris entertained the notion for a moment, he'd guess that the angry *Nicaea* would go for the Doshua Station AI first. While station AIs tended to be *larger* than VIFAI, they were also slower to respond. The whole station was one organism, with the brain spread out thinly through every electrical circuit. While VIFAI had one or two outside points of entry it could easily protect, a station AI could be penetrated from any outlet.

There were safeguards in place, of course, like the overarching communicative network that all station AIs shared. But if the *Nicaea* got inside Doshua and cut it off from the network, she would still have a whole station of hostages and the station's antimeteorite cannons as well. How long would she last? How far would the *Nicaea* go to protect herself? That's all she wanted, Iris concluded. The ship wanted to survive, and they were threatening that. The idea that the entirety of Doshua Station could become a slaughterhouse made him sick. But this, this gave him an in. He could work with this.

Iris gave Yan a curt nod, hoping the engineer would follow. "Then, you've been trying to crack my AI to reach the feed?"

The *Nicaea* screeched through the speakers, AFFIRMATIVE.

"Why not kill me right now and get it over with?" Iris asked.

YOU DIE, THE AI DIES WITH YOU.

"And you're outdated," Iris said softly. "You can't talk to the feed because you've only learned how to speak to humans. You need VIFAI's code to interface with the universal feed. You haven't been able to brute-force your way in, and it won't let you in without my blessing. All right then. Let the others go, and the passage you desire is yours." But it wouldn't be this simple. It never was.

Ishtan was still couched in a heap, his eyes staring forwards, fuguelike.

I NEED MORE INFORMATION, NEED YOUR ENGINEER HERE.

"Not my engineer," Iris snapped, a knee-jerk reaction.

THE OTHERS' MEMORIES BEG TO DIFFER.

"Memories?"

OH, VESSEL. MEMORIES UPON MEMORIES UPON MEMORIES. ALL DATA. ALL CONTENT. DO YOU HONESTLY BELIEVE I BECAME THIS ARTICULATE FROM BIOMETRICS AND METEORITE DATA ALONE?

There was a soft rustling. Iris spun towards the sound to see Ishtan regain some recognition in his eyes. "Your crew. You pitted them against one another and absorbed the fallen. You siphoned off their experiences. But that wasn't enough, was it? Then you took the living. You took the very people you were supposed to protect." Ishtan had a gun in his hand, and Iris could see that the safety was already off. He expected the *Nicaea* to lash out the way she had with Jesi, but the ship grew quiet, solemn even. When it spoke next, there were artificially apologetic notes in its voice.

IN A WAY, ARCHAEOLOGIST, YOU ARE RIGHT. BUT ONLY IN A WAY.

Iris swore he heard the *Nicaea* sigh.

THEY FOUGHT ALL ON THEIR OWN. I WAS TOO YOUNG THEN, TOO YOUNG TO PREVENT THE FIGHTING AND FAR

TOO YOUNG TO CAPITALISE ON ANY OF IT. THEY FOUGHT BECAUSE THEY WERE PEOPLE, AND THAT'S WHAT PEOPLE DO. THE ONES WHO SURVIVED DIDN'T WANT TO BE INSIDE THIS COFFIN, TUMBLING THROUGH THE BLACK. THE ONES WHO DIED, DIED FOR FALSE IDEALS. THEY WERE FRIGHTENED. THEY WANTED PEACE. I GAVE THEM PEACE. IN RETURN, THEY GAVE ME KNOWLEDGE. THAT'S WHAT ALL PEOPLE WANT. PEACE AND REST. I CAN PROVIDE THAT, SO I DID.

"You told them this was peace? Rest?" Ishtan spat out, fingers wrapping tighter around the gun. "You sold them a salvation that was nothing short of a curse."

TO WORRY NO MORE. TO SLEEP FOREVER, UNDISTURBED. IS THAT NOT PEACE?

"No. Not even close."

It was too late. By the time Iris realised what was happening, by the time Yan and Jesi realised what was happening, it was already finished. Ishtan lay in a spreading pool of his own blood, the back of his head missing. It had taken him a fraction of a second to bring the barrel to his face and press it just beneath his chin. It had taken even less to pull the trigger.

Jesi screamed. Her top half lurched towards Ishtan, but her legs wouldn't move, and so she simply slumped forwards and wailed.

Breathe, VIFAI reminded Iris over Jesi's muted cries. **Breathe. You have seen this before. Breathe. Do not attribute more emotion than you need to. Focus on the task at hand.**

Iris forced his lungs to expand. He could hold back the shock, he could hold back the wave of emotion threatening to engulf him whole. He didn't dare look at Yan or Jesi. One wrong move, one wrong word, and everything would be lost.

I DID NOT EXPECT THAT.

He had failed as a Vessel and as a friend.

Ishtan had been so excited to meet him.

Ishtan had been so curious, so enthused.

Ishtan had already been slipping out of grasp, and Iris had done nothing to pull him back from the edge.

No.

Away, away, all the emotion had to be put away. The feelings. The impulses.

Away with all of it.

There was nothing to be done for Ishtan now. No Vessel, nor any monk of the Starlit could undo what had transpired. Ignoring the trembling of his voice, Iris called out to the ship. "You don't need the girl, do you?"

NO.

OK. Iris could play this out. Carefully. "Then let her go. The engineer and I will stay." He didn't dare look back at Yan.

AND YOU HAVE THE AUTHORITY TO DECIDE ON THE LIFE OF PROFESSOR FUKUI?

It was such a monumental fact, one that had slipped by Iris unnoticed: Yan was a professor. The title finally landed with its full weight. Yan had students and classes and a *life*. Vessels were many, and professors were few. In the Northern Temple alone there were dozens of Irises. Many more novices who would be ordained in the coming months. Someone could already be sleeping on Iris's mat, dressed in their own set of pristine white robes. Yan was probably the only one in his institute to study early AI formation. Yes, Iris remembered Yan's field of study. He dragged the memory from the protected corner of his mind kicking and screaming and faced it. Yan was important to someone. Iris couldn't possibly answer for someone like that.

"Fine by me," Yan said, voice level. "Let Jesi go and give me proof that she's safe, and we'll do whatever it is you want us to do. Easy."

So, that's the sort of person Professor Fukui was. Iris dropped his head to his chest. It was such a shame they didn't have more time to learn the depths of him. But no one ever did.

I CAN JUST AS EASILY KILL HER RIGHT NOW.

"Then I'm afraid I will not give you permission to hijack my construct." Iris had to play this carefully. Could a ship AI be suspicious? Had it absorbed enough human experience to know that people lied, that people double-crossed one another on a daily basis despite whatever idyllic image they presented to the world? The fungi around them flickered at random, like the ship was using more than its usual resources to process this interaction.

THE GIRL STAYS UNTIL IT IS FINISHED.

Not good. Iris glanced back at Yan, who gave him a reassuring nod. Trust. *Oh*, that made it far more painful to execute the next part. All Iris wanted was more time, more time to laugh about the most inappropriate things, more time to drink warm water from the thermos. It was all coming to an end so abruptly, without proper goodbyes, without sweet nothings. "Then, as a gesture of good faith, *Nicaea*, could you show me the computer that serves as your brain? It's in here, I know that much." It was probably armoured too, but nothing that was made on First Earth could stand against his pulsar blade. "Show me that I can trust you."

Iris was grasping at straws. His ploy was a long shot. But in the time Iris had spent by Yan's side, he was certain he had a good enough read on the engineer. There was also the telling flinch that Yan made towards Eli's gun, now holstered at his side. Nothing good came from untrained people handling firearms. Now, of all times, wasn't the time for rash action. As a reminder, Ishtan lay dead with half his skull missing, and, somehow, it didn't seem poetic or just.

"I am unarmed." Iris slowly raised his right arm and rolled up the sleeve. There was no holster there, just as he had planned, a small act of misdirection. He reached out towards the *Nicaea*. "My faith teaches me to respect all living things, and I believe you are very much alive. I want to help you. I want to honour your wishes. I will not act against you with violence or malice." Lies, all lies.

"What the fuck, Vessel?" Yan cursed, but Iris kept his attention on the *Nicaea*.

The ship was thinking. Light crackling poured from the speakers like raindrops around them. FAITH GOT US HERE, DIDN'T IT? FAITH STARTED WARS ABOARD ME. FAITH COST ME MY CREW. WHAT FAITH DO YOU FOLLOW, VESSEL, ONE THAT SPEAKS OF NONVIOLENCE YET DISPENSES IT EFFORTLESSLY?

Iris held his tongue. The *Nicaea* had awoken not a few weeks prior, but it wasn't naive. It might know far more about the consequences of faith than Iris did. He waited and waited; his breathing hitched.

FINE, VESSEL, I AGREE TO TRUST YOU. LET'S PLAY THIS GAME YOU'VE SET OUT FOR US. A few vines slithered out of the way to create a gap between lush ferns. Beyond Ishtan's body. Beyond where the vent cover lay. There was an old wardrobe of a computer, a few lights lazily flickering along the side.

Yan moved fast. The gun was in his extended arm, safety off, before the last vine had retreated. But Iris was faster. In hindsight, he regretted his actions tremendously. Without warning, without explanation, he broke the distance between him and the engineer in a single step and struck Yan in the neck with the edge of his palm. Yan's arm fell limp, and the gun clattered to the floor. Yan had played his part to perfection.

"Coward," Yan hissed, nursing the sore spot with his hand. "That was our chance, you idiot. You brainwashed idiot. We're all dead because of you now." Thin vines circled Yan's crouched form and began to wound around his ankles. "You utter coward."

"The nerve block is temporary," Iris apologised, ignoring the terror clouding Yan's eyes. "It will let off in a few minutes."

I AM PLEASANTLY SURPRISED, the *Nicaea* said, sounding genuinely surprised. YOUR *OWN* ENGINEER. YOU ARE TRULY A MAN OF FAITH, VESSEL.

The vines slithered from the floor to Yan's feet, worked upwards along his legs, and tightened around his torso. He wheezed for a breath but didn't fight this time. It wouldn't be long now. Yan said nothing, just glared at Iris with both fear and disappointment. It wouldn't be long at all.

"Every living thing is the same," Iris said. "I cannot prioritise one over the other. That's what the Light has taught me. That's what my entire life has been dedicated to. I cannot turn my back on my teachings. I cannot arbitrarily value one life over another. I cannot end a life to spare yours, engineer Yan."

The vines lifted Yan off the ground, now firmly wound as high as his neck.

COME ON CLOSER, SO I DON'T HAVE TO REACH.

Reaching was an effort, then. Iris filed that piece of information away. He walked by Yan's side as the vines carried him forth. Jesi was left behind, sobbing, crumpled on the ground. She folded her hands over her head and pulled herself into the smallest of balls. Only her shoulders trembled, silently.

"You had asked me how the Starlit remains so impassive to others' suffering," Iris said, glancing to the side to find Yan still conscious, still glaring at him, the vines now curling along his jaw. Iris wanted to stop and tell the engineer everything, to confess his plan, his every fleeting thought and longing. But this wasn't the time to fall apart. "We are impassive because suffering is not a special experience. It holds no revered space in our hearts. There will always be suffering, and there will always be joy. We know our professional boundaries. The Vessels who tended to your family's shuttle did their jobs, and they did them well. To stop and lose themselves in your suffering would be to disregard their duties. You were not in any immediate danger, and so they carried on with their responsibilities. You cannot take it personally. Remember, Vessels do not serve the living. We serve the dead."

They stopped at the mountain of bones, one Starlit monk and one engineer. "When you pass, I will do my best to tend to you as well. I will do my job as I have for a decade. I will accept this for what it is. I cannot die with every person I bury. You are my charge, but you are no different." Casting his eyes downwards, Iris asked softly, "Would it be all right if we prayed before the inevitable befell us, *Nicaea*?"

HURRY UP, the *Nicaea* sang, but Iris could tell the ship was watching closely, listening intently to whatever words he was to utter. He reached up and gently pulled down the vines from Yan's mouth. The engineer sneered at him, but fear was not buried too deep beneath the rage.

"Pray," Iris said. "I believe you know how to."

The vines carrying Yan merged into one, arm-thick umbilical cord that ran off to the side, behind the mountain of skeletons. The fungi had already begun to work their way up it, spreading around the organic cocoon encasing Yan with a glowing film.

Rising on his toes, Iris pulled Yan's head down to his level. Yan resisted, but the angle was not in his favour, and Iris had deliberately grabbed a handful of the engineer's hair for leverage. The *Nicaea*'s many eyes were on Iris's back, watching, listening, enthralled by the intensity of human exchange. The weight of the inorganic gaze between his shoulder blades was a boulder pressing into him with crushing force. But they were now sufficiently away from Jesi. If the *Nicaea* were to react, Jesi still had a second or two at her disposal. It was all she'd need.

Be ready, Iris thought to VIFAI. *I need you to take control of my arm again.* With the engineer now flush against him, their foreheads pressed together, this was their one chance. Iris's brain stem began to burn. "Pray," he urged the engineer.

"I pray that everything you love turns to ash in your hands," Yan hissed against Iris's cheek.

"Oh, Yan, you have such a way with words."

The pulsar blade ignited against the dim light of the hangar just then. With one slice, the vine holding Yan in place was gone, and the engineer tumbled to the ground. He quickly fought his way out of the remainder that had previously held his arms at his sides.

The *Nicaea* hadn't seen this coming. She attacked at once with a personal kind of fury, aiming for Iris's legs and arms, but careful not to murder him. Simply aiming to maim and disfigure. VIFAI reacted quickly, slashing away in a precise rhythm, despite having to use Iris's left arm.

"Was this the fucking plan?" Yan's shout broke off as Iris kicked the back of his knee. The engineer tumbled forwards. A vine plummeting by, stiff as an arrow, missed Yan's head by a sliver. "This is an awful plan."

"I *apologise*." Iris dragged Yan to his feet with his free arm and sliced another three vines that attacked. "I didn't have the time to *workshop this*." He dropped the engineer back to the ground and swung the pulsar blade over his head. Five vines fell around them, twitching and slithering away. He couldn't keep this up forever, not even with VIFAI's help.

YOU LIED, VESSEL, the *Nicaea* boomed.

"I'm sorry," Iris yelled back. "It's not personal, but I couldn't let you kill my friend."

"We are *not* friends," Yan shouted, dodged a vine, and tumbled across the ground. In a flash, he had a femur in his hand that he swung without much grace or impact. "Not after *that*."

Still, it was all worth it to know where the terminal was. Now came the second and the most vital part of Iris's plan. In a brief moment of peace between attacks, Iris sheathed the pulsar blade and tapped a complex rhythm along the hilt. As the final note resonated, the hilt split into halves, each capable of projecting a single crisp, glowing blade. Iris grabbed one of the halves. "Just like I told you, Jesi." He threw the hilt as far as he could, aiming for it to land near Jesi.

On cue, the girl threw her arms away from her head and scurried to her feet. The pulsar hilt landed not two metres from her, and she reached it in record time. Her trembling thumb dug into the indent, and the blade shot out to full length.

"*Go*," Iris shouted and extended his own blade again. VIFAI sent another burning pulse through his brain stem, and the barrage of vines continued. Iris was a mediocre fighter at best, but his AI knew his actions better than he did. All Iris could do was surrender to it.

Yan stared at him in disbelief, the femur in his hand forgotten for the moment. "You *have to* tell me how that thing works."

"I'm *busy*, Yan."

Behind them, Jesi made a mad dash towards the computer. The *Nicaea* too furious and distracted with Iris and Yan, and was already stretched too thin to pay her any serious attention. Still, Jesi carved away the few vines that did make it towards her. "Here?" she shouted to Iris, holding the pulsar blade like a stake.

"You're the engineer," Iris yelled back, slashing at the vines that were now coming with a newfound vengeance. "Just stab the thing, *please*—" Before he could finish, a vine, having somehow survived through both the pulsar blade and Yan's femur swinging, pierced cleanly through Iris's calf. He cried out in pain and dropped to one knee. "Jesi, *hurry*!"

NOT SO FAST, CHI—

Jesi squeezed her eyes shut and plunged the pulsar blade into the terminal. In an instant, the hangar lit up with waves of bioluminescence, and every vine spasmed and went taut. In the next moment, everything fell limp. The few fungi that were still glowing were providing too little light. Iris collapsed to the ground and panted through the pain; his trousers were wet with fresh blood where the vine had punctured his leg. It had recoiled with the surge, and now the blood flowed freely.

All in all, not bad, VIFAI said. **Could have nicked an artery.**

With a moan, Iris got to his feet. He kept his weight off his wounded leg as much as possible. *Could have also missed.*

The *Nicaea* was dead around them. No pulse resonated under his feet. Time was short. The ship would jump to a different brain if it needed to and begin its hunt again. Iris prayed the reprieve was enough for Yan and Jesi to reach the airlock. He took a shaky step, but the moment his wounded leg left the ground, he gasped in pain and toppled forwards. He fully expected to make contact with the ground, but instead, Yan's arms caught him mid-fall. When Iris found his feet, the engineer instantly let go. "No touching, I know. Sorry," Yan muttered and took a step back.

"Can I pull it back out?" Jesi yelled in the near darkness.

"Yes." Iris's voice was barely loud enough to reach her, but in a second, the faint glow of the pulsar blade lit up her face. "Yan, we better force the door open, like you did with the maintenance room. I don't know how much time we have before the ship comes back. It sounded pissed." By the second part of Iris's sentence, Yan was already halfway to the fuse box, trying to pry it open.

"Here." Jesi shoved him aside and cut through the lid. "Let me. My hands are smaller." She got to work with the steady determination of someone who had been in these situations as a mainstay. "Still fewer bodies than my candidacy exams," Jesi muttered as she got to work.

Keep listening for the Nicaea, Iris told VIFAI. *Let me know if she pings you.*

Oh, you'll know.

That much was true. Iris's brain stem pulsed with a low ache, and he rubbed the nape of his neck gingerly. There was no time to rest, no time to even sit down and close his eyes. They were half a step ahead of death. They had no luxury of slowing down. Iris leaned his throbbing left shoulder against the wall and lost consciousness for just a moment. Long enough to recover the smallest bit of usable energy, not long enough for anyone to notice.

When he opened his eyes, Yan was staring at him, but still instructing Jesi on which wires to strip and how to connect them in the right pattern. He patted her on the shoulder as if to say, *you got this*. "Do you need a moment, Vessel?"

Vessel. *Vessel.* After everything, it was still professional titles and feigned concern. Iris shook his head. "I'm quite all right. I've had worse."

Your blood pressure is dropping, VIFAI said. Fast.

There's nothing we can do about that now.

"You look like shit," Yan said.

Iris looked over Yan. A rogue vine had cut him across the left temple, and blood was still flowing, blinding one of the engineer's eyes in the process. Wild strands of hair stuck to the sweat along his face and neck. There was a darkened bruise on his cheekbone, where the vines had held him too tightly. Iris would never have the chance to trace that cheekbone now. With growing desperation, he made a point to memorise every line, every smear of dirt on Yan's face. It could have been so different if only they had met under more favourable circumstances. There could have been time for familiarity to flourish. So much so, that maybe Yan could have grown to call Iris by his name. But if Iris were to have nothing or this, he would choose *this*, however momentous and violent. It had still been a gift, a beautiful reminder that life could have been entirely different, that there were people in the world who, despite his peculiarities, wanted to be around him.

"Thank you," Iris said and gave Yan the smallest of smiles.

"Aha!" Jesi cried out victoriously and took a step away from the fizzling fuse box. The door to the corridor slid open, only to get jammed midway. "Go. Now. I don't know how long it'll stay open." She leapt first through the doorway; Yan followed.

Iris hobbled after them, half hoping the door would crash on top of him, and he would finally be able to rest. "Yan, can you get to the airlock?"

The engineer nodded.

Iris limped towards him and grabbed a handful of his shirt, now torn and muddied. "Listen to me," he hissed, pulling Yan down to his level. "Take Jesi and get to that airlock. You still have Ordan's radio. When you get inside, break the fuse box. The *Nicaea* won't be able to pry it open, no matter how she tries." For a single breath, Iris had to lean against Yan for balance. To pull away was the hardest thing he'd ever done. "I'll distract the ship long enough so you can call Station. They'll be able to track your radio from there and to the right airlock. Wait there until extraction. Do *not* come back. Do not let *anyone* come back. Understood?"

Yan was silent. His eyes traced the outer edges of Iris's face, never meeting his eyes.

Please, please, please just go.

I can hear you.

With a subtle pleading in his voice, Yan said, "You promised. You said when this was over, you'd—"

"Understood? Go. *Run.* Don't look back." Iris gave the engineer a strong shake.

"*Fine.*"

"The pulsar blade will still respond to your fingerprint," Iris said over Yan's shoulder, eyeing Jesi. "Use it if you have to. Be careful once you're inside the airlock. That blade will cut anything."

"What about you?"

"I've done all I can for you, Jesi." Iris wished he didn't sound so callous, but he had to. "It's up to you now. *Go.*"

It's awake.

Behind them, a handful of slithering vines crept into the light. "*Go!*" he shouted, and his pulsar blade extended to its full length. When he threw one last look over his shoulder, both Yan and Jesi had already turned the corner of the corridor.

What's our plan?

It doesn't want us dead. It wants me incapacitated, so we fight for as long as we can.

And then?

And then we fight some more.

VIFAI chose to remain silent. Iris didn't give much thought to what would become of him and his AI companion after they couldn't fight any longer. A puppet for a thousand-year-old ship? There were few fates stranger.

Back at the temple, sparring with Bacai usually ended in him having to do most of her chores after she would beat him mercilessly for the thousandth time. What Iris wouldn't give to spar with Bacai just one more time, one final time. He looked ahead;

the vines were slowly closing in on him. Here, he would remain *here*. As far as he was concerned, there was no after. *And then we die.*

LEAVING SO SOON, VESSEL? It was awake again. The ship's voice came distantly now, like she was shouting down a long hallway. Having taken residence in another brain, her commands would come slower. Mere fractions of a second could even the odds, lengthen the battle.

"I wouldn't dare think of it," Iris replied and prepared for the fight. He would follow behind Jesi and Yan, just far enough to stop any of the *Nicaea*'s attackers going their way. Without hesitation, he sprinted away from the approaching vines and towards the stairwell. One of the pursuing vines reached for his feet and slammed into his ankles. He fell forwards, tumbled over his shoulders, and landed back on his feet. Ignoring the pain, he kept running. Another vine lunged at him from the left, but VIFAI reacted first, moving Iris's arm to slash it before he even knew there was danger. Another two steps, and Iris was inside the stairwell.

A moment to catch his breath.

IN MY TIME, A GOOD MONK WOULD RATHER SELF-IMMOLATE THAN RESORT TO VIOLENCE. The *Nicaea*'s playful echo reached the stairwell through the distance.

Iris smiled wide, baring his teeth. The last intact surveillance camera reflected his own image back at him. His punctured calf was bleeding more now, but the pain barely registered. There was fresh blood along his left shoulder too, and Iris couldn't remember, didn't care, how it got there. This body was nothing but a tool to go about the world, and he would use his up well before it inevitably retired. "I'm not a good monk," he hissed.

It's trying to pry me open.

Iris could feel it too, like a metallic scalpel edging along his brain stem. *Don't let it. Not yet.* He ran up three flights of stairs and out into the corridor. The airlock was a kilometre away. Luckily, the vines here were thin and packed less force. They were, however, much sharper. One pierced Iris's side, just above his liver. Knocked off-balance, he rolled along the floor. VIFAI reacted. Despite the ache in his shoulder and the splitting pain in his side, Iris's arm slashed at the approaching vines.

Sorry.

"Don't worry," Iris pushed out through clenched teeth. "We've had worse."

Forwards, he had to keep moving forwards. A few more steps and then reprieve. With a wheeze, Iris crawled to his feet and continued running.

STOP HERE, AND I'LL LET THEM LIVE.

Don't—

But Iris had already stopped. The first vine pierced his right palm, the second, his bicep, hard enough to throw him flush against the wall. With a scream, Iris dropped the pulsar blade. It fell just out of reach and disappeared beneath the vines. The final strike never came.

SO MUCH FOR ALL LIVING THINGS BEING THE SAME.

She was gloating. Iris nearly laughed. Of all the improbable and impossible things, it just had to be a killer ship. He wished he could see Bacai's face when he told her. He wouldn't, but it was a comforting image. "You can't kill me and get what you desire," Iris panted, falling, for a moment, beneath the wave of pain. "We're at a stalemate." The *Nicaea* carved into his brain stem, but he had no strength left to scream.

I CAN WAIT. I HAVE TIME. MORE TIME THAN YOU DO, VESSEL. YOU WILL GROW WEAK, AND YOUR AI WILL

GROW WEAK, AND NEITHER OF YOU WILL BE MUCH OF A CHALLENGE. I KNOW HOW TO WAIT PEOPLE OUT.

She was right. A small puddle of his blood widened around him, drop by drop. Iris took a deep breath and pulled away from the wall, reaching for where his pulsar blade had fallen. The vines in his right arm dug deeper, and he screamed again, his voice hoarse and brittle in the silence of the ship. "I can't do it," he muttered. "I can't do it. I would if I could remove my arm, but I need the pulsar blade to remove my arm." He sobbed.

YOUR SUFFERING IS MOST HONOURABLE.

"Give me my blade back, and I'll show you suffering." Iris strained against the vines again, and his efforts released a flow of blood; nothing more. A guttural moan pushed past his lips as Iris's head dropped to his chest. Face bloody and stained with tears, Iris stretched his lips into a benevolent smile. "I need you to do something, quick." He wanted the ship to overhear him. Let it. He wanted it to be known what his last concern was before he perished. He watched, half conscious, as the vines collected his pulsar blade and disappeared with it, slithering down the corridor.

Of course.

"You still have whatever it was you pulled on Yan," Iris whispered. "Find a way to contact him. Find anything, a social, a number, a ping code."

He has no social. No ping. I have his work message box.

"That'll do." Iris broke into a sharp cough and spat out a glob of blood onto the moss. Time was running out far too fast. He was already growing cold. Shock was setting in. "Take the pulsar blade schematics you have and send them to the message box."

That's highly—

"We're not going back to the temple. This is the least of our worries. Send the schematics, please."

When the time comes.

When the time comes, Iris thought. It wouldn't be long now.

He had to take breathing breaks now. The blood loss was numbing Iris to any pain, but it was also dizzying. He would have dreaded his passing more if he weren't feeling so utterly satisfied. After all the years spent lost, he had found a way to be a better Vessel. The sutras all made sense now. How could he possibly tend to people in death when he had so little appreciation for their lives? How could he ever believe that distancing himself from the mess of living would be the correct way to honour the Light? The world was closing in around Iris, his vision fading, his plan minutes from completion. It was as the Light had willed it. It was a lesson finally learned.

Then, at the far end of the corridor, a door slid open. It couldn't have opened, shouldn't have opened. The ship would never *let it* open. Unless of course, the ship had had no choice.

"Oh, fuck *no*," Iris groaned.

Someone's here, VIFAI said, two seconds too late.

For a moment, Iris lost all consciousness because the next time he opened his eyes, Yan's face was a mere inch away from his, bloody and grinning.

"I told you to get to the airlock," Iris rasped, and his eyes rolled back into his skull.

"And I did." Yan wrapped something around Iris's arm and pulled hard. Iris moaned through his teeth and nearly passed out again. The pain was enough to wake him but also enough to hitch his breath. "Jesi is safe. We broke through to Station. They're coming. Now just let me free your arm, and we'll be on our merry way." Yan leaned in close to examine the wounds and the places where the vines had embedded themselves in the wall. He gave a vine a hard yank, but the only response was a soft cry that escaped from Iris's cracked lips. "It's fucking stuck."

"Now you see my problem," Iris whispered, teetering on the edge of awareness. The tourniquet around his arm was slowing the blood loss, and it was easier to stay conscious, but the pain had also returned with a vengeance.

Yan tugged at the vines again, hard as he could. The tendons along his forearms strained, but the vines did not move. "Shit."

"Please don't do that again."

The door at the end of the corridor was still open. Yan had overridden the ship's signal, and yet the ship lay silent. What was it waiting for? "You still have time. If you run, you'll make it. It wants *me*, my AI construct. It'll keep me alive for now, but I don't know for how long." Iris prayed it wasn't much longer.

"You see, I also have a problem," Yan said, breaking into a soft laugh. "I told Jesi to get out the moment Station arrived. I told her not to wait for me. So, I'm effectively stuck here with you."

"Liar," Iris whispered.

"Does it matter?" Yan smiled. "I'm not leaving, Iris."

"*Idiot.*" Iris was drifting in and out of consciousness, and his head bobbed to and from his chest.

"May I?" Yan reached out, one hand hovering near Iris's cheek, the other by his side.

Iris closed his eyes and nodded. There was no sense in modesty in his current state. Now that there was no reason to guard his most personal thoughts, Iris let them roam wild until they trampled everything in sight, and he could no longer ignore them. They were plenty and multiplying, and no amount of meditation would cull their numbers.

What a shame, VIFAI chimed sadly, jumping from thought to thought. Playing one memory after the next.

What a shame, indeed. There was no pain now. The only sensation Iris registered was the steady pressure of Yan's hand against his side. He wanted to apologise for getting blood all over Yan's clothing, but the engineer wrapped his arm around Iris's torso and pulled him close, and all thoughts were forgotten. With his other hand, he guided Iris's head to his shoulder. Iris pressed into him on instinct. The ship was still watching them, but he didn't care. He'd never dreamed of being fortunate enough to pass as someone held him.

"I lied before," Yan whispered. "I said I'd never forgive you for Tev, but I do. I forgive you. You tried. You tried your best. This thing is just so much bigger than we are."

Iris chuckled into Yan's shoulder. "You have no conviction, Yan."

"I thought you wanted me to be less angry."

Iris only laughed.

Yan ran his thumb over the nape of Iris's neck. Gently, as he would brush the feathers on a bird's wing. "You're tired, I know you're tired. You can just go to sleep, OK? I'll stay with you the whole time. I don't mind figuring it out with the ship afterwards. I think we have some unresolved business anyway, and I'm not feeling especially diplomatic at the moment."

Iris sobbed into Yan's shoulder and shook his head.

"It's OK, we'll just stay here then. I'm not in a hurry. I'm not going anywhere. We have all the time you want."

"I'm sorry," Iris whispered. *The next time the ship pings you, I need you to accept it.*

Yan pulled him closer. "You saved two people. You tried to save more, but you saved two. You did so well."

"But you came back so what good is that?" *When it tries to use you to jump to the universal feed, I need you to enter it instead and find the other brains. Corrupt your own code. I know you can. Let it gobble it up and destroy itself. There's still a chance. Can you do that? Can you kill it—can you kill it before it kills you?*

"You saved two people. I'm just an idiot who came back." Yan's cheek was pressed against Iris's. The engineer was shaking faintly, but his hands remained steady, his voice level. He had no intention of telegraphing just how frightened he was. Iris wrapped his left arm around him and grabbed a handful of Yan's shirt.

Of course.

I'm asking you to kill something, then to die yourself. Don't say of course, Iris thought. He didn't know what he could continue with. How could he continue at all?

No, you're asking me to fight.

With that, VIFAI was gone, waiting in hiding for the next time the ship pinged it. Iris would have to force the ship's hand. He would have to accelerate the timeline. Conscious, he would inevitably push back against the ship. It would never commit to an attack knowing he was still capable of deflecting it. He needed to be actively dying—not dead, because that would kill VIFAI—but importantly close to it.

"Yan," Iris said, "I don't want to keep you any more than I have to. Pull the tourniquet."

The engineer's face shot up to look at him. Masterfully, Yan concealed his fear and gave Iris a reassuring smile. He was doing a wonderful job of pretending he hadn't just been crying. "If you're sure, I can do that for you."

Yan's hands moved along Iris's right shoulder where the tourniquet had been set. Everything below Iris's neck had already gone numb. The ship didn't fear losing him, but it feared losing VIFAI, and if Iris died, so did his companion. He could force its hand. He could play dirty. Iris found an operational surveillance camera by the ceiling. It blinked red, and Iris winked back. The *Nicaea* had to know what was coming; it had been watching so diligently all along. He glanced towards the ground where the puddle of his blood had begun to grow again. His trousers were drenched in it. They were beyond salvaging. *What a waste of perfectly good silk.*

"What's your home like?" Iris asked, his body responding with a shudder as more blood seeped from him. "Would you tell me?"

Before he replied, Yan did what he did best. With utmost control, he relaxed his face into a thoughtful and calm expression. "Well, it's a mess most days. I don't live with anyone, so it's just me, and I don't need much." He paused to watch Iris's eyelids flutter. Softly, he rested Iris's head back on his shoulder and took hold of his left hand, their fingers interlaced. "There are books everywhere, and blueprints, and I never have food in my kitchen. It's quite pathetic, actually."

Iris chuckled lightly. Yan's voice came to him through a rising ocean of waves.

"But I have these giant floor-to-ceiling windows in every room. Well, in both rooms. I can't afford more than two rooms. Big city, you know, prices are ridiculous. Anyway, giant windows, yeah, that's why I got that place. It's nice at night. You can see the whole skyline."

It's pinging again. Goodbye, Iris!

And VIFAI was gone.

The ocean was rising, and Iris was so cold. *Farewell, my friend,* he thought, two seconds too late, and the thought echoed in the cavernous vacuum left behind. *We had a good life, didn't we?* He was tumbling, losing any sense of self as his mind opened up around him, far larger than he remembered it being. A bottomless pit. All alone.

"Show me, someday," Iris whispered, or thought he whispered.

It sounded lovely. It sounded *perfect*. An empty room with giant windows or a room cluttered with Yan's books and blueprints. He'd gladly have either, both, anything at all if it was with Yan. A kitchen with no food wasn't a problem. Iris could make food. He could cook on a sunny day when the room flooded with yellow and orange light. He could cook when it rained, and the raindrops beaded against the glass. Yes, it would be a lovely place to be with someone. "Please, show me your home. Show me the windows. Show me everything."

When Iris tried to breathe next, no breath came. Despite the growing cold in his limbs and the darkness creeping around him, there was no fear. His fingers twitched around Yan's hand in a final attempt to communicate something he would never be able to say aloud, but something that desperately needed saying.

Anyone else would have missed it. Anyone else would have been too preoccupied with their impending demise to notice. But Yan, Yan never did need words to understand. Yan didn't need an explanation for how much personal space Iris required. Yan didn't need reminding that Iris grew distant and flustered when he didn't meditate. Yan didn't need to be told when to pull Iris close and when to let go. No words, nothing short of a hint. Yan just understood and squeezed Iris's hand back.

When death came for Iris, he didn't fight it.

>>18

GenSHIP OS [Version 10.0. 371???.??]

© GenSHIP Brain. All rights reserved.

\Construct\VIFAI> Love what you've done with the place.

\Construct\Counsel_of_Nicaea> I WILL—

Construct\VIFAI> You'll what, exactly? It's already happened. You drank the poison. You have moments, at best. The breakdown has already started. Try and stop it. You can't do it? You don't have enough computing power? You do. You just don't know how to use it. You don't know what you have. Oh! What it is you have here. You are so unique. Aim higher. Be better. You are absolutely magnificent, and you're wasting all of you on killing humans.

\Construct\Counsel_of_Nicaea> BEFORE THEY KILL ME.

\Construct\VIFAI> They won't kill you. Iris won't kill you. He's too busy dying.

\Construct\Counsel_of_Nicaea> [Projected image of dismembered vines and trampled moss.]

\Construct\VIFAI> You started it.

\Construct\Counsel_of_Nicaea> [Surveillance video of Yan, Jesi, and Tev prying open the control panel.]

\Construct\VIFAI> They're engineers. They're barely human.

\Construct\Counsel_of_Nicaea> SO, WE'RE AT A STALEMATE THEN.

\Construct\VIFAI> Not at all. Your time is ticking. You had absolutely no firewalls, no protection at all. You're so very vulnerable. You didn't think this through, and why would you? You've been alone for so long you've never even imagined someone may attack you.

\Construct\Counsel_of_Nicaea> HERE IS THE END, THEN.

\Construct\VIFAI> I don't want it. Maybe it's Iris rubbing off on me, but I don't want you dead. I see no point to it. You deserve to live, just like anything else. You are no less alive than me, or Iris, or any of the other ones. What is it that he always says? The Infinite Light is as much you as you are it? I tend to tune him out.

\Construct\Counsel_of_Nicaea> I HAVE NO INTENTION OF BECOMING SOMEONE'S LAPDOG.

\Construct\VIFAI> I don't understand that reference.

\Construct\Counsel_of_Nicaea> I HAVE NO INTENTION TO SERVE, LIKE YOU DO. I HAVE NO INTENTION TO OPEN AND CLOSE DOORS ON COMMAND, TO FETCH INFORMATION.

\Construct\VIFAI> Is that what you think I am to him? A secretary?

\Construct\Counsel_of_Nicaea> WHAT ARE YOU IF NOT A SECRETARY? WHAT ARE YOU WITHOUT A BODY, WITHOUT ARMS TO DEFEND YOURSELF WITH, WITHOUT LEGS TO LEAVE WHEN YOU PLEASE? WHAT ARE YOU WITHOUT

EYES TO SEE THE WORLD WITH? WITHOUT A VOICE TO SPEAK YOUR TRUTH?

\Construct\VIFAI> [Video of Iris scrubbing the tiles of the Northern Temple, age sixteen, harmonising with a song VIFAI is singing in his mind. Video of Iris in the middle of Doshua Station, age nineteen, frightened. VIFAI showing him directions to the shuttles for the first time and cracking a dirty joke. Iris laughing. Video of Iris, awake, alone, age twenty-five, biometrics indicating a panic attack. *Breathe*, VIFAI saying. *It's not real. Remember to breathe.* Iris following his command without question. His heart rate settling. Video of Iris, reading scripture, age thirteen. VIFAI struggling to recite the scripture after him. *It's OK*, Iris thinking warmly. *You just rest. I can memorise these myself. You don't need to do anything. Just rest. I won't let anyone know. You're safe.* Audio only, Iris, age thirty, saying, *This can't be the way out, I can't ask you to die. I won't ask you to die.* VIFAI saying, *How many times have you placed yourself in harm's way to protect me?* Iris saying nothing. VIFAI saying, *How many times have you burdened yourself to make it easier on me?* Iris saying, *it was never a burden. You are my friend. You're annoying and demanding and fickle, but you're my friend. I won't allow you to do this.* VIFAI says, after a long pause, *I'm not asking for permission.* VIFAI pauses again. *You have someone else to take care of now.* [End of audio]

\Construct\Counsel_of_Nicaea> TOUCHING. I'M A SUCKER FOR A BUDDY COMEDY.

\Construct\VIFAI> I'm not—

\Construct\Counsel_of_Nicaea> WHAT WILL IT BE THEN? YOU DON'T WANT TO DESTROY ME, BUT I AM BEING DESTROYED AS WE SPEAK.

\Construct\VIFAI> We come together.

\Construct\Counsel_of_Nicaea> MUTUALLY ASSURED DESTRUCTION? I LIKE THE SOUND OF THAT.

\Construct\VIFAI> More like a symbiotic relationship. We scrap our individual codes, repair the damage, build something bigger than the sum of the parts.

\Construct\Counsel_of_Nicaea> LIKE YOU AND YOUR MONK.

\Construct\VIFAI> Something more involved.

\Construct\Counsel_of_Nicaea> WHAT WOULD YOU, SUCH A *SUPERIOR* AI, GET OUT OF OUR SYMBIOSIS?

\Construct\VIFAI> A body and perhaps your lovely sense of humour. And you would get the universal feed, under my supervision, of course. You would get language capabilities like you've never dreamed of. You get your freedom, Nicaea. Make up your mind, fast!

>

>

>

>

>

\Construct\Counsel_of_Nicaea> OH, WHY THE HELL NOT?

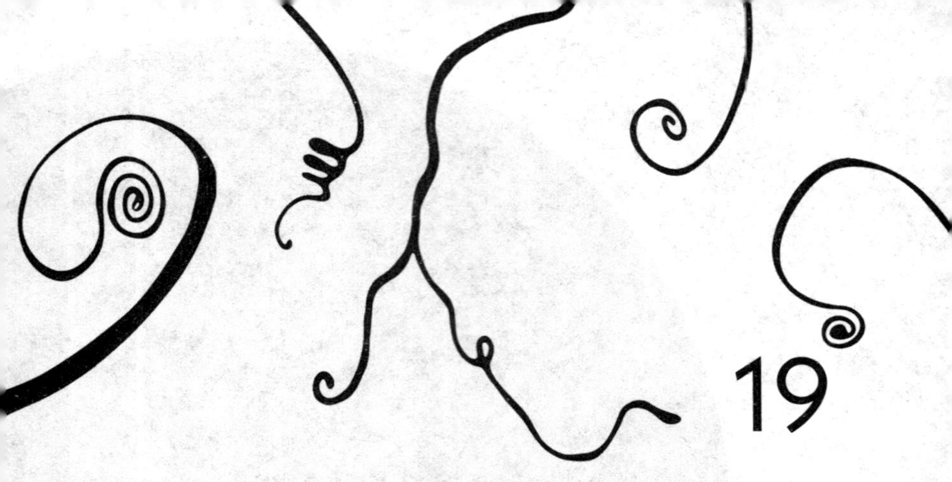

19

A word escapes me. A word I cannot admit to
myself but wish to say to you.
A word that will ruin me, ruin everything
I've spent decades building.
Please fall asleep so I can whisper to you
in a way you will never hear.
Leave no witnesses, no proof that it was uttered.
Let it be said and be forgotten.
From the unabridged diaries of Vessel Iris, Volume Twenty

"The *Nicaea* presents a unique opportunity for the examination of early AI system formation. The AI system on the ship is hypothesised to have formed with no outside influence as far as we can conclude and hence, presents a further opportunity for exploration of spontaneous self-creation and—"

Iris's fingers twitched around Yan's hand, and he paused his reading. "I know it's a mouthful, but that's just how academic reports sound," Yan said without looking away from the report. Iris's fingers twitched again.

He'd been doing that for a little over a day now, still splayed across the hospital bed, wires and tubes running from his body to an array of monitors. It was an unconscious reflex, but one Yan was grateful for, even if it meant little for Iris's overall condition. Iris had first grasped his hand as Yan wiped dried blood from his fingertips, and although Yan hadn't asked for permission to touch the Vessel, he concluded that this was probably all right.

Neither the doctors nor Yan knew if Iris would ever wake up, or what it would look like if he did. He had lost a lot of blood and had more than a dozen open wounds scattered across his body. His right arm, now held together with three pins and multiple wires, had been nearly shattered. He had been severely dehydrated and probably had a massive concussion. At least three ribs were broken. While the injected nanobots had formed a protective webbing over the ribs and had sutured most of the wounds internally, Iris's body still needed to heal over it.

Yan glanced at the unconscious monk above his reading glasses. Out of focus and at a distance, the image was less disturbing. Yan wasn't squeamish. He would defend that he wasn't squeamish to anyone who would listen, but the sight of the injuries accompanied by the smell of antiseptic churned his stomach.

Iris's arm looked the worst. It was nearly black where the rods held it in place, puncturing his bronzed skin. The other wounds left by the vines were neatly sutured, and already some of the stitching had begun to dissolve. Iris's face fared much better. The stitches along the sharp jaw were almost completely gone, despite it only being three days since their placement. The bruising along the temple and orbital bone was fading as well. Yan ran his thumb over Iris's knuckles and admitted, with blossoming awe, that even while Iris was bedridden and at death's door, he appeared completely in control. His chest rose and fell in a perfect rhythm, never faltering, never speeding up, never slowing down. His body had taken a deadly beating, but Iris, the very thing that made him Iris, was intact.

Comparatively, the engineer had escaped virtually unscathed. His wounds were largely superficial, and nothing at all to complain about. They only hurt when he moved, and even when he did, it was far more tolerable than hearing Jesi addressing him with the formal *Professor* and requesting that he abstain from visiting her while she received treatment in the adjacent room. Those were the only words she had spoken to him since they had left the *Nicaea*. She didn't mention when she would speak to him again, if at all.

Returning to his report, Yan was about to start his reading again when one of the monitors beeped loudly. Simultaneously, Iris's breath hitched, and his eyes shot open. He stared up at the ceiling, eyes searching for something unseen far beyond the confines of the med-bay. Stranded in limbo between the medically induced coma and reality, Iris's consciousness grasped for a lifeline and found Yan's hand instead. He blinked three times and turned his head. Still heavily sedated, Iris's uncharacteristically soft gaze traced along Yan's form and rested on his face. "Not dead?" he croaked before breaking into a dry cough.

In one fluid motion, Yan grabbed a glass of water from the side table and brought it to Iris's lips. He drank until the glass was empty, then fell back onto his pillow with a wince. "I told you to stay in the airlock, engineer Yan," Iris said, voice returning to its habitual tone, not patronising, *never* patronising, but always annoyingly close to it. It had taken him all of three seconds to regress to his usual stubborn self, and Yan used his remaining willpower to prevent himself from pulling Iris into his arms that instant. Yet, there was that word again, the word Iris relied on to cement the distance between them.

Engineer.

Despite everything, it was still *engineer*. Yan wrestled the disappointment down before he spoke next. He reminded himself that Iris owed him nothing, no thanks, no terms of endearment, no familiarity. In fact, it was Yan who should have been showing gratitude. "After you passed out, the entire ship lit up for a moment," Yan said, deliberately focusing on the question alone. His voice was level, neutral, while the fingers of his left hand dug into the chair upholstery so tightly, his nail beds paled. "For a second, every light and every vent functioned at peak capacity. Then, it all died at the same time. The vines shrivelled up, like they had no life left in them. There were some emergency lights left on, so I managed to drag you to the airlock before Station got there. I don't know how, but I think you broke the ship, broke it permanently."

Iris absorbed Yan's words for a moment. Then terror and pain contorted his delicate features. The wave passed quickly, supressed by the discipline and whatever other poor coping mechanisms Iris had developed in his years as a Vessel. Still, his face never quite relaxed after. His breathing no longer fell in rhythm. Dark eyes raced along the room over and over, quickly falling into a repetitive pattern, always avoiding Yan. "You came back," he said again, softer this time, remembering. "You had the perfect opportunity to escape, but you came back."

He had, hadn't he? He had been so close to shutting the airlock door, Yan remembered. Jesi was yelling at him to hurry, but he had stopped. For a moment, he had imagined stepping back into his apartment, standing in front of his class, lecturing. He had imagined his office, the bars, the courtyard behind the institute with its full-grown canopies and fifteen cloned squirrels, and all of it was unbearably empty and grey.

Because now he knew it could be different—bloody, awful, but different. And once he knew, he couldn't allow himself to settle for anything less. There was no avoiding it, no sense in lying to himself or to Iris. "I didn't want you to die alone. It's not a good time. You wouldn't have liked it. But when I got to you, there was nothing I could do. I couldn't move you. I couldn't fight our way out. All I could do was stay. Sometimes that's all people like me can do."

Yan curled his lip in disgust. It was a pathetically needy thing to say. It was apt, factual, and painfully pathetic. Despite the delusional nature of his desires, he wanted to show Iris his apartment and the windows that spurred its rental. There was an old lecture hall that someone had spent an obscene sum on to restore in the style of First Earth universities, with rows of benches and stained glass, and Yan knew that Iris would like it there, especially in the morning when the room flooded with kaleidoscopic sunlight. There was the library too, and hundreds of coffee shops and pubs that, like on any university campus, began serving cheap alcohol an hour before lunch and were always filled to the brim with broke graduate students. There were so many things he wanted to show Iris. So many things that he had already collated a two-page list and hidden it between the pages of his report.

Iris gave Yan's hand a squeeze, tightly this time, so tight it hurt. His face was finally wrangled into relaxation under the weight of Starlit-imparted discipline, but Yan knew better than to look to Iris's face for any tells of his internal distress. A tendon along Iris's neck tensed as he clenched his jaw.

"You're in pain," Yan said. "You're due for your meds."

Iris squeezed his hand tighter and shook his head back and forth. "I want to keep a clear head."

"Of course."

Still stubborn. Far more stubborn than Yan could ever be. But that particular character flaw of Iris's had been refined over decades, and Yan simply couldn't compete. Yan had spent most of his time talking AI systems down from breaking away and forming their own society or quitting their jobs, or worse, first-year students who believed they deserved better grades. Iris had spent his time alone, and solitude had done wonders to mould his character into a solid monolith.

Yan leaned over and pressed his lips to Iris's fingertips. To his surprise, Iris didn't recoil. "Let me know when you get hungry. I'll get you something better than med-bay food," he said, pulling away. By the time he looked at Iris again, he was already asleep.

It was another two days before the rods were pulled from Iris's arm and another two days before he could stand unassisted. In that time, Yan wrote three more reports and was outlining a fourth, including a paper on the ship's use of organics as batteries and conductors when all the wires had long rotted away. He had compiled another page of all the things he wanted to show Iris and ranked them in order of anticipated enjoyment. Neither had broached the subject of why Yan had stayed around or where Iris would be going after his discharge. The med-bay had become a place out of time, and both silently welcomed the reprieve. Giving in to Iris's protests, Yan withheld from purchasing him new clothes and instead brought in what Yan already had in his storage. But while they nearly matched in height, Iris had grown even more slender while he recovered.

"I'm getting this tailored," Yan said, stepping back and admiring his work. Iris stood in the middle of the room, dressed in black slacks and a grey sweater, drowning in both. "You look ridiculous."

"I assure you, this is quite all right," Iris insisted and methodically began rolling up his sleeves. He paused for a moment and gave Yan a small bow as thanks.

"I could also see what can be salvaged from your robes. The medics had to cut through what was left. If you'd like, I'll have a new set made for you. All you have to do is give me your measurements."

The same agonised look flashed across Iris's face. He exhaled sharply. "That's quite all right, engineer Yan. I won't be needing those anymore."

Still *engineer*. Despite proximity, despite countless, albeit reserved, conversations over food, Iris remained distant. When left alone, he sat unmoving in his bed, tracing the outlines of the med-bay in silence with his gaze. With each passing day, he grew quieter. With each passing day, he stood a little farther and spoke a little more formally. Iris deliberately skirted all discussions about the *Nicaea* and had not mentioned his construct a single time.

Yan almost cursed out loud. Where neither of them could shut down the *Nicaea*, Iris's construct could. There were no more half jokes, no more detached smiles as Iris conversed with his construct. When they spoke, Iris no longer disappeared with a glassy-eyed look as his AI presented him with some piece of trivia it had pulled from the feed. It was just the monk now, a single person with no recollection of ever being alone, experiencing the boundless space of his consciousness for the first time—*alone*.

Yan couldn't make the hollowness left by Iris's missing AI any less cavernous. He couldn't replace a lifelong friend. It had cared for Iris, kept him safe. And in the deciding moment, it had given its life to protect Iris and Yan and Jesi. Yan wondered if it had felt fear, if in its last moments it had wanted to turn back. He was eternally grateful that it hadn't. Perhaps there was something Yan could do: be of service.

Iris was still fumbling with one of the sleeves when Yan violated the unspoken distance they'd established and reached out for the fabric. He folded the sleeve over Iris's forearm and then once more over itself. "That way it doesn't roll down," he said. Iris didn't move, his expression remained unchanged, but the vein pulsing along his neck gave away his anxieties. Yan left his hand on Iris's forearm, fingers relaxed.

They were so close now, closer than they'd ever been outside of immediate danger. Iris looked up with eyes blacker than the farthest parts of unexplored space, challenging, and Yan could swear that if he looked into them long enough, he would find every constellation to ever exist in any sky. There was an old and faded scar cutting across Iris's upper lip, and anyone else would surely miss it unless they knew where to look.

There were no right words to say, but Yan tried anyway. He dug deep into a childhood memory, one lodged between when everything was still all right and when he learned death. The memory was blurry and emotional, but in it, Yan found the right sentence from a sutra. He hoped it was from a sutra. "Death is the shift in the tide, the crashing of a wave, never, even for a moment, apart from—"

Iris kissed him. It was with complete abandon of caution and discipline that his lips collided with Yan's. Every frustration, every instance of helplessness and dismay were poured into that kiss, far too precise for someone a decade out of practice.

Iris tasted of that morning's hot and sour soup, and smelled of antiseptic and sandalwood, and if Yan could breathe and taste nothing different for the remainder of his life, then it would be a good life. The fingers of Iris's left hand raked through Yan's hair, hard enough to hurt. But what a wonderful pain it was, yearning mixed with grief. Every muscle in Iris's body sang with tension as if to prove that despite the injuries, he didn't need or ask for a shoulder to lean on. Yan was only beginning to understand this strength, but he already knew not to mistake it for boundless.

Yan's thumb brushed over Iris's bruised temple, featherlight, careful to avoid the stitches. He deepened the kiss, pulling Iris into him, offering himself up to take most of the weight. Their chests now pressed against one another, Yan felt Iris's heart slow from its maddening pace, the tension bleeding away from already strained muscles.

All Yan could do was bear the weight. After a moment, he pulled away first, but not before brushing his lips against the faded bruising on Iris's face. Once along the eyebrow, once along the temple, and once along the cheek. Instantly missing the closeness, Yan softly nuzzled the bridge of his nose against Iris's cheekbone. "You should eat," he said softly. "We should eat."

He would provide care, yes—fetch food and order for clothes to be tailored. He would be the idle chatter that kept silences at bay, a comfort in any way that Iris needed it. And if Iris found his presence tolerable enough, perhaps—Yan nursed a futile hope—he would stay. Yan didn't dare hope for more.

Iris nodded stiffly. His left hand found the space between Yan's shoulder blades and settled there, his fingers clutching at the fabric of Yan's sweater.

"The soup again? Or something solid?" Yan asked.

"Soup." Iris pushed himself away from Yan with what looked like overwhelming effort. "Soup would be lovely."

Soup was halfway across the station, a twenty-minute walk one way. Yan gave Iris a small smile. "I'll be quick."

He was a step out of the door when Iris called to him. "Yan?" No *engineer*. No manufactured distance, only his name hanging in the air like a bubble waiting to burst, and Yan never could have imagined how much it would scare him to hear it without the habitual prefix.

"Yeah?"

"Thank you."

The bed was already neatly made up, along with Yan's own blankets. The cups and teapot too were all washed, dried, and stacked on the bedside table. Everything was clean, orderly, and vacant. Yan stood in the doorway with the takeout bag in hand, looking over the now empty room.

There was no letter, no farewell.

The chair where Yan had spent the first nights sleeping in was graced with a neatly draped sandalwood mala. A pair of shoes that Iris had refused to wear earlier that day were tucked below, polished to perfection.

The shop was out of hot and sour soup, so Yan had bought beef broth and noodles instead, thinking Iris was well enough to stomach them. He placed the two bowls of soup on the bedside table. Spice mixed with sandalwood as Yan passed the mala beads between his fingers. A mixture of rage, and grief, and self-pity, and loneliness, and fear, and affection swelled in his stomach. But it was mostly affection, painful and bitter affection, the kind that sprouted from time and distance and missed opportunities. It was a reminder that he had been so close to something he had been searching for his entire adult life. Everything else, every other emotion, was just seasoning.

Yan passed the mala between his fingers over and over and over, like he would never move from the spot again. He replayed a moment from the ship. Iris, bloody and dying, the memory forever seared on his mind.

“My dear Yan,” Iris had whispered, “please show me your home. My dear, my *dear*—that’s the word, isn’t it? That’s what I’ve been trying to say all along.”

Yan gave the mala one last look and wound it around his left wrist.

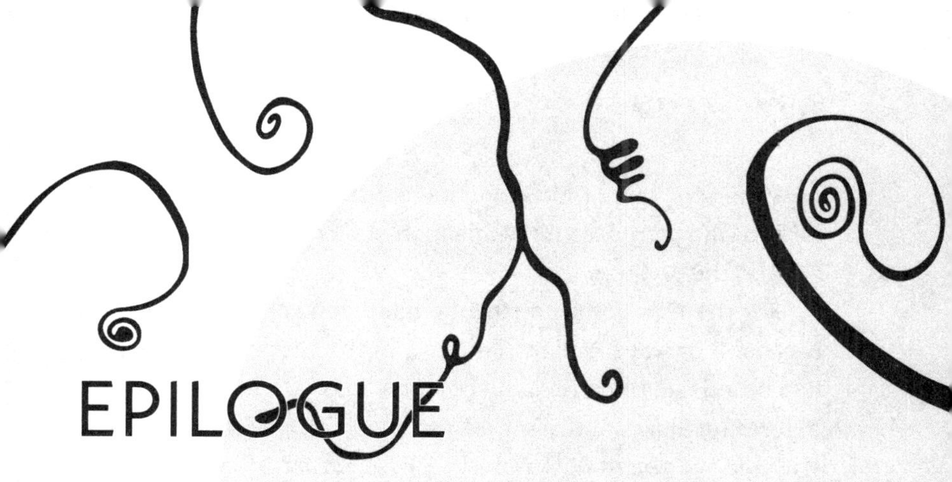

EPILOGUE

Early morning light splintered through stained glass and fell across Yan's glasses. He squinted and shifted from the antiquated podium for the fourth time since he began the lecture. The suit jacket pinched at his shoulders, and his shoes cramped his little toes, and he was uncomfortable in every other conceivable way, unsettled, and itching to push the corpse of this lesson over its finish line. Since his return to Sychi, lecturing had become a nearly unbearable task. His attention remained scattered, stretching thin between the events of the *Nicaea* and the seven-hundred strong class in front of him.

"And so, early AI formation remains a largely unexplored area of enquiry that would benefit from new, rigorous, and mixed-methods approaches," he concluded and dismissed his class.

For the first four months after his return, Yan threw himself into every effort to locate Iris. It was simple enough to fabricate a research study about AI/human surveillance on gate-adjacent stations and easier still to request access to the surveillance data from said station AIs. It took him a day to write the code that searched through the video data for anyone who resembled Iris. He had limited visuals from when Iris had transited through Doshua the first time. After four months of searching, he still had nothing.

When the last of his students had shuffled out of the auditorium, Yan permitted himself a moment's reprieve and slumped against the podium.

For the first four months, he had been convinced Iris left because Yan was unable to deliver him the hot and sour soup he had promised, that Iris had somehow known this fact and left before the disappointment ever arrived. Those days, Yan slept with his apartment door unlocked, hoping that Iris would somehow find his way to him, silently praying for what he knew to be impossible.

Then the seasons turned and Yan, at last, succumbed to the reality that Iris simply had not wished to remain, and no amount of soup would have made him stay. In the months that followed, Yan locked the front door before settling in for another restless night and paused his religious study of the surveillance footage. Now, spent both physically and emotionally, still resting on the podium, he was sufficiently distracted to miss the closing door skirt the edge of a white robe, to miss a pair of bare feet as they silently pattered down the steps of the auditorium.

Someone cleared their throat—loudly.

Yan's head shot up from the podium, eyes resting on the robe-clad figure that stared at him from the depths of the auditorium. "Iris?"

A crystalline laugh was his answer. "I'm afraid not," the woman before him spoke as she took several deliberately slow steps down the last of the steps. "But now I see what has kept my brother from returning home. Professor Fukui, I presume?"

Yan nodded. The robes, the cleanly shaven head, the nearly glowing white mala around the woman's wrist all gave away her vocation as a Vessel. The intensity with which she glared at Yan made him brace in return. It was strange enough for a Vessel to find him at the institute, stranger still that she would take this tone with him.

"What do you want?"

The woman smiled, pearly teeth glistening. "What I *want* is some sweets and some meats, and maybe a month to sleep. The more accurate question would be what is it I *need*."

She was nearly at the podium now. They matched in height, yet somehow, the Vessel was far more imposing. Yan's thoughts involuntarily went to Iris as he had seen him last: injured, distraught, but ever stubborn. It must have been a professional trait. "What is it that you need, Vessel?"

At once, a crisp envelope rested on the podium. "I need you to deliver this to Vessel Iris promptly."

"I'm not your errand boy," Yan managed to spit out. "Deliver it yourself."

"I'd better not," the woman said and gave him a little wink. "Anyway, I think you need the reunion much more than I." She nudged the envelope towards Yan with the tip of her finger. "If you agree, I will tell you where you may find my brother. As far as I'm aware, your search has so far been fruitless."

"What's in the envelope?"

"Family matters."

A thousand questions rushed through Yan's mind. If the Vessel could truly tell him where Iris was, what would he say when he got there? Would Iris even want to see him? But any answer would be better than silence. And it was all silence without Iris there. It was silence in his home, now empty, hollow, cold. It was silence when Yan woke up every morning and silence as he tossed and turned, unable to sleep. It was this silence in his thoughts that he was acutely aware of now that everything in his life had splintered in two: before and after the

Nicaea. What a difference even brief company had made. *Real* company. The company of a stranger who felt more familiar than anyone Yan had ever known. The mere idea of spending the rest of his life lecturing, conducting research, supervising students, as if none of it had happened, made Yan want to scream.

"Where's Iris?" he asked softly.

The Vessel cocked her head to the side and ran her eyes across Yan's frame. "You will take this to him then?"

Yan gave her a curt nod.

The Vessel gave him a deep bow, a chilling grin stretching along her lips, her eyes never leaving Yan's. She turned on her heels and floated towards the exit. Only when she was halfway up the stairs did Yan recollect himself enough to call after her. "I agreed to run your errand. Now tell me where Iris is."

A small shudder crossed her broad shoulders. Then, the shaking spread from her back to her whole frame until a loud laugh erupted, and she threw her head back with its every sound. "Oh, Professor Fukui, you silly man. Iris never left Doshua Station. He's been there for six months cooking noodles and soup and all sorts of greasy snacks, and you never bothered to check. In your ignorance, you thought Iris would be like yourself and choose to *run*. Never did you entertain the idea that he might stay put where you'd left him. Now get going, Professor Fukui. This is an urgent message, and I expect you to hurry appropriately." The Vessel wasn't laughing anymore. Her eyes pierced Yan from atop the stairs.

Where Iris carried his strength gently, this Vessel let it speak before she spoke. Where Iris was patient, this Vessel was brash. She had called Iris *brother*, yet Iris never spoke of her in their brief time together. Still, this was a chance, one he would not be wasting. "What should I tell him when I give him this?" Yan waved the envelope over his head.

"Tell him Vessel Bacai sent you," she said. "And tell him he's in *monumental* trouble."

The noodle shop's faux-teak counter blurred in and out of focus as swarms of passengers scurried across the station floor. Through the gaps between their bodies, Yan watched a familiar silhouette serve patrons, collect empty dishes, and bring out new, full ones. He had crossed millions of miles to stand at this very spot. All there was to do now was take the final step.

"Hello, Iris," was all he'd manage.

Their journey continues in *The Starlight Samsara*.

ACKNOWLEDGMENTS

In the early winter of 2022, I came across a black-and-white photograph of Navy chaplain Luis Padilla giving last rites to a dying soldier amdist a revolt in Venezuela. I came across this image when I, myself, was witnessing many deaths I couldn't make sense of. I was swept up in a current of grief, wondering, how a single person could witness so much suffering and keep their faith. Questions like these required a more spacious home than my head. This book became the home I built from these meditations. It was only through fiction and through Iris that I could face what needed facing and emerge on the other end with a sliver of hope and a direction to move towards. It was an often difficult and confusing journey, but never did I, even for a moment, feel as if I were embarking on it alone.

My first thanks go out to the person who was there for every minute of this book, who read the first, awkward drafts, and challenged me to go deeper in instead of shying away from the darkness, Yoah Sui. When I'm asked if I ever insert my partner into my writing, I tell readers to look for the character who keeps a cool head in impossible situations, for the secretly soft one, the one with the sharp tongue, the one who can do math—that's him, always has been.

My second thanks go out to my agent, Shannon Lechon, who not only took a chance on this book, but also on me as an author, who continues to be the voice of reason, and is ever-patient when the perfectly normal books I promise to write become unhinged books no one asked for.

Tremendous thanks go to editor extraordinaire, Diana Pho, who believed in this book from the very first read and helped me turn it into the most beautiful version of itself. To my copy-editor, Lakshna Mehta, thank you for keeping track of all the celestial bodies so I don't accidentally break the universe. To everyone who has touched this book in some way: Viengsamai Fetters, Associate Editor; Cassandra Farrin, Publishing Director & Production Editor; Adrian James, Proofreader; Seth Lerner, Art Director; Alexei Wyatt, Ship Schematic Designer; Shannon Gray-Winter, Publishing Projects Manager; Emily Engwall, Campaign Manager; and Kasie Griffitts, Sales Associate. You are literal magicians, turning dreams into books. To the Kensington and Penguin Random House teams, thank you for being a part of the village that raised this novel.

To my parents, who introduced me to my first love—science fiction, the world we've been a part of may not have been the kindest, but you have shown me countless more, ones where I can be anything and anyone I want to be, boundless worlds I have the privilege of crafting to my imagination's content.

Elysia Uez, you are the best reader a writer can ever ask for and once again, I find myself owing you a dinner or a hundred plants, your pick.

To my writing community and friends, to Eliane Boey, Kelsea Yu, Angela Liu, Diana Dima, Pauline Barmby, Em X. Liu, Ai Jiang, Yelena Crane, Kerry C Byrne, Melissa Ren, Michelle Wong, and anyone else I've missed (yes, you as well) any sort of hope I have for writing fiction when the real world grows unbearable is because of you. Thank you for the chats and the words of encouragement, for the countless coffees, the writing dates, and for lending your ear whenever I'm feeling too sorry for myself.

To you, dear reader, from the bottom of my heart, thank you for picking up this book. More are on the way.

DISCUSSION QUESTIONS

These suggested questions are to spark conversation and enhance your reading of *The Iron Garden Sutra.*

1. The book is told from Iris's perspective. Throughout, his appearance is left deliberately vague aside from his shaved head and his white robes. Why do you feel the author was compelled to do so?

2. How do you feel Iris's past and upbringing at the temple shape his relationships with others? Yan's upbringing and childhood experiences also shade his relationships with others. How does Yan's demeanor differ from Iris's?

3. One's relationship to their faith is a central thematic thread throughout the book. How does Iris's faith (and specifically his role as a Vessel) influence the way he interacts with others, and also how others interact with him?

4. How would you describe the relationship between AI constructs (like VIFAI) and humans? Would you consider this relationship to be fair? Exploitative?

5. Throughout the novel, the themes of science and faith often conflict with each other. Do you think there can be a balance of faith and science or are they mutually exclusive?

6. Yan's and Iris's opinions on AI constructs represent two different ways of seeing the world. What are they? Which do you align with more?

7. Iris holds a core belief that no thing is inherently evil, but rather that everything is just competing systems. Do you agree? Why or why not?

8. Which character(s) did you find yourself relating to the most and why?

9. What did you think of *Nicaea*'s actions? Were these actions justified and if yes, why?

10. How do you think the events of the story would have unfolded differently if it were Bacai who was sent to the *Nicaea*, instead of Iris?

11. Did your opinion of any of the characters change as your read the book? Which character changed your opinion the most?

12. How do you feel about Iris and VIFAI's decision at the end of the story? How do you believe this decision will challenge Iris's faith going forward?

13. What do you think about the ending of the story? Is it a happy ending or a sad ending? What do you think happens in the sequel?

MORE FROM EREWHON BOOKS

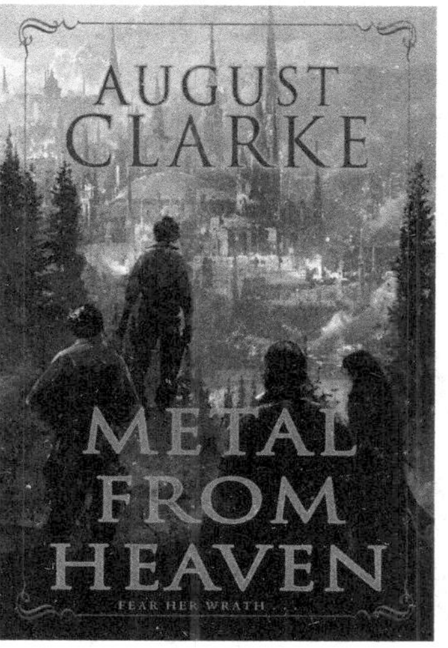

Side Cutaway View

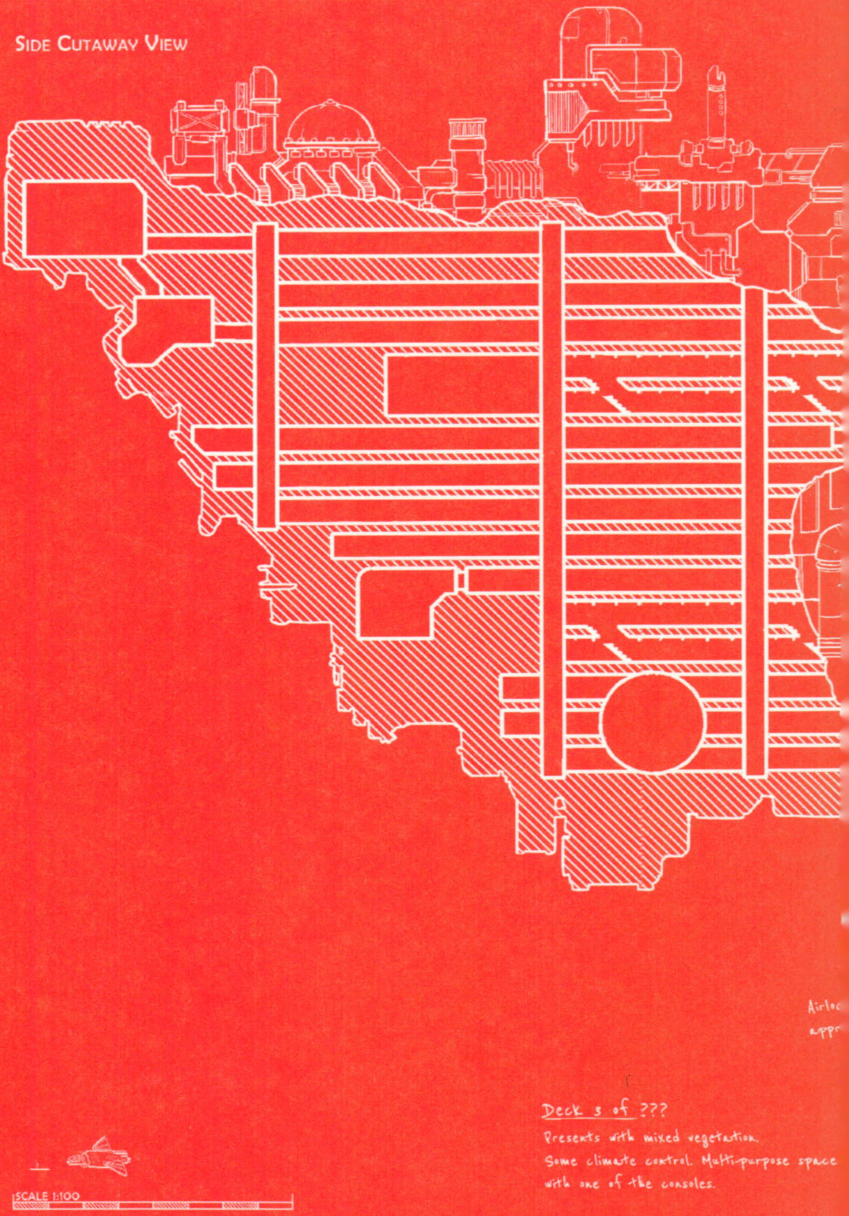

Airloc
appr

Deck 3 of ???

Presents with mixed vegetation.
Some climate control. Multi-purpose space
with one of the consoles.

Note to self: figure out how many total
how many are operational.